S0-BUB-261

Wyndano's Cloak

by
A. R. Silverberry

Tree Tunnel Press
Capitola, California

This book, including characters, incidents, and dialogue,
is a work of fiction. Any resemblance to actual events or
persons, living or dead, is entirely coincidental.

Wyndano's Cloak. © 2010 by Peter Allan Adler, writing as
A. R. Silverberry. All rights reserved. Printed in the United States
of America. No part of this book may be used or reproduced
in any manner whatsoever, or stored in a retrieval system, or trans-
mitted in any form or by any means, electronic, mechanical,
photocopying, or otherwise, without written permission from the
publisher, except in the case of brief quotations embodied in critical
articles and reviews. For additional information or permissions,
contact Tree Tunnel Press, P.O. Box 733, Capitola, CA 95010

ISBN - 13: 978-0-9841037-6-8
ISBN - 10: 0-9841037-6-7
Library of Congress Control Number: 2009931576

Cover and interior illustrations © 2010 by Sherry Adler.
All rights reserved.

Published by Tree Tunnel Press,
P.O. Box 733, Capitola, CA 95010
First Edition. Printed in the United States of America
0 9 8 7 6 5 4 3 2 1

For my mother,
more wonderful than Mother.

And for Sherry,
who walked with me in Aerdem.

ACKNOWLEDGMENTS

WYNDANO'S CLOAK grew with the care and support of many people. I am deeply indebted to my wife, Sherry, for believing in me, pulling me through the dark moments, and listening to me prattle for five years. She provided an astute perspective on my characters and audience, and how these relate to larger questions about politics and society. She did more tasks on this novel than I can list; the book would not exist without her. Under her artful hand, Jen sprang onto the cover.

A world of thanks go to my editor, Walter Kleine, for making the editing process painless. He helped me tighten, clarify key points, and clean up little details without losing sight of the whole. His devotion to the story was miraculous.

Heartfelt thanks go to my cousins, Elisa Adler and Selena Jayo, for enthusiastically critiquing the novel, giving suggestions for pruning, pointing out where to make improvements, and helping me sort out my concerns. The wonderful writers Andrea Walker, Delight Reimers, and Ruth Lofsted helped me grow into a writer. I will treasure our evenings at Borders, and the friendships forged there.

I'm grateful to Madison and Dave (M^2 Productions) for creating such a powerful book trailer. Linda Joy Kattwinkel provided legal counsel; Alan Gadney gave needed marketing guidance. My brother, Mark, was a sounding board, and seemed to have the right ideas to get me back on track. Dr. Lena Osher answered medical questions, and Dr. Joan Baran clarified early child development questions. You helped make it real.

Oceans of appreciation go to my neighbors, Cathy and Chad; and to Irene Archer (interior design); Ian and the gang (exterior design); Chris and Bill (LaserLight); Alisa Davies; Roy Wallace; Anna Storck; Diane Whiddon-Brown; and the other Mark, for putting the book first.

Part One

The warning whispered in the leaves

rustling in a windless dawn. Jen always knew it would come, but the danger had drifted to the back of her mind like a fading nightmare, leaving only a vague clutching beneath the common activities of the day.

She'd been running along the western side of King's Loop, dawn just pushing above the Aedilac Mountains. Silhouettes streaked by, a farmhouse, a barn, a peach orchard heavy with fruit. Her hair streamed behind, catching the wind like a sail. She almost flew, feet barely touching the ground.

Kicking up a cloud of dirt, she veered off the road and cut through a meadow. She spread her arms, feeling the waist-high grass brush her palms as she whizzed by. Leaving the meadow, she ducked into a thicket of trees, dodging low-lying limbs with the thrill of a bird that's found its wings.

She broke into a clearing and headed toward a stream. With a surge she leaped over the water and made for the lone oak near the bank. Here, a ring of rocks collected water in a quiet pool. Only a few hungry skeeter hawks skated across the surface, looking for an early breakfast. Ducks slept in the grass.

They raised their heads and started waddling toward her as she untied a leather pouch.

Taking out a handful of breadcrumbs, she flung it to them. They scrambled with straining necks and blaring trumpets. She threw some toward a runt standing uncertainly on the side, but a big white quacker beat him off with a showy rattle of wings.

Jen pretended to slip the food back in her pocket and waited until the others glided into the water. Then she poured the crumbs into her hand and held it out. The runt hesitated, then crept forward until his beak nibbled her palm.

"You're small," she said softly, "but you can be quick. Dart between them."

When the food was gone, she leaned against the tree. King's Loop looked like a ribbon from here, winding through farm and woodland until it met the great gates of Glowan. There it zigzagged through the little town until it came to the Rose Castle, shining like a jewel in the rising sun. The sheer cliff beyond beckoned. She looked away and exhaled, sighing with frustration and longing.

That was when she heard the whispering. Alert, she backed away from the tree and studied it at a crouch. The air was still. The grass motionless. But the leaves stirred and fluttered. Words floated down. At first they were indistinct, as if someone called through a distant snowstorm. One word emerged clearly, and an icy finger traced down her spine.

She heard her name.

She backed away until she squatted on some rocks that extended into the pool. Every muscle—sun-hammered and wind-hardened like metal in a forge—was poised to spring. Phrases whispered down. The only sense she could make was that something was coming. Something dangerous.

She thought of her family. Fear tightened around her

heart. She was a hair's-breadth away from running to them. Her feet stayed rooted to the spot. Maybe she'd hear more.

A small splash made her look at the pond. Two more followed, as if someone had thrown pebbles. Nothing had fallen into the water. But ripples spread out and ran into each other. More splashes erupted like tiny volcanoes, until the whole pool was agitated with colliding rings. A circle of calm emerged below Jen's feet, pushing the waves back. Pale and ghostly, a face rose from the muddy bottom of the pool until it floated just below the surface. Little hills and valleys lined the features of an old woman, as if olives lay under the skin.

"Medlara." Jen spoke under her breath, unwilling to believe her friend could hear her.

Medlara smiled, but her expression hardened. Words whispered from the pool. Jen leaned forward, straining to hear. She got little more than fragments, as if a storyteller jumbled the pieces of a tale. One phrase repeated, like a riddle. "If you meet . . . a harp, you must . . . If the worst happens, seek the answers—"

Jen dropped to her knees, hoping to catch more. Medlara's hands appeared just below her chin. She clasped them, and lifted her eyes as if she were imploring Jen. She mouthed two words. They might have been, "Forgive me."

Streaks of blue snaked and flowered in the water, as if someone had dropped in dye. Tendrils of mist rose from the surface and licked the ring of rocks. Soon the whole pool was covered. Spilling over the edge, the cloudy vapor surrounded Jen. She backed onto the shore, but the stuff sprouted up on all sides, walling her in, and formed a ceiling above. It crept along the ground until it met her feet. There it paused like an undulating sea.

Jen studied the mist. "She's trying to show me something. But what?"

There was no time to wonder. Fog rose before her like a giant shadow. Black. Forbidding . . .

She stepped back. Looked behind for an escape route. The fog surged forward and pulled her into the inky darkness. She could no longer feel the ground, as if everything solid and beautiful that she cared about was being ripped away. She tried to scream but terror rose from the pit of her stomach and froze in her throat.

The rest was a dizzy kaleidoscope of tilting and falling, of wandering lost, with no way out, no way home, no way back to a world of light and love, until the mist melted away and she collapsed, shaking in a pool of sweat.

How long she lay there she couldn't say, but at last she stopped trembling, her heart slowed, and she gulped some big breaths of air and rose. She staggered to the pool. It looked ordinary enough now. A handful of skeeter hawks glided peacefully on the surface.

The morning sun of Aerdem sparkled on the stream. A few birds sang in the tree. Shaking off numb shock, she splashed water on her face, wiped her hands on her breeches, and ran for King's Loop. She streaked through the fields and leaped onto the road, where a few farmers were carting goods to market. Tearing past them, she was vaguely aware they'd stopped to bow to the king's daughter.

2

Jen wanted to run the full length of

the castle directly to her father. But she didn't want to attract attention. Instead, she walked briskly through the corridors. The castle was buzzing with activity. Servants whisked carts of linen or trays of bread and fruit down the halls. A crew of carpenters carried lumber for construction on a new library. Jen could hear the rap of hammers in a room beyond. Everyone smiled and bowed when she passed. She smiled back, trying to hide the cold shivers running through her.

She thought she knew what the danger was. The whole family would guess the same thing. There was only one thing that could threaten them.

But how would it happen? And when?

She eyed the castle wall. Deep inside the translucent stone, green and turquoise flickered and shimmered like fire. Jen heaved a sigh of relief. Red-hot flames would have meant the danger was upon them.

Still, Medlara hadn't taken the time to send a messenger. That could only mean one thing. Whatever was going to happen would occur in a few days.

Jen had to understand what Medlara had shown her. As frightening as it was, she forced herself to relive it in her mind. One memory stood out. She'd been seized. Held powerless. Then thrown like a sack of potatoes. Was that a way of saying the family might lose control of the throne? Could be overthrown? That didn't seem likely. Since the family had been reunited, after years of separation, Aerdem had prospered. Her father was a popular king.

She stepped into an inner courtyard used as an open-air market for the small city of nobles, servants, and emissaries that lived in the castle. Cobblers, fishmongers, tailors, candlemakers, potters, and a dozen others bargained with customers at stalls around the edges of the square.

Jen approached a man hawking flowers, and purchased a spray of marigolds for her father. When she reached the end of the courtyard she hesitated, fingering the vertical scar across her left eyebrow while she tottered between two routes. The fastest way to her father was to the right, across the walkways and bridges. In the past, Jen would dash across these, leaping from merlon to merlon, or tightrope-walking the handrails like a daredevil. She longed to do that again, but a wave of dizziness turned her left into a safe inner corridor.

Father would want to call a family meeting. This route would take Jen past Bit's apartment. Aside from being Jen's best friend, Bit was engaged to Dash, Jen's half brother. Everyone would want to include Bit.

Jen turned left again onto the corridor leading to Bit's apartment. Ahead, standing in front of Bit's door, a girl argued with a servant. Her back was to Jen, but the strawberry blonde ringlets falling to the shoulders made her instantly recognizable as Countess Petunia Pompahro.

"Let me in this instant, you impertinent thing," the

Countess scolded.

"I can't, Miss. Bit has forbidden anyone to enter," replied the servant, a girl about twelve with an oval face and button nose. Her blue eyes challenged the Countess defiantly.

"It's Lady Bit to you," said the Countess. "If you were my servant, I'd have you flogged for talking like that. Now open that door or I will have you flogged."

"She doesn't mind me calling her Bit. She insists I call her that," the girl replied boldly.

"I don't care. Now open the door."

"No, Miss. No one's to pass."

"I'll be the judge of that. I'm quite sure she did not mean me. Step aside. I am one of Bit's closest confidantes."

"Perhaps, but you're not going through this door. Bit is working on a surprise and no one's to see it 'til it's done."

By this time Jen had joined them. "It's okay, Sally. Let Bit know I'm here."

Sally nodded and stepped inside the room.

Petunia turned to Jen and gave a slight curtsy. "You really must take a firmer hand with your domestics."

Jen ignored the remark. Petunia's long nose and chin—which would be cute on a poodle—did nothing to flatter the Countess. Her only attractive feature was her long lashes, which she fluttered like an agitated butterfly whenever a handsome gentleman passed. She never lost a chance to flutter them at Dash, even though he was engaged to Bit.

Bit peeked shyly out the door. "Jenny! Pet! Are you here to see me?" Bit's soft, brown eyes were wide and earnest.

"Of course we are." Petunia smoothed her dress. "Why wouldn't we come to see you? We're friends, aren't we?"

Bit's face lit up. "Wonderful. Give me a second, I'll be right out."

A moment later, Bit stepped out, leaving the door ajar. Petunia craned her head to see what was in the room.

"Bit," Jen said, "can you come with me to the Crystal Room? I'm calling a family meeting."

"Sure. What's it about?"

"I'll tell you when we get there."

"Is something wrong?" Petunia pried.

Jen eyed the Countess and shrugged. "No. Just family stuff."

"I'm so glad to see you both," Bit said. "I'm planning a surprise birthday party for Dash and want to know what you think of my idea."

"Maybe that should wait," said Jen, taking Bit's arm and trying to lead her down the hall.

But Pet grabbed the other arm and stopped them. "No. Let's hear all about it."

Bit smiled, her face warm and dreamy. "I thought I'd throw a cozy affair in the Hearth Room. Just family and a few close friends. Jenny, I thought your mom and I could cook Dash's favorite recipes. You know how he's always asking me to learn them. Then we can sing some songs by the fire, and after dessert, I'm going to give him this."

Bit looked around to make sure no one was looking, then pulled a velvet pouch from her pocket.

"What is it?" asked Petunia.

"I made it myself," whispered Bit. "It's not quite done." She untied the leather strings at the top of the pouch and pulled out an exact replica of the castle: the walkways, courtyards, towers and spires, the gardens and fountains, it was all there.

"Bit!" Jen exclaimed. "That's incredible! How did you do that?"

Bit blushed. "Do you really like it? I still need to carve the windows and glue on the flags. I thought if I put it over a small candle, it would glow, just like the Rose Castle."

Petunia stroked her chin shrewdly. "You could make a bundle selling them. I wouldn't ask less than thirty gold petals apiece."

"Oh, I don't think I could make another. This one took me far too long." Bit looked proudly at the carving, then returned it to the pouch.

"You know, Bit," said Petunia, "you really ought to wear a white sash instead of that blue belt."

Bit looked down at her belt. She wore a long, airy, white gown, and the belt gathered snugly around her elfin waist.

"What's wrong with it?" she asked, as if she had done something terrible. "I thought these were popular."

"No one's going to be wearing those anymore. Vieveeka— a duchess from Trilafor—is visiting Father and me. She's really quite wonderful and knows all kinds of important people. She says that in the courts of Laskamont and Trilafor everyone is wearing sashes, and that belts, especially blue belts, are totally passé. See? Look at mine."

"I . . . didn't know," said Bit, her eyes growing large. "Should I change it? I wouldn't want Dash to see me in anything . . . old-fashioned."

Jen looked at Petunia's sash. It did look striking against the Countess' scarlet dress. But Bit needed no style consultant. Her thick auburn hair fell in heavy tresses over her shoulders, framing a creamy complexion broken only by a whisper of freckles. Nothing looked bad on Bit, who moved with the mysterious grace of a forest fairy. She was the most beautiful girl Jen had ever seen, except perhaps Jen's mother.

"You look fine, Bit," Jen said. She had to find a way to ditch Petunia, who was becoming a nuisance. Jen grabbed Bit's arm again and turned down the corridor. Pet followed at their heels.

"Pet, could you do me a big favor?" Jen asked. "It would save me a trip if you'd let the Pondit know the family is meeting in the Crystal Room."

Pet wrinkled her nose. "That old fool. What does anyone want with him?"

"He's Chief Counselor to my father. You know that."

"He's old and his clothes smell. I wish I could help you, but I just remembered, I have to run an errand for my father. I'd go to your Pondit, but it's really in the wrong direction. Well, see you later."

With a rustle of her gown, the Countess took off in the other direction down the hall, pausing only to flutter her long lashes at a handsome duke.

Jen hurried forward, tugging Bit with her. When she was sure that Petunia was out of sight, she pulled Bit aside.

"I wouldn't confide so much in Petunia if I were you," Jen said.

"Why? What have I done?"

"Maybe nothing. But I don't think she's really your friend."

"I thought she was. She's always nice to me."

"Always?" Jen asked. "Was she nice before you became engaged to Dash?"

"That's different. I suppose it was right for a countess to treat me like a servant. I was a servant."

"You don't treat any of the servants that way, do you?"

Bit shook her head.

"Neither do I," Jen said. "Or Dash, or my father or mother." She hurried forward again, pulling Bit along.

"What's wrong, Jenny? Has something happened? You're acting strange."

Jen chose her words carefully. "Something might happen.

Something bad. I'll tell you more when we're all together."

"Is it about Dash?" Bit asked. She twisted a corner of her dress as she trotted to keep up. "Is Dash all right?"

"It's about all of us. None of us may be safe."

Bit stopped and clutched the top of her collar. She leaned against a wall, her face white. "Jenny. You're scaring me."

"I'm sorry, Bit. I didn't mean to. Maybe it'll turn out to be nothing." Jen didn't think so, but Bit was no good to her like this. "Mom and Dad will know what to do."

Bit nodded absently, her face still pale.

"Bit, I need you to do something for me. Go to the south wing and tell the Pondit to meet us in the Crystal Room. And send a message to my mom and Dash."

Bit agreed, and Jen watched her walk, still dazed, down the corridor. Jen turned a corner and hurried in the other direction. She worried about Bit. Bit was fragile and delicate. But she would need to be strong. They all would, if they were to get through what lay ahead.

Jen made her way up several stories to the east wing. She slowed when she reached the stairs leading to the Crystal Room. It wasn't the lack of a banister on the right that bothered her. She could take stairs without getting dizzy. It was her father. How would he react to the news? He had been strong, once. But he had been broken. Broken by the very thing Jen now feared. He was healing, but how would this affect him?

Now that she was here, Jen went up the stairs reluctantly. The door at the top was closed. She hesitated, biting her lower lip. With a deep breath she turned the handle and slipped silently into the room. Her father was playing a lute, his eyes closed as he listened to the vibration of the strings. Jen moved quietly past and sat on a loveseat opposite him.

The Crystal Room had become her father's workshop. By

the window a telescope angled toward the sky. A desk in one corner had two large volumes, one of poetry, the other her father's journal. Behind were the makings of a small library. On the other side of the room was a wooden table. A sextant, a globe, and a large map were spread on top. A series of shelves, rising from floor to ceiling, were lined with antique objects. Her father said most of them had a purpose long forgotten. Several were laid out on the table and disassembled. On a small end table were a cup and teapot decorated with roses. The scent of lemon slices filled the air.

She listened as he played, feeling the tension in her shoulders relax. His hands caressed and stroked the strings, making them sing and sigh. He struck the last chord with a flourish. When the notes faded, he looked up and smiled at her.

"That was beautiful," she said. "I liked the part where your thumb kept brushing the bass note."

"Most people miss that," he replied. "It takes a subtle thumb, listening to the other fingers, supporting them in what they do so the whole piece is unified."

"Sort of like the way you rule."

He looked at her curiously. "I could never rule Aerdem alone. I need all five fingers. Perhaps I was the thumb once. But now Dash is, sturdy and reliable."

"Then who's the forefinger?" Jen asked with a laugh.

"You are. Strong. Agile. Never backing off. I'm the fourth finger. Musicians call that the poet."

"That fits."

"Your mother is the middle finger. Being in the center, she is the heart in all we do."

"So Bit's the pinky."

"Right. It's the weakest finger, but the hand is stronger because it has one."

"What would a hand be without a pinky?" She laughed.

They rose and she handed him the bouquet of marigolds. After placing them in a vase, he hugged her tight. Tilting her head up, he smiled as he looked into her eyes.

"Green, with flecks of fire, just like your mother," he said.

She gazed back and studied his face. He was ruggedly handsome, his features chiseled with a few perfect strokes. Jet black hair, just beginning to frost around the edges, fell in loose curls over his forehead. He was sensitive and gentle, yet underneath she felt his strength and power. Still, she hesitated to tell him what had brought her there.

"You're up early," he said.

"Uh-huh. The carpenters are making progress on the new library. I saw them moving a lot of lumber for shelves." She shifted her feet, unable to calm the feelings boiling inside.

"Jenny, is there something wrong? You can tell me."

Still she hesitated, looking into his magnetic gray eyes, searching for some sign of how he would take it. "I got a message . . ." Once started she couldn't stop. It came pouring out. The whispering leaves. The wall of fog. The inky darkness. Medlara's face rising from the muddy bottom of the pool.

And there was her father—strong, commanding, and kingly—falling to the sofa, clutching his hand to his throat.

"Father! Are you all right?!

I'm sorry, Father," she cried.

"No," he gasped. "You were right to tell me." Beads of sweat glistened on his forehead and his lip trembled. "It can mean only one thing."

Jen patted his brow with a cloth napkin. "You don't have to say it."

"No, it's better if I do." But when he did, his voice was strangled. "Naryfel . . . We must tell the others."

"Bit's bringing them. I knew you'd want to meet."

He nodded absently, a haunted look on his face. He tried to pour himself a cup of tea, but his hand shook and he spilled the hot liquid on his fingers.

"Let me get that," she said, pouring the tea. She took his arm and led him to the table where he had been tinkering.

I have to keep him from slipping back, she thought.

"Do you want ice?" she asked, pointing to his fingers.

He shook his head, his eyes still far away.

She handed him the tea and made him sip it. "Have you figured out what these are?" she asked, pointing to the antique objects on his worktable.

He looked down absently at a copper sphere inlaid with fiery red jewels. Like a man reaching in the dark, he extended his hand and traced his finger on the surface. Slowly his eyes refocused. "I think this goes with that silver mirror," he replied. He picked up a triangular mirror and slipped it into a groove at the top of the sphere.

He just needs a little time, she thought. *See, the color's returning to his face.*

She kept him going with small talk. All the while, her mind raced. Naryfel! How could one person have so much power, to reach over time and distance and make her father quake so? Even as she asked the question, she knew the answer. Naryfel had nearly destroyed him. When Jen found him, he was barely alive, with no memory of his kingdom, his family, or his own identity.

The morning sun passed through the translucent walls of the Crystal Room, bathing it in a warm, rosy glow. While Jen waited for Dash and the Pondit to arrive for the meeting, she watched her mother polish off a second cream puff. This one had chocolate icing.

"How can you be so calm?" Jen asked.

"Life is to be relished," her mother soothed. She licked the chocolate off her fingertips. "I see no shadows here, only sunlight."

Jen had noticed a curious thing about her mother. Whenever she entered a room it seemed like there was more light. Not like lighting candles or opening shutters on a sunny day. But it felt brighter, as if her mother were a fairy, or some ethereal being who radiated a warm glow wherever she went.

Jen had watched the room when her mother arrived with

Bit. Ever so slightly, the shadows seemed to shrink; the antique objects gleamed. The pink striations in the walls were pinker. The air fresh and alive.

"Only sunlight," her mother repeated.

Jen had no reply. True, it was a glorious day. But despite her mother's presence, Jen had been feeling cold all morning. The iron grip of the mist on her body lingered like a bad smell, and she couldn't shake the queasy sensation of falling.

Bit sat next to her on the loveseat, braiding Jen's long tresses. "I hope I can eat like that when I'm your age," Bit said to Jen's mother. "What's your secret?"

Jen's mother was trim, despite a steady diet of sweets. Her hair was brown like Jen's. But the resemblance between them stopped with her mother's birthmark, a curious cluster of five circles on the left side of her forehead.

Jen had told her briefly about the warning. The details would get filled in when Dash and the Pondit arrived. She had blanched a moment on hearing the news, then quickly recovered.

Jen wasn't surprised. How many times had her mother put others first? Once, riding in a ravine, she and Jen had gotten caught in a flash flood. The driver had been pinned beneath the overturned carriage. While Jen stayed to keep him sheltered from the rain, her mother hiked three miles for help, through washed-out trails and mudslides. It came out later she'd suffered a broken wrist.

Now her first thought would be for Father. As soon as she heard the news, she was beside him, holding him, whispering in his ear. When his shoulders relaxed and his hand stopped trembling, she ordered breakfast. With easy talk and soothing laughter, she persuaded him to eat.

He sat now at the table, tinkering with the copper sphere.

The color had returned to his face.

"What *is* your secret?" he asked. "If I ate like that, I'd weigh four hundred pounds."

Mother laughed. "You'd burn it off, Elan, taking your exercise with Dash."

"That I would. But soon I'll throw out my back. I can barely keep up with him."

"I've watched. He goes at it like a lion," Mother said.

Father gazed at Jen, almost shyly, and his voice softened. "How goes your own exercise? Have you tried climbing?"

"I like running," she lied.

"There are some beautiful trees at Glindin Lake. We could go together and try them. How does that sound?"

Jen's mouth went dry. She was saved from answering when Dash strode into the room, followed by the Pondit.

"Have you heard about Vieveeka?" asked Dash, his face glowing with excitement. At sixteen, he was the image of his father. Coils of jet black hair. Magnetic gray eyes. A body rippling with strength and vigor. The only difference between them was Dash was still not as tall, or as broad across the shoulders as Father. But he would be.

"No," Mother said. "Who is she?"

"There's quite a buzz going around court. Everyone's talking about her. Everyone wants to be seen with her. She's wanted at all the best parties."

He sat next to Bit, holding her hand absently.

"They say she's enchanting, beautiful, graceful, and intelligent," he said.

Bit withdrew her hand and looked at Jen. No one else would notice, but when Bit's eyes got that big, it meant she was scared.

"In that order?" Jen said sourly.

He ignored her remark. "Father, we must have her over."

"We will then," said Father. "Dash. Something important has happened. Jenny. Tell them."

The second telling wasn't easier—the whispered warning, the strange words about a harp, the engulfing darkness—it left her covered in a film of clammy sweat. And she remembered more: of wrists and ankles seized in an iron grip. She rubbed them now. Saw faint, finger-like bruises where she'd been held.

"What does it mean?" Dash asked.

"That Naryfel's coming," she said.

"How do you know? It could be something else."

Jen folded her arms. Dash had better take this seriously or they were sunk. "Like what?" she asked.

"It could be another plot to usurp the throne. I stopped one before."

The Pondit stepped forward. His body was like a long noodle, bent forward so others didn't have to look up so far. Twinkling blue eyes looked out from beneath a waterfall of eyebrow hair. "That was before your father returned. Some of the nobles could not accept a boy king."

"No, they questioned my right to the throne," Dash said. "They challenged our bloodline."

"True, but since your father's return, there's been unprecedented prosperity," the Pondit replied. "Why would anyone want to change that?"

"Jealousy. Greed," Dash said. "But we still don't know it's Naryfel. It could be a natural disaster. Like an earthquake. Or flood."

"True," said the Pondit. "But we must take all precautions. If it is Naryfel, we will be up against immense power."

"Agreed," Dash said. "I'll put a watch on the borders and extra guards around the castle. She wouldn't dare bring an army here, but she might try and slip in with a small band. What does she look like?"

They all turned to Jen's mother. Her eyes, usually sweet and mild, were filled with pain and sadness. Naryfel was her half sister.

"It's okay, Love," Father said. He put his hand on her shoulder. "You don't have to talk about it."

"I'm all right," Mother replied. But she poured a glass of water and sipped before continuing. "She would be about forty now. Her hair is dark. The last time I saw her, it was turning gray. She has long lashes, and thick black eyebrows, like . . ."

"Like a man's," Father said.

Mother laughed. "Like a man's."

"Good. If she tries to sneak into Aerdem," Dash said, "I'll spot her."

Jen chewed on a corner of her lip. No one was bringing up the obvious. "Father, what about Wyndano's Cloak?"

He glanced at the scar above her eyebrow and looked away. "What about it?"

"Shouldn't we get it back?"

Father shifted his feet uneasily. His fingers tapped the copper sphere and he shot a glance at Mother.

Jen pressed him. "We could use it against Naryfel."

"How?"

"Like using the Cloak to turn into a squirrel or a fox," Jen replied, "and slipping behind enemy lines to spy."

Father turned the gadget back and forth, his eyes fixed on a point a few inches beyond. "Medlara has the Cloak."

"I know. She wanted to see how it worked. But if you needed to, you could use it, couldn't you?"

"Jen, the Cloak is dangerous."

Jen tried to quell the fear gnawing inside her. She wanted

Father to be strong, to protect the family. "You could turn into a dragon if you wanted to. No enemy could face you then."

He sighed. "I never tried a dragon."

"But you could."

"Before, yes, when I was . . . not myself."

"But afterward, when you were yourself, you flew."

Dash slapped his fist into his hand. "Father, she's right. The Cloak's a perfect weapon."

Father's throat tightened. "Don't ask this of me."

"But Father, if I'm to defend Aerdem, I want every advantage."

Father looked imploringly at the Pondit, but got no support there. "He's right, Sire. With the Cloak, you can attack as a lion or spy as a bird. Even now, Medlara is probably sending it. She will know we need it."

Father's shoulders sagged. "Very well." His gaze, sad and troubled, rested on Jen.

"Thank you, Father," said Dash. "Now, what about Bookar and Penrod? They should be able to help."

"They're still in Medlara's valley," Father said. "If she's sending the Cloak, they will accompany it."

"Then all we can do is watch and wait," said Dash grimly.

"No," said a small voice.

Everyone turned in surprise and looked at Bit who sat forgotten on the loveseat, twisting a corner of her sleeve.

"That's not enough," she said. "I can't let anything happen . . . to any of you." She looked at Dash, her eyes wide.

"Don't worry," he replied. "I've been building and training the army for over a year. They're sharp, fast, and disciplined."

"I know. It's just—"

"Shh," soothed Dash, taking her hand. "I promise, everything will be all right."

"No," the Pondit said. "Let her speak. Go ahead, Bit."

"We need to . . . protect the Cloak . . . don't we?"

Everyone looked at her, thunderstruck.

"She's right," the Pondit said. "If Bookar and Penrod return with the Cloak, Naryfel will try and steal it."

"I don't think she knows about it," Father said.

"We can't count on that," the Pondit replied. "She may have spies. And we must protect Bookar and Penrod too."

"I'll send a party of soldiers to escort them home," said Dash. "So that's it. There's nothing more we can do."

"No." Jen jumped to her feet. "Bit's right. We've got to do more."

"Like what?" asked Dash.

"I don't know. But I can't just freeze like a chicken waiting for the snake to strike." Jen clenched her fist. "We have to fight back."

"But there's nothing to fight. There's a danger—we don't know what. Maybe it's Naryfel. Maybe not. Give me something real, and I'll act. I can't battle smoke and fog."

"It's Naryfel, all right. You just don't want to see it."

"If it is, I can handle her."

"Can you? Don't you remember who she is? What she did?"

Even as she said it Jen regretted her words. He had suffered as much as any of them. Everyone in Aerdem knew the tale. Dash's mother died in childbirth. After two years of grief, his father journeyed afar in search of a wife. At last, in a distant land he met Queen Naryfel, a handsome woman with a quick mind. At first he thought they would marry. But one morning he heard singing from a lonely tower window, and his heart was captured. He found the tower locked, but gained entrance with the aid of a servant. The singer was as lovely to his eyes as she had been to his ears, and they quickly fell in love. The queen's half sister, she had been imprisoned for years out of jealousy and spite.

He helped her escape and they fled. Enraged, Naryfel pursued them relentlessly. A powerful sorceress, she sent evil sprites and imps to find them. Obeying her call, fiendish nightwalkers, crawlers, and sniffers joined the search. When these failed to locate the couple, she summoned ghouls and geists with gruesome spells, and unleashed unspeakable horrors from the bowels of the earth. Still the couple eluded her.

Ever on the run, they married and conceived a child. Jen was born and hidden. And still Naryfel pursued them.

It was only a matter of time. Weaving a trap of deceit and lies, first the king, then his bride was captured at last. Now the full force of Naryfel's fury was felt. Without mercy or compassion, she punished them with horrible enchantments. Dash grew up without a father. Jen was an orphan for nine years, with only vague memories of her mother. The King of Aerdem was driven nearly mad. And his sweet bride was lost . . . until Jen . . .

Jen had reversed all that . . .

What would Naryfel do to her?

4

While Jen met with her family in the

Crystal Room, the morning found Count Pompahro pacing his study. It was a bright and sunny day, but he pulled the curtains shut. He'd spent a restless night. Before going to bed he'd drunk a cup of chamomile tea, in hope that sleep would not evade him another night. After several hours of tossing and turning, he rang for hot milk. By four, he tried the fiery spirits he swore he would no longer drink. At five he was in the leather recliner in his study, working on a second glass. Six o'clock found him at his desk, poring over his accounts. He lingered on one page in particular, resisting the urge to tear it out and toss it into the fireplace, where a crackling blaze provided the only light in the room. If he did crumple up that page and burn it, he knew it wouldn't do any good. He slammed the account book shut and threw it across the desk.

"One page," he said to himself. "How could one page mean so much?"

He paced the room, then over to the window, where he parted the curtains an inch and peeked out. Turning, he rang a brass bell that hung by his recliner.

"Where is that useless Geoffrey?" he grumbled. "How many times do I need to ring for that worthless, dimwitted slow-poke? Mother told me never to hire a Deastyer. 'They're useless and shifty.' That's what she used to say. I'll let him go the moment I see him."

He returned to the window and peeked out cautiously. He heard a soft tapping from the door.

"Enter," he called, still staring out the window. He heard the door open behind him. "How dare you keep me waiting. You try my patience, man. My patience."

"Father?"

The Count turned. "Oh. Pet. It's you," he said coldly. "I thought it was that lazy Geoffrey. Have you seen him?"

"No. He didn't greet me when I came in."

"He's probably stuffing his mouth in the kitchen. If I don't let him go soon, he'll eat us out of house and home." His eye lingered on the account book.

Petunia followed his gaze. "Is it that bad, Father?"

"It couldn't be worse."

"I wish you had listened to me. I told you those seeds were no good."

"Everyone said they would triple my crop. How was I to know I'd get less than half?"

"Because no one knew the man who sold them. He was probably a gypsy. Look, Father. How much is the debt? I can help."

The Count laughed. "You? How can you help? I owe three hundred grand petals." He pulled violently on the brass bell. "Where is that worthless scoundrel with my coffee?"

Petunia sank onto a burgundy sofa. "Three hundred . . . I didn't know it was that bad."

"Yes, well, I borrowed on what I expected the grapes to

bring. Now the loans have come due. With interest."

"What if we sold off the crystal and the silver? That should be worth at least a hundred grand petals. I have some shoes I've outgrown. We could sell those, and I'm sure there's some furniture we don't need at the country estate. We could get another fifty there. Even that looking glass would bring in twenty-five." She pointed to a large mirror, hanging over the fireplace, which had gold leaf around the edge. She ticked off a dozen more items, calculating the price they would bring.

"You forget, we have an important guest," he replied. He always spoke through his nose to communicate an air of sophistication and privilege. "What kind of impression would we make without crystal and silver? And I won't sell the furniture. It belonged to my mother."

"Father, I have this idea for a business. We could make the money."

"Now, now. Don't worry your little curls over this."

"But Father—"

"We have a plan, remember? Once you marry Prince Dashren, our worries are over."

"But he's in love with Bit."

"Bit? She's nothing more than a servant. You are a countess. Never forget that."

"But he never even looks at me."

"Oh, he'll look, all right. Trust me. Now, no more talk of selling and businesses. That's for the little people. Remember, we're practically royalty. Now run along and powder your nose. And put more rouge on your cheeks. It will make your face rounder. Then see what you can learn at the Rose Castle."

"I was just there. I found out Bit is planning a party for Dash. She's making him a surprise."

The Count stroked his long chin. He was a short, slight

man with dainty hands and feet. He looked remarkably like his daughter, but his strawberry hair was straight.

"That is interesting news," he said. "Stay close to Bit. Try and find out what she's making."

"I already know. She made a replica of the castle out of rose quartz."

"Well done, Pet. Well done." The Count rubbed his hands. "You must be my eyes and ears in the castle."

He held out his hand, the signal that she was to go. She kissed the tips of his fingers and left the room. When she was gone, he removed a silk handkerchief from his pocket and vigorously wiped where she had kissed.

He returned to the window and peeked out again cautiously. A soft tapping turned him toward the door.

"Enter," he called.

Geoffrey entered, carrying coffee and pastry on a silver platter.

"I ordered that thirty minutes ago," the Count snapped.

"Yes, Sir." Geoffrey set down the platter, poured the steaming coffee into a cup, and dropped in three lumps of sugar. He added a dash of cream. "I was delayed, Sir."

"Delayed! What could possibly delay you? What could there possibly be between here and the kitchen to delay you?"

Geoffrey was a tall man, portly in the middle, with a shiny bald head. He stuck his hands into the pockets of his vest.

"There was a caller at the door," he replied quietly, glancing at the Count's black account book. "A Mr. Tite. He was most insistent on seeing you. He said that he knew you were here and would not be turned away again without seeing you. I told him you had left early this morning to inspect your country estate. He laughed, I'm sorry to say, Sir, quite heartily at that, and insisted I take him to the carriage house. He wanted to see for himself if you had left. I hope you don't mind, Sir. I took the liberty this morning to suggest to your lovely guest, Lady Vieveeka, that she take a country carriage ride." He glanced meaningfully again at the leather account book. "I hope I did right, Sir."

"But I had a meeting with her, scheduled for eleven this morning," the Count replied, disappointed.

"I took the liberty of suggesting that you and the Lady could meet at the corner of Linden Lane and Old Mill Road. Have I done right, Sir?"

The Count brightened. "Quite right, Geoffrey. Marvelously, splendidly right." The Count moved to the curtained window, threw it open, and let in some fresh air. The spring had returned to his step. "To show my appreciation, you may retire an hour early this evening!"

"That is quite . . . generous, Sir."

The Count waved his hand. "Think nothing of it. I always treat my servants right."

"I took the liberty of laying out your riding clothes, and your dapple gray is saddled."

"Geoffrey, you're a gem. I'm off to meet Vieveeka. If anyone asks, I've taken ill and I'm recovering in the country. I may not be disturbed under any circumstance."

"Very good, Sir." Geoffrey bowed and closed the door behind him, leaving Count Pompahro feeling like he had slept a week.

The Count stood beside his horse and watched the carriage approach along Old Mill Road. It was a warm day. Only a few puffy clouds hung lazily on a corn-blue sky. If things went well, all his days would be sunny and lazy, too. He inspected his suit while he waited. He'd abandoned the riding clothes for something more attractive. A pastel pink shirt with matching silk trousers. A gray handkerchief tucked neatly in his breast pocket. Patent leather pumps—polished to perfection—with shiny gold buckles. His head was topped with a jaunty cap, mint green with a peacock feather pinned on the side. He felt flushed with excitement, like a boy going on a first date.

The carriage was drawn by two dapple grays, the Count's favorite breed. He recognized his own driver, Owen, up top. The carriage stopped beside him. Before climbing in, he told Owen to drive them up Old Mill, then make a circle that would bring them back to his horse. He wanted to show Vieveeka the peaceful countryside. This was a lovely road, with a pleasant view of rolling green pastures, grazing cattle, and peach orchards.

In the carriage, the Count settled into a cushioned seat opposite Vieveeka. *Oh my*, he thought, with a pounding heart. *She is even more breathtaking than I remember, and I only saw her just last night at dinner.*

"Good morning, Count," came a voice young and sweet, with just a hint of a rasp, as if she had attended too many late-night parties. It was hard to place her age. She could be sixteen, he thought, but hoped she was a few years older. She held a white fan, which covered the lower part of her face. Her eyes were spellbinding, one a luminous brown, the other a cool blue. Fiery red hair spilled about her bare shoulders in a cascade of enticing curls. She wore a long yellow gown held by two thin straps.

Oh, thought the Count. *If she were only a little older and I were young again, I would marry her. She's young, rich, and beautiful. That would be the end of my troubles. After what the Countess has done—a divorce would be easy.*

"You look dashing today, Count."

He blushed. "And you look enchanting."

"How goes our little plan?" Beside her, near the back window, was a toy dog he had given Petunia when she was four. The dog's head was on a spring. Every time the carriage bounced on the road, the head nodded.

"It couldn't be better. I found out just this morning that Bit is having a party for the prince. She is planning to surprise him with a model of the Rose Castle."

"That is interesting news. And how clever of you to find out."

"But how can we use it?"

"Yes . . . how?" She gazed out the window. Tall poplars lined the road. They were evenly spaced so that sun or shadow fell across her face as the carriage ambled along. Turning back to him, she lowered the fan and revealed a pair of red lips and a dainty cleft chin. Her mouth curled up on one side in a bewitching smile. "A masked ball."

The Count stared at her. "I beg your pardon?" He could hear the horses clopping on the dirt road, and the carriage groaned over a pothole.

"A coming out party."

"For who?"

"Me." Her face was in shadow again.

"Forgive me, but what's the point?"

"The point my dear Count, is we need to break up Dash and Bit." The little toy dog nodded.

"How will you do that?"

"By making the prince fall in love with me."

"But what about Petunia? I want her to marry the prince."

"And so she shall. After I break the prince's heart, she'll be there to pick up the pieces."

"It won't be that easy to break them up. He's quite taken with the girl."

"Leave that to me. I'll sweep her aside like a leaf. It will be my coming out, and also his birthday party. Nothing could be better to throw us together. We'll have it at your estate."

The Count turned white. "My estate. That would be difficult. I find I lack . . ."

She reached behind her and produced a pouch.

"This should cover any expenses."

The Count looked eagerly inside. It was filled with gold coins. "This is most generous."

"A trifle. If you do your part well, there's more."

"How much more?"

"Enough to settle your debts. And . . ." The carriage hit another pothole, sending up a fine dust.

"And?"

"My dear Count," she said with a laugh, and played with the gold buttons on his shirt with her fan. "Have you not thought of having more for yourself? Why should you settle for second when you can have it all?"

His throat went dry and he licked his lips. "What do you mean?"

"We could sweep them all aside." The light and shadow from the passing trees flickered on her face.

"That wasn't to be the plan. It was to be Petunia . . ."

"Yes. It will be Petunia. But come, Count. She's no beauty. We need a backup plan."

"It's one thing to break up two lovers. It's another to commit treason."

"Pooh. Call it what you will. The royal family holds you in contempt. You told me so yourself. Why shouldn't you sit on the throne? All Aerdem could be yours."

The carriage creaked and swayed gently as he eyed her silently. She reached out the window and tapped with her fan.

The carriage came to a stop beside his horse. She extended her hand. As he touched her fingertips she quickly grasped his whole hand and held it tight. At the same time, she reached with her other hand and plucked out his handkerchief. She patted her cheek with it.

"Don't disappoint me, Count. I so hate to be disappointed." She still held his hand, which was intensely cold. "I know I can count on you to do your part. In all I say."

The little dog nodded.

5

After an early morning run, Jen

usually relaxed on her veranda with a mug of steaming coffee. She was up one story, and liked to look at the garden below. There, gladiolas lined a meandering path, which ended at a fountain beside a blooming oleander. The day after the warning, she sat facing her bedroom, her coffee untouched and cold beside her. She stared at the eaves above.

Shortly before sunrise, a dream had awakened her. At first it seemed like a woman was in her room, laughing.

Naryfel! she'd thought.

As the cobwebs of sleep dissolved, she'd realized the laughter was scratching and cooing from outside. She tried to go back to sleep but thuds and whaps pulled her out of bed to investigate. She'd been out on the veranda ever since, watching suspiciously.

Strange birds swooped and fluttered about the eaves. Their feathers were dull gray, except for a brilliant star of gold and blue that blazed on the breast. There were half a dozen of them, dropping clumps of dirt, twigs and leaves. They must have found a garbage pile, because later they dumped rotten fruit and vegetables. Jen even saw fish bones.

Any other day, this would have been fascinating. But after Medlara's warning, the birds alarmed her. She wondered if this was an omen. Another warning. Or worse, one of Naryfel's weapons.

Sunlight reflected off the luminous star of one of the birds. He circled over the pile, now dank and dark, and added a lump of manure. Fortunately, a breeze blew the other way.

Jen's mother stepped onto the veranda, her face serene and untroubled. "Hi, Sweetie. Can I join you?"

Jen nodded. Mother pulled up a chair, glancing at the untouched coffee. She raised her eyes and studied the birds. A faint smile curled her lips.

They sat together quietly. Her mother was giving Jen space, and she appreciated it. After a while her mother drew out a brush and stroked Jen's tresses. The brush against her scalp was soothing, the motion hypnotic. She felt her hair part into three and the slow weaving of a braid. When it was done, her mother laid it gently over one shoulder, where it hung like a long anchor rope.

She swept her own hair back and the scent of wildflowers floated past Jen's nose. That fragrance was her earliest memory of her mother, who claimed she wore no perfume.

"Do you think Naryfel sent them?" Jen asked at last, nodding toward the birds.

"No."

"How can you be sure? Isn't it strange they've shown up now?"

"It's a blessing."

Jen's eyes narrowed. It was hard to see why.

"They are Starbirds," said Mother. "There is a legend in my country about wondrous birds that live among the stars. In times of tribulation and sorrow for us, the young ones fall to earth. Try as they might, they cannot fly high enough to return home. So they build a mound out of whatever they find and bury themselves. They stay in the mound until a great change takes place: They will fly only when a rainbow of feathers covers them. Then, when the time is right, they burst from the mound, soaring higher and higher until they reach the stars."

"Why are they a blessing?"

"It is said that if a Starbird nests on your roof, you will soar with them. Prosperity and happiness will come to you and those you love."

Jen watched one of the birds drop a lump of dung on the pile. "I hope you're right."

Mother left, and the wind shifted. The smell drove Jen off the veranda and down to the garden below, where she continued the vigil among the gladiolas. She sat on a stone bench beside the fountain, hoping the tinkling of the water would calm her nerves. She could see her veranda and much of the rest of the castle. Strangely, she didn't see the birds anywhere else except on the eaves above Bit's apartment.

She heard footsteps behind her.

"Hi, Jen. What's wrong?"

It was Petunia. The last person Jen wanted to see. She should have known the Countess would find her here.

Jen shrugged. "Why do you ask?"

"You look tired."

"I didn't sleep well."

"Why not?" The Countess' eyes were wide and earnest.

"I had a bad dream. I've had it before."

"What happens?" Petunia sat on the bench and smoothed her dress. This one was bright red, tied at the waist with a green sash.

Jen sighed. "Nothing. I just hear this woman laughing. It's awful."

"I know what you mean," Petunia replied. "Laughter is a funny thing. You can giggle or bubble with laughter. And you can chuckle. But you could also *burst* with laughter, *crack up, break up, or fall in a fit* of laughter. Worse, you can split your sides, be in stitches, double up, double over, rock, roll, shriek, and roar with laughter."

Jen found herself smiling.

"Even worse," Petunia said, "you could *choke* with laughter, *die* laughing, *or kill yourself* laughing."

"How about laugh your head off?" Jen suggested.

"Right. That wouldn't be fun."

Jen nodded toward the birds above her veranda. "Have you seen those anywhere else?"

"They're roosting outside my bedroom window. What a nuisance."

"I know."

"And they stink. I tried to get rid of them with raw garlic, but they just added it to their pile. Well, got to run. I'm getting a manicure with Bit. See you."

Petunia's rustling dress faded down the path. Jen looked at the eaves above her veranda, just in time to see one of the Starbirds drop a small fish skeleton.

The path Jen followed broke out of

a thicket of oak and wound up the belly of a hill toward the top. The grass on either side was dense and long. At this time of year, the dominant color wasn't green, or even the wild lavender that bloomed in broad strokes on the hillsides. It was the vast fields of plenderil flowers that painted the meadows and slopes crimson.

She knew she shouldn't have left the safety of the castle, or the family unguarded. She had to risk it. Watching. Waiting. It was getting to her. She felt cooped up. She had to move. Get away.

And there was something she had to do.

The sun felt good. Warming. Bees, a few moths with small, delicate white wings, hovered about the wildflowers. She drank in a breath of air, clean as the sky above.

The trail forked, one running directly to the top, where a water tower crowned the summit like a hat. The other trail sloped more gently, coming upon the tower gradually from the other side. She chose the slower path. She was in no rush to get there.

Her mind turned to Medlara's warning, trying to sift through the words and sensations. The forbidding fog. The riddle about a harp. The urging to "seek the answers." What did it all mean? She'd been over it a hundred times, but no new ideas came. Only more questions.

The trail wound around the hill and dipped into a shady copse. When she emerged from the trees, the path turned down into a meadow, where someone sat in a field of plenderil.

Jen slowed, coming up quietly behind until she recognized the thick auburn tresses. "Bit, what are you doing out here?"

Bit's shoes and socks were off. Her shoulders jumped and she plunged her feet deep into a cluster of crimson flowers. "Jenny, you startled me." She gave a little laugh of relief.

"You shouldn't be away from the castle."

Bit gazed at the patchwork of orchards, farms, and pastures below. "I know, but it's so beautiful here. I had to come."

Jen sat beside her. "How did you get away?"

"No one will notice I'm gone." Bit gave a little laugh, but her eyes were sad.

Jen frowned. "But Dash, Father . . ."

"Dash is running patrols. Your father and mother are meeting with dignitaries."

Bit ran her fingers gently up the stem of a plenderil. "Did you know, these grow nowhere but in Aerdem?" She held the plant near the top, where the crimson flower bowed like a poppy. "You can snap it off here." Her thumb and forefinger slid down the stem. "And here." Then she grasped the base. "But you can't pull it out."

"I didn't know that."

"Try."

Jen tried. Grasping the narrow stem with both hands, she pulled as hard as she could. The stalk broke off in her hand, but the rest of the plant remained embedded in the soil.

"See," Bit said. "Your father told me. The roots go too deep."

"I'm sorry I broke the flower." Jen laid it on Bit's lap.

"It will grow back."

A lavender bush within arm's reach reminded Jen of a great head, the stalks like hair stirring in the breeze. Buzzing droned from within the bush as bees floated lazily among the blossoms. Bit began gathering long blades of grass, plenderil, and baby's breath, arranging them in groups on her lap.

She glanced at the scar on Jen eyebrow, then nodded toward the water tower. "Are you going up there?"

Jen swatted at a fly. "Yeah."

Bit plucked a dozen lavender stalks. The bush buzzed like a hive, but she moved gently, calmly among the blossoms. The bees paid no more mind to her hand than if it had been a tree branch or a cluster of leaves. "This is your first time up there since—"

"Yeah. First time." Jen felt ashamed, angry with herself.

"What happened up there?" Bit braided two stalks of lavender and a plenderil flower, and tied them with a stout grass blade.

Jen watched her braid another set before answering. "You know the story."

"I don't. No one will talk about it."

"There's nothing to say. I fell. That's all."

That wasn't all. She'd been with her father at the top of the water tower, trying to use Wyndano's Cloak. Then . . . the rest was a black nightmare she refused to think about.

Since then she'd been frightened of climbing trees, rocks, ladders. Anything going straight up. How could she be frightened of what she loved most?

But whatever danger was coming, her family needed her, counted on her to be strong. That's why she'd come here. She needed to climb that tower. When the Cloak came back, she might have to use it. How could she, if she was afraid?

Frustration and anger nipped at her like a snarling dog. Fortunately, Bit didn't push her to say more. Instead, her friend tied a flower braid to the end of another, and did the same with four more braids.

"Let's go up there together," Jen said hopefully. Maybe she'd feel calmer if Bit was along. "We can go skinny-dipping."

Bit blushed and pushed her feet deeper in the plenderil. "I want to finish this wreath."

Why was she hiding her feet? Come to think of it, Jen had never seen her get dressed. She'd always written that off to Bit's shyness. But there was much about Bit that was mysterious. Coming to Aerdem in rags with a group of refugees. Where had she come from? What happened to her parents? Bit couldn't say.

Still, if she needed privacy about her feet, she could have it. Jen loved her too much to push the point. She took a knife from her belt. "Hold out your hand."

Bit set aside the wreath and held out her hand obediently, fingertips laced with the scent of lavender. Jen gave her the knife. Bit held it in her palm like it was a snake or a poisonous spider and let it fall to the ground.

"Look, Bit, it might not be safe out here. The danger can come any time. You need to protect yourself."

"I know, but I couldn't, wouldn't use a knife." Her eyes were open and pleading.

Jen put the knife near Bit's knee. "Okay. Just keep it near you. In case. I won't be gone long."

꙳

Jen moved up the trail, but glanced back at Bit. How do you explain a girl who was frightened of knives, but put her hand in a bush humming with bees?

Jen shrugged. She had her own problems to worry about. The water tower loomed above, and she felt her heartbeat quicken.

The sun was falling toward the hills, but Jen felt hotter. Sweat trickled down her face and back, doing little to cool the nest of prickles at the back of her neck. She paused to tie her hair in a knot and stuffed it down her shirt.

A few minutes later she stood at the bottom of the tower, a cylinder of wooden planks, shiny with pitch, rising thirty feet. A ceramic pipe from a higher hill siphoned water into the tower. Boards nailed crossways formed a crude ladder. Little trickles of green at the seams marked the leaks.

Morbid curiosity drew her away from the ladder to the other side of the tower. There, jutting out of a cluster of daffodils like a strange, deformed flower, was the rock that had opened the gash above her eye. Dried blood still stained one side.

Her knees wobbled and she steadied herself against the tower wall. "That's the last thing you should've looked at," she muttered.

Retreating to the ladder, she reached for a rung and felt her heart bolt to a gallop.

Take it slow, she thought, but her hand was shaking. She lifted one foot to the first step, but kept the other firmly rooted on the ground. "What's wrong with you?" she cried. "It's only one step."

It might have been a mile, the way her body trembled. She forced the leg up and waited for her limbs to quiet. They didn't.

One step at a time, she told herself.

She reached for another rung and her foot found the next board. All she had to do was push down with that foot and the other one would join it. Her heart drummed inside her chest. She waited for it to calm. It didn't. She pushed on anyway, drawing the other foot up. A wave of dizziness overtook her and her head swam.

She clenched her teeth until her jaw ached, then forced herself to reach for the next rung. One foot followed on the next step and she froze.

"It's only three steps," she said bitterly. "You could fall right now and not get hurt. You've jumped farther."

It didn't matter. Sweat soaked her clothes. A queasy snake twisted in her stomach. "Don't look down."

She did. The ground tilted and spun. Quickly backing down the ladder, she stumbled to some bushes and threw up.

Afterward, she collapsed onto some grass, thoroughly disgusted with herself.

7

The peaceful waters of Glindin Lake

did little to soothe Jen. Everyone was on edge. Father wandered the castle at night like a ghost. Bit followed Dash like a lost puppy, until Jen told her to stop. Bit agreed, but twisted her way through three dresses a day, "So Dash doesn't see me all wrinkled."

Dash insisted he wasn't scared of Naryfel, but drilled the troops until they were exhausted, "So Bit feels safe."

Jen was a taught rubber band. She kept a wary eye on the Starbirds in the mornings, and spent the afternoons watching Dash wear the soldiers to a frazzle. Neither made her feel better. Worse, Bookar and Penrod still hadn't returned with the Cloak.

Even Mother showed the strain. She couldn't be everywhere at once, and little lines of worry had crept around her eyes. Coming here for a picnic was her way to calm everyone. Just outside the city, they were beside the shore in the shade of some willow trees. Dash had hidden a perimeter of soldiers around the area for protection. Unlike the castle, there would be no spies here. Father stood at an easel near the water, painting the scene in oils. Mother was barbecuing skewers of vegetables over a fire, the smoky aroma of onions and peppers filling the air. They only awaited Dash's arrival.

"Is Pet coming?" Bit asked. She sat on a pale blue blanket folding cloth napkins.

Jen paced the edge of the blanket like a guard dog. "Remember? It's just family."

Earlier, Pet had shown too much curiosity about where they were going, so Jen had told her that Baron Endare was having a luncheon party with all the most eligible bachelors. There would only be a few girls there. Could Pet figure out where and when the party was? Pet promised she could, and scurried off to sniff it out. The only problem was there was no party. *That should keep her poodle nose out of our affairs for a while,* Jen thought.

"Oh, right," Bit said. She pulled a shawl over her shoulders. A few clouds had moved over the sky, and a wind had picked up. "When is Dash coming?"

"Any time."

Father picked up some yellow paint with his brush and sketched in a boat. A moment later, he frowned.

"Why don't you help him?" Jen whispered to Bit.

Bit shrank into a ball and shook her head.

"You're the artist in the family," said Jen.

"They're just silly little pictures. Anyway, no one can capture Aerdem. It's too beautiful." She looked around her, eyes drinking in the sky, lake and trees.

She was right, of course. The first thing that struck Jen about Aerdem was the colors. The blues were bluer, the greens greener, as if the world were painted in a collage of peacock feathers.

"It must have been awful growing up in the Plain World,"

Bit said. "Was it really gray?"

"Pretty bad. If Nell hadn't loved me all those years, I'd have died."

"There must have been some nice people."

"I liked the doctor's wife."

"And the doctor?"

"Always busy. But he could cure anything. How's your present coming?"

"I just need to paint the flower gardens." Bit waited for Mother and Father to turn away. Then she pulled her little castle from a craft bag and held it up. Little flags waved gaily in the breeze and sunlight flashed on the towers in rosy sparks.

Jen caught her breath. "It's magic," she said softly, half expecting little people to march out the doors or wave from the windows.

"Will Dash like it? Maybe I should get him a bridle instead."

"He's got a dozen bridles. Nothing like this. He'll love it."

"I hope so." Bit tucked the present away.

Jen turned and paced the other way, scanning the willows and flowering acacia beyond. A branch quivered in one spot.

Bit watched her. "Dash said we'd be safe here."

"I know." Jen watched the branch. It stirred again, but the nearby foliage remained motionless.

"We are safe, aren't we?"

"I just want to make sure."

Bit studied the foliage and pointed. "It's just one of Dash's soldiers, behind that tree trunk."

Jen looked but saw nothing.

"See," Bit said, "there's his plume."

Now Jen saw the edge of a crimson feather. Her face went hot with shame. She'd missed that. "I think there's something behind that branch." The branch quivered again and a thrush burst out of the foliage. A minute later she glided back with a twig in her beak.

"She's building a nest," said Bit.

"Right." Jen sank onto the blanket and tried to relax, but a few minutes later the thunder of hooves brought her to her feet.

A moment later Dash galloped up on Nightflyer, leaping off before the giant horse skidded to a stop. "Father! Have you heard? The Lady Vieveeka is throwing a masked ball!"

Father wiped paint from his brush. "When is it?"

"Tomorrow night, at Count Pompahro's. We're all invited."

"But Dash," said Bit, eyes suddenly round, "tomorrow's your birthday."

"Exactly," he replied. "It's a birthday party for me, and a coming out party for Vieveeka. We'll all get a chance to meet her. Isn't it nice of the Count to host something for me?"

"But I was planning something for you tomorrow night," said Bit, twisting one of the napkins.

"Can't we do that the next day? I've never been to a masked ball."

Bit looked helplessly at Jen, who had no idea what to say.

Mother pulled two skewers off the fire and weighed them thoughtfully in each hand. "Bit's worked hard to do something special for you."

Dash grabbed a carrot off a platter and munched on it while he paced before them. "Look. It's a chance for us to get out. Meet someone extraordinary. They say Vieveeka's been everywhere. Think of the stories she could tell."

"Can we trust the Count?" Jen asked.

"I don't see why not," Dash replied. "He's never done anything wrong except be overly pleased with himself."

Jen folded her arms. "We shouldn't leave the castle. What

if Naryfel strikes?"

Dash shrugged. "We're outside now, and we're safe enough. I can have my soldiers provide extra security."

"In the Count's house?"

"No. But nearby."

"That won't protect us against poison."

"Jen. Don't be foolish. The Count is not going to poison us. If he wanted to do that, he would have done it long ago."

"I don't like it."

"Then don't like it. I'm going. It's my birthday. I can do what I like, can't I Father?"

Father set down his brush and studied Dash. "Will it make you that happy?"

"More than anything."

"Then we all go. But Jenny's right. We'll need to keep our eyes open."

"Father, is this wise?" Jen asked. "What do we know about this Vieveeka? What does she want in Aerdem?"

Dash rolled his eyes. "She's coming out, and wants an introduction to fine society."

Jen snorted. "You couldn't do finer than the Pompahros."

"She's a duchess of Trilafor."

"She's a stranger."

Dash's eyes blazed. "If a stranger offered you a hand you'd spit at him."

That hurt. Jen felt the fight draining out of her. "But Pet's been spying, and strange birds are roosting, and something bad—"

"Bad things can happen anywhere, any time," said Mother. "Hopefully not too often. We can't stop living. Every moment counts."

Jen had no reply. But she still didn't like it.

"Right," said Dash. "I'm not going to stick my head in a hole." He sat next to Bit and held her hand. "We'll still do your party. I promise," he said gently. "You know I'm all yours."

"Are you?" Bit replied. "Are you still?"

"Of course I am." But he had a far-off look in his eyes.

The lake was no longer peaceful. The wind whipped the trees and etched white chop on the water.

Dash pulled a cape from his saddlebag and flung it over his shoulders. "Where did those clouds come from? The sky was clear this morning."

Father stopped painting and squinted at the sky. "Those are thunderheads."

"Nonsense," Dash said. "It never rains this time of year."

"I know," Father replied. "But a storm is coming. A big one."

❧❧

Dressed in a black leather riding outfit, the Lady Vieveeka slipped out of the Count's mansion and headed for the stable. Passing through the garden and across the yard, she was nothing more than a shadow in the moonless night. As expected, the stable door was open, and the groom waited for her with a saddled horse. She had paid him well. He would keep quiet about her activities.

She left the stable and avoided the cobblestone driveway that ran from the Count's house to the road. Instead, she circled the horse silently across a stretch of soft turf. At the road, she mounted and cantered north. The occasional barn was no more than a silken silhouette against an ebony sky.

A few miles passed, and she left the road and entered a thick grove of trees. She followed a narrow path that ended at a clearing. A crisp wind picked up the scent of eucalyptus.

She swung lightly off the horse and gave a soft whistle, like a mockingbird. From the trees on the other side of the clearing the whistle was returned. Tucking her riding crop under her arm, she walked to the edge of the trees and peered in. A figure stood among the shadows, barely visible.

"How goes it with the Count?" said a voice like dead leaves crackling underfoot.

"All is in place," Vieveeka replied. "Tomorrow night is the masked ball. The royal family is sure to attend. Are your men ready?"

"They've been ready, and grow impatient."

"Can you keep them under control?"

"Of course. They wouldn't dare defy me. But why not move now?"

"I want a little fun first."

"You want to play with your food before you eat it, huh!"

With a whisk and a crack, Vieveeka lashed with the riding crop. Instead of a scream, a hoarse cackle came from the shadows.

"I want to look them over first," she said.

"I think maybe you've grown soft on them."

"Never," she replied coldly. "Be ready on my command. There's a storm coming." She spun on her heel, mounted the horse, and rode off.

Deeper in the shadows something watched and listened—unknown to the other two. Only a tiny, unblinking eye of red marked its presence. Unseen, it melted into the woods like a ghost. A short time later, a song hung on the wind, high and mournful and haunting.

Jen settled reluctantly into the carriage

and began the journey to Count Pompahro's estate. It was the night of the ball, and despite her continued protests the family was going. Worse, while putting on her costume she had received another warning from Medlara.

The message—coming out of a watering pot with snowy static and missing words—ripped at her heart. There was the same warning about danger. Something about a harp. And if the worst happened, she was to seek—

But the words were cut off.

Then there was something new. Beyond a ring of swirling mist, she saw Bookar and Penrod standing beside Medlara.

"We're trapped," they said. "The valley is besieged . . . Darter leaves tonight . . ."

Medlara's eyes dilated. "Things are not as they seem . . . look beyond appearances . . ."

The old woman clasped her hands until the knuckles whitened. She managed to make one point clear. Whatever was going to happen would happen tonight.

Jen had told her family, hoping they would seal the castle

and stay inside. To her surprise, everyone insisted they should go to the ball anyway. Only Bit disagreed, but no one heard or noticed.

"I'm ready for anything," Dash had said, pacing the floor of the Crystal Room, brandishing a sharp knife before concealing it under his costume. He was going as a tiger. He wore a jacket and pants with orange and black stripes. A mask covering his eyes and half of his face was also striped. He refused to wear the tail. "I've ordered my men to keep an extra-sharp lookout."

"Let it come," he added. "I want this over with. Right, Father?"

Blue vessels swelled around Father's eyes, framing a new crop of furrows. "I don't think we can back out now. All the guests have been invited. Everyone expects to celebrate your birthday." He studied and turned the mask in his hands. A noble nose tipped with black velvet sprang from the face, and magnificent horns crowned the top. He was going as a buck. "Rumors are circulating that something is wrong. It might cause fear and unrest if we aren't there."

Dash agreed. The last thing they needed was to look weak. Besides, he argued, Naryfel wouldn't attack them openly. "Doesn't she prefer to slink through the night and set dirty little traps?"

"She does," Father replied. "But she thinks she is cleverer than anyone else. If she thought she could get away with it, she'd relish a bold, public display."

That didn't make Jen feel any better, and she said so. She made one more plea. "Have you all forgotten what Naryfel did?! Tore us apart for nine years! Almost killed us!"

But Mother insisted she would not live in fear. If something were to come, let it come. She would face it.

Jen hoped Bit would back her up, but Bit insisted that since

Dash was going, she needed to stay close to him. She wouldn't leave him for the world.

But she did. To confuse any enemy, Dash divided the family into two carriages, and sent a third ahead as a decoy. He included an armed escort—not unusual for public appearances—and guards disguised as drivers. Dash rode with Mother and Father. Jen went with Bit, who stared silently out the window at the damp, dreary night.

At last, she asked, "Do you think Dash has changed?"

"Changed?" Jen replied. "How do you mean?"

"When I'm with him, he seems far away."

"Maybe he's thinking about Naryfel. Father puts our safety in his hands."

"Maybe that's it."

Bit looked out the window. So did Jen. Dark, threatening clouds had been piling up all day. An unusually strong wind blowing from the northeast had been knocking over flowerpots on Jen's veranda. Now, fat raindrops formed circles on the carriage windows and drummed on the roof.

"He seems awfully interested in the Lady Vieveeka," Bit began again.

"So that's what's bothering you," Jen said. "Don't worry. You know how devoted Dash is to you."

"That can change. What if I don't have enough to hold him?"

Bit smoothed her dress and placed her mask on her lap. She was going as a rabbit. Jen had tried to convince her to wear a different costume. Something like what Jen's mother was wearing. Her mother was going as an angel. The gown was a rich blue. The fabric was light and airy, surrounding her like clouds. The wings shimmered, as if someone had captured the delicate vapor of a rainbow. Her dark hair billowed about her shoulders, bringing out the color in the wings and the softness in her eyes.

Something like that would have been better for Bit, but Bit thought a rabbit would be cute. At least Jen convinced her not to wear a one-piece jumpsuit with a cottontail. That would have looked ridiculous. Instead, Bit wore a white satin gown. The mask had whiskers, and long white ears were pinned to her hair.

"You've got plenty, Bit. Trust me."

Bit replied with a look that said, I hope so.

Jen put her arm around her friend's shoulder. "You still have your present. He'll be thrilled when he sees what you've done." The paint had dried, and Bit's little replica of the Rose Castle looked wonderful.

Jen was satisfied with her own costume. She was going as a pirate. She wore a black patch over her eye, but had punched a small hole in the center so she could see. The costume let her get away with wearing white pants that fell loosely to her ankles. If she needed to move fast, she wouldn't be hindered by a dress. Even better, her costume allowed her to openly carry a cutlass. Dash had been working with her on her swordplay for months. She didn't have his strength, but she had speed and endurance. Several times she'd managed, just as Dash was tiring, to send his sword flying out of his hand. The cutlass would feel different, but would be effective. Knowing it was there made her feel a little safer.

Rain ran down the window in little streams. Jen thought she saw a flicker of lightning. A while later, there was the distant rumble of thunder. *The worst of the storm is coming*, she thought.

Darter was starting home tonight. They could really use him, despite his being one of the most unusual members of the household. A sparrow with one wing shorter by half a length, he had followed Jen to Aerdem from the Plain World. She realized there was magic here when Darter started to talk. Her first friend after Nell died, he'd helped Jen find her parents. He'd even saved Dash. When a giant Kishwar—a dumb brute the size of a house—threatened to crush the prince, Darter swooped in front of the monster. After pestering and distracting the beast, Darter led him on a merry chase away from Dash.

If Naryfel attacked, they could really use Darter, who wouldn't back away from her if she were living fire. But he wouldn't make it here sooner than a day. Not in this storm.

By the time Jen reached the Pompahro mansion, the rain poured in curtains. Lightning flashed as she stepped out of the carriage, illuminating a dark mountain of thunderheads that loomed only a few miles away. The wind blew harder. On a barn across the way, a weathervane whipped in frantic circles. It gave Jen a bad feeling.

She and Bit ran for the entrance to the house, finding the rest of the family already there. They took a minute to remove their rain-soaked cloaks, adjusted their costumes, and were escorted down a long hall to the ballroom.

Most of the guests had already arrived. At least a hundred bodies twirled around the dance floor, and a jumble of buzzing chatter and clinking glasses competed with a small orchestra, which played the *Airs of Aerdem*. The musicians, dressed as frogs, were surely the finest in the land. The strings and horns sang like a mellow chorus. Shimmering cymbals and a pulsing drumbeat made Jen want to move her feet.

No time for that. She needed to check out the ballroom. It was a large square. Two staircases centered on opposite sides led to a second floor balcony, which surrounded the room and led to various chambers upstairs. A huge chandelier hung from the ceiling, spinning prismatic circles on the dancers. The orchestra played in one corner. Along one entire wall was a lavish buffet.

Jen hated everything about the room. What if that chandelier crashed down on everyone? Or the doors were sealed and they were trapped inside with a fire? A skilled archer or knifethrower could attack from the balcony. For that matter, someone could slip a dagger and strike right on the dance floor. It would be hard to keep track of everyone's motions among the whirling bodies. There were at least four men dressed as devils, three foxes, and two executioners. Jen even saw another tiger that looked like Dash. She quickly became confused following who was who as they waltzed about the room. This seemed like the perfect setup for an attack. Or a trap . . .

Her mother headed for the buffet, and the family followed. There were royson-apple pudding, sugarplums, delicate crispels, and pears simmering in honey and wine. Heaped and steaming on platters were roast boar, coneys, pigeon, and rack of lamb—floating on a sea of mint jelly. Enough here to tempt a monk from a fast.

Jen had no stomach for any of it. She took her mother's arm. "Maybe we shouldn't eat or drink."

Mother pulled gently away and stepped to the salad table. "Hush. The Count isn't going to poison everyone."

Jen watched in dismay as Mother filled a plate with marinated artichokes, pickled eggs, stuffed mushrooms, and chocolate-dipped strawberries, and began sampling each like she'd never tasted it before.

The Count might not use poison, thought Jen, *but Naryfel would.*

At that moment, a peacock and the Queen of Hearts spun off the dance floor and greeted them.

"Good evening, Your Highnesses," said the peacock. Long

colorful feathers covered his mask and the same colors repeated on his jacket and shoes. The voice coming from his nose—
which was held high, followed closely by his chin—identified
him as Count Pompahro.

"This is a splendid party, Count," said Father. "You've really outdone yourself."

"Thank you. Do try the punch. I think you'll find it has a
bewitching flavor."

"Sure," Jen cut in, "let me pour you a cup, Count."
She grabbed the ladle before he could reach it and fixed
him a glass.

"Why . . . thank you." He sipped from the glass. "Splendid!"

"Jenny," said her father. "Pour me one too."

She did. Reluctantly.

The Queen of Hearts stepped forward. Her mask was
bright red. Her gown was gold and embroidered with crimson
hearts. Rubies adorned her fingers. And a giant heart-shaped
ruby crowned her tiara and sparkled amid a profusion of strawberry curls. It was Petunia, and she'd never looked better.

"This is a lovely waltz, Your Highness," she said to Dash.
"Would you like to take me for a spin?"

"Maybe later," he said. He looked distracted, and had barely a glance for either Bit or Petunia.

"Those jewels are magnificent," said Jen.

"Aren't they?" Petunia replied. "My friend Vieveeka loaned
them to me."

"Vieveeka?" asked Dash, suddenly alert. "Which one is
she? Is she here?"

"No. But she will be. Later."

"Oh," said Dash, disappointed.

"Can you imagine?" said Petunia. "She refuses to let the
servants help her dress. Our Jane brought her hot water for a

bath and Vieveeka chased her out of there like a harpy." A little discomfort crept into her laugh.

Jen wanted to hear more, but a tall figure approached her. His suit was white, his mask the one used in plays to represent comedy.

"Might I have this dance?" he said, in a voice that crackled like dead leaves.

Jen thought she recognized that voice, but couldn't recall where. She didn't like what she heard. "No thank you."

"Later then," he said. "We'll dance in the moonlight."

"It's storming outside."

"Yes. And more is coming." He turned and walked away. The back of his suit was black, and he wore another mask on the back of his head. Tragedy.

"Who was that?" she asked the Count.

"Why . . . I don't know."

Just then a lad with a powerful chest and sturdy legs approached Jen. He had something furry with large round ears covering the top of his face.

"Endare!" Jen laughed. "What in the world are you supposed to be?"

"A bear," he replied. "Don't I look like one?"

"Well . . . now that you mention it."

"Would you like to dance?"

Any other time, Endare, any other time, Jen thought. He was the handsomest, most eligible bachelor in Aerdem, now that Dash was engaged. But she couldn't take the risk. Father was dancing with Mother, and Dash had taken Bit onto the floor. Someone had to keep watch. She pushed Endare and Petunia together.

"Not right now, but if you're quick you can steal the Queen of Hearts."

Petunia's red lips mouthed "thank you" to Jen, as Endare swept the Countess onto the dance floor.

That settled, Jen tried to find Tragedy-Comedy. There he was, staring at her from a corner. An uneasy tension settled in her shoulders, but she stared back until he turned away and talked to one of the executioners. Through the ballroom windows, Jen could see the trees waving wildly in the wind. Bright flashes of lightning tore the night sky. The thunder still wasn't close enough to be heard above the orchestra, which blasted out the lively *Trilafor Trot*. For a moment, Jen thought she saw a tiny, unblinking eye of red hovering just outside one of the windows.

Must have been the reflection of someone's costume, she thought.

She walked along the edge of the ballroom. Unable to see her family on the floor, she went up the stairs and circled the balcony. She forced herself to the rail. With a knuckle-white grip, she looked down. Perfume, mixed with sweat and wig powder, struck her nose. Everything swirled in a mass of dizzy color. Her head swam and the room tipped. She fought the urge to step back, and the feelings passed. She picked out Dash dancing with Bit. And Mother with Father. It all looked normal enough. But Jen couldn't shake the uneasy feeling churning inside. Something was going to happen. She was certain.

She searched the crowd for Tragedy-Comedy, scanning for black or white among the colored costumes. She spied him at last, standing by a window. As if he felt her stare, his mask slowly tilted until the wide, empty mouth grinned up at her.

Goose bumps crawled up her arms and she pushed back sharply from the rail. Who was he? Why was he interested in her? The face that went with that dry voice hovered just on the edge of her mind, like a man standing in a dark shadow, taunting her.

She was certain of one thing. He wasn't going to dance with her. She went downstairs and lost herself in the crowd of gyrating dancers so he couldn't follow where she was. Then she made her way back to the food buffet. The Count's servants, dressed as mice, freshened the punch and carried in a whole deer, still steaming on the spit.

The music stopped and Jen's family had just rejoined her when a drummer started a timpani roll. Count Pompahro ascended several steps and called for everyone's attention.

"Ladies and gentlemen. Tonight we celebrate two wonderful events. First, the birthday of our beloved Prince Dashren."

Everyone applauded.

"And second, the moment I know many of you have been waiting for . . . the entrance into fine society of a lady whose wit and beauty have already captured so many hearts. From one of the noblest bloodlines in Trilafor, and, may I say, a personal friend of *ours*," he put a feathered glove on his breast, "I present to you, the Duchess Vieveeka!"

On her name—there was a final flourish of the timpani, a cymbal crash, a door on the second floor was flung open, and a sparkling snowflake with flaming red hair floated down the stairs. Her gown, mask, and tiara glittered with a thousand diamonds. Everyone caught their breath. The ladies murmured. The men stood transfixed. Bit clung tightly to Dash's arm, as if afraid he would float away.

Vieveeka glided across the room, the crowd parting before her, until she stopped before the royal family. Behind the mask, Jen could see one brown eye. The other was a cool blue and shone like a polished moonstone. She wasn't sure she liked what she saw there.

Vieveeka removed a white cloak and tossed it to a servant. "Your Majesty, thank you for allowing me the honor of this ball," she said to the king. "I hope I have not gone beyond what is right and proper—joining with your son in this celebration, his birthday, and my debut."

"The honor is ours," said Father. "I'm sure Dash has never had such a splendid party."

"Never!" Dash agreed, nodding like a puppy.

Vieveeka smiled. "And this must be your queen. Look how lovely she is!"

"You grace us with your kindness," Mother replied.

The moonstone eye twitched.

"And you have a daughter, I am told. Where is she? Oh, is that her, beside that handsome bear?"

Jen stepped away from Endare and closer to one of the candelabras so she could be seen.

"A pirate! Oh my! Young Prince," Vieveeka said to Dash, leaning against his arm, "please save me!"

Dash bowed low. "My Lady, if ever I could serve you that way, I'd do it in a moment!"

Why don't you just grovel, Dash, thought Jen.

"Your Majesty," Vieveeka said, turning back to Father, "what an impressive family. A bold daughter with such fire in her eyes. (I'll have to get just such a pair of pantaloons. I declare, all of us girls should run around like little sailor boys. It's just the thing.) And such an angel in your queen. But really, Your Highness, can she be naughty too?"

Father looked shocked, but before he could reply, Vieveeka turned to Bit.

"And what is this, hiding behind the young prince? Oh! Are you a little rabbit? How cute. If I say—BOO!—"

Bit drew back in alarm.

"—would you scurry down a hole?" Vieveeka looped her arm around Dash's. "Save me now, Prince—I'm dying to

67

dance!" The band struck up a tune and she whisked Dash onto the dance floor.

Bit looked like she was about to cry as she watched her rival spinning and twirling across the floor with Dash. He was holding Vieveeka awfully close.

"I must look like a fool," said Bit, taking off the bunny ears and throwing them on the floor.

"Don't worry, Bit," said Jen. "It's only one dance."

But it wasn't.

Dance after dance followed, the orchestra surging with *Tender Feelings, A Love So Rare,* and *O My Quivering Heart.* Dash looked mesmerized as Vieveeka gazed at him with sparkling eyes.

Even Petunia seemed disturbed. She put her hand on Bit's shoulder. "She doesn't even live in Aerdem," she said, trying to say something comforting.

"She doesn't have to," Bit replied. "All she needs is his heart."

"I'll try to get her to switch partners," Jen said as she grabbed Endare's hand and pulled him onto the dance floor.

The orchestra throbbed with *Hearts Entwined,* a slow dance done with a sultry tangle of arms and legs. Dash and Vieveeka didn't hold back as they glided across the floor, locked in a passionate embrace. Jen couldn't get near them. One of the executioners always spun by with a partner, blocking her way into the center of the room, and she had to lead Endare away from Tragedy-Comedy, who seemed bent on switching partners to get at her.

Just before midnight, another timpani roll brought Count Pompahro to the stairs.

"Ladies and gentlemen!" he called. "May I have your attention. Please clear the center of the floor."

Everyone but Vieveeka and Dash moved to the edge of the room and formed a circle. Jen struggled against the bodies crushing front and behind.

"It is my privilege," Vieveeka announced, "to present to his Highness, Prince Dashren, this gift in honor of his birthday."

A servant gave Vieveeka her cloak, and she draped it over the floor. With a wave of her hand, half the candles were extinguished, leaving the room semi-dark. Jen gripped her cutlass and tried to push through the crowd. Lightning flashed and for a moment a clap of thunder drowned out the timpani roll. She managed to squeeze through to the front of the circle and found herself standing beside Bit.

The floor vibrated and a section in the center of the room began to rise, drawing Vieveeka's cloak up with it. There was something under there, and it stopped at eye level. Jen took a step forward, loosening the cutlass in its scabbard.

Vieveeka grasped the cloak with one hand and pulled it away. At that moment, all the candles were lit. A murmur of astonishment swept through the room. And a piercing cry of agony from Bit.

There before them, carved from a single crystal, was a three-foot-high replica of the Rose Castle, glistening and glowing with pink-velvet light.

Bit burst into tears and ran from the room. Jen wanted to follow her, but would it be safe to leave the others? She didn't have to decide.

Blinding lightning, an explosion of thunder, and the whole house shook. A blast of wind shattered the windows and a torrent of rain streamed in.

"Oh my! Oh my!" the Count cried.

Still wearing his mask, he dashed about the ballroom like a pendulum gone mad. With his elbows out and hands clutching his temples, Jen thought he looked (and squawked) more like a bird than at any point that evening.

A few guests gave him a polite bow and thanks for his hospitality, but most faded toward the exits.

"Oh my. This is a disaster," he cried, flapping his arms. "Please don't leave. It's just a little water. Oh, my floor, my floor. It's ruined. I'm ruined. No. Don't leave. Please, the evening is young. It's just a little water. Oh, the water, the water. The wood will warp. Oh! Oh! What shall I do? What shall I do?"

Petunia threw aside her mask and huddled with some servants. A moment later the servants rushed off, and returned immediately with tools and boards and began sealing the window. Then, under Petunia's direction, they pulled down a huge curtain and swabbed the floor.

By this time, the guests flowed steadily out the exits. The party was officially over when Vieveeka blew Dash a kiss, glided upstairs, and disappeared into a room above. Jen looked for Tragedy-Comedy. He was gone, and the executioners had melted into the stream of departing guests.

A unit of Dash's soldiers rushed in from a side entrance and surrounded Jen's family.

"Let's get out of here," Jen said.

"You go to Bit," said Mother. "I need a few minutes here."

"We should go before the storm gets worse."

"We'll be right behind you. Go."

Jen looked to Father, but he nodded in agreement with Mother. Unable to change their minds, Jen turned to leave.

"I'll go with you," Dash said. His chest swelled, but he avoided her eyes.

Jen whirled on him. "Haven't you done enough damage? You're the last person she needs to see."

Dash went limp. "But—"

Jen flashed him a warning that made him step back. Grabbing an escort of five soldiers, she stalked off. Glancing back, she saw Mother speaking softly to the Count, an arm over his shoulder. He was standing still now, holding his mask and nodding.

Jen found Bit in the carriage. She held her little carving in her hand, tears streaming from her eyes. Jen took Bit in her arms, stroked and rocked her. She took out a handkerchief and patted away the tears, but more cascaded down her friend's face. Jen spoke softly. That it was nothing. Dash would come around. She'd see.

Each word made Bit shake her head more violently, and deeper sobs wracked her body.

I'm making it worse. Jen sagged back in her seat, and watched the storm as the carriage rolled through the dark countryside.

The wind screamed and shook the carriage. Hail pelted the roof. She put seat cushions over the windows in case they shattered. She felt sorry for the horses and driver. Hopefully the carriage would block some of the storm, which blew from behind. But there was no protection for the escort of soldiers riding beside them.

So the attack hadn't come at the ball. It could still come. Jen pulled away one of the cushions and peeked out the window. All she could see was a blur of slanting gray. The storm was a perfect cover. Enemy troops could hide anywhere along the way and ambush them. Dash's men had been ordered to surround the Count's estate, not the road.

A jagged burst of lightning and a flurry of hail made her recover the window.

On the other hand, maybe Dash was right. Maybe Medlara was warning them about this storm. A hurricane wouldn't damage the Rose Castle, but a lot of houses and farms would be ruined. Anyone caught away from home tonight would be in danger. Jen would be on pins and needles until she knew everyone was safe.

Still, there were a lot of strange things about the ball. Vieveeka had found out about Bit's gift, and used the information to upstage her. Poor Bit. Her surprise was ruined. How could she give Dash her present now? It would look small and insignificant beside Vieveeka's.

Vieveeka had been awful. Insulting Mother and Father. Mocking Bit. For a moment, Jen wondered if Vieveeka was Naryfel, the master of disguises. But no. There had been dozens of opportunities to attack the family in front of everyone. And Vieveeka seemed bent on capturing Dash's heart, not his head. From the look of things, she had succeeded.

Bit's heart was broken. She was a girl who cried when a cat

caught a mouse or a baby bird fell from a nest. Fragile and sensitive, she might never recover.

Then there was Tragedy-Comedy. Where had Jen heard that voice? She couldn't recall, and no one seemed to know him. He was no one good, she was sure of that. Just thinking about him made her flesh crawl.

The carriage stopped and Jen put a cloak over Bit's shoulders. Together they ran against the wind and rain for the castle door. Once Jen was sure the rest of the family had returned safely, she went to Bit's room and found her sobbing on the bed.

"I've lost him forever," Bit cried.

"Maybe not," Jen lied. She was relieved Bit could talk now.

"I have. I saw the way he looked at her."

"She didn't impress my parents."

"That won't matter. If he wants to marry her, your father will never stop him."

"Father will."

"No. He won't. But if he does, Dash will run off. He'll marry her anyway. You know how stubborn he is."

Outside, the wind shook the trees. Jen closed the storm windows and latched them tight.

"Look, Bit, Vieveeka is all on the surface. There's nothing beneath all the glitter."

"She's clever. I could never be like that. Dash must find me boring."

"If she was that clever, she wouldn't have to steal your idea."

Bit looked up. "What do you mean?"

"Look. You've got to win Dash back. Don't let her get away with dazzling him with cheap parlor tricks."

"But how?"

"I don't know, but you've got to show him what's inside of you."

Bit nodded slowly. "What's inside . . ."

⁊❧

By the time Jen got back to her room, it was almost two in the morning. She was dead tired. Setting her cutlass aside, she removed her boots and crawled into bed with her clothes on. As she fell asleep, her last thought was that Medlara had been wrong—the danger hadn't come.

Outside, the castle guards relaxed too. No one walked the walls in this wind and rain. They huddled in the guard towers, playing dice or dozing. If anyone had patrolled the walkways, there would have been nothing to see through the storm's blinding veil.

East, north, and west, hundreds of dark shadows slithered up the outer wall and down the other side. They snaked through the courtyards and scaled the inner walls to the gardens. Avoiding the footpaths, they wound around the fountains and slipped between the shrubs. The castle glowed more brightly than usual, but no one saw as the shadows glided up the trees leading to three verandas. From there, they slid to the windows. A white stone was held a few inches from the pegs that fastened the storm windows down. The stone glowed, and the pegs turned and slipped from their holes as easily as if they had been dipped in oil . . .

Maybe if the storm were not blowing Jen would have heard something to warn her. But the shaking trees tapped on the window. The wind cried long and mournfully, and the rain pattered with a lulling rhythm. With barely a scrape, the inner window opened. Shadows slid inside, crossed the floor, and surrounded Jen's bed.

The first thing she was aware of was a strong hand locking on her right arm. It felt like a vise with thorns, squeezing, sticking her. Almost immediately another hand gripped her left wrist. It

74

was dark, but she was aware of darker shadows surrounding her. She tried to scream, but something was clamped and tied over her mouth. She fought like a tiger, kicking, wrenching, twisting. There were too many of them. They held her ankles and legs. She was blindfolded, and something snaked around her body. Starting at the ankles, it wound up her legs, looping over and over. The hands let go, and the thing wound around her torso, pinning her arms to her sides, sticking her like a briar.

She was lifted roughly. She thought she heard screams from somewhere in the castle. She felt a rush of wind and rain on her face and knew she was being carried out the window. She was tossed, and tumbled through the air. She struggled frantically at her bonds. They were too tight. Her heart was in her mouth. She braced for impact. Instead, she was caught, carried, pushed, and thrown several more times. She guessed she was past the outer wall by now. She was thrown like a sack of potatoes and landed on something hard. Metal clanged. A latch snapped in place. From behind, the castle alarm bell pealed deep notes of doom.

Then there were only hours of bouncing and creaking. And cold stinging wind and rain.

Part Two

10

Jen wasn't always a princess. She
grew up in the Plain World, a gray, cloudy, rain-shrouded land.
The dreary climate had seeped into the people. They sputtered
through their lives like a candle flame running out of wick.

The motto of the *Daily Picayune* read, "No News is Good
News." A story on the back page observed that no innovations,
no inventions, no scientific discoveries or breakthroughs had
occurred for forty years. Another article reported that nobody
had dreamed for the same forty years. People plodded through
their lives, and that's the way they wanted it. You put up plums
in the summer, and did laundry on Monday in the washtub, with
homemade soap of lye, fat, and borax. You marched through
the State Fair, not to see last year's cows and pigs, but because
it was on the calendar, and don't ask why.

Jen tore through this world like a tornado. Her guardian,
Nell, kept her safely in their mountain cabin as long as she
could; otherwise her little firecracker would get into a world of
trouble. But Jen needed clothes and shoes and had a natural
curiosity about what was down the road. On her first day in the
village, there was no way to quell the thousands of questions she

asked. "Why do they keep pickles in a barrel? Won't they taste like wood?" "Why are taffies wrapped in newspaper? Won't the ink come off?"

Nell left her only a moment to look at some cloth. In less than five minutes, Jen knocked down a jar of seed and a row of pitchforks. Mr. Meklton, the general store owner, escorted her out by her ear, telling her she would come to a bad end.

"Why?" she asked as the door slammed behind her.

She tried to be good when she went to the village, but there was always a puppy or butterfly that she chased with a single-minded focus. Blind to all else, she sent a pail of paint flying off a ladder, knocked the minister's prayer book out of his hands and into a horse trough, broke a window, and trampled Mrs. Farley's nasturtiums.

By the time Jen showed up for her first day in school with short pants and skinned knees, all the children had an earful from their parents about the new "bad ender."

The name stuck. By the end of the week, she was Bad En', or Baden. She tried to join in hopscotch, and the other children drifted away. She offered to share her pie, and they said it had worms. They passed notes about her, some of which Jen intercepted: "Don't play with Baden. She's got scabies." "The old woman she lives with is loony." "No, she's a witch." "When she dies, they'll throw Baden into the orphanage." "Her real parents didn't want her. They left her under a bridge."

No one went near her. When Clem Pickett was asked to sit next to her in class, he boldly told the teacher, Mr. Grimm, "Naw, Baden'll give me lice." Jen looked hopefully at Mr. Grimm. At last, she'd get some help.

He looked at her muddy clothes and wind-ratted hair, and looked away, embarrassed.

To all this, Jen turned her cheek. Why Nell thought that

would help was a mystery. She turned her cheek right, left, up, down. The taunts only came harder. Stolen books and jackets. Frogs, snakes, and spiders in her schoolbag. Honey on the out-house seat, and ants under her desk. The last straw was when Clem Pickett dumped her lunch in a puddle. When she was finally pulled off him, her fists were raw. But Clem sported a split lip, bloody nose, and an eye that swelled shut.

The feud was on. Clem kicked over a chair and declared to the teacher, "It was Baden." He unhitched Mr. Grimm's horse and sent the mare trotting home. Clem swore he saw Baden do it. Jen tackled him to the ground every day at lunch and pum-meled him. These battles earned her dozens of trips across Mr. Grimm's desk, where the switches broke on her backside.

But not her spirit. Her tormentors listened outside the window and she refused to cry.

At last, a new teacher arrived with a better way to reach Jen. Make the girl with the perpetual-motion feet stand in a corner. When Jen couldn't stay still, she was made to stand on one foot each for fifteen minutes, with a sign around her neck that read, "I will come to a bad end."

Jen ended her day doing the only thing she could. She ran. Leaping over puddles and cart ruts, cutting through woods and fields to get to the one smiling face she ever knew: Nell. Then she was off again, climbing the trails and trees behind her cabin. Then up the mountain. What did it matter that she ran through wet curtains of slanting gray? There was something she desper-ately wanted to bring home. She climbed, shimmying up cracks and crevices. Scaling ledge after ledge. Higher and higher. If only she could climb high enough, she'd find an eagle's nest. When she reached it she would make friends with the mother. Climb on her back. Then they'd sail higher. Break through clouds. Then reach, reach, reach, for a piece of blue . . .

11

Bit barely felt her feet as she left the

Pondit's room. The only clear sensations were in the fingers of her right hand—which twisted at her sleeve—and the fearful weight crushing her chest, smothering every breath.

She tried to focus on what she needed to do, but a dozen images swam in her mind. Jenny and her mother, the king, the Pondit. Above all was Dash's face, pale, turning slightly blue.

She shuddered and passed through the castle like a sleep-walker, vaguely aware she stepped around debris littering the walkways. Torn branches. Broken vases. Shards scattered on the floor like puzzle pieces.

She made her way by instinct; down a corridor, a flight of steps, through a courtyard, around servants picking up, sweeping, and mopping. Water still dripped from the eaves and shone in little pools on the floor. The morning sun kissed the castle, gently drawing up tendrils of mist, the ghostly remains of last night's storm.

She'd promised herself she'd be bold, but already resolve slipped away, like sand spilling from a tiny tear in a sack. Then Dash's face appeared and she twisted her sleeve tighter, stemming the tide of sand, rooting herself. She was doing this for Dash—and for herself. How could she ever face herself, knowing she hadn't done everything she could? She'd rather die.

A familiar voice broke into her thoughts.

"Bit, what's wrong?"

Bit stopped and the hall came into focus. She stood by her door. Feeling poured back into her body and she swayed a little. Petunia stepped beside her and held her steady.

Bit didn't want to cry, but with a rush of emotion she burst into tears. "Oh Pet. It's awful. Haven't you heard? We were attacked last night. Jenny and her mother were kidnapped, and I have to go get the doctor Jenny knew, and Dash and his father are . . . are . . ."

"Hold on, one thing at a time. First, tell me what happened."

"Horrible creatures attacked . . . there was a terrible battle. Dash and his father tried to protect Jenny's mother. There were too many to fight. By the time help arrived, her mother was gone and . . ." Bit broke into sobs.

"And?" Pet asked.

"And now two of the creatures have Dash and the king all tied up."

"Tied up?"

"Yes. The Pondit took me to see them. It was dreadful. The creatures are like blackberry vines, wrapped around them head to foot."

Petunia gasped. "Can they talk?"

"No. It's like they're asleep."

"Why don't you just cut the plants off?"

Bit wiped her eyes, but the tears kept pouring out. "The vines are tied around their necks. The Pondit thinks if we try and cut them, Dash and his father will be strangled. Yalp thinks the same thing."

"Yalp! Don't listen to him. He's just a funny little man who can't find a robe to fit him."

"Oh, no! He knows lots of magic. He thinks some kind of enchantment holds them captive."

"Then why doesn't he break the spell?"

"He's tried. Nothing works. The best doctors have tried, too. They're all afraid of killing the king. Someone has to go get the doctor Jenny knew in the Plain World. Lots of things are beyond us there—machines that go faster than a horse, boats that cross the ocean without sails. We're hoping he'll know a way to remove the creatures. I'm going to get him."

"You?" Pet smoothed her dress, a pale lavender that set off her strawberry blonde curls. "Send a servant or messenger."

Bit turned away and entered her room. "No. I have to go."

Pet followed. "Look, ladies don't go scampering all over the countryside. Send the Pondit."

Bit went to her closet and pulled a knapsack from behind a row of gowns. "He has to stay and rule."

"Then send one of the Royal Guards."

"Don't you see?" Bit cried. "I have to go. I can't just wait and watch Dash die. I have to do something."

"No, I don't see, and I can't see you going, either. Look at you right now, crying like that. You're a mess."

"I know," Bit sobbed, trying to pull herself together. "But I have to try. I don't know what I'll do if I lose him."

Pet shook her head, as if someone told her they planned to jump over the moon. "You don't have a clue how to survive such a journey. It's far too dangerous. I can't believe that old fool of a Pondit is letting you do this."

Bit crossed the room and put her knapsack on the bed. Going to her dresser, she took out some thick socks. "He wasn't going to. I convinced him."

"How?"

"I told him I'd take five soldiers and Yalp." Arms loaded with socks, woolen shirts, and a pair of cotton pants, Bit carried the clothing back to her bed and began packing them neatly in her knapsack.

"Please! He's the last person you should take. He'll make a mess of things."

"No he won't. Besides, I'll need his help getting into the Plain World. It takes magic."

Pet stared, the edges of her eyes wrinkled with worry. "This is madness. What if you get stuck there and can't return?"

With shaking hands, Bit closed the knapsack. "I die trying."

❧❧

The Count was sitting at his desk reviewing his account book when Vieveeka entered the room. She was no longer dressed as a snowflake, but still seemed to float.

"Well, Count, how do you find your finances?"

"The ball cost more than I'd planned," he said wearily. "I'm worse off than I was before."

Vieveeka smiled. "Not to worry. If you do as I say, your problems will be over."

He looked at her without replying. He'd been listening to her, but things had not gone to his liking.

"I heard there was some kind of attack on the royal family," she said, watching the slow progress of a pill bug that circled the edge of a flowerpot on the Count's desk.

"Did you. And you wouldn't happen to be behind it, would you?" he replied coolly.

"Silly Count," she laughed. "I'm a duchess, not a kidnapper! No, I find your country far too frightening. If the king is not safe, what about the rest of us! I've decided to leave for a while."

"Leave? But how will I pay these bills? You promised you'd finance the ball."

"I promised no such thing. I gave you more than enough to cover expenses. Any news from your little spy?"

"Pet? She told me this morning that Bit is going on some kind of journey, to find a doctor to save the king and prince."

"Is she now. Well, Count, you must see that little Bit does not return." The pill bug was coming around the other side of the pot.

The Count stared at her. "How am I to do that? I'm not a murderer."

"I don't care how you do it. Just see that it is done." She smiled; a frosty edge crept into her voice.

"But if she doesn't return, the king and prince may die. How does that help our plans?"

"If they die, that leaves the way clear for you and me to take the throne. But it may not come to that. I know a wonderful doctor in Trilafor. If I bring him back before Bit returns, Dash is sure to love me better."

"How does that help me?"

"I've told you before. After I break Dash's heart, Petunia will pick up the pieces. Once they're married, she'll send all the wealth in the royal treasury to you and me. You can control her can't you?"

"She'll do what I say." The Count stroked his chin, adding up the money in his head. Aerdem was a small kingdom, but was famous for the mountains of gold and diamonds piled in the treasury.

"Bit must not return," Vieveeka repeated. The pill bug was back where he started. She flicked him off the pot and he rolled into a ball on the desk. "Do what I say Count, and you'll be richer than you could possibly dream. Fail me, and I'll collect on your debts."

"But you gave me that money!"

Smile lines curled at the edge of her brown eye. The moonstone eye was glacier-hard. "I never give money away, you silly man. It was a loan. You can start repaying me by giving me a long-distance horse. I need to leave immediately." Another flick of her finger sent the pill bug spinning off the desk.

❧❧

The drumming hooves of a steed were fading when Petunia entered the Count's study. He had a thunderous expression on his face and drummed his fingers on his desk.

She caught her breath. "What is it, Father? Have I done something wrong?"

"No. Sit down, Pet." He walked around the desk and stood over her.

"Has something happened?" she asked. "Please don't stare at me like that. Has something gone wrong?"

"I'm trapped, Pet. There's no way out."

"Is it the money? Please, Father, let me help. I have this wonderful idea. A million things can go wrong on a farm. You know how it goes on our vineyard. Farmers lose all kinds of time and money bringing their goods to market. But if someone picked up their goods and brought them to the city in wagons, they could stay home and watch over the farm. Whoever runs the wagons could make a bundle of money."

He waved her idea aside. "Business is not a suitable occupation for a countess. And it would reflect poorly on me. Besides being a ridiculous idea—carting goods for farmers, who ever heard of it?—what makes you think you can do it? It's far too complex."

"But Father. I know I can. All I need is—"

"Silence!"

The Count paced the room a few minutes, then stood over her again.

"I have something else I want you to do," he said.

"Sure, Father. Anything." She searched his face, looking for some sign he was pleased, but he occupied himself polishing a gold button on his coat.

"Good. You are to go with Bit to find this doctor. Make sure she does not return."

Petunia caught her breath. "Father, what are you saying?"

"It's very clear what I am saying. Bit must not return."

Petunia fluffed her curls. "It would not be fitting for me to go. I'm a countess. Send Geoffrey or one of the other servants."

"I can't trust this to anyone else. And no one must know. *No one.*"

"But no one knows if Jenny's story about a plain world is even true. I've become quite convinced she made up the whole thing, and the queen, feeling sorry for the little orphan girl, adopted her."

"True or not, you must follow Bit wherever she goes. After that . . . no doctor, no Bit . . ."

"This is madness. It's too dangerous. I could get killed. Besides, I haven't the slightest idea what clothes to take."

"You'll figure it out."

"But how am I to keep her from returning?"

"Whatever it takes," he replied, studying his nails.

"You can't mean—"

"I say nothing. I leave it up to you to find a way."

"But Father, if she doesn't return in four days, the king and prince will die."

"Why?"

"Creatures are tied around their bodies. Every hour the knots pull tighter."

"That's not our concern."

Petunia burst into tears. "But I'm a lady, you always said so, I can't go running all around the countryside picking up stickers and burrs and who knows what else; I can't live outdoors like some homeless gypsy. Besides, it's wet and miserable. I could catch a cold." She stamped the floor with her silk slippers. "I won't do it. I won't—"

A bright light flashed and stars floated around her. Her cheek burned red hot and her jaw ached. When the stars faded, she saw her father's hand raised for another blow.

His voice was icy. "Bit doesn't return or you don't return."

12

Jen drifted in and out of sleep. There

was no change in the monotony of wind and rain, or the bump and rattle of the wagon. She was gagged. For a time, the briar-thing had been wrapped around her body, sticking her with thorns. Later this was replaced with strong ropes around her wrists and ankles. She wrestled briefly with the ropes in an effort to free herself, but gave up. Her bonds were secure.

Her hands were pulled behind her back. Her neck and shoulders were a mass of cramps and spasms. Her hands went numb. The wooden floor was rough. The rocking motion of the wagon worked splinters under her exposed skin. The position of her hands made it impossible to rest on her stomach or back. The only comfort she could find was to lie on one side or the other.

Bars above and on the sides formed a cage. Into this, the wind drove the rain like a frosty whip. Her clothes were soaked. She shivered continuously.

The night was dark. She was vaguely aware of several wagons rolling ahead.

No one talked to her. The only sounds were the hissing

wind, the drumming rain, the squish and suck of the horses' hooves in the mud. The grating cry of the left rear wheel.

She was unfamiliar with this road, but by the silhouette of the mountains ahead, she knew she was moving north. She figured she was somewhere near the border. How would they get her across? Dash had placed extra guards there.

A short time later the wagons stopped. A tarp was thrown over her. She heard grunts, and animal bodies were packed around her. Pigs. One of them stood on her. At least the tarp protected her from the rain, and the pigs kept her warm.

The wagon heaved forward. A short time later she heard a call to stop, then muffled conversation. She tried to scream through the gag, to move, to bang against the bottom of the wagon, but the animals hemmed her in. Then they were rolling on, and her heart sank. The border guards probably couldn't hear her above the wind and the grunting pigs. Now she was outside Aerdem. There were no towns or villages for miles. Just open country. She could be taken anywhere. The rain would turn the wagon tracks into mud. Who could follow that? And who was there to follow?

She'd never felt more alone. A strangling terror gripped her throat. Where was her family, and what had happened to them? Were they in the wagons ahead? Why had she been taken rather than killed? Perhaps she would be killed. Later.

This thought spurred her to focus on escape. She wormed her way through the pigs to the side of the wagon, and pushed free of the tarp. Rising to her knees, she backed against one of the bars, rubbing and worrying the rope, back and forth, trying to weaken and loosen it. She rubbed until she was exhausted and her wrists were raw and blistered.

The wagon was beginning to stink from the pigs, who relieved themselves where they stood.

Hours passed. She clung to the memory of her mother, the day she told the story of the Starbirds. How reassuring her mother was. How soft and gentle and warm. At last, the wagon became a cradle and her mother rocked her to sleep . . .

The dream changed. One of the Starbirds stood on the edge of a cliff. Chains encircled the bird's body, imprisoning its wings. Jen approached to remove the shackles. But every time she reached out, the bird became frightened, thrashing its wings against the metal. Feathers flew off and littered the ground. Holes of bare skin appeared, sore and bloody.

Angry, Jen kicked up a cloud of dirt. "Why won't you let me take off the chains?"

The dirt sprinkled onto the bird, covering it with a coat of dust. The chains melted away like water.

A cougar appeared ten feet away and began stalking the bird.

"Fly," Jen called. "You can fly now."

The bird stood frozen on the cliff edge.

"Fly," Jen yelled. "Why can't you fly? What's wrong with you?"

The bird stood as still as if it had been stuffed and mounted. Only its eyes grew round and made little jerking motions.

"Fly! Why don't you fly? He'll tear you to shreds."

The cougar crouched to leap. In desperation, Jen grabbed the bird and threw it over the cliff. The bird's eyes fixed plaintively on Jen as it plunged down the abyss.

The snorts of the pigs shuffling out of the wagon jarred her awake. She felt thirsty and dazed. It had stopped raining, and she could see the stars. A sliver of moon illuminated a tree-shrouded meadow. Rough hands hauled her to her feet. Her captors wore black masks and carried halberds. They tied a long rope around her neck and cut the bonds around her ankles and wrists. The circulation had not returned. Her legs and feet were racked with pins and needles. She felt so stiff and wobbly she could barely walk. They pushed and kicked her toward a large rock, and allowed her a private moment to relieve herself.

She could try to slip the rope from her neck, but figures lurked in the shadows beyond. If she tried to escape, she'd run right into them.

When she came out from behind the rock she was led to a circle of guards. A solitary figure stood in the middle. He wore a white mask with a wide, empty grin. It was Tragedy-Comedy. He put one hand on her shoulder blade and forced her to him, smashing her cheek to his chest. He smelled like rotten cactus. Still wobbly on her feet, he held her up and danced her round and round the circle. He brought his lips to her ear and whispered, in a dry, crackling voice, "I told you we'd dance in the moonlight."

Then she was back in the wagon and passed out. She woke with her hands and feet tied. She wondered if it had been a dream. But the Comedy mask lay nearby, leering up at her.

Then there was nothing for miles but the complaining wheel and the beat of the horses in the mud. In the distance she thought she heard someone playing a pipe. The notes bent strangely, like a crying baby, and hung high and mournful on the wind.

Next morning, the wagons rattled across a broad plain. Scattered mesquite, rocks and tumbleweed dotted a stark landscape. Jagged hills floated like a mirage against the horizon. Jen felt like she was floating too.

Her wagon rolled to a stop beside a dirty waterhole. She

listened jealously as the horses drank. She hadn't been given a drink and her throat felt like a scab.

A wagon stopped beside her. Her heart pounded as she saw a figure kneeling facedown inside a cage. The person's clothing—black boots, riding pants, leather jerkin—were splattered with mud. Jen couldn't see the face, but a spray of bright red curls spilled onto the floor.

The masked captors had moved off and were talking softly beside a supply wagon. Jen ventured a call to the victim across from her.

"Are you awake?" she asked, her voice a fragile croak.

The head stirred, looked up.

"Vieveeka!"

"They got you too, Jen?"

Jen's mind swirled in confusion. This was the last person she thought she'd see. She didn't think Vieveeka was Naryfel, but she wasn't a friend, either. Why would anyone kidnap her? She wasn't connected with the royal family, and was only a visitor to Aerdem. Jen thought about her moonlight dance with Tragedy-Comedy. Maybe he was the danger, not Naryfel. Jen wished she could place that desiccated voice.

"Who are they?" Jen asked. "Why were we taken?"

"I don't know. I was riding to Trilafor to get a doctor when they took me."

"A doctor?"

Vieveeka looked down and stifled a sob. "It's your father—"

"Father? What's happened?"

"—and Dash. Strange creatures attacked them—"

"—are they alive? Please tell me they're alive."

"Shh. The guards." Vieveeka nodded toward the supply wagon. "Yes. They're alive. But creatures are wrapped around their necks. If they are not removed properly, Dash and your father will die. I was going for a surgeon I know. If anyone can save them, he can."

Jen felt like someone had grabbed her heart and twisted it. "Why?" she asked, her voice tiny and plaintive. Any remaining strength drained out of her, and she sagged against the bars of her cage. "Why would anyone want to hurt someone so kind?" She was thinking of her father. "Or noble." She was thinking of Dash.

"Jealousy. Spite. Revenge. There are a million reasons and life is cruel. But Jen. There's more."

"More?" Jen's voice fell to a strangled whisper.

"It's your mother."

"Mother?!"

"Yes. She's here."

"Mother?! They've taken her too? Is she all right? Where? Where is she?"

"Shh. The guards. Yes. I think she's all right. She's in that cage beyond the supply wagon."

Jen saw another cage largely hidden behind the supply wagon, but couldn't see inside. She gripped her bars fiercely. "We've got to escape and free her."

"We will. Tonight."

"How?"

"I've managed to loosen the rope around my wrist. I think I can slip it off."

"What about the lock on the cage?"

"I've got a hairpin in my boot. I think I can pick the lock. I'll free you and we'll go to your mother."

Jen felt a pang of guilt. "I guess I had you all wrong."

"A lot of people do."

"I'll never forget you."

"I do make an impression," Vieveeka replied with a laugh.

"But save that until we're out of here. I haven't done anything yet."

"Right. Did they hurt you?"

"No, I'm all right. Just a little stiff. You?"

"I'm fine," Jen lied. "What about Bit?"

Vieveeka looked surprised. "Bit?"

"Father and Dash were attacked. Mother and I were taken. Bit is part of the family. Is she all right?"

"As far as I know. I heard she also went in search of a doctor."

Bit! Jen thought with a surge of hope. *I knew you had it in you.*

Now anything was possible.

Around midnight, the wagons stopped in a pine-covered valley. The sky was moonless. The air crisp. The horses were watered, and fed on shoulder-high grass that surrounded the campsite. One of the guards lit a fire, and the odor of sizzling bacon and smoke wafted passed Jen's nose. She hadn't eaten or drunk in over a day. Her lips felt like a cracked desert, but she didn't care. They were going to free her mother. And Bit was going for another doctor. Since Vieveeka had been captured, Dash and Father would need another doctor.

Vieveeka's wagon had been moved to the front of the line, and Jen hadn't seen her the rest of the day. There had only been glimpses of the wagon holding Mother, with no clear view inside. Jen had spent the rest of the day trying to loosen the knot around her wrists, without success.

But she felt hopeful. There was a plan, and with Vieveeka there, she didn't feel so alone.

An hour later, the camp was still. The fire had died down. The guards, wrapped in blankets, looked like potato sacks flung haphazardly across a nearby belt of grass. No watch was set. They appeared confident the prisoners could not escape.

Jen listened for a scrape, a creak, any noise that would reveal Vieveeka had opened her cage. The only sound was a slight breeze rustling the grass and trees, carrying the dark scent of pine.

Without warning, Vieveeka appeared at the side of the wagon. She placed a finger to her lips to stop the startled cry at the back of Jen's throat. Vieveeka moved to the hatch at the back of the wagon. With a sly smile, she held up a pin and began picking the lock. A moment later Jen heard two soft clicks and the lock was removed. Her eyes darted anxiously to the guards. None moved. Then Vieveeka was beside Jen, untying her bonds. She was free!

She was so stiff she could only crawl to the hatch. Outside the wagon, she felt unsteady on her feet. Returning circulation brought pins and needles to her muscles, but these soon passed. Vieveeka glided silently ahead, red hair glimmering in the starlight.

Jen followed, eyeing the sleeping guards for movement. One snored and rolled over, but the others remained still. Jen caught up with Vieveeka on the other side of the supply wagon. A second wagon with a cage was parked a few feet away. A woman lay facedown inside. Her hands and feet were in metal shackles. Her hair was disheveled. She wore what might be a torn and soiled nightgown. Jen couldn't tell if this was her mother, but her heart ached for the woman. She reminded Jen of the delicate petals of a rose, cruelly torn and crushed underfoot.

"Mother?" she whispered.

There was no response.

"Mother? Is that you?"

The woman didn't stir.

"Unlock the hatch," Jen said to Vieveeka. "We've got to get her out of there."

"We won't be able to carry her. Try and revive her with water."

Jen nodded and grabbed a water skin off the side of the supply wagon. Meanwhile, Vieveeka worked at the cage lock.

"Mother?" Jen tried again. "I've got water." She pushed the skin into the cage, unmindful of her own parched throat.

The woman stirred and looked up. A nasty sunburn peeled in patches across her forehead and cheeks. She tried to speak, but could only mouth the words. A single drop of blood sprang from a cracked lower lip and rolled down her chin. Jen stifled a cry. It was Mother!

"Sip a little water," Jen whispered, trying to contain the anguish ripping her heart. "Then we'll get you out of there."

Mother shook her head and tried again to speak. She looked to Vieveeka.

"Look, Mom. It's Vieveeka. She's going to free you."

"Run—" Mother managed to say, her voice cracking.

"Not without you."

Mother shook her head, eyes wide. "She's—"

"I know," said Jen. "She's on our side. Give her a moment. She's picking the lock." Jen called softly to Vieveeka. "What's taking so long?"

Vieveeka moved away from the hatch and walked toward Jen.

"What's wrong," Jen asked. "Can't you pick it?"

Vieveeka didn't answer. She stepped beside Jen, a faint smile on her lips. She began to laugh. A low, mocking laugh . . .

13

In her bedroom, Bit still had half an

hour before meeting the Pondit and Yalp at the stables. To calm her nerves, she checked her backpack once again. The canteen was full. There was a supply of dried fruit, nuts, and hardtack, all wrapped carefully in parchment paper. She had several pairs of thick socks and a woolen sweater. Toothbrush, cup, and gear for cooking on a campfire were stowed in the side flaps. A slicker and blanket were neatly rolled and tied at the bottom.

She bent over and inspected her boots. They were sturdy and made for hiking. She felt carefully around her toes. There seemed to be plenty of room, as she knew there would. She'd ordered the boots for long walks with Dash. They were a little bigger than her size, so nothing would rub. Still, if there were hours of walking, she worried whether her feet would hold up.

There was nothing she could do about that, so, feeling all was ready for the journey, she made one more round about her room. She tried to fight it, but she felt like she might never return, never see her things again. They were such little things, but they meant the world to her. She started at her bed, running her fingers across the smooth surface of her bedspread, feeling the texture of the little white doilies she had sewn on the edge.

She straightened the row of porcelain dolls and stuffed animals that beseeched her from the pillows, giving a final hug to the pink bunny, which had been so held and squeezed it was almost worn to the inner cotton. Pulling away, she moved to the window and watered the sky-blue forget-me-nots on the sill. Then she stepped onto her veranda and looked for the funny birds Jenny called Starbirds. Bit hadn't seen them since yesterday morning, but taking breadcrumbs from her pocket, she scattered them anyway. The pile they'd built on the eave of the roof was still there, baked hard from the sun. Maybe they'd return.

Back inside, she turned to her art area, set up in a corner by a window. Golden light streamed in here most of the day. She sat at the chair and ran her hands along the side of the round table, restraining the urge to touch anything else so she wouldn't cry. She never had such wonderful things before. There was a whole world here to get lost in. Pigments for egg tempera, watercolors, chalk, paper as soft as felt. Then there were the little treasures to make crafts. Shiny beads, pieces of interesting driftwood, feathers, yarn, leaves, and colored sand. On her easel was a painting of one of the castle gardens, a present she was making for Jenny's mother. Would she ever get a chance to finish it?

Tearing herself away from the table, she stepped to her dresser, where a small mirror sat on top. She traced her finger around the silver flowers on the border. Dash wanted to give her something big and ornate, but she felt too embarrassed when she saw it. Fortunately, Jenny was there. Seeing Bit's reaction, she told Dash he didn't know anything about girls and gave Bit this one instead.

She opened the top drawer of the dresser and gazed at her diary and an album where she collected all things Dash: his first card; an awkward poem penned in bold script; a flower plucked on one of their walks and placed in her hair; each precious beyond compare. A sharp pang at her heart kept her from opening the diary or the album.

Forcing herself to close the drawer, she moved next to her little desk and tucked in the chair. On the far right corner was a small portrait she'd drawn of Dash. She picked up the picture and softly brushed his cheek with her fingertips. Choking back a sob, she replaced the picture and turned away, busying herself with straightening the already neat row of gowns in her closet.

She didn't see them. All she could think about was Dash's pale face. Would those eyes ever open, would she ever see him smile again? And what if she failed? The weight of her task was sinking in, plaguing her with a million doubts.

But she had to try. She turned back to the room. Through a mist of tears threatening to overflow her eyes, she saw the little dolls and animals still beseeching her.

"I'll be back," she promised them, wishing with all her heart it was true.

A bold knock startled her. She wiped her eyes and smoothed her hair to compose herself, but before she could open the door, Pet strode in. She wore a wide-brimmed hat and a red and green plaid shirt. Khaki shorts held up by suspenders, thick woolen socks folded below the knees, and a pair of brown hiking boots completed her outfit. She'd slung a pack over her shoulders, and a spyglass, compass, and whistle dangled from loops on the side. Poking out the top flap were a makeup box, a long loaf of bread, and a stick of cured meat.

"Let us sally forth," she said, cocking her head like a sea captain gazing at a far horizon.

Never having seen Pet outside a gown, Bit stared in amazement. "Pet! What are you doing?"

"I'm coming with you."

"You . . . you are? I thought you were against me going."

"I am. But as long as you insist, I'm going too. To make sure you're all right."

Joy and relief sprouted in Bit's breast. Pet was funny and smart and nothing would be better than having her along. For her to want to help only proved what Bit had felt all along. "I knew it. I knew you were really my friend." She restrained herself from crying, knowing how much Pet hated tears. Instead she threw her arms around the Countess, as far as the backpack would allow.

"Of course I am. Why wouldn't I be?" Pet walked to the bed and slung the pack off her shoulder. The makeup box tumbled out.

Bit reached for the box but paused halfway there, a warning flashing in her mind like one of Dash's military flares. "I can't let you go. It's far too dangerous."

"Nonsense. We'll be safe as long as we stay together. Wherever you go, I go."

"But we know nothing about the Plain World or the people there. The risks—"

"If you can take risks, so can I."

"But your father, your mother . . ."

"Father thinks I'm going to visit my mother, and my mother is out of the country."

Bit shook her head. "I'd never forgive myself if anything happened to you."

"Enough! I'm going. It's settled. We stick together like glue, whatever may come, 'til the end." Pet picked up the makeup box and stuffed it back in the pack.

Out of arguments, really wanting Pet to come, Bit let all objections go. Bursting into tears of happiness she flung her arms around her friend.

Pet took a little step back. "Whoa! Stop blubbering all over me. Save that for when we're in trouble."

"I'm sorry. I've mussed you up." Bit drew a kerchief from her pocket and started fussing over Pet's face and shirt.

Her friend whisked the kerchief out of her hand. "I'm fine. When do we go?"

"Right now. I'm meeting the Pondit and Yalp at the stables."

"Now that I'm going, you don't need Yalp."

"I do need him, and the Pondit will insist that he go."

Pet flashed a mischievous smile and winked. "Let's ditch him. He's a silly little midget. It's all I can do to keep from kicking him like a ball."

"We'll need his magic to get into the Plain World."

"I thought Jenny used some kind of key to pass between worlds."

"She did. But no one can find it. She must have hidden it."

Petunia's shoulders sagged. "Then let's get on with it."

Bit took one last look at her room. The bedspread was smooth, the pillows fluffed, the dolls and animals set in a row. Her shoes had been polished and lined up along the floor of the closet, and the forget-me-nots on the sill had been watered. She was about to turn away but ran instead to her pillow. Underneath she found the little replica of the Rose Castle. Going to the window, she placed the carving in the shade of the sky-blue flowers and whispered, "Come back to me, Dash. Come back to me . . ."

Before coming to Aerdem, Bit had seen tents, lean-tos, huts, and sheds. She'd seen shacks, small villages with thatched

roofs, and a few ramshackle farmhouses. None of these prepared her for the grandeur of the Royal Stable. She still felt a
little awed when she saw the building, which rose two stories at
the end of a vast lawn. It was painted pure white, and the sun
reflected so brightly off the walls that she had to shade her eyes
as she approached. Trim around the windows and ornate railing along the roof made it look like a fine boardinghouse. A set
of double doors was large enough to drive a carriage through.
Walking up a short ramp, Bit passed through the door, and
stepped into a world of cool shadows and aromatic leather.

Pet followed her in, pack slung over her shoulders, feet
falling softly on the plank floor. A wall running nearly the length
of the building divided the interior. This side was home to carriages, buckboards, mud and hunting wagons, phaetons, and
buggies. They seemed to be sleeping, and Bit passed each with
hushed reverence, admiring the workmanship—lacquered
wood, wicker armrests, polished lanterns, peacock-blue wheel
spokes. She lingered when she reached the barouche.
Raindrops from last night's storm still jeweled the black surface,
catching sunlight from the open back door. Sadness wrapped
her heart. She had ridden to the masked ball in the barouche.

The sharp ring of metal roused her from a blanket of
melancholy. Outside, Hom the Smith had begun hammering.
He had a long shed behind the stable, where, in addition to hot
coals and bellows, a flotsam of old wheels, hubs, spokes, discarded wagon cushions, and rusty tools crowded his stall.
Fifteen shoes of various sizes were nailed on a beam above his
open-air window. A deep, soulful tenor sang from his hammer,
and Bit guessed he was beating on number ten, a shoe for a
heavy draft horse.

Shifting her pack on her shoulders, Bit passed the barouche
and entered the other side of the stable. Lines of horse stalls

ran on either side. Pausing to pick two apples from a barrel, she stepped to the first stall and whistled. Dash's stallion, Nightflyer, greeted her with a trumpet call and greedily snatched an apple from her fingers. She caressed his nose while he munched, but wondered why she didn't see her own horse next door.

Halfway down the line of stalls, she found Yalp sitting on a small wooden crate, his legs hanging over the side. He stared at a halter in his hand. When he saw Bit and Pet, he pushed off the crate and approached them. He'd usually bow so low he'd almost stand on his head. And his body—two feet tall and shaped like a chicken egg—usually rolled and tumbled when he walked. Now his little legs rocked him gently from side to side, and his head was lowered in thought. He wore a deep-blue robe, far too big for him, which trailed behind gathering dust and blades of straw.

Bit could guess what was wrong. "You've been to see Dash and the king."

He looked up, his eyes sad. "Yes." His voice was high and sweet, like a tiny child. His face—boyish for a man in his forties—was creased with worry.

She clutched his arm. "Is there anything you can do for them?"

He shook his head. "I've tried. Maybe the problem is with me."

"Why?"

"My magic is based on happiness and laughter. I'm struggling to make it work."

Bit felt her heart twist. "But you can do it, right?" she said, trying to bolster her confidence.

Yalp looked down at the halter in his hand. "I've been trying for the last hour to get this to levitate and go on my horse. I can't seem to do it."

"But you have to get us into the Plain World," Bit cried.

"I know." He looked lost as a lamb searching for its mother.

"Please, you have to try."

"I will, now that you're here. Come." He led them back to the crate, which he climbed on top of so he stood taller. He gave a little whistle and a happy whinny answered from one of the stalls. A moment later, his miniature horse trotted out. She buried her nose in his neck and tugged playfully on the collar of his robe. He stroked her face affectionately and giving her a pat sent her to stand a few paces away.

Picking up a straw, he held it near Bit's chin. "You won't mind dear, will you?"

Bit was anxious for the magic to work. "Of course not."

He touched the straw under her chin and ever so gently traced it from side to side. Butterfly wings couldn't have felt lighter, and she felt a tiny smile and the whisper of a giggle escape her lips.

At that instant, Yalp dropped the straw and, cupping his hands, caught the little breath that carried the giggle. Nodding, he began to mumble a series of strange words that Bit didn't understand. Soon a rustling like wind in the leaves accompanied the words, only there was no wind in the stable. Instead, the halter stirred straw on the floor as it wound like a snake toward the little pony. When it reached her forehoof, the halter rose in the air and with a rocking, swaying motion fitted neatly over the horse's nose.

Yalp gasped for breath and swayed on the crate. Fearful he would fall, Bit steadied him. "Thank you, I'm fine now," he said, mopping beads of sweat from his brow. "That shouldn't have been so difficult."

"But it worked," Bit exclaimed, with a rush of relief.

"Yes. Let me try putting that pack on your horse. I've already got her saddled."

He whistled again, this time like a nightingale, and Bit's white mare, Snow Dancer, trotted out of another stall. She shook her head and nickered when she saw Bit. In a moment, Bit's arms were around her and the horse pressed her moist nose into Bit's neck. Bit always felt a thrill when she saw Snow Dancer. She had a wild spirit—though she was always gentle with Bit—and when she galloped her long mane and tail tossed like ocean waves.

Still standing on the crate, Yalp motioned for Bit to remove her pack, then he held out his hand palm up. Cupping it with the other, he mumbled a few words. Taking the second hand away, he revealed a blade of straw.

Delighted, Bit clapped her hands. "See, you can do magic."

Pet frowned. "Hardly. It's just sleight of hand. Any street magician can do it."

"But he raised the halter."

Yalp hung his head. "I did. But the Countess is right about the straw. It never hurts to throw in some drama."

"Drama won't get us into the Plain World," said Pet, slinging her own pack to the ground.

Yalp looked surprised. "Us?"

"Pet's coming with us," said Bit. "Isn't that wonderful?"

Yalp studied the Countess' face. She stared back evenly. Something seemed to pass between the two of them. Bit couldn't imagine what, but was too concerned with whether the magic would work. She pressed Yalp to try again. He tickled her again with the straw, this time along her earlobe. Again he caught her little laugh in his hands and began chanting over it in a low voice.

The pack stirred at Snow Dancer's feet. Yalp chanted

louder and motioned with his hands, as if he were lifting the pack with a great effort. One end rose off the ground, then fell back. He tried again, straining at the air. His body trembled. Beads of sweat formed on his brow. His voice grew hoarse. The pack rose a few inches off the ground and rocked back and forth as if it hung from a single rope. Whatever magic held it up snapped. The pack dropped with a thud.

Yalp coughed and sputtered as if he were drowning. He staggered on the crate and Bit kept him from falling off. She lowered him gently until he sat on the edge and leaned against her.

There must be something we can do, she thought. Her mind raced, but no solution presented itself. Without Yalp's magic, they were stuck. A feeling of helplessness overtook her, and with it a bleak despair.

Cradling his head in her arms, she gave him water from her canteen. "Is there no other way?"

He took a few grateful sips. "There is another magic."

"Then you must try it."

"Yes, but not now. I need to rest. We need to travel to the pool Jenny came out of when she first arrived here."

"The Portarien Pool—where the magic water is."

"Yes. It's linked somehow to the Plain World. I'll try again there."

Outside, there was a pause in the smith's pounding, probably to turn the shoe. The hammering resumed as the Pondit appeared at the back of the stable. He wore the same robe he'd worn earlier that morning, a dusty rose now dimmer in the shadows. He approached with weary steps, bent over as if he carried a burden. Bit knew he'd been up all night and probably hadn't slept since the attack. "Is all ready for your departure?" he asked Yalp.

Yalp drooped. "The spells aren't working."

The Pondit leaned down and placed a hand on each of Yalp's shoulders. "Trust, my friend, trust. It will come." He turned to Bit. "And you, little one? Are you prepared?"

Bit hesitated, feeling resolve melt away. Without Yalp's magic, they'd never get into the Plain World. And if they managed to get there, could he get them back? And there was a malevolent power out there, capable of penetrating the safety of the Rose Castle. How much more powerful would it be outside the castle walls? She wanted to yell, "Stop. What can I do? Let someone better go." It was all she could do to keep from running out of the stable.

The Pondit seemed to sense the panic rising within her and gave her an encouraging smile. "Don't be frightened. You have all you need, right in there." He pointed to her heart.

Bit wasn't sure what he meant, but nodded and managed to ask, "Is there any change with Dash and the king?"

His smile faded. "Alas, I fear the worst. The creatures draw more tightly around them every hour. At this rate, they will die in four, maybe five days."

Bit felt her legs wobble and her throat tighten, as if she too were being strangled. "What if I fail?" she gasped.

"You won't." From beneath a wild tangle of over-pouring eyebrow hair, his eyes were steady, patient, but a little hard. He was making it clear she would be going.

"But if I do fail and they die, it will be because of me."

"And if someone else tries and fails, it will be because of them. It's the trying that matters, not the failing. Besides, you have as much chance of failing as anyone, but more of succeeding."

"Why?" she asked in surprise.

"Because your love for Dash transcends all obstacles."

Bit swallowed, wishing, hoping, praying with all her heart that it was true. Outside, Hom the Smith stopped pounding. A sharp hiss rose and faded, announcing the red-hot shoe had been cooled in water.

"But you must hasten," said the Pondit.

She nodded and lifted her pack onto Snow Dancer's back and fastened it down with straps. "At least I'll have a friend along. Pet is going with me."

"What?" The Pondit's face went blank as he looked at Pet.

"Yes! Isn't it wonderful?" Bit said.

He started to reply but a yawn seized his mouth and twisted it open like a giant cave. When it closed at last, he rubbed a pair of puffy and bloodshot eyes. "That wasn't the plan."

Bit adjusted her horse's stirrup. "I know, but I'll feel so much safer if she comes along."

The Pondit didn't answer. At least that wasn't no. He stared at Pet with the confused face of a schoolboy trying to put together puzzle pieces that didn't fit. At last he spoke. "This isn't a stroll in the country, Countess."

"My family wants to do their part." Pet studied a loose thread at the bottom of her shorts.

"It's far too dangerous."

"Then why are you sending Bit?"

The Pondit rubbed his eyes again, but still looked dazed. "Too much is riding on this mission."

"That's why she needs a friend, someone our age to talk to. You're old. You wouldn't understand."

He seemed to recover a little at that. "Are you a friend?"

Pet worried the thread between her fingers. "Of course I am. Why wouldn't I be?"

The Pondit tried to stifle another wrenching yawn. "But . . . have you asked your father? Does he know?"

Bit knew they had him. Now Pet looked him straight in the eye. "Of course he knows."

The Pondit was out of questions, but to make sure Bit added, "Please. I don't want to go alone."

"Very well. Benden and some soldiers are going with you. They'll protect you both." He continued to stare uncertainly at Pet, who avoided his eyes and went back to pulling at the thread.

Bit threw her arms around the Pondit and thanked him before he changed his mind. Then she saddled a horse for Pet and helped her tie down her pack.

"I guess I won't be missed much," said Bit, adjusting the horse's bridle.

"We'll all miss you," replied the Pondit.

Bit turned in surprise.

"Sally is crying right now. Don't you know? Everyone loves you. You are sweet and gentle and kind. Even an enemy would find it hard not to love you. Isn't that right, Countess Petunia Pompahro?"

Pet wound the thread around her index finger and yanked it out. "If you're done with your little pep talk, let's get on with it."

14

A secret teased the corner of

Vieveeka's mouth and curled the upper lip. Eyes narrowed to sharp points, she lifted her hand above her head and lowered it slowly, as if pulling down a shade.

"Jenny, run!" cried Mother. "She's—"

Jen faced Vieveeka with cocked fists. But Vieveeka was changing. She maintained the form of a woman. But inside that shape she broke into chaotic pieces, like the tumbling fragments of a kaleidoscope. The pieces fell into place and resolved into a new image, that of a woman in her forties. Dark brown hair with a gray stripe fell to her shoulders. The brows were thick, hairy, and mannish. The eyes a frosty blue. Where Vieveeka's figure was small and supple, this woman had powerful hips and shoulders. She towered over Jen.

"—Naryfel!" Mother finished. "Run!"

Jen would never abandon her mother. Even if Jen wanted to, it was too late. Shadowy figures formed a circle around her, cutting off any escape. The halberds in their hands glinted in the starlight. A tall man stepped beside Naryfel. He lit a lantern, illuminating the grin of Tragedy-Comedy, and lowered his mask.

His nose was long and pointed. Thorny growths jutted from his skin. He leered at Jen with bloodred eyes and held out his arms for a dance.

She knew him instantly. The Desert King. He'd captured her briefly when she had first searched for her mother. He'd thought of Jen as a toy for his amusement, as one might collect coins or butterflies. But why was he here, and with Naryfel?

"She paid me," he said, guessing her question.

"I'll pay you more," Jen said stoutly. "All the wealth of Aerdem if you release us."

"She's already promised me that, and more," he said. If a mummy spoke, the voice could not sound more withered. "You've had your little game," he said, turning to Naryfel. "Did you enjoy it?"

"Nothing could give me more pleasure," Naryfel replied. "The look on her face when I changed was priceless," she said, cocking a thumb at Jen.

"Let her go," said Mother. "It's me you want."

"Not true, little sister," replied Naryfel. "The look of horror when you saw she'd been kidnapped was worth the whole thing. What better way to hurt you than through her?" She reached into the cage and withdrew the water skin.

"Let her drink," Jen cried. "Can't you see she's ill?"

Naryfel felt Mother's forehead. "She's hot. Very well," she said, tossing the skin back in. "Drink."

Mother reached gratefully for the water. Removing the plug, she raised it to her lips. A moment later, she sprayed out the liquid and coughed violently. "Vinegar," she gasped.

As she was dragged fighting and screaming back to her cage, Jen heard Naryfel laughing.

Jen seized the bars, and dug her nails into the wood until

her knuckles were white rocks. She'd been played for a fool, a marionette forced to dance for someone's amusement. She should have seen this coming, should never have trusted Vieveeka. Images of Mother—head hanging, face blotchy and red, eyes swollen—tore at Jen's heart. Once free, she should have run, then found a way to free her mother.

Strangely, Naryfel relented on food and water. It wasn't out of kindness or compassion. She was keeping her prey just strong enough to play with, like a cat pausing with a prize, waiting for it to wriggle and move. Still, Jen was grateful. After a long pull at a canteen, she devoured a plate of beans. An hour later her old energy returned.

She was no longer tied up. She was sure this wasn't out of mercy, but only to let her know she was completely in Naryfel's power, that there was no escape.

The camp had grown quiet. Jen couldn't sleep, so she inspected all the bars of the cage to see if any were loose. She tried the rear hatch. All were solidly fixed. She busied herself massaging her legs and arms, and stretched. If she got the opportunity to run, she wanted her muscles to work. Using her fingers, she tried to comb out the masses of knots in her hair. Then she braided it so it would be out of her way.

The night was unusually dark. In the distance she thought she heard that strange piping. She decided it must be a bird-call. Otherwise, whoever was playing would have to be following. But what bird sounded like a baby wailing for its mother? The last notes bent plaintively, longingly, like they were trying to find a home.

The song repeated for a while, then stopped. Curling arms of fog rolled down the valley walls and reached long fingers through the tall grass. Jen hugged herself to keep warm, and mournfully watched the campfire shrink to a bed of glowing embers. A light wind sent up a few twirling red sparks. One hovered in midair.

Jen felt the hair stand on the back of her neck. Like a tiny red eye, the spark floated toward her. She lost it for a moment in a patch of fog, then it emerged again.

She peered into the darkness. A shadow emerged, moving soundlessly with the spark. As it approached, it resolved into the form of a boy. He was Jen's age, maybe older. He chewed on a long straw, the end of which burned with a tiny ember. He paused a few feet away and held his fingers to his lips. Then he smiled, exposing red-stained teeth.

He had round cheeks, sprinkled generously with freckles, and sandy bangs that fell to sparkling eyes. Under other circumstances, Jen would think he was cute. Out in the middle of nowhere, who could he be but Naryfel in disguise?

He moved to the back of the wagon and fiddled noiselessly with the lock. A soft click sounded and he winked at Jen. He removed the lock, and opened the hatch.

Jen shrank to the back of the wagon and glared. "I'm not falling for your trick a second time, Naryfel," she hissed.

"Naryfel!" he whispered with a roll of his chestnut eyes. "Puh-lease! I've been called a lot of things, but nothing bad as that."

"Move away from the hatch," Jen demanded. If she could get a little space she could make a run for it. Still, the Desert King probably had sentries posted just beyond the grass.

"What's your problem?" he whispered. "I'm saving you." He reached out a hand. "Come on, I know a place. They'll never find you."

"Stay away or you're grave grass."

The boy shrugged and spit out the straw. "Suit yourself."

He turned and headed for the supply wagon. There was

now a good twenty-five yards between them. She could run for it.

She slipped from the wagon and headed for the perimeter of tall grass. Glancing back, she saw the boy disappear under the cover of the supply wagon. She stepped inside the grass and parted the blades just enough to watch what he was doing. A few minutes later he left the wagon, a canteen slung over his shoulder. He stopped at the fire, removed a straw from his pocket and lit the tip. Then he walked straight toward her.

She slipped farther back and crouched where the grass was thick and towered above her. A moment later the boy's head poked through the blades.

"Miss me?" he said with a red-toothed smile.

Jen didn't know what to make of this. If this was a shape-shifting Naryfel, she was not acting as expected. The artful Vieveeka had been convincing. But could Naryfel pull off this boy, whose eyes were open, frank, and candid? That seemed unlikely. How could she be something she wasn't? Still, the best policy was to be wary.

"How did you find me so fast?" She watched him closely, ready to spring away if he tried anything.

He wore loose fitting shirt and pants, crudely made of rough burlap. Rope-soled sandals covered his feet. He tamped out the ember on his straw. "You left tracks like an elephant." He pulled two sourdough rolls out of his pockets and handed her one. "Courtesy of Naryfel."

Squatting beside her, he tore off a big chunk of bread with his teeth and chewed with gusto. "Better eat," he said. "We don't want to be here when they find you're missing."

Jen dug into her roll, realizing just how famished she was.

"I left her a thank-you note," he said, chewing with his mouth open.

"Who?"

"Naryfel," he said, thumbing back to the campsite. "Come on," he said holding out a hand to pull her up, "I'll tell you on the way."

She rose, ignoring his hand. "Where?"

"Anywhere but here, unless you want to be thrown back into a cage." He moved off into the grass, the blades barely stirring as he passed.

Jen hesitated, watching him disappear. She knew she needed to hide. But she didn't want to be far from her mother, either.

"Well?" she heard him whisper. "You coming?"

Her feet moved before she was aware of deciding. In a moment she was beside him and they were stepping quietly through the grass.

"What was your note?" she asked.

He grinned. "I dumped the flour and beans and poured vinegar in the water."

"What?" Jen cried, stopping in her tracks. "My mother's still back there."

The boy looked stunned. "I didn't know that. Yours was the only uncovered wagon."

"She's ill. She won't survive without food and fresh water."

"Don't worry. I didn't have time to spoil it all. What does Naryfel want with you and your mother?" He eyed her clothes. She was still wearing her pirate outfit from the ball.

"It's a long story." She'd want a lot more information out of him before she told him anything.

"What's your name?" he asked. They were slipping through the grass again.

"Jen."

"You don't look like a Jen."

117

"It's short for Jenren."

"I have many names. Round these parts they call me Will o' the Wisp. I'm Tom Tumble in Laskamont. In Upper Trilafor, they call me Jack Quick."

"And in Lower Trilafor?"

"There I'm Jack Nimble. In Shaklesberry, it's Fast Eddie."

"In Aerdem they call you Al Otto."

"Al Otto?"

"A lot o' hot air."

"Fine. Don't believe me. But it's all true. Where she comes from," he waved a thumb back toward the campsite, "they call me Naryfel's Bane."

"Why?"

"I make her life hell. I'm her thorn. Her personal gnat, buzzing about just to annoy her."

"Why?"

"It's a long story." He gave her a wry smile, as if to say, "You tell me more, and I'll tell you more."

She followed him out of the grass and into a clump of pines. The only sound was the murmur of crickets. A scattering of periwinkle blossoms dotted the ground, which was piled with a soft carpet of pine needles. After running on the hard earth, the needles were a welcome relief to her feet, still bare from when she'd been pulled out of bed.

"This way," he said, bearing left toward a steep hillside. They walked a short distance to some broom bush growing up against a rocky wall. He grabbed some twigs and retraced his steps. Then quickly swept the path they had taken to cover their tracks. When he returned, he pulled aside one of the bushes and revealed a cave.

Inside, a flickering candle threw a warm glow on the cave walls. The embers of a small fire smoldered below a coffeepot.

An old woolen blanket was spread over a pile of straw.

He winked at her. "I found this place last year. Nice, huh?"

Jen followed him in. It seemed safe. If this was one of Naryfel's tricks, something would have happened by now. Still, it seemed best to be wary. What was a boy doing out in the middle of nowhere. As far as Jen could see, there had been no villages for miles.

He dragged the bush back in place to camouflage the entrance. Then he kicked off his sandals, and stretched out on the blanket. He held out the canteen. "Want some?"

She shook her head.

"Look what else I got, courtesy of Naryfel." He took a small bag of morslittes out of his pocket and poured half of them into her hand. They were dry morslittes, tidbits of roots and fruit peels that had been spiced and sugared.

She sucked gratefully on a green one, and mint burst on her tongue. The accompanying scent was welcome. The cave smelled of old sweat. When the boy moved near her, she was aware of a strong body odor she found hard to ignore. She wondered how long it had been since he had bathed. Or washed his clothes, which were splotched with food stains.

"What's wrong?" he asked, looking at his clothes.

"Nothing."

"You're lying," he said matter-of-factly, but without offense.

"I'm not."

"You are. Go on. You can tell me."

She hesitated. The smell was getting to her. She didn't think she could stay in the cave much longer.

"How long has it been since you've bathed?" she asked.

"Never. It's bad for my health."

"Now you're lying." She laughed and her shoulders relaxed.

He grinned. "Am I that bad?"

"Terrible."

"Then if you don't mind, I'll do the honors now. I want my guest to be comfortable." He rose and started to take off his shirt. Then hesitated.

"It's okay," said Jen. "I'll look away."

He stood with his fingers at his collar. "I have other names," he said. His voice was hoarse and he coughed. He waved a thumb back toward Naryfel's campsite. "In her land, I'm sometimes called . . . Blue—"

"Blue," exclaimed Jen. "That's a wonderful name."

"You like it?" His face brightened. "Then call me Blue."

He pulled off his shirt and washed his chest and under his arms with canteen water. Then he wet the shirt and rubbed it vigorously.

"Better?" he asked, when he was done and the shirt was spread beside the fire to dry.

"Better," she said with a smile.

He finished the last morslitte and pulled some kind of nut out of his pant pocket. He cracked it open with his teeth and showed her the red meat inside. "Want some?"

She shook her head. He popped the nut into his mouth and began chewing.

"They're like sour cherries," he said with a grin. His teeth were soon covered with crimson juice. When he was done, he wiped his mouth on his arm.

"I wish I'd had more time back there," he said. "I would have grabbed some bacon and eggs. We'll need something for breakfast."

"I'm not staying for breakfast."

He looked at her quizzically.

"I've got to free my mom."

"Jen, you can't go back there now."

"I have to."

"Any minute they're going to find you're gone and start a search."

"I can't leave her with that monster."

"We won't. But we have to wait for the right moment. That's how I got you out."

"How did you know I was there?"

"I've been following you since they nabbed you in Aerdem."

"Why?"

"I told you. I like to mess with Naryfel."

"Aren't you scared of her?"

A gust of wind penetrated the bush doorway. For a moment, the candle wavered and Blue's shadow swayed on the wall behind him.

"Naw. She's shown me the worst she's got. I survived it."

Jen was about to ask what Naryfel had done, but a blood-curdling shriek cut through the night.

15

Bit's journey to the pool passed like

a dream . . . the questioning faces of the townsfolk as they rode down the cobbled streets . . . passing through the tall gates of Glowan and wending through the pastures and orchards and farmlands rich with black, fertile earth. The clopping horses, the creaking saddles. Pet falling into a sulky silence. A half dozen stern-faced soldiers ahead and behind for safe passage, the broad shoulders of Benden, their captain, rising and falling with his steed. Yalp's furrowed brow—was he thinking whether the magic would work? Then they crested a hill and looked back at the whole of Aerdem, stretched out in a hazy valley, the Rose Castle sparkling like a jewel at one end, splitting the light of a golden sun and bathing the little city and surrounding land in a rainbow glow.

Nowhere in the world was so beautiful.

The castle was left reluctantly behind as they plunged into woodlands alive with the heady scents of eucalyptus and pine and chattering wildlife.

At last, the dirt road broke from a cluster of trees and Bit had her first view of the Portarien Pool. A waterfall splashed in graceful steps off a low hill, then tumbled into an opalescent pool of turquoise. The pool was surrounded by a ring of smooth rocks and spilled over at one end into a brook, where, tinkling like wind chimes, the water passed under the arches of a stone bridge, before winding its way through a landscape of rolling hills and farms.

They dismounted by the bridge. The soldiers remained there with the horses while Bit, Pet, and Yalp, followed by Benden, carried their packs down to some flat rocks by the pool.

Pet put down her pack and it tumbled over. The top flap fell open and half the contents spilled out. Aside from food, a change of clothes, and the makeup box, Bit spied a bottle of Artesia Works Ginger and Lavender After Bath Rain, a jar of Rose Petal Facial Infusion, Dr. Owon's Apricot Foot Therapy, Royal Pistachio Hand Lotion, and Mrs. Jolola's Cucumber and Melon Body Butter.

Bit stared in wonder at the creams and lotions. "Won't they make your pack too heavy?"

"A girl has to be prepared. You never know. There might be a handsome duke or prince in the Plain World." Pet started throwing everything back into her pack willy-nilly, but her gaze strayed to Benden, who found a rock at a respectful distance and set down his gear. He blushed and turned away when he noticed the Countess staring.

"Why did that fool of a Pondit send Benden?" Pet asked. "He's as green as a new shoot. A girl could lead him around like a baby calf."

"Benden loves Dash and will do anything to save him. That's what the Pondit said."

"He's a fool, and should have been put out to pasture long ago."

Bit didn't know what to say. If the Pondit was wrong about

Benden, he could be wrong about her too. She pushed the thought aside and tried to see Dash's face, as he'd appeared the day she'd sketched him, filled with morning light.

Pet reached for her bread. "I'm hungry."

"We shouldn't eat our food yet. We might need it," Bit replied.

The scent of orange and pear drew her attention to the surrounding trees. Willows rustled in the breeze and bowed like graceful dancers. Peach, pear, orange, and pomegranate trees cast their fruit in a mosaic carpet. "I'll get us something to eat."

A few steps, and she was collecting the fruit. In the foliage above, a chorus of blackbirds, goldfinches, robins, and larks flitted from branch to branch, caroling sweetly. It was all a wild and perfect garden. When this was over, if it was ever over, she would linger here with Dash.

She returned with a napkin of fruit and handed it to Pet.

Pet tore into a pear, chasing a fly with her hand. "Well, now what?" she asked Yalp.

Shading his eyes, he surveyed the pond. "I must try and find where Jenny first appeared."

"How long will that take?" She looked longingly at the long loaf and the sausage sticking out of her pack.

Yalp frowned. "As long as it takes."

Bit glanced at the sky, a crisp marine blue deepening with the approach of sunset. "Oh, but please hurry. We can reach the doctor in a few hours and bring him back tonight."

His voice softened. "I'll do the best I can." He cast a worried glance at Pet, then skipped over some steppingstones, which led partway across the pool, and sat down. A moment later he was chanting under his breath.

Pet gazed at him skeptically. "Can we really put our lives in his hands? He's like a little child."

"I think he's sweet," Bit replied.

"He'll foul things up."

Bit fought the urge to twist her sleeve. "Please don't say that. He's all we have."

Pet turned to her and gripped both her arms. "Look, it's not too late. You don't have to go. Yalp and Benden can do it." Her voice was urgent, a little shrill.

Bit still felt like running and hiding. She couldn't. She felt a flame inside—little more than a spark, but still it burned! And pushed her forward despite her fears. "Have you ever wanted to be more?"

Pet stared at her a long time before answering. "To do something no one thought you could."

"Even yourself. That's why I must go. Anyway, if I don't, I'll be abandoning Dash."

"You love him that much?" Pet studied her nails, which were still decorated with red hearts from the ball.

Bit felt her shoulders sag, thinking of Dash spinning across the dance floor with Vieveeka clasped in his arms. She looked at Pet through a film of tears. "Yes," she murmured. She cried softly, wiping her eyes. What could she expect from Dash when this was all over?

"You'll win him back," said Pet, as if reading her thoughts.

"Will I?"

"Sure. You just have to know how to turn a man's head." She nodded to Benden, who sat a dozen yards away sharpening a battle knife. "Watch."

Pet rose. Dusting herself, she straightened her shirt and took off her hat. Reaching into her pack, she fished out a brush. She stroked and primped, but no matter what she did, the curls snapped back into unruly corkscrews. Pet was frustrated, but Bit loved her hair, which shone like honey in the setting sun.

Pet tossed the brush aside. "Benden?" she called, with a coquettish tilt to her hips.

He looked up, startled. Blond bangs and baby fat on his cheeks made him look younger than his nineteen years. He rose and bowed awkwardly. "Yes, Countess?" He tried to make his voice sound deeper, something he'd been doing all afternoon.

Pet sauntered over until she stood beside him, looking up at him alluringly. "Fetch me a bouquet."

Benden blushed. "Miss?"

"A big bouquet."

He shifted from foot to foot, looking from Pet to Bit to Yalp. "My duty is here."

Pet fluttered her eyelashes. "Have you no duty to a lady?"

"Yes," he mumbled, his face burning redder.

"Then take your men and gather me the largest plenderil you can find. Nothing smaller than my hand will do."

Pet reached out and toyed with one of his buttons until he backed away stumbling.

"No," Bit called. "We have to stay together." In her mind she cried out. But her voice was painfully weak and inadequate. Even the birds singing in the trees sounded louder.

Benden didn't hear. He gathered his men and took them into the surrounding fields. A few minutes later Yalp skipped back over the steppingstones and took her hands.

"I found the spot," he said. "We must act quickly. Timing is everything."

Bit looked anxiously for Benden and his men. They were already out of sight. "But—"

Yalp drew her to the edge of the pool. "I need you to stand here. And Countess, you must stand beside her."

Pet rejoined them. "Why me?"

"Because I need a giggle from both of you."

"Get two from Bit. I don't want you touching me."

"No, no, you don't understand. I must capture your giggles at the same time."

"Please, Pet, for Dash," said Bit.

Pet swatted at a gnat buzzing around her head and exhaled sharply. "Fine, but be quick about it, before I'm eaten alive out here."

"And we must get Benden," said Bit.

"I'll get him before we go," Pet replied.

Bit didn't like Benden's absence, but Yalp had already started his magic and insisted they stand still. He dampened his hands in the pool. Holding them palms up, he slowly cupped one over the other. He muttered in a strange tongue, concentrating so hard the lids of his eyes fluttered. When the words stopped he opened his hands. There, looking like it would float away any moment, was a perfect dandelion seed.

Holding it by the stem, he raised the seed and let the delicate tips touch Bit's cheek, then Pet's, then Bit's. Back and forth he went. Softer than baby's breath or caterpillar fur, Bit barely felt it. But the whisper of a giggle escaped her lips, and a moment later Pet giggled too. Yalp caught both giggles, cupping his hands over them. When he opened his hands again, a small bubble floated in the air, filmy and iridescent. Something stirred inside, not exactly light, but warm and golden, and beating like a pair of hearts.

Even Pet looked in wonder.

With a motion of his hands, Yalp sent the bubble floating out over the pond, until it hovered above the last steppingstone. He waved the seed and began chanting, quite loudly this time, every atom of his being focused on the bubble. Perspiration sprang to his face. He trembled, swayed, and tottered so, Bit feared he would fall.

And the bubble expanded. Bit thought at any moment it would burst, from a gust of wind, or tension from within. But some magic lent strength to the surface.

When the bubble grew to the height of a man, Yalp dropped the seed at Bit's feet. "Crush it," he exclaimed.

She stepped back, horrified. "It's too beautiful."

"You must. It's the only way." He continued chanting, waving his arms. "Hurry, I can't keep this up much longer."

Bit still hesitated. None of the little seeds had blown off; a breath of air rocked the ball gently on the rock like an innocent baby. "But the seeds will be ruined."

"They won't. They will separate from their brothers and sisters and blow on the wind, finding root wherever they fall. Now, Bit. Now!"

With a cry of anguish she stamped the seed with her boot.

At that instant, the bubble popped, revealing a curtain of rain that fell only over the steppingstone and a few feet beyond. Beyond the rain it was black, and a deafening roar struck Bit's ears.

"Go," yelled Yalp. "Through the door."

Bit swung on her pack. "But Benden—"

"I'll get him," cried Pet. She scurried over the rocks and disappeared beyond the bridge.

Yalp continued chanting and waving his arms in circles. "Hurry," he shouted. "I can't hold the door open very long."

A sharp wind blew through the opening and some of the rain struck Bit's cheek. "We can't go without Pet and Benden."

"Here's Pet. Go. Now." Yalp's face turned ashen, his eyes glazed like he would faint.

Pet ran up panting and put on her pack. "Benden's coming."

"But the horses," cried Bit. "Snow Dancer."

Yalp shook his head. "The steppingstones are too narrow and slippery. She could fall and break a leg."

"But—"

"Go. You first. Then the Countess. I'll hold the door open for Benden."

Bit swallowed, stepping carefully across the slick stones toward the opening. There was something monstrously big on the other side. Only the thought of Dash moved her forward. She reached the threshold and looked back. Pet, then Yalp had followed, but she didn't see Benden.

Yalp urged her again. But she paused for one last, desperate look at Aerdem, inhaling every color, every sound, as if this would be her last breath. She took in the soft lilac mountains in the distance, the sea of crimson plenderil. The afterglow of the sun spread through the valley like dream dust. She would awaken, and this fairytale would be gone forever, forgotten little by little like melting snowflakes. No castle. No family. No prince. All vanished.

She turned to the dreaded door, which was like a dark sore against the emerald trees and azure sky. The rain pattered on the pool, agitating the surface.

Still no Benden. Yalp quivered and swayed like a dizzy drunk. "It's closing," he cried. "Only . . . a moment . . . more."

Bit understood. Yalp was spent, exhausted. He could work no more magic today. She had to go now. She stepped past the curtain of rain, feeling a momentary shock like thousands of little needles pricking her skin. Yelling behind made her turn. Pet was just outside the doorway, desperately fighting off a bird that beat its wings about her head.

Yalp shouted, "The door . . . the door."

The bird darted through the opening and zoomed by Bit.

Pet followed, but turning halfway around, leaned onto Yalp and clutched him. He fell backward. Before he could rise, Pet rushed through the opening and it closed, fading like a dying lamp.

Leaving them alone . . .

In the dark . . .

With the terrible roaring . . .

16

The shriek was a knife in Jen's heart.

"Mother!" She jumped up and darted for the entrance of the cave.

"Jen, wait."

She hurtled the bush door aside and bolted through the trees, Blue right behind her.

"It's a trap," he called.

She ignored him. Trap or not, she had to rescue Mother. She plunged into the tall grass, the blades whipping her face. There was no trail. Twigs and rocks cut her feet and made her stumble. She barely felt them. Her only thought was to get to her mother. Another shriek pierced the night, driving her on. *"Mother!"* she screamed in her mind. *"What are they doing to you?"*

"Jen, it's not your mom. They're slaughtering a horse."

No. Why would they do that? It's Mother. I know it is. Naryfel hates her. The cries of anguish spurred her into a wild, mane-flying mustang, streaking full tilt.

"Not that way," Blue called, running two steps behind. "At least circle around."

Jen ignored him. This was no time for clever tactics. She

had to act before it was too late.

Ten yards ahead she was blinded by a burst of light. A wall of flames shot up, blocking her way. She turned and sped on. Nothing would keep her from her mother. She was about to pass the fire when another barrier of dancing yellow sprang up. She ran around that only to be confronted by another, and another. Soon she'd turned so many times she wasn't sure of the right direction. Smoke stung her eyes. The air smelled like fire-crackers. Every inch of her wanted to race on, but her lungs were red-hot coals and a fit of coughing staggered her to a stop.

Blue caught up with her, carrying his shirt in his hand. "Take this," he yelled above the roar of flames. Tearing off a poorly sewn section of his shirtsleeve, he forced it over her mouth. He tore a piece for himself and tied it around his face.

He looked around. "This way."

Jen followed him down a ten-foot corridor of unlit grass. Walls of fire rose on either side. At the end of the passage, another wall flared up and spun them right. They ran through corridor after corridor. Each ended in a curtain of flames.

Another scream of agony cut through the night. *Mother!* It was all Jen could do to keep from running straight through the fire.

"Maybe if you were wet," shouted Blue, as if reading her thoughts. "But you're dry as cork. You'd light instantly."

She knew he was right. But maybe this was her funeral pyre and she would die here anyway. Tongues of fire darted at her and spurred her down another corridor. Furnace-hot walls scorched her face and arms. Columns of brown smoke billowed up and muddied the sky. Breathing was useless. All the air had been sucked out of the world.

The fire zigzagged through the field. The grass only

burned where it had been lit, leaving a maze of square turns, forks, dead ends. She was forced to turn this way and that, forward and back, but strangely, always toward Naryfel's camp. She felt like that marionette, stepping against her will to the crackling music of the flames.

Maybe Blue was right. Maybe she should go back to the pine forest and circle the blaze. She could come at the camp from the west and hope to escape detection. Even as she thought this, a line of fire raced across the space behind her, closing off the exit.

"What now?" she called to Blue.

His eyes were bloodshot and tears from the smoke cut across his soot-darkened face. "I'm working on it." He took a quick look around and pointed forward. There was nowhere else to go.

Another line of fire raced across the path behind them. If they didn't get out of the field soon, they'd pass out from smoke and heat.

Jen felt a sharp pang of guilt for Blue. "I'm sorry I got you into this," she yelled.

He shrugged and gave her a red-toothed smile. "We're not dead yet."

He led the way down another corridor. Another turn. Another long hall of fire. Then Jen saw the camp. She grabbed Blue's arm and raced forward. Just as she was about to exit the maze, soldiers rushed from either side of the grass. They fell into two lines and held up halberds that glinted in the firelight. Jen paused. To leave the maze she had to walk down the gauntlet. The formation was like the jaws of a dragon. The halberds were teeth. And at the end, ready to clamp the mouth shut, was Naryfel. With a small motion of her finger, she drew a shape in the air.

Another line of fire roared up behind Jen. She looked desperately for an opening to dart through, a stone, a stick, something to fight with. There was nothing. All she could do was walk down the line of soldiers, Blue beside her, until she stopped in front of Naryfel.

"What took you so long?" Naryfel asked Blue, with a smile.

Part Three

17

"**Where are we?**" Pet yelled above the

roaring. She was drenched with mist and spray.

Bit held tight to Pet's hand and looked around. It was night. The silhouette of a tree rose beside her. She seemed to be standing on the small outcropping of a cliff. On either side, something vast and powerful thundered and crashed.

"I think it's a waterfall," Bit yelled back.

Pet crept to the edge of the outcropping and peered down. "Great. Just great. The miserable little clown put us right in the middle of a waterfall."

"Can you see the bottom?"

"No, it's too dark. But I think it's a long way down."

"What do we do?" Bit asked.

"Let's feel around and see if there's a way out."

"Okay, but be careful near the edge. The rocks are slippery."

It took only a few minutes of exploration to take them back to where they started. The cliff jutted about twenty-five feet, forcing the waterfall to part and go around them. The entire area was wet, and little rivulets flowed through cracks in the rock. A lone pine clung to the outcropping, constant erosion exposing its roots. They could find no way down.

"Now what?" Pet asked.

"Maybe we can build a fire."

"With only this tree? Even if we break off branches, it's green wood."

Bit shivered from the wet and cold. "We have to dry off and get warm. We'll get sick if we don't."

"Right. What do you have in your gear?"

"I've got a slicker and a blanket."

"Great! We can sit on my tarp and get under your slicker."

They dried off with one of the blankets and quickly changed their clothes. Huddling under the other blanket, they pulled the oilskin slicker over them.

"I'm still cold," Pet complained after a few minutes.

"Let's look for wood," Bit suggested. She was still shivering. "Maybe twigs blew off the tree, or the waterfall brought pieces from a forest above."

Pet looked dubious, but they scoured around the outcropping. Twigs and small branches had broken off the tree, and a dozen pinecones were scattered about. They left the green ones, and piled dried ones, along with the dead wood. Then they searched the perimeter of the cliff and found some chunks of oak and spruce, and more pinecones.

While Pet broke twigs for kindling, Bit took a knife from her pack and used it to strip bark off the branches. The wood was dry underneath, and the scent of pine filled the air.

"Let's rake some of these pine needles and make a little dam," Bit said. "That might keep the ground drier."

Her idea worked. They stacked kindling beneath the tree, hoping the upper branches would provide some shelter from the continuous drizzle and spray from the waterfall. They had flint and steel, but Yalp had provided them each with a box of little firesticks he said would light anywhere. Bit pulled hers out. Striking the tip of one on her boot, the stick instantly flared. Sheltering the flame with her hand, she held it beneath the drier pieces of wood. The wood sputtered. She held it there until the firestick burned close to her fingers and she had to drop it. A moment later it died out.

"Now what?" Pet asked, sounding more miserable by the minute.

Bit thought a moment. "Let's put all my firesticks under these twigs. We'll keep your box for later."

"If we use up yours, that will leave only enough for one more fire."

"No, we're getting off this rock in the morning."

"You don't get it. We're stuck up here. There's no way down."

"There has to be," Bit cried. "If we don't, Dash and the king will die."

"Not to mention us."

Bit fell into a gloomy silence. "Okay," she said at last. "We'll use half my firesticks. Then we'll try to keep the fire going, so we won't have to relight it. Once the fire is going, we can try drying off more wood."

She piled half her firesticks under the kindling. Striking another, it flared and ignited the others. Soon a happy blaze was throwing off a cheerful heat. After placing more wood near the fire for later, they got back under the slicker and blanket and watched the flames. Sparks spiraled about the branches of the tree.

"Will the tree catch fire?" Bit asked.

"I doubt it. It's too wet."

"I hope you're right. It's a wonderful tree."

"It's a miserable tree, sitting all alone up here."

"No, it's a courageous tree—using all it has—surviving where it shouldn't, with everything against it."

"Let's hope we do as well."

They fell into another gloomy silence.

"What happened back there?" Bit asked at last.

"Back where?

"Back there. With Yalp."

"I suppose you're going to blame me and say I pushed him," Pet replied defensively.

"No I'm not. It looked like your foot slipped."

"It did, so leave it at that. Are you hungry? I'd like some of this bread." Pet pulled bread out of her pack and handed Bit a chunk.

"I don't know if Yalp can open the door again," Bit said.

Pet stopped chewing. "What do you mean?"

"He said something about the magic working only one time in one direction."

"What are you saying?"

"That he may not be able to open the door again."

"But he gave you a way back, right?" Pet asked hopefully.

Bit felt her eyes grow round. She stared at her friend and slowly shook her head.

"Great. Just great. Then we really are stuck. Even if we get off this stupid rock, we can't get home."

"Don't say that," said Bit, her voice shaking. "We have to. Dash and the king will die if we don't."

"That's the least of our problems. Since we can't get off this rock, and Yalp can't open another door, we're as good as dead. Give me the rest of that bread. We need to make it last."

Bit felt tears coming on, but held them in. If she cried now, Pet would feel worse. "It can't be over so soon. Jenny found a way to our world, all alone. There has to be a way."

"Jenny had a locket or a key or something. We have nothing."

"Maybe when we find the doctor, he'll know a way."

"Look, Bit. If it was easy for people to leave the Plain World, we'd see them all the time."

Bit decided not to argue further. Her mind kept going back to Dash, with that awful creature around his neck. Even though it seemed impossible, she had to find a way to save him. And Pet too, who wouldn't be in this mess if it wasn't for her. Poor Pet. She was a real lady—not used to being out at night in the wet and cold.

Bit put more twigs on the fire and watched the yellow flames lick at the darkness. A gust of wind and spray sent the sparks dancing like fireflies among the branches of the tree. She thought she saw something move up there. Now she was sure a small pair of shiny eyes stared back.

"Pet. What is that?" She pointed.

Pet squinted. "I don't see anything."

"There. Behind those branches."

"It's nothing. Just a shadow. Don't start imagining things on me. I have enough to deal with without you going crazy on me."

Bit rose. Stepping to the tree, she peered into the shadows. "It's a bird."

"Fine. It's a bird. Now get back under here, it's cold."

"What if it's Darter?"

"It's not Darter."

"It could be. When you were fighting off the bird in the doorway—it looked something like Darter. Maybe this is him."

"That bird was awful, beating at me. I tell you it wasn't Darter."

"But it looked like he had half a wing, just like Darter."

"Don't be absurd. Why would Darter attack me?"

"I . . . I guess he wouldn't." Bit held out her index finger and called to the bird, "Come on down, little fellow."

To her surprise, the bird flew from the branch and landed on her finger.

"Is that you, Darter?" she asked.

There was no reply.

"See," said Pet. "Darter talks like you and me."

"It is Darter!" exclaimed Bit. "Look! His right wing is half as long as his left."

"Then why can't he talk?"

Bit stroked the bird's belly. "Maybe the magic doesn't work in the Plain World."

"I think I'd know Darter if I saw him," said Pet. "He's a very good friend of mine."

The bird stopped pulling at the edge of Bit's sleeve and stared at Pet.

"I tell you that's not him," continued Pet, "that's some other cripple bird."

The bird stopped staring and turned his back on Pet.

"It is him. See, you've hurt his feelings."

"Stop this nonsense and get back under the blanket. It's cold."

Bit threw another branch on the fire and stepped to the blanket.

"You're not bringing that filthy creature in here," Pet said. "He probably has fleas."

Bit laughed. "Now you're being silly. Birds don't have fleas."

"Fine. Keep him on your side of the blanket."

Bit settled under the blanket and felt a little thrill as the bird nestled under her chin. She tried to sleep, but one memory kept running through her mind. The Pondit had taken her to the king's bedroom. Dash lay on the bed, his father beside him. They appeared to be slumbering, except their faces were deathly white. And starting at the ankles, brambles thick as ropes wound around each of their bodies, ending with a knot around the neck. The Pondit said the knots were tightening. Slowly, but tightening. He had put a mark on one earlier that morning and showed her how much it had moved. She couldn't see the creature's head, but the Pondit said it was there, buried beneath the coils of its body. Earlier, he'd seen red eyes glaring back at him. Now he thought the creatures had fallen into the same enchantment as the king and Dash.

Bit shuddered and felt Pet stir beside her. She tried again to sleep, but the rock was uneven and hard and pressed into her back. The wind picked up and made the slicker flap. Pet snored softly. That was good. She wouldn't feel the cold.

Hours seemed to pass. Bit was finally drifting to sleep when she heard a soft tap on the slicker. A moment later there were two more, falling on different spots, a little louder, followed by a stuttering pat-a-pat, then another. The waterfall seemed to rumble louder for a few seconds, then a continuous drumbeat of rain smacked the slicker.

The fire! She had to keep it lit. Slipping quickly out from under the slicker, she piled on more wood.

It was too late. The fire had burned low, and the rain came down in sheets. The flames sputtered, fought to stay alive, and winked out, leaving everything in inky darkness. She tried to cover the backpacks with branches, as best she could. By the time she made her way back to the slicker she was soaking wet.

"Great. Just great," grumbled Pet.

A few minutes later the little dam of pine needles washed away and tiny rivers invaded the tarp. Bit shivered, and Pet shivered beside her, teeth chattering. They were too miserable to talk. The bird was gone.

Bit awoke. The rain had stopped, and daylight penetrated the slicker. She peeked from beneath the cover. Mist and spray billowed from falling walls of silver, obscuring her view. She was on her side. Pet had fallen asleep spooned against her back, one arm wrapped around her tummy. She slowly rolled out from under Pet's arm so as not to wake her, and stood. The pine tree glistened with raindrops. Beyond, she could see a dark forest breaking through swaths of low-lying fog. The sky was overcast, and everything appeared dull and gray, as if some essential ingredient had been left out. Looking upon this world filled her with longing and sadness.

She stepped carefully to the edge of the rock. She was on an outcropping of a vertical cliff. The waterfall roared on either side and plunged violently into a pool far below. She had heard that striking water from a great height was like smashing into granite. There was no surviving such a fall. She'd be pulverized, and dragged to the bottom of the pool.

The sharp chatter of a bird made her turn. For one terrifying moment she saw the tree, leaning back, the arms of its split trunk thrown wildly back, as if to keep from toppling off the cliff. The bird streaked toward her from a branch. Pet, arms outstretched, fingers splayed, was only inches away. Bit's mouth dropped open. Then she swayed . . .

18

Jen stared at Blue from the other side

of the prison cell. Seated on a low wooden bench, he leaned against the stone wall, knees pulled to his chest.

"What?" he asked, like a child unsure why he is being punished.

Jen didn't reply. Since her recapture, she didn't know what to think. She had started to believe Blue was who he said he was, a homeless tumbleweed, drifting through the world. Naryfel disturbed that picture, the way a stone tossed in water sends ripples through a reflection. "What took you so long?" she'd said, with a smile. Why say that unless she was expecting him?

After she was captured, Jen had begged to see her mother. To her surprise, Naryfel consented, and allowed Jen to give her mother water and a little food. Her mother shivered. Beads of perspiration dotted her forehead. A deep liquid cough doubled her over. She needed a blanket, and Jen convinced her captors of that. Then she'd clung to her mother, stroking her hair, patting away the sweat, holding her hand. Mother's thumb caressed back, softly, almost imperceptibly. She tried to speak words of comfort, but Jen hushed her, begged her not to weaken herself further.

Mother managed one hoarse whisper: "Soar, my love . . ."

The visit was far too short. When it ended, they had to drag Jen kicking and screaming back to her cage.

Blue was already there. Why? If he was Naryfel's lackey, why lock Jen up with him? Naryfel reveled in tricks. She gloated on her prey. Why else would she bother with a maze of fire? Maybe the game wasn't over and Blue was to keep it going.

Jen had been too exhausted and confused to puzzle it out further. As the wagon rolled over a rutted road, she retreated to a corner of the cage and fell asleep with the wheel complaining in her ear.

Some time later, she awoke to the glare of a bright light. Before her was the strangest sight. The wagons had stopped before a narrow mountain pass. Jagged mountains rose on either side, their icy tops blue against the night sky. The road ahead led to a towering wall of white light, stretching like a curtain from one side of the pass to the other. It flickered and flashed as bright as lightning. Jen could not see what lay beyond. Crackling filled the air, reminding her of the snowstorm static during Medlara's warning.

"It's Naryfel's Pass," said Blue from his side of the wagon. "Instead of taking a month, she'll get us to Purpura by morning."

Jen ignored him. He seemed to know a lot about Naryfel.

The wagons rolled onward. The ones ahead of Jen disappeared from sight as they entered the towering brightness. Then it was her turn. She closed her eyes, but it was still like staring at the sun. As she passed into the light her skin prickled and crawled.

Then she was through. She opened her eyes, and the pass, mountains, and wall of light were gone. The road cut through a field. Pale yellow daisies, illuminated by a crescent moon, swayed lazily in the breeze.

She slept.

By morning, she and Blue had been thrown into prison.

"What?" he asked again, stretching his feet out on the bench.

Jen gazed at him, trying to size him up.

"What's wrong with you?" he asked. "I've risked my hide twice for you."

"Did you?"

"You know I did."

"Maybe there wasn't much risk."

"What're you talking about? I got you out of that cage. Then I tried to stop you from running into a trap. If that's not risking my life, I don't know what is."

"Unless you and Naryfel planned it all along."

Blue gaped at her. "You're crazy."

"Am I?" Jen stabbed a finger at him. "She was happy to see you."

"Of course she was. She's been trying to catch me for years. I got sloppy. She knew I was out there, and used you to catch me."

Jen stared. That made sense. If he was telling the truth.

Blue took a nut out of his pocket and offered her one. She shook her head. He shrugged and popped it in his mouth. Soon his teeth glistened with juice. Afterward, he wiped a red smear on his sleeve.

He took a harmonica from his pocket and held it to his lips. Closing his eyes he began to play. Sad creases lined his face as the harmonica wailed.

That melody, Jen thought. It was the haunting birdcall she'd heard in the cart.

"Before," she said when he was done, "that was you I heard."

He looked up and smiled. "Probably. I'm Wailin' Willie in Nallendor. Mothers lock up their babies when they hear my harp."

Jen inhaled sharply. "Your what?"

"My mouth harp," he said, holding out the harmonica.

Beware . . . Medlara's warning flashed in Jen's mind. *If you meet . . . a harp . . .*

"What's wrong?" asked Blue. He stood and looked about him. "It's like you've seen a ghost." He stepped toward her, reaching out.

Jen shrank back. "Stay away."

"Aw, it's just a legend. I've never stolen a baby."

So far, Medlara had been right about everything. Two warnings of danger, the second predicting something would happen the very night Jen and her mother were kidnapped. The very night her father and Dash were attacked.

Things are not as they seem. Look beyond appearances, Medlara had warned. Vieveeka had surely been far more than she had seemed.

And now Blue. *Beware . . . If you meet . . . a harp . . .*

"What's spooking you?" Blue asked, his eyes wide. "You're giving me the heebies."

"You're in with Naryfel." Jen planted her feet firmly on the floor, ready to spring if he came too close. "Don't try and deny it. Your harp gave you away. I don't know why she's got you locked up with me. But stay on your side of the cell." Her heel touched the chamber pot under the bench. She could throw it if she needed to.

"I hate Naryfel. You have no idea how much I hate her." He clenched a brown fist and shook it. "Just give me the chance and I'd chop her into little pieces and feed her to the crows."

The crack of a whip and a scream of pain echoed down the corridor beyond the cell. Jen flew to the prison bars.

"Mother!" she cried. "They're torturing her."

"No, the voice is too low. That's a man . . . getting Naryfel's Tears."

Three more lashes, impossibly loud. Each answered by an

agonized shriek. Then a fourth stroke. Jen waited for the scream. The silence that followed hurt more.

"He passed out," said Blue. "Poor soul. Probably did nothing."

"What are Naryfel's Tears?" Jen asked, apprehensively.

"You heard it. If you want to be scared of something, be scared of that. Not me."

Jen felt tears well up. She didn't know what to think or do. Everything about Blue seemed right and honest, worldly but innocent. Everything he'd done had been kind and brave. He'd saved her. Twice. But everything Medlara had said told her to beware.

"Look, Jen, I'll get you out of here. I promise."

She let him lead her to one of the benches. She dropped her head in her hands and fought off tears. He put an arm around her shoulder. It felt comforting.

"I can't leave without my mother," she said plaintively.

"I know. We'll get her too. Trust me."

She felt herself soften. Somehow, she did trust him.

An icy snicker made her look to the bars and corridor beyond. Naryfel stood there, stroking the bloody strands of a whip. Two guards armed with swords stood on either side of her. One had a large ring of keys at his belt. The other held a small lead box. A pair of leather gloves lay across the lid.

"Did you like my little concert?" Naryfel asked.

"Your timing was off and you play out of tune," Blue replied. "But hey, some of us are just born talented."

Naryfel glared at him, her thick eyebrows narrowing to a V. "I'll deal with you later. It's her I'm interested in."

Blue stood back with his hand on his chin. "I do declare, you're grayer than before," he taunted. "Where's the pretty red-head? I want someone nice to look at."

149

Naryfel's lower lip quivered. "First her, then you," she said, grinding her teeth. "Let me in," she hissed to the guard with keys.

He let her in. She tucked the whip under her arm, then took the gloves from the other guard and put them on. He handed her the box.

"I have something special planned for you," she said to Jen.

"Where's my mother?" Jen asked, stoutly. "Let me see her."

"First I have to dress you up." Naryfel opened the box and drew out a few jagged leaves. "Do you know what this is?"

Jen did. Poison oak, or something very similar. It grew all around the mountain near Nell's cottage. She'd gotten a weeping case of it all over her body that felt like a million bee stings. It took two weeks of Nell's salves and pastes to recover.

Jen clenched her fists. They wouldn't take her without a fight.

Naryfel smiled. "I see you are familiar with this delightful herb. Poison sumac." She said the name as if she were savoring a rare wine, then turned to a guard. "Grab her."

Blue bounded forward. "Take me, you rotting lump of maggot meat—" he yelled at Naryfel. He locked arms with the guard, and was swung about like a rag doll.

"Blue! No!" Jen cried, surprised at the protective feelings that welled up. "What are you doing?" Maybe she wasn't sure about him, but she couldn't let harm come to him on her account. "Don't hurt him," she yelled at Naryfel. "It's me you want."

With a heave, the guard sent Blue crashing against a bench.

"Blue!" Jen screamed.

The guard—a big bruiser with a nose like a pit bull and a tattoo of a bloody knife on his cheek—reached for Jen.

"Wait," said Naryfel. "She cares for the little guttersnipe. Take him. It'll hurt her far more. She's just like her mother."

The guard made it one step. Jen leaped on his back and

pummeled his ears. He twisted and jerked to buck her off, but she wrapped her arms under his chin in a stranglehold. His face swelled like an overripe plum ready to burst. But the second guard drew his sword and Jen felt the tip prick her neck. She dropped helplessly to the floor and backed away.

Blue wobbled to his feet. Bloody Knife grabbed him by the collar, took the sumac, and dragged him from the cell.

Naryfel turned to Jen, one corner of lip curled in a smile. She pointed to the floor. "Lie down."

"What?" Jen looked apprehensively at the whip.

Naryfel set it down. "You heard me."

Jen hesitated, but Naryfel nodded to the guard. In a moment his sword was out and pressing Jen's arm. She dropped to the ground, her face against the cold floor. She watched a cockroach crawl from a crack between the flagstones.

"Don't move," she heard Naryfel say, "or he'll skewer you."

The sword traced down to the small of her back. Jen had no intention of moving. Her head was pulled back, not roughly or kindly.

Then snip, snap, snip, snap. Time slowed . . . A lock of hair floated down like a lost feather.

Jen paced in front of the bars like a panther. An hour that was an eternity later, the guard with the tattoo brought Blue back. He shuffled into the cell with his head hanging and Jen's heart twisted.

The guard left and Blue slumped on a bench and hid his head in his arms.

"Are you all right?" Jen cried.

He jumped up like he'd been out for a stroll and flashed her a red-toothed smile. As soon as he saw Jen his face fell. "Your hair . . ."

Tears sprang to Jen's eyes. "Never mind about that. You're all right? They didn't harm you?"

"Naw. I told you already. I'm not afraid of Naryfel."

"She . . . she didn't whip you?"

"One of the guards rubbed sumac over me, that's all." He reached in his pocket and drew out a fishbone. "I guess you won't need this. They stepped out for a moment and I got this out of the garbage. I thought you could use it as a comb."

What was left of Jen's hair was still quite ratted. She took the bone gratefully and began working at the knots.

"Don't worry," said Blue. "There was a bucket of water. I washed it."

"I wish you hadn't. The water will make the sumac spread."

"Maybe they'll call me the Sumac Kid," he said with a wink. He put a hand on her shoulder. "Jen, I'm sorry about your hair. It was pretty . . ."

Jen wished it still covered her ears, which were burning. "It'll grow."

"Anyway, now it looks like mine." He held out uneven lengths on either side of his head. "See? I cut mine with a knife."

Jen continued working at her hair. Blue was lost in thought for a spell until he raised his eyes to hers. "Do you still suspect me?"

"No."

"But it looks bad. Giving you a comb right after Naryfel chops off your hair. It's just the kind of trick she likes."

Jen had thought of that. She touched lightly near his ear, swollen where the guard boxed him. "Does she beat her friends?"

"She's capable of anything."

Jen awoke to the shuffle of footsteps. The first gray light of dawn filtered through a tiny window at the back of the cell. Blue slept in a ball on the floor beneath one of the benches. The footsteps stopped and Jen looked up. Naryfel stood alone at the bars. Her face was lost in shadow, but her eyes glimmered like pale icicles.

She unlocked the door and entered the cell.

Jen sprang up, her fists clenched defiantly. "Where's my mother?"

Ignoring her, Naryfel crossed the floor and gave Blue a kick. "Get up."

Blue moaned and pulled his burlap shirt over his head. "Leave me alone."

Naryfel smiled and kicked him again. "I want to see how red you are."

"Please . . . don't hurt me anymore." He mewled like a sick cat.

"Poison sumac," she said to Jen. "So easy. So effective. See how it's curbed his spirit? It'll take the fight out of you too."

"Must've been a bad batch." Blue stood behind her. His voice was strong. There wasn't a spot on him.

Before Naryfel could turn he sprang and gave her a kick that sent her sprawling.

"You're losing your touch," he laughed. "I don't get poison sumac."

Naryfel leaped to her feet and lunged at him.

"Slowpoke," taunted Blue. "Catch me if you can." He darted about the room with Naryfel in pursuit. Jen backpedaled to avoid them, until she jumped on one of the benches and pressed her back against the wall.

Naryfel's fingers spread out like hooks. "You little wretch. I'll tear you to pieces—"

"Oh, help me, Jen," Blue cried in mock terror. He raised his hands above his head and shook them. "I'm frightened. I'm frightened."

He skittered about the cell, feinting, ducking, nearly scampering off the walls as Naryfel lunged after him.

"Save me," he cried. "Save me from the bad old queen."

Without warning he veered straight toward Jen. She leaped to avoid colliding, sending the bench flying across Naryfel's path. Naryfel flung up her hands reflexively. But her legs carried her forward like a charging bull. She crashed into the bench and sailed over, landing with a hard thud on the stone floor.

Blue backed away and watched. Jen held her breath.

Naryfel lay motionless a moment, then slowly rose to her feet, her face a storm of fury. "You'll pay for that," she hissed through her teeth.

She limped to the door. Once outside the cell, she locked it and hobbled away.

Naryfel limped down the corridor. A swelling cherry formed on her shin, but she barely felt it. Her only thought was to skin some hide. She entered her torture chamber. Arranged in a semicircle were a whipping post, a rack, and a fire pit for heating oil and branding irons. Yanking a thick cord, she rang a bell violently until two guards rushed into the room. Grabbing a five-strand whip off the wall, she waved at the guards to follow.

She led them back to Jen's cell. A grim smile twisted her lips. *First the boy. Then the girl. Then my dear sister.*

She froze at the cell door. It was still locked. But the little rats were gone.

19

Bit swayed on the edge of the cliff.

Pet stood close behind, eyes pinched, hands poised only inches away. Beyond, the bird squawked in protest and dove for Pet's head.

Bit's heart leaped to her mouth. She tottered back. Her arms spread like wings. She flapped them helplessly, violently.

Pet's eyes narrowed. She took a quick step forward and her hands shot out. Latching onto Bit's shoulders, she pulled her to safety. Then the bird was all over Pet's head, beating with his wings and body. She screamed and swung her fists until he flew to a branch of the tree, where he chattered angrily and glared down at her.

"Pet! Are you okay?" Bit cried, reaching for her friend's face.

"No thanks to you. I was almost blinded by that pest."

"I'm sorry, I—"

"What were you thinking? You could have fallen!"

"I . . . I didn't know you were there. You startled me."

"Don't blame me. I was going to pull you away before that bird interfered. Don't do that again. The rock is slick. You could have slipped." Pet stood with her hands on her hips. Her face was red and her ringlets shook.

"Don't be angry with me, Pet."

"Stop calling me Pet. Why does everyone call me that? I'm not a dog or a pampered housecat."

"I . . . I thought you liked it."

"Well, I don't."

"I'm sorry—"

"*Stop* apologizing all the time. It's not your fault we came to the Plain World with no way back. It's not your fault we're stuck on this stupid rock and I'm cold and wet, and I just spent the worst night of my life shivering on a frozen slab of granite with a waterfall roaring in my ears. Who could blame you that we only have two days of food before we starve to death? Stop saying you're sorry, or I swear I'll scream."

Bit burst into tears. "But it is my fault. If it wasn't for me, you wouldn't be in this mess."

All the courage she had tried to show last night melted away, and she sank to the ground and sobbed. "I'm nothing," she cried. "I might as well die here. My life is over, anyway. I'm a fool to think I could save Dash. I couldn't save a fly. I'm no better than a worm. Fool that I was to think that Dash could love me. It was only a matter of time before a Vieveeka took her rightful place beside him. I'm nothing, I was always nothing, I'll always be nothing," and she sobbed harder.

"Bit, I was only blowing off steam. Don't talk like that. You'll make me cry too."

Tears streamed down Bit's face in hot rivers. Her hair, limp from mist and spray, swung back and forth as she shook her head.

"Look now, enough of that," Pet said. "See? I am crying now. Here's a tear."

"I . . . don't want to make you cry."

"Well, you have. Look. There's another."

"Please don't cry, Pet. I couldn't bear making you cry."

"Well, I am. See? Big, rolling tears. I'll be blubbering soon." Pet squatted beside Bit and patted her shoulder. "We'll find a way down."

"But we can't. You said so yourself. We're stuck." She was still crying.

"Come on, I'll help you look."

"Will you! Then maybe there's a chance. You're smart and clever. You'll help us find a way. I couldn't have a better friend with me."

Pet turned away. "Yeah. Fine. Just stop crying."

"I'll try. What shall we do?"

"Don't ask me. You're leading this expedition."

"That's what worries me. But I'll lead us anywhere, if I just know you're helping me."

"Okay. I'm helping. Now what?"

Bit looked around the outcropping. "Let's search the rock one more time."

"Shouldn't the troops have breakfast first? It would be good for morale."

Bit wiped her eyes and laughed. "Sure. Eat first. Then look."

Pet took out a knife and started cutting her meatstick into slices. Meanwhile, Bit managed to light the fire and got some hot water boiling for tea. In a few minutes they felt warmer, and finished a breakfast of sandwiches and dried apricots. Afterward, they made a careful search around the perimeter of the rock. Nothing new turned up. Above and on either side was a mountain of crashing water, below a sheer vertical drop. Pet surveyed the surrounding landscape with her telescope, but saw no road, no house, no hopeful sign of smoke.

"How long is your rope?" Bit asked. "Maybe we can tie it onto the tree and lower ourselves down."

"Forget it. It's not long enough."

"How about smoke signals? If we can get someone to come here, maybe they can get us down."

Pet looked at Bit, surprised. "That might work."

It didn't. No matter how much they built up the fire, the spray from the waterfall scattered the smoke. Exhausted from pulling the blanket on and off the fire, they sat to catch their breath.

"This is a wretched world," Pet grumbled, as she surveyed the drab landscape. "No wonder Jenny left."

"If we could only fly," said Bit wistfully. She was watching the sparrow. He still sat on the tree, contemplating her. She tried to entice him down with an offering of breadcrumbs.

"Leave him be. I don't want him near me," Pet said.

It didn't matter, the bird refused to come. Instead he hopped down to a bed of pine needles and began scratching.

"What's he looking for?" asked Bit. "There are no pine nuts here."

Pet shrugged. Bit watched him over her tea mug. He was ten feet away, where the rock dipped into a shallow trench. He was raking clumps of pine needles with his feet, sweeping them aside, piling them in a circle around him. He stopped scratching and looked at Bit, then ferociously dug at the needles.

"There's something there," Bit said.

"Probably worms."

The sparrow stopped scratching. He looked at Bit, chattered loudly, then began digging again.

"What if it's Darter, and he's trying to tell me something?"

"Don't start that again. He's just some stupid bird.

Probably not even the same one you saw last night."

Bit decided not to argue. This bird was a sparrow, with a plain gray breast and dull brown stripes. And he had half a wing, just like the one she'd seen last night. Just like Darter.

She rose and approached him cautiously so she wouldn't scare him away. "What're you looking for, fella? Can I help?"

The bird cooed back, but kept scratching. Bit moved beside him and started pulling away the needles. There weren't any earthworms, and she could see no reason for him to be digging there. He kept at it, so she picked up handfuls of the stuff. It was dry a foot down, but a foot below that it was rotting. He jumped into the hole she made and raked excitedly with his feet. She scooped up another clump and felt the earth fall away below her fingers. For a moment, little holes the size of a coin opened up, but quickly filled with needles sifting from above. She shoveled out another bunch of needles, pungent with the scent of decaying pine. Suddenly a patch of ground the size of her hand fell away, leaving a black hole.

"Pet! Come quick! There's something here."

Pet ran over, and together they dug away the pine needles. Another hole opened, then a third. They cleared away the remaining needles and found a rock about two feet long and a foot wide. Around the edge were a number of dark gaps and fissures. The bird whistled and chirped happily. The two girls looked at each other.

"Are you thinking what I'm thinking?" Pet asked.

"A way down," Bit said, almost afraid to breathe.

Together they cleared away more needles and found two more stones. One was small enough to lift out, leaving a gaping hole. Bit tried to see inside, but the sunlight penetrated only a few feet. They quickly lifted out another rock, and could see further.

"It looks like a shaft," Bit said. "If we pull out this last rock, we can squeeze through and see how far it goes."

The last rock was too heavy to lift.

"Great," said Pet. "Now what?"

Bit thought a moment and looked around. "If we can break off that branch, maybe we can use it as a lever."

"Don't we need something else to make that work?"

"I think it's called a fulcrum. We can use one of the rocks we just pulled out. What about the branch? It's halfway up the tree."

"You'll have to climb up there and get it."

Bit looked at the branch and felt her eyes widen. "I don't think I can. It's too high."

"Well, I'm not going to. I think I twisted my ankle when I came through the door."

Bit hesitated. The tree looked slick and glistening from last night's rain. One misstep and she'd go flying off the cliff.

"Look, Bit, you have to start showing some courage. If that shaft leads down to the bottom, you'll have to climb anyway. Come on, I'll help you."

Bit replied with a nod. She agreed about the courage. How to get some was what worried her. She approached the tree apprehensively, telling herself she had to do this for Dash. Pet gave her a boost and she pulled herself up to a Y in the trunk. Wrapping her arms and legs around the left side of the Y, she inched her way up until she could reach the branch. She bent it toward her as far as she could, but it wouldn't break.

"You'll have to hang from the branch," Pet called. "Then I'll grab onto you and we'll both pull."

"What if it breaks first?" It looked like a long way down.

"I don't think it will," encouraged Pet. "It's too thick. Trust me."

Bit hesitated. She tried to stay calm, but her shaking hands and knees made the leaves around her quiver.

"Hurry up. I don't want to stand here all day," said Pet.

Reluctantly, Bit grasped the branch firmly and slid her hands down the length until only her feet remained on the trunk. Suddenly her feet slipped and she was dangling in the air, the limb bobbing up and down. Once, twice, Pet jumped for her feet, finally reaching her on the third leap and dragging her to the ground. They both held the branch now, and walked it back and forth until it cracked, splintered, and tore off in their hands.

Bit's heart was still pounding, but she helped Pet carry the branch to the rock. They placed one of the smaller stones there, and jammed the lever into one of the crevices that ran along the edge of the rock. Together they pushed down and the rock lifted!

"Bit! You're a genius," Pet said.

Bit could only blush. The rock was balanced on its end. She held it there while Pet tipped it over and out of the way, revealing a gaping hole. Together they knelt at the edge and looked down. A natural shaft in the rock descended almost vertically in rough and jagged steps. Daylight illuminated the opening for fifteen feet before the passage disappeared behind a turn.

"How far do you think it goes?" Bit asked.

"There's only one way of finding out. Lead on."

Bit hesitated. "It's going to get awfully dark in there."

"So? All we have to worry about are a few bats. Maybe some spiders. It's not like there are snakes or goblins."

"Spiders?"

"Yeah. But I doubt they'll be very big."

Bit swallowed.

"Anyway, I've come prepared."

"What do you mean?"

"I packed candles." Pet drew out two long candles, each twisting in a silver spiral.

"Now you're the genius," Bit said. "Those are fancy. Where'd you get them?"

"Nothing but the best for the Count's little girl."

Bit started to laugh until she saw Pet's eyes were pinched. She wasn't smiling.

"Are you okay, Pet?"

"Yeah. Fine." Pet shifted her feet back and forth and seemed anxious to leave.

"We'll need your rope," Bit said. "I heard somewhere that climbers tie a rope around their waists to keep from falling."

"No way. If you fall, you'll pull me with you."

"But if I slip, you can hold me with the rope."

"No. I can't. I told you already, I twisted my ankle. I can't hold your weight."

Bit didn't think it was safe, but Pet insisted, so they packed up their gear and stepped to the opening.

Bit turned.

"Now, what are you waiting for?" Pet asked.

"For Darter." Bit called to him. He sat placidly on the tree, nibbling at his feathers.

"Leave him be," Pet said. "He's a menace."

Bit called again, but the bird ignored her.

"See," Pet said. "If that was Darter, he'd come to you."

"I . . . I guess you're right."

"Of course I'm right. Come on."

Lighting her candle, Bit turned and led the way into the shaft. Jutting rocks provided footholds, allowing her to step and climb down. The candle threw a soft, wavering light. The air smelled stale, but without the wind and spray from the waterfall it was warmer. Spider webs clung to the corners and stretched across nooks and crannies between the rocks. She was careful not to use any of those for a handhold.

Climbing was difficult. She had to hold the candle, and water dripped and trickled over the crags, making them slippery. The hours ticked by, marked by an occasional rest, a drink from the canteen, and few words. Pet pulled inside herself. The few times Bit tried to start a conversation, Pet snapped back. It seemed best to leave her alone. Once, Bit thought she saw the bird, hopping from rock to rock in the shadows above.

Several times a precipice brought her to a stop, and she found Pet behind her, eyes pinched, hands hovering and flexing spasmodically.

"Don't worry," Bit would say with a little laugh, "I won't fall."

Pet only shrugged and looked away.

In places, the tunnel opened into a chamber. Other times it became so narrow they could barely squeeze through, and had to take off their packs and lower them with a rope. Elsewhere, the passage sloped sharply, and they had to hang from the edge and drop to the next level.

Pet stopped occasionally to yank and tug at a thread that tore loose from her shoulder strap. Otherwise, she climbed in stony silence. After a lunch of cured meat, pickles, peach nectar, and chocolate-covered cherries—all from her pack—she opened up again.

"Assuming we find an exit to this shaft, how do we find the doctor?" she asked.

"There's a maze of trails below the waterfall—"

"A maze. Great. How do we find our way out?"

"If we go southwest, hopefully we'll run into a road."

"Hopefully? I suppose you heard all this from that silly Pondit."

"And he heard it from Jenny. She lived in a cottage on the edge of the forest. The doctor lives only a few miles south of there."

That seemed to satisfy Pet, so they packed up their gear and continued to climb down. The rocks became jagged and sharp, tearing their clothes and leaving fat blisters on their hands. Pet got the worst of it. Her short pants did little to protect her. Soon she had long scrapes and cuts on her knees and calves.

After another hour, Bit thought she saw the bottom. Thirty feet below, the shaft widened into a cave. There was something black down there. A faint turquoise light glimmered on the walls. The rock below her feet was smooth, slick, and wet. Water trickled and dripped around her, and she thought she smelled something sour.

"Why have we stopped?" asked Pet, coming up behind.

"I think that's the bottom."

Pet squinted. "Why don't I see a rock floor then?"

"I don't know."

"It could be a bottomless pit."

Bit sucked in a breath. The only way to find out was to climb down and see. Four feet below was a shelf. Covered by a thin stream of water, it ended at a precipice. Bit jumped and landed on the shelf, squatting so she wouldn't slip on the slick surface.

"Don't climb until I get there," Pet called. "I don't want you falling on me."

"Okay."

Pet handed Bit her candle, then jumped. Her feet struck the shelf and slid out from under her, propelling her to the precipice. She scrambled to keep from flying off. Bit threw aside the candles and lunged for Pet's arm. She grasped at the wrist and leaned back. Her feet had nothing to brace against. She skidded across the rock. Pet stared back in horror, her mouth a gaping O. Bit was pulled to the edge, then tumbled over. Still hanging on to her friend, she plunged into the yawning blackness.

20

"What are you mad about now?"

Blue asked. Jen plowed through knee-deep water cold enough
to make her bones ache. She was in some kind of tunnel. Dim
light illuminated the drains and spill pipes of the castle above.
Blue was a silhouette splashing beside her.

She whirled on him. "You knew how to get out all this time
and you didn't say anything?"

"Keep your voice down. It'll carry through the pipes."

"I ought to strangle you."

"Why? I got you out, didn't I?"

Something soft and squishy floated by, brushing her calf.
She didn't want to think about what it was. "You don't get it. I
spent all night worrying you'd get poison sumac. And my mom's
sick. I've got to free her."

"I forgot that. Really I did."

"She has a fever. She's suffering . . ."

"Jen, I'll free her. I promise."

Jen softened. She clutched his arm tight and fought back
tears. "Can you?"

"Of course. They don't call me Jack Nimble for nothing.
Follow me."

The drip and plop of water reverberated against the tunnel walls. "Where are we?" she asked.

"The sewer."

That explained the smell. The air was heavy and she labored to breathe.

"You really worried about me?" he asked.

She could see his red teeth shining dimly. "Shut up." But she was smiling too. "How did you know about the secret passage?"

After Naryfel had left, Blue scurried to a corner of the cell. He'd jiggled a rock on the wall. Racing to an opposite corner, he'd slid back one of the flagstones on the floor and revealed a crawlspace, which sloped down into darkness.

He said it would lock behind them in a few seconds, so they scurried down the hole and he replaced the stone. It was pitch black. He'd placed a finger across Jen's lips to keep quiet. A few minutes later she heard Naryfel screaming in the room above. Blue waited long enough to hear one of the benches splinter against a wall. Then with a pull on her sleeve, he'd led the way down to the sewer.

"Last time I was here, a prisoner told me about it," Blue replied. "I found another way out, so I never had to use it. He never got a chance to . . ."

"But won't she find the passage and follow us?"

"I doubt it. The rock in the corner unlocks the one across the room. She'll never think to look there." Blue gave Jen another of his red-toothed smiles. "Come on. I know the castle like the back of my hand. We'll have your mother out before you can say Jack Quick."

Jen crawled on her hands and knees, following Blue up a steep chute. The sewer was lost in the darkness far below. She was glad she couldn't see it. The last thing she needed was a shaking body that refused to move. If only she'd conquered the water tower that day she met Bit among the plenderil.

The chute was narrow, covered with something wet and sticky. The smell made her gag. "Where are we?" she asked.

"The garbage drop."

She should have known. "Where does it end?"

"A storage closet just off the kitchen."

Jen could see a dim light ahead. A short time later, they tumbled into the kitchen through a pair of swinging doors. Blue scooted behind a storage bin, pulling Jen with him. They were just in time. A stout woman wearing a grease-stained apron entered the closet carrying a pail. She went to the chute and dumped a load of rotting garbage.

Blue raised his eyebrows and exhaled silently, as if to say, "That was close."

When the cook was gone, Blue led Jen on a zigzag, darting course out the closet, behind counters and sacks of potatoes and onions, and out the kitchen. They reached a corridor and ducked into a shadowy alcove. He held Jen back with his arm while a pair of washerwomen walked by with laundry sacks. Then he was out and waving her to follow. Her bare feet patted the tile floor as she raced down the hall behind him.

They flitted through the lower levels of the castle like thieves. Darting, dodging, stealing, there were plenty of places to hide. A table standing on end. A tower of old boxes. A pile of broken armor. Some big paintings leaning against a wall. This part of the building was used as much for storage as quarters for the servants.

Jen took more than a passing interest in her surroundings. This had been her grandfather's castle. And where her mother had grown up. The walls were blue and white on the lower levels, the paint old and peeling. Many of the walls were covered haphazardly with curtains and tapestries that were musty, torn, or moth-eaten. Everything appeared dark, yellowed, dim. The smell of dust and decay hung in the air.

Jen's furtive ascent through the lower levels was largely unnecessary. Hidden behind a stairwell, she only saw a few guards sweep by. The servants walked glassy-eyed through the corridors.

Before ascending to the upper levels, Blue slipped into a closet and stole a pile of folded blankets. He loaded half of them up to Jen's chin.

"You look just like a servant." He grinned, and the big freckles on his cheeks swelled. He led the way confidently up the next flight of stairs, blending in with the streaming hubbub of domestics and dignitaries.

The décor changed dramatically on the fourth level. Polished furniture was attentively placed along the walls. Sparkling chandeliers hung from the ceilings. Giant vases of flowers were set on alabaster pedestals. The smell of fresh paint filled the air. At one end of the building, workers labored on a scaffold with large brushes, covering the walls with another coat of white. The same blue Jen had seen on the lower levels came through faintly.

She saw more painters on the next level, and the next, on one end of the building or the other.

Blue nodded at them from behind his blankets. "As soon as Naryfel finishes painting the building, she starts all over again."

"Why?" Jen asked.

"No matter what she does, the original color keeps coming through. Come on. One more level and we'll get to her Audience Chamber. That's where she does all her business."

"I thought we were going to my mother."

"Jen, I don't know where she is. But Naryfel will tell us."

⤳⤲

"Are you sure this is safe?" Jen asked. "We could get trapped in here."

They stood in a dark closet. Blue pulled aside a curtain, revealing Naryfel's Audience Chamber. The walls were stark. Pale rectangles showed where paintings once hung. White curtains fluttered at an open window, which was the only source of light. A large rug with black and red interlocking triangles covered a marble floor. Upholstered chairs surrounded a teak table. One chair, raised above the others on a dais, dominated the room.

"It's a one-way mirror," Blue replied, tapping the glass in front of them. "No one can see us from the other side."

"But what if someone comes in here, or finds the door locked?"

"We'll have to risk it."

There was no time to argue. Naryfel limped into the Audience Chamber, followed by a bald man of about sixty. He looked weary.

"That's the Royal Steward," Blue whispered.

Naryfel sat on the raised chair and kicked one leg onto the table. She iced a nasty lump swelling on her shin. "The servants are spying on my bath."

"Impossible," replied the Steward. "I post a heavy guard on your quarters."

"See that there is, or I'll remove their eyes."

The Steward paled, evidence this was no idle threat. He rubbed his hands nervously. "I understand you've taken prisoners."

Naryfel's eyes narrowed. "What of it?"

"The law requires formal charges."

"The law, the law," she mocked. "You're a slave to the law."

"Nonetheless, regulations are specific. I am duty-bound to follow them."

Naryfel smiled. "One of the prisoners destroyed my supply wagon. The other attacked my guards. Isn't the law specific on that point?"

The Steward's shoulders sagged. "Yes . . . No formal charges are necessary following a direct attack upon royalty."

"Precisely." Naryfel studied the ice, which she held in a piece of flannel. "Send in the Desert King. When I'm done with him, bring my sister."

Jen felt her heart skip. She gripped Blue's hand.

The Steward bowed and left the room. A short time later the Desert King entered, threw himself into one of the chairs, and crossed his boots on the table. He grabbed an apple from a fruit bowl and chomped off half in one bite. While he chewed, he eyed Naryfel's shin.

"I've dealt with the little spitfire before," he said. "You should have killed her when you had the chance."

Naryfel's eyes hardened. "I won't make that mistake twice. Find her, and the street urchin, too."

"I have a price."

"You've been paid."

He pulled thoughtfully at one of the thorny protrusions on his face. "That was for kidnapping the mother and daughter. I fulfilled that bargain."

"Fine," Naryfel said with a wave of her hand. "Name your price."

"Give me the girl."

Naryfel studied him. "What would you do with her?"

"Add her to my collection."

Jen clenched her fists.

"Done," Naryfel replied. "But I get the boy. He and I have unfinished business. Do whatever it takes to find them. Use sniffers."

The king's smile sent chills down Jen's spine. He rose and left the room.

Naryfel summoned the Steward, and he returned with Jen's mother. Jen felt her heart race to a gallop. She wanted to rush into the next room. To throw her arms around her mother and never let go. Instead she bit her lip until she tasted a drop of salty blood.

Naryfel ordered a heavy guard on the door and dismissed the Steward. "You've recovered from your cold?" she asked, looking down from her dais.

Mother nodded. The color had returned to her face and she was steady on her feet. "Please, take me to Jenny. Is she all right?"

"She's quite the little hellcat—nothing like you or Elan."

Mother gazed at Naryfel's shin. "Did she do that?"

"I tripped. You are comfortable, I trust?"

Mother nodded. "Let her go, Naryfel. It's me you want."

"Do you think so? Does my wise sister understand my motives?"

"I never understood you."

Naryfel stepped down from the dais and led Mother to the very mirror Jen looked through. Jen touched her fingertips to the glass, her mother's face only inches away.

"Look at my beautiful sister," said Naryfel.

The curtains fluttered. Light streaming from the window cast golden rings around Mother's hair. "It can't be about looks," she replied. "You were cruel even when I was little."

Naryfel laughed. "It can't be about looks when I can do this." She reached for a spot above her and drew her arm down.

A moment later Vieveeka stood there, a wealth of red hair tumbling gaily to her shoulders. Her eyes sparkled mischievously. "Which beauty would Elan have chosen? Yours, soft and vulnerable, or Vieveeka's—sultry and spicy?"

"Surface means nothing to Elan. He would look for beauty inside."

Naryfel flung her arm up and down angrily, returning to her true appearance.

Mother turned, reached out a hand that her sister evaded. "It's not too late. You can still do good in the world. Your people long for it."

"Haven't you heard what they say about me?" Naryfel asked. " 'Her appetite for power is insatiable.' 'She twists noble hearts to her purpose, or destroys them.' 'She craves wealth to fill the empty spaces.' "

"No!" cried Mother, shaking her head. "There are gifts, treasures inside, if you'd only trust yours—"

"Wait! There's more! 'She drains everything that is pure and beautiful, and leaves a hollow skeleton.' Here's my favorite. 'Her heart withered away; horrified, her soul fled.' "

Mother grasped Naryfel's arm. "You have a heart, but you're too in love with your mind to listen to it."

"Ah, the wonders of a clever mind."

"The heart is never clever. The heart is only happy when others are happy. Never with itself."

"Precisely," said Naryfel, wrenching away. "I'll never place my happiness in the hands of others."

"You will never find happiness that way. Only emptiness. People will flock to you for power or wealth. But they will never love you."

"I have no need for their love."

"Don't you? I never saw someone more in need of it. More

in need of giving it. You have a niece who would love you if you would only try to love her."

Never! Jen thought, clenching her fists.

"It's not too late," said Mother.

"I could kill you now," Naryfel gloated. "I could kill her."

"You can't. If you could, you would have done so long ago."

Naryfel snickered. "I have a little present from her."

She picked up a silver box from a side table and held it out to her sister. Mother removed the lid and gave a strangled cry. Tears sprang to her eyes and her lip trembled as she drew forth a length of hair. A wave of anger surged through Jen. Only Blue's restraining hand kept her from rushing to her mother.

"What have you done?" Mother gasped.

Naryfel put her hand innocently to her breast. "I thought she wanted to be a little sailor boy. Now she can make a long apprenticeship aboard one of my slave galleys."

"No!" cried Mother. She sobbed and choked through her words. "You spite me for having a child. That's it, isn't it? Oh, Naryfel, if only you'd had your own."

Naryfel froze. Then her face ignited. "My wise sister thinks she understands. You understand *nothing*."

She stormed to the door where she called the Steward. "Take her," she hissed. "Triple the guard on her room. Ready my carriage for sunup."

When they had left she added, "Watch me, dear sister. I'll dispose of you at the Ice Falls."

21

Blue held Jen back. His face

was lost in shadow, but his eyes glowed in the dark closet.

"No," he whispered. "We can't just go to your mother's room and march her out."

"But Naryfel's going to kill her," Jen cried. Prickles of sweat needled the back of her neck.

"Shh! Guards are looking for us—"

"I can't leave my mother."

"If you don't, the Desert King will take you."

"She thinks Naryfel has me." Jen balled up her fists. "I have to let her know I'm all right."

"She's too heavily guarded. We'll get caught." He tugged sharply at her sleeve. "We've got to get out of here fast or the sniffers will find us."

Jen's shoulders sagged. "I've got to do something."

"Come on," he said. "I've got an idea."

After loading her up again with blankets, he peeked out the door. "All clear." Grabbing his own blankets he slipped out the door.

He walked casually down the corridor, whistling softly to

himself and bowing to passing nobles. They looked away indifferently. Jen tried to follow Blue's example, but wondered whether her shaking knees gave her away.

"Why did we leave the castle?" Jen asked, looking at the great building behind her. With red shingle rooftops and white wooden walls, it was more like a grand old mansion. The front of the building was round. Rising eight stories, it was capped with a tall, conical roof. The rest of the mansion stretched behind in a long rectangle. An army of workers labored around it in the late afternoon sun, hauling blocks of granite. Levers and cranes lifted and placed the rock on a growing battlement. Most of the stone, as yet unused, lay scattered pell-mell in piles and heaps. Viewed from the side like this, the old mansion reminded Jen of a ship adrift on a stormy sea. How could she abandon her mother there?

"We can't rescue your mom alone," Blue replied. "We need help."

Jen turned away reluctantly and followed Blue over a low marble fence. She landed like a cat on a manicured lawn and scurried with him along the perimeter. They darted from a pool to a bathhouse to a gazebo. Beyond a garden and a tinkling fountain was a three-story home, pristine and white. Avoiding the streets, Jen and Blue had been hopping into back yards like this. All the houses had been this prosperous.

They went over one more fence to the next street, and Jen stopped short. On the side of the road, a discarded mattress leaned against a faded, rain-stained sofa. Straw stuffing jutted out of both. Empty bottles and broken glass clogged the gutters. A few steps away, the houses teetered uncertainly on their foundations. The windows were broken or boarded up, and grime obscured the original color of the stucco. A group of men loitering on a corner stared at Jen with narrowed eyes.

"What happened here?" she asked.

Blue hooked a thumb behind him. "Naryfel lavishes wealth on a few to stay in power." He nodded in the direction they were going. "These folks can't find work."

"Why?"

"Naryfel won't pay them. She brings slaves in to work, and lets her own people starve."

"Slaves?" Jen followed Blue through the streets.

"Around here they're called Bluebacks. They had a king-dom of their own nearby. They were a peaceful folk, known for their craftsmanship. Silversmiths, potters, painters, violinmak-ers—you name it, no one made anything finer. When Naryfel's father ruled, he returned their land and restored their king. When Naryfel took over, that was the first place she attacked. She killed off the heirs, squashed rebellion, brought the people here as slaves."

A woman glared from an open doorway. Hanging on the edge of her faded dress was a little girl no more than three. Jen smiled at her. The little girl giggled and ran toward Jen. Before she was halfway the woman grabbed the child and gave her three sharp spanks. The girl cried, looking fearfully back at Jen.

"Why are they so suspicious?" Jen asked.

"Who can they trust? The folks living the high life look down on them, and strangers took their jobs. They hate anyone they don't know—especially Bluebacks."

He turned into an alley that dead-ended at some garbage barrels.

Jen looked apprehensively around. "Why are we going here?"

"We've got to get you some sandals." He grinned at her. "You can't save your mother barefoot."

He stopped at a low window near the trash barrels. His smile dropped. He fixed Jen with an intense stare. "Here, people call me NB. Best call me that."

Jen nodded. He turned and tapped the window. When there was no answer, he called out, "Klak, you old snake, open up. It's NB."

The window opened and Jen saw a gaunt man with hollow eyes and a few straggles of long white hair. He stared a moment at Jen, then turned to Blue. His tongue darted at the space between his missing front teeth and he whistled.

"Look what the cat dragged in," he said. "Where've you been hiding?"

"Oh, here and there. You know me. Here today, gone tomorrow."

He pointed to Blue's sandals. "I do recall that 'tomorrow' you was gonna pay me for those."

"That's just why I've come." Blue removed a small wooden statue from his pocket and held it up. Sanded to a fine polish and stained a dark red, it depicted a woman serenely nursing a baby. "I never forget my debts."

Klak examined the statue with interest. "Stolen?"

Blue placed his hand innocently over his heart. "I never steal."

Klak leered at him. "Sure you don't. How much?"

"The pair I'm wearing and three more."

"One more."

"You old skinflint, that statue's worth three, and you know it."

"Two."

Blue shook Klak's bony hand. "Done."

Klak produced two pairs of rope-soled sandals, but Blue sent him back to find a pair that fit Jen.

With the sandals on her feet and the second pairs dangling from Blue's shoulder, Jen followed him to the edge of the city.

Again she stopped short. A lid of brown dust hung over the sky. Below that, the road wound down to a flat meadow where hundreds of shanties spread out like odd mushrooms.

Jen soon walked in the midst of them. They were little more than ramshackle huts stitched together with wooden planks and canvas. The ceilings were low, barely high enough to stand in. Many had open walls and roofs, allowing Jen to see inside. Bits of carpeting were scattered on dirt floors. Crates or upside-down jugs served as stools; old barrels or cork from a ship were tables. An old drawer nailed to the wall became a shelf. A burlap sack was a door.

They entered a central square. Women shuffled with bent backs and downcast faces to a community bath. It was little more than a muddy ditch. Beyond the bath, men gambled with dice or squatted before an open fire, roasting turnips. One had a scar from ear to jaw, and kept flicking a knife into a log, where it quivered in the center of a crudely drawn target. There were no children.

Jen clung to Blue's heels, wishing she had a knife. "What is this place?"

"Desperation. You can buy and sell anything—mostly illegal." He nodded to a man sleeping against a jug. "They pass out on melon mash, hugging the last of their dreams." He swatted away a horsefly and turned down a narrow alley. "The slaves— Bluebacks live here. Stay with me and you'll be safe."

The smell of a latrine hung in the air and Jen took small breaths through her mouth. "Why are we here?"

Blue smiled. "I need something."

He pulled out his harmonica and blew that strange, haunting song. He stopped beside a ditch and jumped in, waving Jen to follow. Lying on his stomach, he rested on his elbows and continued playing while he watched the open window of a shanty that stood apart from the others.

Jen wondered how any of this was going to rescue her mother. But Blue seemed confident. Who else did she have to turn to?

She could see inside the shanty through the window. There was a bench with two mismatched cushions. The far wall had shelves lined with little candles and clay statues. Someone had drawn pictures of a girl with charcoal, and tacked them neatly above the shelves.

The wind rustled the burlap door, bringing with it the aroma of onions, thyme, and roast meat.

Blue stopped playing a moment and smiled. "Pigeon pie. The best you'll eat."

He kept playing and a short time later Jen saw a woman set a pie on the windowsill to cool. When she was gone, Blue put the harmonica in his pocket. Then he started crawling forward.

Alarmed, Jen stopped him with her hand. "You can't steal from these people. They don't have anything."

"I'm not going to," he replied. "Watch."

He slipped away from her hand and slid along the ground until he was beneath the window. In a flash he snatched the pie, and just as quick replaced it with the extra pair of sandals. Then he started sliding back to the ditch.

He was halfway there when the woman appeared at the window. Her head was long and shaped like a potato, and a peasant scarf covered her hair. She had large hands and she tucked them now under crossed arms. Jen held her breath.

"Shame on you," the woman said.

Blue turned and held out an innocent hand. The other held the pie. "What? The sandals are worth three times the pie."

"It's not that. Ain't you even gonna have dinner with an old friend?"

"I can't, Elda. I'm in a hurry."

"You're always in a hurry."

"I really am this time. It's life and death."

Elda held firm. "Ya don't leave with my pie without playing a jig."

Blue gave her a red-toothed smile. He waved Jen over and handed her the pie. Elda came out and sat on a barrel. Blue slapped his thigh a few times to set the tempo, then tooted a lively dance on his harmonica. Elda clapped and stomped, and the music lit a fire under Jen's feet.

Blue finished the jig, and Elda hugged him and mussed up his hair and gave him a handful of his favorite nuts.

Jen followed Blue out of Desperation. They plunged back into the poor section of the city. Soon they meandered through a maze of narrow streets. The sun sank below a line of western hills, bathing the buildings crimson.

She bit her lip. Time was running out, but she could think of no other plan than to follow where Blue led. He knew the area. Where to go. Where to hide. But could he evade the sniffers?

"Why do we need the pie?" she asked him.

"I told you. We need help." He bounced from side to side, a little spring in his step. "We can't go empty-handed."

He stopped before a door. Unlike most of the others, this one was still on its hinges.

"Who lives here?" Jen asked. The lower windows of the building were boarded up, but the ones on the second floor had white curtains.

Blue grinned. "Naryfel's carriage driver."

22

"Let me do the talking," said Blue.

He rapped with the brass knocker. A short time later a small panel in the door slid aside and a pair of gray eyes stared out. Jen heard an exclamation when they rested on Blue. After many rapid clanks and clinks the door flew open.

"Cap! My boy, it's been an age!" the man cried. He swept Blue in his arms and hugged him tight.

"Too long, Tubole," Blue said, his freckles expanding with his smile. "This is my friend, Jen."

"Pleased to meet you, Jen. Any friend of Cap is a friend of mine."

He was a short man with a thin mustache. His face was round and pleasant, although it appeared too narrow at the forehead.

"Pleased to meet you," Jen replied. "We brought you pigeon pie."

"Pigeon pie! Now that's rare. You must join us for dinner and have some." Tubole stared both ways up the street, which was deserted, then bolted and chained the door.

He led them down a dim hall to a snug living room. A

bench covered with a faded tapestry and pillows faced a stone fireplace. A clock on the mantle was made of glass, and Jen could see the gears and swinging pendulum. Below, a blaze crackled on the hearth. Two straight-back chairs were arranged near the bench. At the foot of one chair was a small pile of wood shavings. A woman sat in the other chair. She was dressed in a high-necked brown cotton dress. Her fingers twitched at her knitting needles, and she glanced up only a moment as Jen entered the room. A little girl about three sat on the floor glued to the woman's calf. She stared with wide eyes, her face flat and expressionless.

"Divida, my love," exclaimed Tubole, "look! It's the little Cap'n, come to pay us a visit. And here's his friend, Jen."

Divida smiled and looked everywhere but at Blue and Jen. *My*, Jen thought. *She's shyer than Bit.* She wondered if Bit had found the doctor for Father and Dash. Time was running out for them, and Mother too. She glanced at the glass clock, aware now of the ticking.

"Forgive the mess," Tubole said, sweeping up the pile of shavings and throwing them into the fire. "I've taken up whittling. Problem is, I never seem to make anything. If only I had *their* talent." He nodded to the clock.

"Blueback?"

"Who else? No one can touch their craftsmanship."

Jen sat beside Blue on the bench. Tubole picked up a piece of wood and a knife and began slicing thin curls onto the floor.

"Where's Darleen?" Blue asked.

Tubole studied his work and made an extra long curl. Divida's fingers flew at the needles. Jen was impressed. The wales and courses were perfectly straight, and the stitches the tightest she'd ever seen.

The curl of wood finally floated down to the floor.

"Darleen's visiting my sister," Tubole replied. "She likes to play with my niece."

Blue looked disappointed. "I wish I could have seen her." He turned to Jen. "She's their daughter. About our age."

"She'd want to see you too," Tubole said. "Divida. Why don't you heat up that pie? I'm famished."

Divida hurried off to get dinner ready, taking the little girl with her.

Tubole continued whittling. There was little left of the wood now. He tossed it aside and selected a new piece to work on.

Blue leaned forward and narrowed his eyes. "How's the Resistance?"

Tubole glanced at Jen.

"It's okay," Blue said. "You can trust her."

"You've been gone awhile," Tubole replied. He held up his work and turned it in the firelight. "Naryfel captured Makken and Tich."

Blue exhaled sharply. "That's a blow. Are they alive?"

"We don't know."

"Who leads us now?"

"That's the problem. No one's stepped up."

"They're scared. They need to see we can beat her. It doesn't have to be big. Something to show she's fallible."

"Interesting," Tubole said. "What do you have in mind?"

"Naryfel captured Jen's mom."

Tubole threw aside the whittling and reached out a hand to Jen. "I'm sorry," he said softly. "I know how hard it is. Everyone in this city has lost someone to Naryfel."

Jen didn't know what to say. There was a lump in her throat and all she could do was swallow.

"What does Naryfel want with your mother?" he asked.

"She's going to kill her," Blue said.

Jen was relieved she didn't have to say it. But the words were grim. Final.

Tubole froze, his mouth halfway open. "Why?"

"Why does Naryfel do anything?" Blue said angrily. "On a whim she'd burn your house down."

"True enough," Tubole said. "How can I help?"

"Naryfel is taking Jen's mother to the Ice Falls tomorrow morning."

From the kitchen beyond, Jen heard a pot crash to the floor. The little girl started bawling. Tubole sprang to his feet, Blue and Jen right behind him.

"No," he said. "Please. Sit. I'm the only one who can soothe her. It will only take a moment. She's just frightened."

He left the room and in a few minutes the girl was quiet. Tubole returned carrying her in his arms. She stared at Jen with saucer eyes.

Tubole settled in his chair. "So. The Ice Falls." He shook his head sadly.

"Will you help?" Blue asked. "There's a good chance you'll be driving."

"I know I will. Naryfel ordered the carriage for sunrise tomorrow. She never tells me in advance where she's going, though."

"How does she work it?"

"She brings the prisoner down in advance, under heavy guard. Then she makes 'em wait."

"Why?" Jen asked, not liking the sound of that.

Tubole smiled wryly. "So they grind their stomachs worrying."

Jen gripped the cushion, digging in her nails. "She takes every chance to torture."

"She does," Tubole sighed. He rocked his daughter, her head nestled under his chin. Her eyes closed and she fell sleep.

"How long does the prisoner wait?" Blue asked.

"Maybe an hour."

"Perfect," Blue said. "If we can get the guards away from the carriage, we can ride off with the prisoner."

Tubole caressed the child's hair, his eyes far away. "You love your mother very much," he said to Jen.

"She's everything to me," Jen replied.

"Yes, I'm sure," Tubole nodded. "As much as a child loves, a parent loves more. There's nothing she wouldn't do for you. You can't imagine the agony she's feeling now."

Jen clenched her fist. "I'd jump off a cliff if it would save her."

"You're brave and determined. I can see that." Tubole's daughter stirred and he kissed her soft hair.

"You'll help then?" asked Blue. "We'll keep you and your family safe, of course. We'll force you to ride off, so Naryfel won't blame you. I could hold a knife to your throat."

"That could work. How do we handle the guards?" Tubole asked.

Blue flashed him a crimson smile. "I have just the plan."

23

I'm dreaming, Bit thought, as she

plunged through the air clutching Pet's hand. It was like falling inside the mouth of a monster, and the jagged rocks of the shaft were teeth. Her candle arced away below her. The puny flame flickered, needing only a breath more to snuff out.

The walls dimmed, and faded out. Time seemed to stop.

She'd heard that when you die, your life flashes before your eyes. But she only saw the wonderful moments with Dash . . .

The first time he held her hand, his fingers wrapping gently around hers, warm and confident. How her little heart trembled . . .

The first time he gave her a flower, they sat in a garden. A nearby fountain tinkled like wind chimes, and he reached behind her. With a smile, he brought back a rose, pale and pink.

"The first bloom of spring," he said, stroking her cheek with it. "See how it blushes at your beauty?"

Afterward, she rushed to her room and put the flower in a vase. She wanted it to last forever. And it seemed to. Months passed before the last petal fell. She saved each precious one, pressing them in a book, and looked at them every night before going to bed . . .

Their first carriage ride. He, dressed in white silk, she in a honey-yellow frock. They drove to the top of a hill, spread out a blanket, and watched cotton-puff clouds go by. He pointed out horses and lions and elephants. She called out bunnies and kitties and cocker spaniels. But all she really saw was Dash, standing on the prow of a great ship, sailing across a foamy sea; Dash charging across the sky in a chariot, hair blowing in the wind; Dash scaling a tower to win her heart—which had been won long before he ever noticed her, when she gazed at him from afar, a shining star too high to hope for . . .

Who was she really? Only a servant girl. Hands and knees rough and callused from scrubbing floors.

"Here's Bit," said the other servant girls. "She don't mind doing a little extra ironing. Do you, Bit?"

"Here's Bit," they said. "Your shift ain't done 'til you've changed all the beds." Her shift had been over hours ago.

"Now, Bit," they said, "we're going dancin' tonight. You'll cover our shift for us." She always did.

"Bit, your balance is better than mine. The outside windows need washing." She hated washing windows the most. Standing outside on a scaffold, it looked like a long way down. Some days, wind rocked the scaffold and the pail of water was ice cold.

There was silver to polish. If a single spot marred the surface, they made her do all the pieces again. She dusted and re-dusted the furniture. She cleared the cobwebs from the corners. She scrubbed clothes for hours on a washboard. Her hands turned red and dry. The skin cracked, and pulling away from the nails, bled. She rose every morning tired, and collapsed every night exhausted, asleep before her head hit the pillow.

She was too shy to complain. Even if she were bolder, she

would have done the work. It gave her a chance to see Dash!

Once he saw her, he never treated her like a servant girl and never allowed her to work again. He stared into her eyes like they were rare jewels where all the mysteries of life were revealed. He left little chocolate treats by her door and love notes under her pillow. The calluses faded, and her skin became soft and silky. "See," he told her. "You really are a princess. Only a princess has delicate hands like this." And he would look deeply into her eyes again until her knees grew weak . . . There were walks in the woods gathering mushrooms, and hot summer days with strawberry-laced snowballs. There were rose-scented cards inscribed "I'm yours," and evenings by the fire reading poetry. Every laugh, every look, passed through her mind. The black locks falling over his brow, the smile full of light, the eyes flashing in the sun.

Memory after memory fell like gentle rain, until she came to the last. Dash, slumbering peacefully in his chamber, the creature wrapped around his body, the coils tightening around his neck. No. Dash must not die. Not Dash. No. Never. No. No—

"No!!" Bit screamed.

A high-pitched singing reverberated off the walls of the shaft, getting closer, until it was in her ear. As if awakening from a dream, she realized Pet was screaming too.

Why can't I see her? Bit thought. Everything was dark, but she had the sensation she was tumbling toward something darker. The odor of rotten eggs rushed past her nose.

Then she plunged into shocking cold and inky blackness. Her muscles felt heavy and numb. She was sinking.

Water, she thought. *I've landed in water.*

The backpack dragged her down like an anchor, so she slipped it off her shoulders. Letting it go, she swam for the surface. Five seconds, ten seconds passed, a crushing weight ripping her lungs. Her hands knifed through something thick and tangled and oozing. Then she was out and gulping air. Slime dripped into her eyes and mouth and she spat. A moment later she heard Pet sputtering beside her.

"Great," Pet said. "Just great."

"Are you all right?" Bit asked, wiping her eyes.

"Just peachy. What is this muck? It smells awful."

"It feels like grass and leaves. The waterfall must push it back here, where it rots."

"Great. Now what?"

Bit looked around. "This must be a cave behind the waterfall. There's a dim light on your left. Maybe that's the opening."

She swam toward the light, Pet following. The cave made a turn and the walls became visible, rough and jagged like the shaft. She thought she heard the waterfall, muffled, like a deep drum roll. Another twenty feet and the water was shallow enough to wade in. The bottom gradually sloped upward.

"I lost my pack," Pet said.

"Me too," Bit replied.

The water was up to her knees now. A few more steps took her to dry rock, where she collapsed to catch her breath. Pet dropped beside her.

"We better find the doctor fast," said Pet. "We lost the food and canteens when we lost the packs."

"I have to find him," said Bit. "Another day has gone by, and Dash is dying."

"Then let's get going. I'm cold."

Rocks littered the floor of the cave. Water collected between the rocks.

"Careful," said Pet. "There could be snakes in there."

Bit scrambled and climbed over the rocks. Ahead she

could hear the roar of the waterfall. Another turn of the cave and she saw the opening. It was a narrow slit between two boulders. Beyond was light-gray sky. She hurried forward and squeezed through. For a few seconds, the sunlight stung and blinded her. When she could see again, she looked around. She had come out among some boulders that ran along a cliff bottom. She stood on a shore. The waterfall thundered to her left, filling a pool. More boulders surrounded the pool like a horseshoe. She wondered how the water got in the cave. Perhaps grass and leaves were carried there when it flooded.

"I'm stuck," Pet called.

Bit turned and saw Pet struggling. Her head, shoulder, and one arm were free. The rest of her was wedged in the opening.

Bit grasped Pet's hand and pulled.

"You're hurting me," Pet screamed.

"Try and push with your feet." Bit tugged again.

"No! Stop! You're making it worse."

"Try going backward."

Bit pushed while Pet tried pulling back.

"It's no good," Pet cried. "I'm trapped." Her eyes widened in panic. "Don't leave me. Please don't leave me."

"Don't be silly. I wouldn't leave you. Try to calm down." Bit stepped back and looked at the opening. It was formed by two boulders leaning against each other, and looked like a very tall and narrow upside down V.

"Don't just stand there, *do* something," Pet cried.

"Hush. You got in there. We'll get you out." Bit studied the opening.

"Well?" asked Pet.

"The opening is a little larger toward the bottom. Try going down and back."

Pet rocked her shoulders back and forth, trying to pull down.

"Bend your knees," said Bit.

Working down and back, Pet freed herself.

"Now come through, but lower down."

"I'm not taking any chances." Pet got down on her side and wriggled through like a snake, tearing the sleeve of her shirt on a sharp rock. She rose, and Bit hugged her.

"You're bleeding," said Bit, looking at a long scratch on Pet's elbow.

"I'll live. Stop fussing over me. I'm not a baby."

Bit stood back and looked at her friend. She giggled.

"What?" Pet asked.

"You're a sight."

Pet's hair was matted and tangled with globs of green muck. More slime dangled like confetti from her shirt and shorts, which were ripped, tattered, and streaked with grime. Her boots were scuffed and swollen with water, and a heel had come off. It looked like she hadn't changed clothes in years. Her face was smeared with mud. Scrapes, cuts, and nicks crisscrossed her arms and legs.

"If you tell anyone—" Pet swore.

"Don't worry, I'm not much better."

Swamp slime hung in ribbons from Bit's hair and clothes. Her pants, filthy and torn at the knee, looked like they came from a poor box. Her hands were raw and blistered. A year of heavy work could not have made them more red and swollen.

"You look like a waif," said Pet.

"You look like a street urchin." Bit laughed.

"You're a beggar."

"You're a tramp."

Bit pretended she wore a dress and curtsied. "Good evening, Countess."

Pet laughed and curtsied back. "Good evening, Your

Highness. I love your gown. Is that the latest style?"

"Yes. Everyone in court is wearing one."

"And what is that rare perfume?"

"I call it Eau de Swampgas."

They laughed, until at last, Pet grew serious again. "Thanks for helping back there."

"You would have done the same," Bit replied.

Pet looked away and played with her torn sleeve. "Not just when I was stuck. When I fell."

"We stick together like glue—whatever may come, 'til the end. Remember?" Bit said with a smile. "Come on. Let's clean off in the pool."

They took off their shoes and dashed into the water. It was icy, forcing them to scrub quickly. Afterward, they rested on the rocks beside the shore, letting their clothes dry on their bodies. The day was warm, but the afternoon sun had not broken through the gray clouds. Bit was relieved she didn't have to take off her socks.

"Where do we go now?" Pet asked, when they were ready to leave.

"There should be a trail on the far end of the pool."

Bit led them around the horseshoe of boulders. Opposite the waterfall, a fast-moving stream poured from the pool and disappeared into a forest. But there was no trail.

"That's odd," Bit said. "The Pondit said there was a trail."

"What do we do now?"

Bit looked around. The hills surrounding the pool were carpeted with thick-growing trees. It would be easy to get lost in there, and Pet's compass was gone with her pack.

"Let's follow the stream," Bit replied.

The banks of the stream were steep, leaving no place to walk on either side, so Bit led the way along the water's edge, where she scrambled over a jumble of rocks or waded knee deep in the cold current. After an hour she stopped and checked her direction by the sun. The stream had turned and she was going the wrong way.

Since they lost the canteens, she was reluctant to leave the water, but there was no choice. Before leaving the stream she made Pet take a long drink, and drank deeply herself. Afterward, she led the way through a grove of giant redwoods. These gave way to fir, then a stand of old oak. The forest was still. The only sound was the crackle of leaves underfoot. Occasionally she thought she saw Darter flitting from branch to branch.

Gnarled roots cut across the path, and patches of low-lying brush grew around the trees, slowing her progress. She found herself turning, circling, doubling back. She worried about getting lost if the sun set before they left the forest. Hunger gnawed at her stomach and her throat was dry. But she wasn't concerned about herself. Before coming to the Rose Castle, she had gone without food. She knew she could survive. She was worried about Pet. Pet's life was pampered. She had never faced hardship. She'd always sat on soft silk cushions. Every meal had been served on porcelain china and eaten with a silver fork. Starvation would be a shock to her.

Maybe that was what she was thinking about now. She'd been lost in thought for several miles now, tugging at a loose thread on her shorts.

That was okay. Bit needed time to think. The tender memories of Dash cascaded through her mind and made her ache. She had to survive for Dash. Four, maybe five days. That's all she had before the creature took him from the world. The thought was unbearable. She had to find the doctor. Then, somehow, she had to find a way back to Aerdem. This worried her the most. Without Yalp's magic, she didn't have a clue how to get home.

Snapping branches broke the silence. Two streaks of brown rushed out of the brush and into a little clearing. The first was a little rabbit, bolting across the ground. A coyote chased behind, gaining with lightning-fast leaps. The coyote was old and scrawny, her yellow teeth bared in a nasty grin. She sprang, jaws locking on the rabbit's neck, then dragged it back into the brush. The rabbit was still alive. Bit could see its eyes, wide, frightened and helpless.

Tears sprang to Bit's eyes. She could only stare at Pet, who looked back in horror.

They continued on. If Pet was quiet before, she was completely withdrawn now. Trees hemmed them in at every turn. Branches grew to the ground like prison bars. The sun was setting. It would be dark soon. There was no choice but to plow through some thick bushes.

"Stop!" Pet called. She grabbed Bit's hand and yanked back.

Bit lost her balance. Together they tumbled into the brush.

"Great. Just great." Pet rose first. "Bit, haven't you seen poison oak before?"

Bit gasped. "Are you sure?"

"Of course I'm sure. It grows all around our back yard."

"Maybe you won't get it. You fell on top of me."

"What about you? You fell in the worst of it."

"I don't care what happens to me. As long as I find the doctor."

Bit led the way down a hill. The trees continued to grow in dense patches, but a few minutes later she found a dirt road going in the right direction. She followed the road, suddenly feeling hopeful. Roads lead somewhere, and this one went away from the wilderness and the mountain behind. The cottage where Jenny had lived was supposed to be the last home on the shoulders of a mountain. Two miles farther was Doc Jenkins' house. Three beyond that was a village. Even if Bit overshot her exit from the forest, she could ask for directions.

"What's that?" Pet asked, pointing down a tree-lined hill that fell away to the left.

Through the trees, Bit thought she saw a building.

"Let's go see," said Bit, a growing thrill fluttering in the pit of her stomach. If someone lived there, they could get help.

She led the way down the hill. At the bottom was a cottage. The windows were dark and dirty, and one of them was broken. Piles of leaves littered the porch. Weeds overran the remnants of a garden. A neat pile of wood was stacked next to a well, an ax still lodged in the chopping block.

"I wonder if this was Jenny's cottage," she said, her heart pounding with excitement.

"Maybe," Pet replied. "I'm thirsty. Let's see if there's any water in the well."

Bit followed Pet to the well, which was made in a circle of stones. The crank was rusty, but a rope still held the bucket. Together they pulled up the bucket. It was dusty, and dry as a cork.

"Come on," said Pet. "The cottage looks deserted. Maybe there's food and water inside."

Bit followed. She no longer felt hungry. She wanted to see the inside of the cottage and see whether it had been Jenny's. Jenny had lived alone with Nell, an old woman who had died.

She knocked on the front door. There was no answer so she pushed it open. The hinges whined, protesting from rust. She brushed away a sticky spider web that clung to her face as she passed through the entrance. The smell of dust and mothballs filled the air. She lit a lantern that hung from the ceiling. To the left was a cozy living room. A small wooden stool and a big, overstuffed chair faced a stone fireplace. A beige shawl hung over the back of the chair. Along the fireplace mantle were little clay animals, such as a child would make.

She picked up a thick book that sat on a side table next to a pair of spectacles. She blew away the dust. The title read: *The Age of Reason.* She thumbed through several pages. There were a lot of words she didn't know.

Opposite the living room was a dining room, with a round table and three oak chairs. The table was covered with a faded yellow cloth. A vase in the middle held a single dead flower.

Through an entryway beyond was the kitchen. There was barely room for a counter, the sink, and a wood-burning stove. Shelves and cupboards lined the walls to the ceiling. A pot had been left soaking in the sink. Pet found jars of pickled eggs, an unopened package of crackers, canned tomatoes and peas, and a tin of candied apricots.

"We could look for wood and heat up the vegetables," Bit suggested.

"I'm too hungry. Come on, I'll fix you a plate."

They ate quickly, then explored the back rooms. The one on the left had a narrow bed. Bit lifted the covers. Underneath she found a thick layer of straw piled on top of wooden slats. There were pink curtains on the windows and a child's desk in the corner. Her heart skipped a beat. Was this Jenny's room? If so, they were close to the doctor. They could find him tonight!

Pet rummaged through a closet, while Bit explored the next room. She found another narrow bed covered with a thick quilt. On a night table were a lantern and a hairbrush. She quickly lit the lantern and looked at the hair caught in the bristles of the brush. She stopped breathing. Gray hair. An old woman!

The nightstand had three drawers. The first was empty. In the second she found a piece of paper, folded in half. A big smiling sun had been drawn, and letters crudely formed by a child's hand. She read the words in a whisper, hardly able to believe her eyes, which filled with tears of joy: "Happy Birthday Nell! Love, Jenny."

"Pet!" she cried, her heart trembling. "We can find the doctor. This was Jenny's cottage!"

Pet ran in from the other room. "Are you sure?"

Bit showed her the card. "If we leave now, we can get there before dark. He's only two miles down the road."

"I'm tired. Let's sleep here tonight and find the doctor in the morning."

"Please, Pet. Every moment that goes by may be Dash's last."

"Okay. Let me just gather some food, in case we get lost."

"Please hurry."

Pet threw some jars, cans, and an opener in a burlap sack. "Calm down. We'll find the doctor soon enough."

Nothing could be too soon for Bit as she urged her friend out of the cottage. The clouds had finally broken and the setting sun had emerged, pink with hope. The color reminded Bit of the Rose Castle. It was like an omen from heaven, she thought, and soon she would be home with Dash beside her.

As she skipped off the porch and down the road, wrapped in dreams of happiness and peace, a bloodcurdling sound sliced through the evening air.

"What's that?" Pet exclaimed.

"It sounds like a pack—"

"Of dogs. They don't sound friendly."

"They're coming this way," cried Bit.

"Let's hide."

They dashed back up the hill and hid just beyond a small clearing of trees. The barking grew loud, sharp and hungry. Bit pulled Pet deeper into the brush. A few minutes later, a boy burst through the trees. He ran across the clearing, face red, heaving with every breath. His shirt was too big for him, his pants too tight. They were nothing more than rags, so frayed and worn and covered with grime that it was impossible to tell the original color. Terrified, he glanced over his shoulder, and hid among some bushes across the clearing from Bit.

The pack sounded like a single, vicious beast, yapping and snarling as it drew closer. The barking stopped abruptly at the bottom of the hill. Bit thought she heard whining. Then a sharp cry of triumph and the yelping pack charged up the hill. A dozen or more bloodhounds crashed through the trees and streamed into the clearing, eyes red, mouths drooling. They raced across the path the boy had followed, clambering over each other in their excitement. Growling, they stopped directly in front of the brush where he lay hiding. Several of them circled the spot, cutting off any escape.

A new sound turned Bit's attention back down the hill. Someone was singing, the voice harsh and shrill as a vulture:

Oh, my little babies,
What have you caught today?
Oh, my little darlings,
Serve it on a tray.

A woman emerged from the trees as she finished the song. She was tall and thin. Her body was bony, all sharp angles and protruding joints. Her gray hair was wrapped in a severe bun, held in place by several knitting needles. Her nose was like a bird of prey, her chin a knife. Her eyes were nothing more than black slashes.

"Ox!" she called. "Where are you, you lazy lub?"

Bit heard the heavy scrape and crunch of leaves moving up the hill. A burly man appeared. His hair was coarse stubble, his face square and sweating. He stood panting, looking stupidly at the woman.

"Well? What are you waiting for?" said the woman. She gave his bottom a hard kick. "Go get him."

Ox grinned viciously as he approached the bush where the dogs were barking. Reaching in, he pulled the boy out by the collar and held him in the air like a rag doll. The boy hung limp, a look of resignation on his face.

"Now, Jeffrey," said Ox. "We're gunna have a nice time when we get home, ain't we?" He gave the boy a little shake. "Ain't we?"

Jeffrey hung his head.

"What'sa matter? Cat got your tongue?"

He carried the boy to the woman, who stood with her hands on her hips. She lifted the boy's chin with a claw-like hand.

"You know the rules," she said to him. "Running away is the highest crime, and shall be met with the highest penalty."

Jeffrey came alive and looked pleadingly at her. "Please, Miss Drath. Don't beat me. I won't do it again. I swear."

Drath's mouth was an upside down U set in a perpetual frown. Now it pulled lower. "I dare say you won't, after Ox is through with you," she replied.

Ox licked his fat lips and smiled wickedly. Jeffrey sagged again. Ox put him down and tied his hands behind his back with a thick rope. Another rope was tied around his neck like a leash. Ox gave it a sharp pull and the boy stumbled.

"Come along, Babies," Miss Drath called, gathering the bloodhounds.

They yipped and jumped around her, but one turned and looked toward the brush where Bit lay hiding. She backed deeper among the leaves, tugging Pet with her. The dog took a step toward the bush and sniffed. His red eyes narrowed. Baring his teeth, he growled.

"What is it, Nose?" Miss Drath called to the dog. "Have you found another treat for Mommy?" She clapped her hands. "Hunt!"

Yipping and barking, the dogs raced to the brush where Bit was hidden. She looked wildly about for an escape route. Her heart swelled into her mouth. She tried to rise, tried to run, but her feet felt like lead. A moment later, Ox peered through the leaves and his eyes locked on hers. With a triumphant smile, he seized her arm and dragged her roughly into the clearing.

"Well done, Ox!" said Miss Drath.

Bit stood beside Pet in the middle of the clearing. The dogs had formed a ring around her. Ox was an arm's length away. He leered at her, making three thick bristles twitch on his nose.

Miss Drath stroked her long chin and circled around Bit, looking her up and down. Bit knew she was a sight. Most of the mud had washed off at the pool, but her clothes were ragged and torn. Pet looked worse.

"Where are you from?" asked Drath. "I haven't seen you before."

Petunia took a bold step forward and drew herself up to her full height. "I am Countess Petunia Pompahro, and this is Lady Bit, betrothed to Prince Dashren. Bring us Doctor Jenkins at once and we will see that you are richly rewarded."

Drath looked amused. "A countess. And a lady," she said in mock surprise. She examined the contents of the sack Pet had filled with supplies from the cottage. "Let's see what you would reward me with. Ah, a can of green beans, a couple of onions, potatoes. Ox! Have you ever seen such riches?"

Ox laughed viciously. Jeffrey had been tied to a tree limb. Ox gave him kick.

"And these are your noble clothes?" continued Drath. As she spoke she leaned her face close to Pet's, tugging with a bony hand at a hole in the Countess' shirt.

"Get away from me you disgusting creature. Your breath stinks," cried Pet.

For a moment, Miss Drath looked startled and put her hand over her mouth.

Bit tried to give Pet a warning look, but her friend was in rare form. She stood with her hands on her hips, her face red and shaking. "Bring the doctor to us at once or the Count will take you severely in hand."

"The Count!" cried Drath with a laugh. "I should like to see your Count. Is he as elegant as you?"

Pet glared.

Drath shook the sack. "Where did you get this?" she said sharply.

"We got them from Jenny's old cottage—"

"Jenny?" said Drath. "What do you know about Jenny?"

"She's a princess," Pet said importantly, "and she'll bring the whole Royal Army of Aerdem down on you if you don't do what I say."

"Pet," whispered Bit. "Don't."

"Oh. The little mousy one talks," said Drath, turning to Bit. "Speak up. What do you know about Jenny?"

Bit felt trapped. If she said Jenny was a princess, she knew she would sound as absurd as Pet. If she said they needed the doctor for Dash, or he would die, Drath would demand they produce him. Still, that part of the truth seemed her only option.

"If you please, Miss," she began, "we have a friend—"

"Jenny," shrieked Drath, "where is Jenny?"

"I . . . I don't know," Bit replied.

"Don't lie to me, girl!"

"Miss?"

"I've been wanting to get my hands on her a long time. I've suspected she's been living in a cave up here. Now I see she's gathering runaways and vagabonds to live with her—then sends them out to steal."

"No, Miss. We were only—"

"You've admitted you stole this food from Nell's cottage."

"The cottage was abandoned, Miss. We didn't think anyone would mind."

Drath grabbed Bit by the hair and shook her. "Tell me where Jenny is or I'll beat it out of you."

Bit cried out. Her scalp burned, like every hair was being torn out. Through a blur of tears she saw Pet raising her fists.

"Leave her alone," Pet yelled.

Drath lunged for Pet. "I'll start by beating it out of you."

"Don't you dare touch me, you dreadful hag," Pet cried, "or the Count will take the skin off your back."

To Bit's surprise, Drath dropped her hands.

"You'll regret those words," she said coldly. "Ox! Tie them up."

Ox gave Bit a nasty grin, exposing a set of yellow, horsy teeth. He pulled a length of rope from around his waist and reached for her. Something streaked from the trees. It was Darter! He beat Ox's head with his wings and body. Ox swung wildly, trying to bat the bird away. But Darter dodged Ox's hands and attacked his face. Jabbing with his beak, Darter cut open Ox's cheek and forehead. Blood streamed into the man's eyes and mouth.

Bit had no time to run. Drath grabbed a stout stick and nailed Darter with a single swing. He sailed ten feet away and fell lifeless on the ground. The battle was over in seconds. Bit's hands were tied behind her back, the knot cutting painfully into her wrists. Another long rope looped snugly around her neck and was tied to Pet and Jeffrey.

The rest of the night was a blur. Dark, lowering clouds. Miles of marching. The leash pulling at her neck. Drath's skeletal silhouette leading them down a muddy dirt road.

One moment was clear. She saw a long driveway branch off the side of the road with a wooden sign at the entrance. Painted in blue letters were the words "Doctor Jenkins." At that moment, the last light of the day expired.

24

Jen dipped her paddle silently into the

water. "Have you seen a sniffer?"

Blue steered the dinghy, his silhouette inky against the night sky. The current whisked them along with only a soft gurgle. A crescent moon turned the stream silver.

"They're ugly as sin." His voice stole back, a notch above a whisper. "Big as a calf, speed of a cougar. The head is mostly a huge, flat nose, with flaring nostrils. Below that are steel-trap jaws and razor-sharp tusks."

Jen shuddered. "Are you sure they won't find us here?"

"Positive. They can't track through water."

A small island loomed ahead. Blue guided the boat there, and soon the bottom rustled on a sandy shore.

"We'll spend the night here," he said.

They grabbed blankets and food from the boat and trudged up a short trail to the crest of the island. Scrub oak crowned the top, and they stashed their gear in some dense brush.

Blue yawned and looked longingly at the blankets. "Come on," he said turning away. "Let's scope out the carriage house."

They returned to the boat and pushed off. A hill rose up

along the left bank, and a mile downstream she saw a series of dark openings along the shore.

"What are those?" she asked.

"Part of the sewer system. Light the lantern just before I go into that one there. I don't want anyone spotting us."

Tubole had generously provided the lantern, blankets, and food. Jen thought he was a good, humble man. He loved his family and understood her agony. Before meeting him, she'd felt herself sinking into an abyss. Time was running out. Unless she did something, her mother would be spirited away— doomed to die. All Jen could count on was Blue. Sure, he was cocky and clever, and people loved him. But he was just a boy. What could he really do against Naryfel?

All that changed with Tubole. Despite the risk to himself and his family, he'd agreed to help rescue Jen's mother. All her fears evaporated. There was a Resistance. Tubole was experienced. He'd fought in clandestine forays. With tears of relief and hope streaming down her face, Jen had tried to thank him. He'd only looked away sheepishly and kissed his sleeping daughter.

"Okay," said Blue. "Light the lantern."

Jen lit it just as the boat skimmed into the tunnel. The amber light extended only a few yards beyond, illuminating the vague outline of a stone ceiling and walls. The air was cold and she regretted not bringing the blankets. The stench of the sewer made her stomach twist.

She was aware of more tunnels on either side, inky mouths within the shadows. Blue turned down one of these, then another. The boat picked up speed and he turned again. He guided them through a honeycomb of dark passages until Jen felt completely lost.

"How do you know where to go?" she asked.

"I can see in the dark like a cat."

"But all the tunnels look the same."

Blue veered toward another tunnel. "Look," he replied, pointing. "We've painted colors above the openings. I've been following the red ones."

Jen thought she saw a crimson mark, but couldn't be sure in the flickering light. "What color did you follow out of the prison?"

"Green. Hold on."

The boat shot out of the tunnel and splashed into a broader channel. Amber rapids boiled and roared on either side, rocking the boat like a toy. Blue side-paddled, furiously fighting for control.

"When I get the boat to that wall," he called, "you'll see an iron ring. Grab onto it and don't let go."

He steered to the left-hand wall, where the boat's wooden side scraped and smacked into the stones. Jen saw the ring ahead, sticking out like an empty eye. Just beyond was a large drainpipe. She braced her feet against a bottom board and grabbed the ring with both hands. The boat lurched, and the ring, rough and rusty, tore at her hands. But she held tight and they stopped.

Blue snatched a rope and secured the dinghy with a slip-knot. He pointed to the drainpipe. "We go up here."

The pipe was just wide enough to crawl in and angled up steeply. The bottom was slippery with a slick of water.

Blue went up first, Jen following close behind. They braced the width of the pipe with hands and feet, and worked their way up a foot at a time. They left the lantern in the boat and Jen was relieved she could not see down. All she had to do was focus on each step of the climb. She'd scaled shafts like this all the time before her fall.

Soon Blue was sucking in air and Jen suggested they stop and rest.

"Sure," he called down. "If you're tired."

Jen wasn't, but she stopped to give Blue a chance to catch his breath.

They started up again. After a while, she saw a growing circle of gray. Just near the top Blue slipped. She saw him coming and braced herself. His knee hit her shoulder, but using her feet as a brake, she kept them both from hurtling back down to the stream.

"Sorry," he said. "Are you all right?"

Her shoulder was screaming. "I'll live. Can you go on?" She was still holding him.

"Yeah. We're almost there."

He climbed up a few more yards and crawled onto a ledge. Jen joined him. The ledge was a short, rectangular enclosure sloping precariously to the street. At the far end was a metal grate.

"Careful," Blue said. "We don't want to fall back down the pipe."

Jen nodded. If she slipped she'd carom down the pipe and the stream would sweep her away.

They slithered on their bellies to the grate and looked out. At one end of an unlit courtyard, she made out the carriage house, a red wooden building with tall double doors. Catty-corner to the carriage house was the back of Naryfel's castle. The guards would bring her mother from there.

Jen helped Blue lift away the grate and they stole out. The cobblestone pavement shone with indigo moon glow. A high rock wall was behind them. To her right, the straw-littered courtyard narrowed to a road. The smell of horses clung to the chill air.

Blue pointed to the sloping roof of the carriage house. "Can you climb up there?"

The carriage house was little more than a barn. The walls were built with rough planking. It wouldn't be easy, but knotholes in the boards and spaces in between would provide foot and hand holds.

"I'll make it," Jen replied quickly, before she could back out or change her mind. This was do or die, and it was for Mother.

"Good. Here's how we'll work it. I'll hide behind that tree up the road. Tubole will bring out the carriage and park it by the barn doors. The guards will bring out your mother and put her in the carriage. They'll stand around bragging and killing time. When they're relaxed, I'll wander up the road and do my act—luring them away from the carriage."

"Then what?"

"While I distract the guards, you jump down from the roof onto the carriage—"

"And force Tubole to ride off. But how will you get on the carriage?"

"Don't worry. I'll dodge the guards and leap on before they know it. By the time they recover, the horses will be moving too fast to stop."

"What if you can't lure the guards away?"

"Then we improvise."

The moon had set. The darker veils of night lifted, hinting at the first gray light of dawn. Jen lay beside Blue, looking out the grate, waiting. Excitement fluttered like a butterfly, dancing in her stomach. Only a few minutes and it would start. They would slip to their stations and free her mother.

"Naryfel will follow after we highjack the carriage," Jen said. "Where can we go that's safe?"

"There's a lawless bunch in the hills," Blue replied. "And nomadic gypsies. I know them. It's a rough region, hard to reach with an army. We can take your mom there."

Blue chewed on a straw, the tip burning like a tiny red eye. "I know some back roads to Aerdem. Not even the sniffers will track us through the bogs and swamps I'll take you through."

Jen traced a star into the dew that had settled on the grate. It could really happen. They could get safely home. And if Bit had found a doctor, then Father and Dash would be all right. They could march a strong army to Purpura and destroy Naryfel forever.

"Are you part of the Resistance?" Jen asked.

"You heard Tubole. They call me Lil' Cap."

"Why?"

"I'm captain of a brigade."

Jen stared at him.

"What?" Blue asked. He tamped out the stub of straw and lit another. "Don't you believe me?"

Jen thought of the way he had talked with Tubole, revealing a carefully thought out plan, then convincing the man to join them.

"I do," she replied. "I just don't understand how."

"I grew up fast," Blue replied dryly.

An owl hooted, and a chill wind blew through the grate. Jen pulled a blanket around her shoulders.

"I guess I know how you grew up," Blue said. There was a slight edge to his voice. He hadn't looked at her much since their brief sleep on the island and journey back here. She missed his smile.

"What do you mean?"

"Naryfel's your aunt. I heard your mother say it."

"I never met her before she kidnapped me."

"But you're a princess." He said it like he was chewing on a bitter apple.

"How do you know? My mom could have married a butcher."

"Sure. But if anything ever happens to Naryfel, your mom would be queen. And you'd be next in line for the throne."

"So?"

"So—queens don't marry butchers."

"What are you saying?"

"I'm saying you've led a soft life."

Jen gave a sigh of relief. "So that's what's bothering you. Trust me, I was far from pampered. To protect me from Naryfel, my mother left me with an old woman when I was two. Her name was Nell, and she pretty much was my mother. I lived in a cabin with her for nine years. It was a five-mile hike to the nearest village. I didn't fit in with the other children—they took every opportunity to torment me—stealing my books and my lunch, laughing at how slow I was in school. And they called me the witch's daughter. But she wasn't a witch. While I was there, hers was the only smile I ever saw. I don't know how many fights I got into over her."

He pointed to her eyebrow scar. "Is that how you got that?"

"No—I fell . . ."

"So when did you find your mother?"

"Three years ago."

"And you're that loyal?"

Jen traced a heart in the dew beside the star. "It's like we were never apart. I feel that close."

"I can see why," Blue said with a smile. "She's wonderful. I wish I'd had someone like her for a mom."

"What happened to yours?"

"Shh! Tubole is here."

Jen saw a short figure cross the courtyard to the carriage house. The sky had turned gray, and she thought she saw Tubole's mustache in the growing light. He passed through the big red doors into the carriage house.

"It's time," said Blue. "You still have Tubole's knife?"

She pulled it out of her belt and showed it to him.

Jen helped him push aside the grate. They rose one at a time through the narrow opening to the street. She turned to push the grate back in place.

"Leave it ajar," he said.

"But someone might notice."

"We'll have to chance it, in case we need an escape route." He took her hands and squeezed them. "Good luck." Then he was off, melting into the shadows along the edge of the courtyard. A moment later she thought she saw him slip behind a tree down the road.

She scanned the courtyard. It was deserted. Taking a deep breath, she ran silently to the side of the carriage house. She peeked briefly through a hole in one of the boards and saw Tubole light a lantern. Then he led one of the horses from a stall.

Jen stepped back and scanned the wall. It was about fifteen feet high. She looked for a spot with knotholes every few feet and gaps between the planks. She curled her fingers around two of the boards and found a foothold and then there was no thought, only motion and grace and the ascent of a cat.

When she reached the roof, it sloped at an easy angle, allowing her to walk upright. The second section of the roof at the front of the building was almost flat. She lay on her stomach near the edge and waited.

The doors opened below and she saw Tubole bring out the carriage. He parked it a few feet beyond the doors. Jen gauged the distance. She could leap to the driver's seat from a crouch. Tubole climbed down and waited by the horses. He stroked their noses affectionately and they nickered.

The sun peeked over the horizon. A band of fleecy cloud balls ignited into flaming roses. The wind dropped, and the air felt warmer.

The door to the castle opened and two guards escorted Mother into the courtyard. Jen felt a swirl of emotions. A burst of joy on seeing Mother, and rage as the guards prodded her with the butts of their swords. They laughed when she stumbled. One of them had a jaw like a wolf. And tiny black eyes. The other had grease and wine stains on his tunic, which hung over a swollen belly. This fellow licked his lips and ran his fingers lasciviously through Mother's hair.

She looked straight ahead and seemed unaware of him. A sweet, silvery voice floated up to Jen, and she realized her mother was singing.

Tubole opened the carriage door, then climbed onto the driver's seat. The guards passed underneath Jen, her mother almost close enough to touch. The guard with the wolf jaw put a black hood over Mother's head and pushed her roughly inside the carriage. He closed the door and leaned against it while he rolled a cigarette.

"Roll me one," said the bloated guard.

"Make your own," said the other.

"I'm out. Lend me some."

"Why should I?"

The fat guard belched and pulled up his pants, which kept slipping off his waist. He pulled a pair of dice out of his pocket. "I'll play you for one."

"What's yer stake?" sneered Wolf Jaw.

The hefty guard grinned and nodded at the carriage. "She's

a looker. We can play for her."

His mate stroked his long chin, considering. "All right. As long as the queen doesn't go with her."

They squatted. The big fellow shook the dice and scattered them on the pavement.

Wolf Jaw scooped them up and rolled. "Ten. I win."

"No. Let's make it two out of three."

"I won."

"I never agreed to one roll." The big fellow grabbed the other guard by the collar.

Jen looked up the road. *Where is Blue?*

At that moment she saw him step from behind the tree. He wore a beaten up old hat, pulled down so you couldn't see his face. He had a long stick in one hand that he tapped on the cobblestones like a blind man. The other hand held a begging bowl.

"Alms for the poor," he cried, walking in the direction of the guards. "Alms for a poor blind boy."

The guards looked at him blankly. Blue stopped halfway between the tree and the carriage. "I know you're there. I can hear you. Won't you please help?" he cried plaintively.

Wolf Jaw scowled. "Go back to town and beg there, urchin."

"Is this not the town?" Blue asked.

"Back the other way."

Blue held out his bowl. "Please. I'm hungry and lost and don't know the way."

"Come on," said Wolf Jaw to the other guard. "Let's show him with a boot on the bottom."

"No," cried Blue. He backed away, trembling so that the stick rattled on the pavement. "Please don't hurt me. I haven't eaten in days."

The guards moved up the road toward him. When they were a pace away, he took off his hat. Swinging it in an arc, he sent a spray of dirt in their eyes. "Now!" he shouted.

Jen leaped from the roof to the seat beside Tubole. She put the knife to his throat. "Drive!"

Tubole looked straight ahead, ignoring her command.

"Drive," she screamed. "Or I'll slit your throat!"

Tubole sat like a statue.

"Go," Jen whispered. "What are you waiting for?"

"My daughter," he said to himself. He shook his head from side to side. "Darleen. My daughter."

The guards stopped rubbing dirt from their eyes and stared at Jen.

Blue pelted toward her. "Run! It's a trap!"

The doors of the barn banged open and ten guards streamed out, followed by the Desert King and Naryfel. Jen leaped off the carriage and ran for the drain, Blue only a step behind. More guards leaped off the walls and surrounded her in a semicircle.

"It's over," bellowed Naryfel.

Jen turned, but continued to back toward the drain. Naryfel stepped through the line of guards. The rising sun was behind her head, setting her hair on fire.

"Drive," she commanded Tubole. "I'll meet you at the pass."

Tubole cracked the whip. Jen's heart sank as she watched the carriage roll away with her mother.

"Holding the children of my servants is an excellent way to guarantee loyalty, don't you think?" Naryfel asked, smacking her lips.

Jen backed to the drain.

Naryfel pointed to her. "Here's your prize," she said to the

Desert King. Her eyes frosted. "Take her!"

The Desert King's laugh was like the screech of a sawmill and the thorns on his face quivered. "Shall we dance?"

Blue sprang in front of Jen, swinging his staff to drive the king back. Jen reached the partially open grate and wavered. Only one of them could enter the drain at a time. If she went first, Blue might not have time to follow.

The guards closed in, tightening the circle. Blue threw the staff at the king, then turned and pushed Jen hard. She lost her footing and fell into the drain. Just before she tumbled into the pipe below, she saw the guards leap on Blue and tackle him.

She tried to stop her fall. She needed to get back up there and help Blue. But there was nothing she could do. Her hands and feet burned when she tried to brake. She banged and slid and caromed down the pipe. Her head did a rat-a-tat on the metal and stars filled her eyes. Finally she shot into space. She could see the boat and the lantern and the stream below. As she came down she reached for the boat, only inches from her stretching fingers. Then the current gripped her and dragged her away, sending her down a tunnel of blackness.

Part Four

25

Bit was first aware of the cold,

penetrating the darkness of a dreamless slumber. "The Castle's an iceberg," she thought vaguely, pulling the blanket over her.

The cold nipped at her feet and ankles. Drawing her knees up to her tummy, she tried to burrow into what seemed like an ever-shrinking blanket.

She was sinking back into the shroud of sleep, when someone coughed. That cough, shattering the illusion that she was alone in her bedroom, startled her awake.

She willed her eyes to stay closed. If only she could pretend she was still in the Rose Castle, and this had just been a bad nightmare. The king would be tinkering in the Crystal Room. She would make cookies with Jenny's mother that afternoon, and Jenny and Pet would join them for tea. But first, Dash would be all right, and would greet her with a knee-melting smile—then they'd ride bareback on his stallion through the crimson fields of Aerdem, and watch the rising sun turn the dew to diamonds.

If only she could pretend, she wouldn't see, for a little while longer, her grim surroundings. She'd seen enough the night before.

After passing through a small village, her forced march with Pet ended when she turned down a long, lonely street. On either side were empty fields, save for an overgrown jumble of crabgrass and tumbleweed. The street dead-ended at a three-story house, which loomed gray and ghostly through a swath of fog. The shuttered windows were bleak and lifeless. An old oak tree, stripped of its leaves, leaned against one side of the house. The building sagged, and Bit was uncertain whether the house held up the tree or the tree propped up the house. The skeletal remains of a gate, fence posts, and railing tilted like drunken sentries around the front yard, which was a neglected wilderness of foxtails and devil's paintbrush.

Ox goaded Bit, Pet, and Jeffrey past the gate and up a short walkway to the porch steps. A nearby street lamp illuminated the entrance. The wooden stairs and planks of the house were sun-bleached and weathered. An ancient coat of paint had all but peeled off. A sign over the door announced the establishment: Drath Orphanage for Lost and Wayward Children.

Bit and Pet were untied in the foyer. Miss Drath told Ox to lock Jeffrey in the chicken coop, where he would be "dealt with severely in the morning." Jeffrey begged once again to be spared, but Ox gave him a kick that started him moving quickly down a dim hallway.

Miss Drath lit a candle and held it overhead. Under the flame, her face looked yellow and waxy. "You two follow me."

Bit twisted at a corner of her pocket and glanced at Pet. Pet's eyes narrowed and darted about the house, lingering on the windows and doors. Then she gave Bit a little nod and they followed the old woman up three flights of creaky stairs and down a series of hallways. The candle barely penetrated the darkened rooms on either side, leaving Bit with only a vague notion of an office, a parlor, and a dining room with stiff, straight-backed chairs around a square table. The whole house was damp, and smelled of mildew.

Miss Drath stopped at a door at the end of a long hall. "Keep quiet," she hissed under her breath. "I won't have you waking the other girls."

Producing a key, she opened the door and led them into the room. They were in a rear corner of the house. The A-frame ceiling was low, suggesting that this had once been an attic. Grimy blinds were pulled well down over the windows. A dozen lumpy cocoons scattered on the floor marked where the girls slept.

Drath led them to a spot in one corner and pointed to a rumpled burlap blanket. "The two of you can bunk here."

Bit stared at the bedding, which looked recently occupied. "Won't this girl need her bed?"

"No."

"She was adopted?" Bit asked hopefully.

"If that comforts you." There was no comfort in the grim smile that creased Miss Drath's face.

Pet picked up a corner of the blanket with her thumb and forefinger and inspected the mattress, which was no more than a few rags stuffed between two straw mats. "You can't expect me to sleep here. Take me to a private bedroom with a proper bed." For all her indignation, she spoke in hushed tones.

"You can sleep here or in the coop." Drath shot a bony finger at Pet. "Mark my words, Missy, I'll have no more of your nonsense. Breakfast is at o-seven hundred. Boys' dorm is off limits." With that she turned on her heel and left the room. A moment later, Bit heard the soft grate of the lock.

Pet sank to her knees and dropped her head in her hands.

"Don't worry," Bit said, "we'll get out of here." She patted her friend on the shoulder.

Pet pulled away. "Stop fussing over me. I'm all right."

Bit straightened the blanket. "Maybe it won't be too bad."

"Sleep there if you want. I refuse. That bed's probably loaded with fleas or cockroaches."

Bit was too exhausted to argue. Every muscle ached and sleep pulled at her eyelids. She crawled under the blanket and used her arm for a pillow. The burlap felt scratchy, but she was beyond caring. She could think about escaping and rescuing Dash tomorrow. What she needed now was a good night's sleep.

Sleep came mercifully, just as she felt Pet slip under the blanket. Then the cough, and the night was over.

How had she ended up in such a dreadful place? Miss Drath and Ox would turn a cold ear to her pleas, but there had to be someone reasonable she could talk to. She thought of everyone Jenny had told her about in the Plain World, but, except for Nell, there really wasn't a friendly face in Jenny's past. The schoolteacher was strict. The sheriff constantly accused Jenny of petty thievery—she was sure the other children set her up to take the blame. Even the doctor had been described as a busy, unfeeling man.

Another cough from across the room interrupted these thoughts. Pet turned, pulling the blanket off Bit.

Bit opened her eyes at last. Slipping softly away from Pet, she sat up and looked around. The other children were asleep except one little girl of about six, who stared at Bit with enormous eyes and broke into another gurgling cough. Dishwater hair fell in limp tangles over her cheeks, which looked sunken and hollow. Bit smiled sympathetically, but the girl looked back vacantly.

Bit spread the blanket gently over Pet, and rose. She tiptoed to one of the windows and drew up the blind. Rain slanted in gray lines and drummed against the building. In a yard below, a child's wagon jutted from a patch of weeds, exposing a rusty underside. Tied to a bay tree, a wooden swing dangling from a single strand of rope pitched back and forth. Clothes left soaking on a clothesline tossed and shivered in the wind.

Pet slipped beside her and looked out.

"Are you all right?" asked Bit.

"Just peachy," said Pet, rubbing her arms to stay warm. Her eyes narrowed as she looked outside. "Just another fine day in paradise."

"I'm sorry I got you into this."

"Let's just worry about how we're getting out."

Bit pointed to the steep, slanting roof of the second floor below them. "We could try climbing down that, and sliding down the drainpipe."

Pet's eyes narrowed. "The shingles are slippery."

"But we can try, right? And now we know where the doctor lives. We can be there in a few hours."

"Sure. A nice little walk in the wet and cold."

"But we'll go, right?" Bit asked.

"I didn't say I wouldn't. I only said it's miserable out."

Bit was about to turn and hug Pet when an old woman stepped from behind a row of tall cypress bushes that lined one side of the back yard. She stooped under a black umbrella and wore a tattered brown cloak over her shoulders. Deep wrinkles crisscrossed her face. Her left eyelid drooped, but she fixed her right eye firmly on Bit.

Bit shrank back. "Why is that woman staring at me?"

Pet scratched her arm. "Maybe she's one of Drath's cronies, keeping an eye on us."

Five hard clangs on a bell from somewhere in the house made Bit turn. The other girls scrambled out of their blankets.

Most had slept in their clothes, a patchwork of dresses with big pockets sewn in front. The bedding was rolled up and pushed to the wall.

"You two," a girl called to Bit and Pet. "Go fetch the bucket." She was about sixteen, with stout arms and shoulders. Dark circles under her eyes made her look like an owl.

Pet smoothed the wrinkles on her shorts. "Were you addressing us?"

"You heard me," said the girl. "Fetch the water."

Pet studied her nails. "We do not fetch. We are served."

Clenching her fists, the girl stalked over and scowled a few inches from Pet's face. The girl was six inches taller. Maybe Jenny could handle her, but not Pet. Bit put a cautioning hand on her friend's shoulder.

"Where's the water?" Bit asked.

"First floor, out the kitchen door. There's a well. Be quick. I won't be punished if we're late."

"Late for what?"

"Get going. You'll find out soon enough."

Bit and Pet found the door unlocked. Making their way down several flights of stairs, they found the kitchen door and the well beyond. Grabbing a bucket, and an old umbrella that leaned near the door, they ran for the well. Pet held the umbrella while Bit pumped the water. Some of it splashed icy cold on her arm.

She looked around, wondering if they could escape. They were in a side yard. A low wooden shack was the only barrier to an open field that lay beyond. Soft yelps and cries came from the shack. Miss Drath's bloodhounds.

"We could make a run for it," Bit said.

"Not now. We're being watched." Pet nodded to one of the house windows where Ox leered down at them.

"Tonight then." Bit carried the pail of water back to the house.

"Did you see the bristles on that Ox's nose," Pet said, as they walked back to the girls' dorm.

"I know," Bit giggled.

"Can you imagine him shaving it?"

Bit laughed again. That's what she liked about Pet. She was crusty on the outside, but could always make Bit laugh. Even now, when things looked bleak.

Back in the girls' dorm, a line quickly formed to use the bucket. The girl that had challenged Pet, First Girl, asserted her position at the head of the queue. As newcomers, Bit and Pet were pushed to the end. First Girl cupped some water in her hands and splashed her face. Then she wet her finger and scrubbed her teeth with it. Cupping more water, she rinsed her mouth and spit it out in the bucket.

"Disgusting," whispered Pet.

Each girl repeated the ritual, washing and spitting in the same water. No one seemed to notice that Bit and Pet didn't wash.

First Girl led the way downstairs to the dining hall. Sunlight was the only illumination, gray and dismal after it filtered through the rain and dirty windows. Peeling yellowed wallpaper lined the walls. A fireplace at the far end was unlit, and the room was as cold and damp as the dorm. There were long wooden tables and benches, and a dozen boys were already seated, chattering and laughing.

Bit and Pet sat with half the girls at a table. Another bell rang, everyone folded their hands, and the room fell silent. A moment later, Miss Drath, Ox, and a woman carrying a pot entered the room. The woman's apron was brown with food stains. She waddled as she walked, making her body jiggle like a vat of gelatin. Her face, red and angry to the roots, looked like a lobster just plucked from the kettle.

"Who's that?" Bit whispered to a girl beside her.

"The cook," the girl replied, under her breath.

The pot was put on a table at the head of the hall. Two lines formed, one of boys, the other girls. One at a time, a child approached the table, removed a wooden bowl from a stack, and held it out. The cook deposited a spoonful of gruel into the bowl while Miss Drath watched with folded arms.

Bit and Pet were pushed again to the end of the line. Hunger gnawed at Bit's stomach. When at last it was her turn, she watched with disappointment as a lumpy, sticky slop slid into her bowl. It smelled like stewed shoes.

Pet wrinkled her nose in disgust and looked like she was going to complain, but Bit pulled her friend away.

They sat, and after a short prayer of gratitude, led piously by Miss Drath, the children around them began eating. First Girl poured her food down her throat in one swallow, and rose. Pushing aside a little girl beside Pet, she sat down.

"Do you want something?" asked Pet.

First Girl batted Pet's bowl so it skated across the table and smacked into her own. Pet eyed her sullenly.

"Please," said Bit timidly. "She hasn't eaten since yesterday morning."

"She'll have to get her own. I found this touching my bowl, so it must be mine," said First Girl, her eyes challenging Pet to disagree.

Pet glowered a moment, then dismissed the whole thing with a wave. "Oh, take the disgusting mess. I couldn't get it down anyway." She scratched her arm, which was starting to look red.

Bit had been prepared to eat the food. She'd had worse

before coming to Aerdem. But she lost her appetite when she saw the cook's arms and hands. They looked like they'd been rubbed raw with a scrub brush, and were covered with oozing carbuncles.

Bit handed her bowl to the little girl with the gurgling cough, who stared at it like she'd received a gift from heaven. She ate the slop just as reverently, licking it off her fingers a little at a time. Bit hoped she'd get a smile out of the girl, but none came.

After breakfast, Miss Drath, Ox and the cook left the room. One of the boys followed them to wash the dishes. Bit expected the rest of the children would file into a schoolroom. Instead, they remained in the dining hall. A group of boys formed a knot of bodies along one wall and played dice. Three girls crawled into the fireplace and walled off the entrance with a tipped-over chair.

"What are they doing?" Bit asked a girl beside her.

The girl shrugged, and continued chewing a splinter in her finger.

"What happens now?" asked Bit.

"What do you mean?" The girl got the splinter out and started worrying at a hangnail.

"Don't we go to school, or do some kind of work?"

The girl looked at Bit as if she had fallen from another world. "This is Drath Orphanage," the girl said, as if that were all the explanation needed.

"I know it's raining, but don't you ever go out?"

"Sometimes Miss Drath takes us on an errand."

"You can't mean she shuts you in all day," Bit exclaimed.

The girl shrugged, lay down on one of the tables, and closed her eyes. No one took notice of Bit and Pet, except the little girl with the gurgling cough. She stared at Bit with glassy eyes and sat shivering against a wall.

"Come on," Bit whispered to Pet. "Let's look around."

They circled the room, checking all the windows. They were locked. Even if one opened, there was no tree or drainpipe to climb down. They wouldn't get far with a jump, which would result in a broken leg or a sprained ankle.

Bit stopped near the fireplace where the three girls still sat. She couldn't see their faces, but she could hear their conversation.

"Where's Jeffrey?" asked one girl.

"He escaped again," replied another.

"Did he make it?"

"Caught again."

"Is he . . . in the coop?"

"Where else? He'll never learn. He's tried more than any of us."

"He'll die trying."

"Naw. The bloodhounds will run him down first."

Pet pulled Bit away and they tried the door. A peek out revealed Ox snoring nearby on a stool. He leaned against the wall, his big belly rising and falling above his belt.

Bit closed the door. "We could try sneaking past him," she whispered.

Pet nodded. They opened the door again and stepped forward on tiptoes. They were barely out when the floor under Bit's foot creaked.

26

" 'Tis a pleasant day for the coop," said

Ox, without opening his eyes. "Nice 'n cold 'n wet. Would you like to join Jeffrey and the other chickens?"

Bit froze. She had to think fast. "No, sir. We were just looking for a blanket. One of the girls has a bad cough."

"That's nothing around here. Get back inside or you'll have more than a cough to worry about."

"Yes, sir."

Back in the dining hall, Bit twisted at her sleeve. Ox made her nervous. He had been watching her by the pump, and now again outside the door. He couldn't watch her forever. Tonight, she and Pet could try escaping out the dormitory window.

No one noticed that she had left the room. The cluster of boys still rattled dice in one corner. The Fireplace Club, as Bit had come to think of them, still met among the ashes of the hearth.

One boy sat on the edge of a table. He was about seven, and his legs stuck out from his short pants like toothpicks. He spent the whole morning pulling at the tongue of his shoe, which dangled from a dirty foot.

"If he doesn't stop, I swear I'll pull out every one of my hairs," Pet cried.

"He doesn't know any better," said Bit. "See, he's wearing two left shoes."

Pet scratched her arm—which looked quite red and angry—and withdrew into a cloud of sullen silence. Bit knew better than to try and pull her friend out of one of these moods. Especially now. Pet must be starving.

The morning ground on, broken only when a lad of fifteen, called First Boy, approached First Girl. His ears stuck straight out from the sides of his head and his lips were too big for his face. He bartered with First Girl for a marble she showed him. He offered her a ball of string, a frayed shoelace, and a pebble. She rejected each with folded arms. Finally he sealed the trade with a faded piece of ribbon.

Bit started to feel as dismal and oppressed as Pet looked. She rose and wandered around the room to try and shake the feeling. How could a place like this exist? How could anyone treat children this way? It made her heart ache.

She made a solemn vow. When she reached the doctor, she would tell him what happened here and make him shut it down.

At last the bell rang, and Miss Drath, Ox and the cook returned with the noon meal. The children lined up once again. They were given a ladle full of mushy turnips and a chunk of stale bread.

Pet eyed the food suspiciously. When they were seated she sniffed the bread and broke it open.

"It's moldy," she cried, flinging it aside.

Miss Drath loomed above her in a flash. "Our food isn't good enough for you?"

"It's not good enough for pigs," Pet screamed, springing to her feet. "The flour is probably filled with worms or boll weevils. Bring these children something decent to eat, and bring it now."

"I warned you, Missy, not to take that high-and-mighty tone with me." Miss Drath turned to the other children with a sly smile. "My dears, we are blessed here with a countess."

First Boy stood up. "A countess?" he said in mock amazement.

"Truly," replied Drath. "Children. I've raised you right, ain't I?"

"Yes, Miss Drath," they all replied at once.

"I've taught you fine and genteel manners."

"Yes, Miss Drath."

"Then show this young lady how we treat countesses in Drath Orphanage."

A mop and bucket filled with dirty suds were brought in. First Boy and several strong lads raised Pet on their shoulders. She tried to kick, slap and scratch herself free, but the rest of the children held her arms and legs. First Girl dipped the mop into the bucket. Standing behind the crowd of children, she placed the dripping mop on Pet's head. Holding it in place, she followed as everyone paraded Pet around the room.

"No," Bit cried. "You mustn't. Pray, don't hurt her. She won't do it again. Please stop. Please."

No one seemed to hear her. Their cheers filled the room. "Good afternoon, your ladyship." "Three cheers for the Countess." "Step aside gentleman, here's a *real* lady."

Bit ran to First Girl and pleaded for her to stop. She tugged at First Boy's shirt, begging him to spare her friend.

"Please," Bit implored Miss Drath, who watched the whole thing with a satisfied smile. "Make them stop. She won't do it again. Have mercy. For heavens sake, have mercy."

Miss Drath flattened a loose hair on her bun, which was

wrapped so severely the scalp at her roots was red. There was no mercy there.

Bit never felt more invisible. Never wanted more to be heard.

At last, a shrieking Pet was lowered to the ground. The children made a circle around her and the bucket of water was poured over her head. Everyone laughed and pointed. Pet sat glowering in a puddle.

"Children," said Miss Drath. "Return to your seats and finish your lunch."

The children filed back to the tables and began eating as if nothing had happened.

Miss Drath's eyes narrowed to thin slashes and she pointed a bony finger at Pet. "That, young lady, is how we treat countesses. Now clean up this mess, and while you're at it, wash all the windows." She spun on her heel and stalked out.

Bit was at Pet's side in a moment. "Oh Pet. It was awful," she cried, trying to dry Pet's face with her shirt. "I tried to stop them, but no one would listen."

Pet pushed Bit's hand away. "Stop fussing over me." Her eyes narrowed to two hot coals and she stared at a spot on the floor.

Ox had left, but returned now with another bucket of soapy water. He nudged Pet with his shoe. "She says you're to mop the whole room. Do it good, or you'll clean out the kennel."

Pet continued looking down.

"She will," Bit told him.

Ox shrugged, and left the room.

"Don't worry, Pet. I'll do it for you."

Bit picked up the mop and put her back into the work. She didn't mind. It gave her something to do. Pet wasn't used to cleaning, and she'd suffered enough. Besides, if the job wasn't done right, she'd be sent to the kennel. Bit couldn't risk that. They were escaping tonight, and she wouldn't leave without her friend.

Bit finished the floor and moved to the windows, using a scrub brush that floated in the bucket. Everyone had ignored her before, but now many of the children watched, especially First Boy.

She had finished half of the windows when First Boy leaned against the wall beside her. He smiled, revealing a space between his front teeth. Boys had smiled like that at Bit before, around the Rose Castle. She didn't know how they could dare, when everyone knew she was engaged to Dash.

"Why you doing that?" he asked.

Bit glanced at Pet, who had retreated to a corner of the room. She twisted her clothes, trying to wring the water out. She was shivering.

"She's my friend," Bit replied, scrubbing the window with a load of suds. "I want to help her."

He scratched his head. "Then why doesn't she help you?" He made a funny whistling sound when he spoke.

Bit removed a rag that was tied to the mop handle and began wiping away the suds. "You have no idea what she's been through."

The water in the bucket had turned brown. "Can you get me clean water?"

His eyes glowed as he stared at her. "Sure," he whistled.

He returned with a fresh bucket. "You're pretty."

Bit felt herself blush. "Can you get me a couple of blankets and some dry clothes for my friend?"

First Boy stood up straight and threw out his chest. "Leave it to me."

He returned a few minutes later with blankets and a bundle

of clothes. The clothes were little more than a patchwork of rags.

"You aren't pretty," he said, "you're beautiful."

Bit gave the girl with the gurgling cough one of the blankets and brought Pet the other.

"Change into my clothes, Pet. I'll wear these." Bit knew Pet would never wear the rags.

"I wouldn't if I were you," grumbled Pet. "They probably have fleas or lice."

"They look clean enough," Bit replied, with a little laugh. "Come on, we can change in that closet."

Bit reached down to help Pet up.

Pet gripped her hand tightly and looked deeply into Bit's eyes. The hard lines of her face softened. "Thanks," she said.

"Hey," Bit replied. "We stick together like glue—whatever may come, 'til the end. Right?"

For a moment the hard lines returned to Pet's face and there was a far-off look in her eyes. Then the moment passed and she smiled. "Right."

After changing, Pet huddled under the blanket to keep warm while Bit finished the windows.

"They never looked better," said First Boy, still hovering about her.

Bit looked the room over. It looked a little brighter.

Later that afternoon, the girl with the cough let Bit hold her. The cough had quieted and the girl curled up in Bit's lap. She stroked the girl's head.

She sat with several of the children at one of the tables. Everyone stopped jeering Pet as soon as the dousing was over. Now they acted as if it never happened. Bit guessed Miss Drath not only used such humiliations for punishment, but to let off steam in the orphanage. Having vented, the children were happy to let Pet into the fold.

Pet was not so willing to forgive, and sat slumped at a near-by table. Quick glances and a cocked ear convinced Bit she was listening to everything the children said. Bit listened carefully too, hoping to hear something to help her escape.

Everyone wondered why Miss Drath had not returned to inspect the room. It was unlike her. She'd usually be up here looking for flaws in the cleaning—any excuse to send Pet out to the kennels.

First Girl was convinced it was to make Pet wriggle. "Drath likes to keep us guessing."

"The old crow's probably cooking up something for all of us," said First Boy.

"But you didn't do anything wrong," said Bit.

"Exactly," everyone replied.

A dozen explanations for Miss Drath's absence were debated. Three were finally settled on. "She's collecting all the blankets so we sleep in the cold." "She's painting a heavy sign to hang around Pet's neck." "She's getting a lock for the basement—we'll be shut in the dark."

Bit shivered. She had to escape tonight.

The mystery of Miss Drath's absence was solved when Jeffrey rushed into the room. "There's an ugly old woman downstairs, arguing up a storm with Miss Drath," he exclaimed.

"Who is she?" asked First Boy.

"I don't know, but she's trying to get you two." Jeffrey pointed to Bit and Pet.

Bit's heart skipped a beat and she shrank back. She looked questioningly at Pet. It had to be the woman they'd seen from the window.

Pet's eyes narrowed. "Why does she want us?" She took a seat beside Bit.

"She says she's taking you out of here," replied Jeffrey.

"Aw, you're batty," said First Boy. "You've spent too much time in the coop."

"I swear it's the truth. Miss Drath shrieked like a vulture that she'd never let them go. The old woman was quiet but firm, at first. Then she threatened to bring the sheriff. Miss Drath laughed. The sheriff never bothered her. The old woman swore she'd never stop until she had them two."

"You heard all this?" asked First Boy.

"I was waiting in the hall for a lecture from Miss Drath, but she never got to me. She was that worked up. She asked what the woman would pay. The woman offered some square copper coins with holes in them. Miss Drath laughed. 'These are worthless,' she cried. She named her price. Two hundred rugdas."

"Is that a lot?" Pet asked. She scratched her right arm, which now looked as red as her left. "We're not from around here."

"Is it ever! The State pays Miss Drath ten rugdas a year to keep one of us."

"She's asking for what she'd get over ten years," Pet replied, tapping her head as she calculated. "Considering we'd grow up in three or four, if we haven't died first, that's a nice profit."

Jeffrey blinked and scratched his head. "I guess so."

"What did the old woman say?" Bit asked. She hugged the little girl tight to her.

"She told Miss Drath not to interfere. That she would have the children, one way or the other."

Bit looked out the dormitory window. She couldn't see the rain, but heard it pelting against the glass. Below, a gust of wind pulled the swing out at a crazy angle. The wind died, and the swing banged against the tree, only to be flung out again by another cold breath from the north. Deep shadows cut through the darkening night.

After dinner, they had marched to the dorm, where the other girls whiled away the time with the same monotonous idle nothings Bit had seen earlier in the day.

First Boy's infatuation with Bit paid off. He was above First Girl in the pecking order, and made it clear that she was not to bother Bit and Pet. Bit thought First Girl would object. But she obeyed like a seasoned soldier, well used to a lifetime of orders.

"Great," said Pet, "just great." She sat against a wall inspecting her arms. They were covered with a rash, and her face was red and swollen.

Bit turned from the window and sat beside her.

"Why didn't you get poison oak?" asked Pet. "You were right in the middle of it."

Bit looked at her own arms. "I don't know. Maybe I still will."

"No. You'd have gotten it by now."

"Pet? Who is that old woman, and what does she want with us?"

Pet's eyes narrowed. "I don't know, but I don't like it. Maybe around here children are bought and sold to the highest bidder, like sacks of potatoes."

Bit shuddered. "Do people really do that?"

"Why not? Miss Drath profits from these children."

"But why us?" Bit twisted her sleeve. She had tried not to twist it all day, but Jeffrey's tale about the old woman had rattled her.

"I don't know. Besides First Girl, we're older than the other girls here. Maybe she saw us last night when we were brought in, and thought we'd fit the bill for one of her customers."

"Fit the bill?" Bit asked in alarm.

Pet scratched her neck. "For servants or field hands, or who knows what else. All I know is she's a grotesque old hag. If she gets us, she'll drag us off to someplace far worse than this."

"We've got to get out of here."

"Not in this rain. The roof is too slippery."

"We've got to try."

"Bit, if I go out there now, the rain might spread the rash into my eyes."

Bit slumped. She felt trapped at every turn. Another day here was unthinkable. She'd managed to get down some dinner, but Pet still hadn't eaten.

And Dash was never far from her mind. Her heart ached every time she thought of him.

Pet pulled up a pant leg and looked at her calf. The rash had moved down her leg.

"I've got to get you something for that. It's getting worse," Bit said.

"I'll ask Drath." Pet stood and moved toward the door. "I can't stand sitting around, anyway."

Bit followed and stopped her. "No. Miss Drath hates you. I'll have a better chance."

Bit met Ox going down the stairs. She politely asked to see Miss Drath. Ox refused. She said her friend was sick. He cared not a whit. She said her friend was suffering, and couldn't Mr. Ox please help? It wasn't his job to help. Pray, couldn't he reconsider? It wouldn't take long. She wouldn't trouble anyone much. Not more than a little. She just needed a little ointment.

Ox was immovable as a block of granite. He caught a loose patch at her collar and pulled her to him, his breath a foul mixture of cigars, herring and whiskey.

"You're new here," he said. "But you'll learn quick." With a sharp pull, he tore off the patch.

"For the hounds," he said with a leer, then sent her scurrying back to the dorm with threats of the coop.

It was just these moments that Bit hated her timidity. She'd felt it when the children doused Pet, and now again with Ox. Jenny would have been tougher, would have been ready to fight—with words or fists.

Bit had to try again. Ox seemed to go off on errands. Maybe she could slip downstairs and go directly to Miss Drath. But would the old woman listen?

Bit pulled at her collar and felt where Ox had torn off the patch. His intent was clear. He'd use it to track her if she tried to escape. She couldn't worry about that now. She had to get Pet some ointment. Maybe if the rash were covered, it wouldn't spread in the rain. And maybe the wind and rain would throw off the hounds and cover her scent.

So the ointment was her first step. She ran her fingers over a piece of burlap on her shirt. She looked down and studied the patchwork. It was the uniform of an orphan.

But it was a good thing First Boy had gotten these clothes and the blankets, or Pet would have pneumonia. Maybe he could get the ointment too.

Bit poked her head out the door. The hallway was empty. Moving quickly to the boys' dorm, she explained what she needed to First Boy.

He combed his hair with his fingers and smiled, exposing the little gap in his teeth. "Leave it to me."

Bit moved nearer him and whispered. "Can you get me the umbrella in the kitchen?"

His face fell. "Don't try it. This is hunting night."

"What do you mean?"

"If the rain stops, Miss Drath will take out the blood-hounds," he replied, his little whistle emphasizing his words. "She says that after a storm, all the wet and homeless urchins creep out of their holes looking for someplace dry. That's when she nabs 'em."

Bit begged him to do what he could, and returned to Pet. A few minutes later Miss Drath herself entered with a small pot and a spoon.

"Well, Missy," she said, bending over Pet and squinting at the rash, "this is what you get for gallivanting like a gypsy. I dare say you've been sleeping in the bushes for months. Here you can stay dry and warm and get three squares."

Pet looked like she was going to reply, but Bit shot her a warning glance. The last thing they needed was another scene, right before they were escaping.

Instead Pet looked suspiciously at the contents of the pot, which looked like homemade paste. "What is it?"

"Never mind," replied Drath. "It works. I've got dozens of cures—for ringworm, measles, mumps—you name it. I avoid the doctor at all costs. He overcharges. Nosey to boot."

She pointed to Pet's clothes. "Take 'em off."

Pet glanced at the other girls, who looked on with mild interest. "Here?"

"Do you want this cure or not?"

Pet looked ready to refuse, but the rash was starting to weep. She began undressing with short, angry jerks at her clothing.

Bit called First Girl over, and together they held up a blanket to prevent further humiliation.

With a stiff arm, Miss Drath dabbed on the paste, poking and slapping with the spoon.

"Pray, can't you be gentler?" asked Bit. "The rash must hurt terribly already."

"I'm gentle enough," grumbled Drath. With short strokes she finished with Pet's face, then stood back to examine her work, not like a painter admiring a masterpiece, but like a tired laborer who has been smearing plaster all day. "There, you'll be better in a day or two."

Swatches of white crisscrossed Pet's chin, cheeks and forehead. Some of the paste had gotten into her hair. She tried to wipe it off, but it only stuck out further.

Reluctantly, Bit lowered the blanket. For a moment all the children stared, then burst out laughing. Miss Drath let them point and jeer long enough to turn Pet's cheeks crimson, despite the white paste.

"Enough," cried Drath. "Not another peep the rest of the night."

She spun on her heel and left. A short time later First Boy tapped on the door and entered with the umbrella.

"I wish you wouldn't go," he said, his eyes sagging. "You'll only get caught—and punished."

"I must," replied Bit. "I must get Doctor Jenkins, or a friend of mine will die."

Several hours later, the other children snored softly, except First Girl who watched from her blanket.

"You won't tell?" Bit asked her. She was afraid First Girl would alert Ox.

"It's your funeral."

"Thank you. If we reach the doctor, we'll get him to help all of you."

First Girl shrugged. Bit turned to the open window, where Pet waited. The rain had stopped. An ochre halo ringed the moon. The swing was still. In the distance, Bit thought she heard the bloodhounds baying. Strangely, it gave her comfort. If Miss Drath was out hunting, this was a perfect time to escape. She only hoped the dogs were tracking in the opposite direction from the doctor.

"Ready?" Bit asked Pet.

"Ready. You slip out first. Work your way down on your haunches. I'll follow with the umbrella."

"Right."

Bit took a deep breath. There was a drop of three feet down to the roof. The shingles still looked wet and slippery. Hanging on to the windowsill, she climbed out, then slowly sat on her bottom and began inching forward. The roof tilted at a frightening angle—scaling it would be a challenge even in dry weather. Wet, it seemed nearly impossible. The sheer slope made her feel she would roll off any moment. A wave of dizziness made her head spin. Flattening her palms against the rooftop, she tried to steady herself—and one of the shingles slipped.

Quickly regaining her balance, she jiggled the shingle. Finding it quite loose, she held it up for Pet to see. Pet nodded grimly.

She climbed out, the umbrella tucked beneath the back of her shirt, and soon squatted behind Bit. Bit moved forward again, little by little. The wind picked up. The swing flew out, then turning like a giant pendulum, crashed against the tree. Startled, Bit jerked at the sound and slid down a few inches before braking. Looking back, she saw Pet reaching toward her with outstretched fingers.

"That was close," Bit whispered.

The bright face of the moon faded behind fastmoving clouds. It started drizzling and the roof became slicker. The swing banged on the tree. The urgent wailing of the hounds grew closer.

Bit had to hurry. She inched forward again, little by little, until she reached the edge of the roof. Pet was right behind her, one hand out, fingers spread, hovering near Bit's shoulder.

Bit smiled back. "It's okay. I'm fine."

Pet dropped her hand.

The drizzle turned to rain. The wind struck with quick, sharp punches. Every motion felt precarious. Any moment they could be sent spinning off the roof.

Bit began making her way to the drainpipe. The wind was shifting erratically, buffeting her from one side or the other. She felt she could be swept off, despite gripping the metal gutter.

Pet also gripped the gutter. But her free hand was always near Bit's back. It darted out with each shift of the wind. Bit slipped a little to the left and the hand was there. She jerked right, and there it was again. Back and forth, back and forth, the hand stretched and withdrew, always present, always hovering just behind her shoulder blade.

At last, Bit could stand it no more. "You're making me nervous," she said, with a little laugh.

Pet nodded. But a moment later the hand was out again, floating near Bit's back.

At last Bit reached the drainpipe. The rain subsided a little, and another howl from the dogs floated to her, farther away this time. Below, the wind stirred the shadows among the cypress bushes.

She tested the pipe. It seemed secure. She slid half off the roof and found the pipe with her feet, which she wedged between the drain and the wall. She slid down slowly until she held onto the roof edge with her fingertips. Pet knelt just above, peering down.

Bit shifted her weight from the roof to the pipe. With a groan, the pipe swayed away from the wall. Still holding on, she fell backward. She wondered vaguely how long it would take to hit the ground. Her back would strike first. And break.

She wondered why she wasn't scared. Then she was. Not for herself, but for Dash. Dash would die because she had failed. And Pet. What would happen to Pet, stuck alone in the Plain World?

Then Pet's hand darted out—

A thought raced through Bit's mind, faster than she could cry out, *No, Pet! Please don't*—

Pet gripped Bit's arm.

—*I'll pull you down too*, Bit finished.

Pet's hand was steady, and with surprising strength pulled her back to the wall.

"That was close," said Bit.

Pet sighed in relief. "Too close."

"Can you hold the pipe while I climb down the rest of the way?" asked Bit.

"I think so."

With Pet holding firmly to the pipe, Bit climbed to the ground. Then she leaned against the drain to hold it steady. In a few moments, a smiling Pet joined her and they hugged each other.

"I can't believe we made it," Bit exclaimed. She paused, listening to the dogs howl in the distance. They sounded farther away. She had a real chance of making it to the doctor.

She started to turn away, when a deep voice spoke philosophically from the shadows.

" 'Tis a lovely night for the coop."

27

Ox emerged from the shadow of a cypress

bush. He wore a long coat, slick and shiny in the moonlight. The rain had subsided, but strings of water still trickled from a wide-brimmed hat. He worked at something in his mouth, like a cow chewing its cud.

" 'Tis a very pleasant night for the coop," he said with a leer, and spit out a brown wad of tobacco.

He grabbed Bit and Pet by the collar, one in each hand. Lifting them like rag dolls, he walked them on their toes to the coop.

The coop was in a far corner of the back yard, opposite the kennel. It was a low wooden shed. A haphazard series of slats formed the walls. Wire fencing inside and out confirmed that the shack's purpose was more than keeping chickens from roaming.

Ox kicked the door open and tossed them inside. He followed them in.

"I'll learn you not to run away. You," he said to Bit, "take off your shoes."

"Sir?" asked Bit.

Ox started unhitching his broad belt. "You heard me. Shoes off. Socks too. Lay down on your back with your feet on that." He pointed to a low bench in the middle of the coop.

Bit realized with horror what he planned to do. She'd never been hit, much less whipped. She had seen a gypsy man flogged once. The screams of anguish still haunted her. But there was something that frightened her far worse than the prospect of pain. A wave of embarrassment and shame seized her. She felt the blood drain from her face and her knees buckled. "Please, sir," she begged, "not there."

"When I'm done with you, you'll think twice about using your feet to get away. Shoes off, or you'll get double."

Bit trembled as she took off her boots and socks. The coop was dark. Along the walls, she could see the silhouettes of the chickens in their nests. A beam of moonlight passed through a gap in crisscrossing boards, but blessedly, it didn't fall on the bench. Maybe it would be all right and no one would see.

Then Ox adjusted the bench and the moonlight fell right on the seat. Her hopes sank that she'd remain in shadow.

He doubled the belt and smacked the bench with it. "Move," he said.

There was nothing she could do. She lay down on the straw, her whole body quivering, and put her feet on the bench.

From behind, she heard a gasp from Pet.

Bit wanted to close her eyes, but instead watched Ox's movements with numb fascination. He removed his hat and coat and tossed them aside. He unbuttoned his right sleeve and rolled it up, exposing a beefy arm. He raised the strap.

His arm froze like a statue. He drew his head back and tipped it a little to the side as he looked dumbly at Bit's feet. Then, ever so little, he winced, and slowly lowered the belt.

"Let that be a warning to both of you," he grumbled. He

didn't bother to put the belt back on. Quickly gathering his clothes, he left, pausing only to chain and lock the door.

Bit slid off the bench and scurried to one of the walls, where she buried her feet beneath the straw and hugged her arms around her knees. She was still trembling uncontrollably. She made no sound, but tears rolled down her cheeks and wet her neck.

She didn't dare look at Pet, but out of the corner of her eye she could see Pet walking around the hut, pushing at the walls, pulling at the chicken wire.

The coop was secure.

"Are you hungry?" asked Pet. "I'm famished. Could we eat the eggs?"

"Yes," Bit replied faintly.

Pet started gathering eggs. "We won't get sick, will we?"

Bit shook her head. To keep from starving, she'd eaten plenty of raw eggs, from the nests of sparrows and blue jays. But she didn't tell Pet that.

Rain fell in curtains around the coop. Pet pointed to a small hole at the bottom of one of the walls. "I suppose we can put them out there and let the rain wash them."

She made a nest of straw and arranged half a dozen eggs just outside the coop. Then she sat next to Bit.

The rain drummed on the roof and streamed dismally from the eaves. The slatted walls gave no protection from the cold night air. But Pet's body felt warm and comforting beside her.

"This won't be so bad," said Pet. "We survived a night in the middle of a waterfall, right?"

Pet drew two of the eggs inside. "How do you eat them?"

Bit showed her how to crack the egg in half, making a cup for the yolk and one for the white. Pet poured one down her throat.

"Not bad," she said. She put two eggs in her lap and handed Bit a couple.

Bit cracked open an egg, waiting with dread for the question that was coming.

Pet held up an egg and studied it. "Maybe this is why Jeffrey runs away so much. He can count on a decent meal." She cracked the egg against a board. "Bit—" she said softly.

Here it came.

"—What happened to your feet?"

Bit's hands trembled. No one in Aerdem knew about her feet. Not even Jenny.

She shivered and hugged herself tightly. She didn't want to think about it. She wanted to shrivel, to shrink away, disappear . . .

The worst was that she really might disappear—back into the blank, lonely times before Aerdem. But there was something else—beyond the bleak, empty years. She felt herself caving in, slipping, sinking. . . . The old horrors rose before her like specters and drew her back—down, down, down into a dark well of terror. . . .

Pet's voice, uncharacteristically gentle, reached out through the darkness and drew her back. "Maybe it'll help to talk."

She tried as best she could, sifting through fragments of memories. Thunderous red explosions, screams of women and children . . . Wandering alone in the wilderness, digging through snow to eat grass, digging deeper into the frozen earth to find insects. The numbness in her feet . . .

Coming out of the wilds and down into villages. The sound of moaning, babbling—the look of fear in peoples' eyes. What was it? Who was it? Looking fearfully around and seeing no one. Only the angry stares of the villagers, who picked up pitchforks and clubs. Then running and confusion and running and wandering and a never-ending aching loneliness. . . .

One of the chickens fluttered her wings, then sank deeper into the nest. The rain had slowed, and drops rolled slowly off the eaves and patted on the earth outside.

"What about your people?" Pet asked, after a long silence. "Was there no one to care for you?"

"There was, once. I barely recall them. I think there was a war. Then I was alone—I don't know how long—until some gypsies took me in. One of their women nursed my feet."

"You had frostbite."

Bit nodded and drew her feet out from the straw. "She had to cut off the tips of my toes, here, and here. She said the whole toe would fall off if she didn't. They were turning black. The red, these wrinkles, these blisters never went away."

She massaged her feet. "I still feel stabs of pain where the tips were."

Pet retrieved her stockings and boots. "You better put these back on."

"Do . . . do you think they're very ugly? Will Dash . . . find them repulsive?"

Pet cracked open another egg and slid the gooey yolk down her throat. "If he does, he'll hear from me."

Bit didn't feel reassured. Telling the story left her drained. She started to cry softly.

"Look, Bit, if you cry, you're going to make me cry. You know you will. See, I'm starting now. There's a tear, I swear. Look! There's another. I'll be a waterworks in a moment—enough to turn a mill—"

Bit felt a little smile form on her lips.

"—Enough to grind wheat for a year."

Bit laughed and wiped her eyes. She wanted to bury her head in Pet's shoulder and hug her and really cry, but she knew her friend wouldn't have it. "Thank you, Pet. You're a true friend."

Pet looked down.

How selfish of me, Bit thought. *Thinking only of myself, when Pet has her own worries.*

"We've been gone so long," said Bit, "your father must be frantic over you."

Pet's eyes narrowed. "Oh yes, he's just pining over his precious little daughter."

Bit didn't understand the sarcasm, or the silence that followed. But she gave Pet space and turned her thoughts to escaping. But how? Ox was always watching, and the bloodhounds would run her down before she got halfway down the street. Worse, time was running out. Every hour, every day that went by, Dash was being slowly strangled.

Try as she might to fight it, she felt gloom overtake her. "Oh Pet, what's to happen to us?"

Pet put her arm around Bit's shoulder and pulled her in tight. "Don't worry. I'm getting us out of here. Missy, indeed. They haven't heard the last from *this* countess."

"Scrub them taters good," said the cook. "They're for Miss Drath's table."

Bit and Pet were at a large double sink in the kitchen, washing a pail of potatoes in some icy well water. Ox had fetched them early the next morning and brought them here for work duty. "So you're properly punished and don't think about escaping," he'd said.

The coop hadn't been so bad. They'd buried themselves under a pile of straw, and, hugging each other, stayed snug all night. The next morning, they'd eaten more eggs before Ox arrived. Bit was relieved to no longer feel lightheaded from

hunger. She needed a clear mind to plan an escape that succeeded. She knew what would happen if she failed again. She
didn't want another encounter with Ox's belt. He wouldn't be
lenient.

The cook leaned a fat arm against a counter and smoked a
cigar. "You," she said to Pet. "Fetch a sack of oatmeal from the
pantry."

Pet nodded, gave a little curtsy, and smiled agreeably. "Yes,
ma'am."

She left the kitchen and returned a moment later with a
small sack. "All I could find was this little sack."

"That's it. Dump it in the kettle." The cook pointed her
cigar at a pot atop a metal stove. Wide and ponderous, the stove
was her twin.

Pet opened the sack. Before dumping it into the pot, she
looked inside. A tiny smile crept to the edge of her mouth.

"You," the cook said to Bit, "that's enough scrubbin'. Fetch
water and dump it in the pot. "You," she said to Pet, "start peel-
in' them taters."

Pet smiled pleasantly and applied herself industriously to
the potatoes with a little paring knife.

Bit took a pail beside the door and ran out to the well. It
had stopped raining, but gray clouds hid the sky and the air
nipped her cheeks. She looked around for Ox, but didn't see
him. It didn't matter. She wouldn't run off without Pet. She
needed a plan that would work.

She returned with the water and was sent out again to chop
wood, which she brought back to the kitchen door in a wheel-
barrow. After loading the stove with wood and lighting it, she
waited for further orders.

The cook still leaned against the counter. Pots and pans
hung on hooks above her head. The rest of the kitchen was

cramped. The double sink had brown and green stains and was rusted along the bottom. Catty-corner to the stove was another counter, home to a long wooden chopping block. In the pantry beyond, shelves filled with jars and sacks lined the walls from floor to ceiling.

"You," said the cook to Bit, "get some onions and peel 'em. Then chop 'em." The ash on the end of her cigar had grown.

"If you please, ma'am, how many?" asked Bit.

The cook's fat face, already red, turned redder. "Some! Don't you know what some means? Get going, or I'll clobber you with a rolling pin."

"Yes, ma'am." Bit scurried into the pantry and found a shelf lined with dozens of small sacks of onions. She loaded four into her apron and brought them back to the kitchen.

Peeling and chopping the onions was difficult. The knife was dull, and the edge uneven, curving in where it should have curved out. The chopping board was warped, and rocked and tapped on the counter every time she came down with the knife.

The gruel sputtered angrily in the pot. It needed to be stirred or it would burn. The cook made no move toward the stove. She still leaned against the counter, one hand cupping a red cheek, the other holding the cigar with an ever-growing length of ash.

Bit looked meaningfully from the pot to the cook, but the stout lady made no move toward the stove.

"Ma'am?" said Bit. "Shouldn't we stir the oatmeal?"

"I'll say when somethin's stirred or not stirred. You just mind them onions." The cook blew out a gray cloud of smoke that burned Bit's eyes more than the onions.

"But . . . won't it burn?"

By this time the oatmeal was erupting like a volcano.

The cook waddled to the pot and glanced down. "I'll say when somethin's cooked or not cooked." She emphasized her words by stabbing the air above the pot with her cigar. The ash looked ready to fall.

"Ma'am, careful—"

Too late. The ash fell into the pot. The cook snatched up a wooden spoon and tried to fish it out, but the oatmeal bubbled too violently. Giving up the quest, she stirred the ash into the food.

"Adds to the flavor," she said, with a wink.

Bit turned sorrowfully back to her onions, which she finished chopping in short order. Then she and Pet were ordered to help serve breakfast in the dining hall. Bit carried up the heavy pot of oatmeal, which smelled a little burned, and Pet carried a tray of wooden bowls. Bit watched sadly as the children ate. They didn't seem to notice anything wrong, which made her feel worse.

Afterward, back in the kitchen, she washed, peeled, and quartered carrots; she peeled and cored a dozen apples and put them in the oven; and kneaded dough for Miss Drath's daily bread, which must be baked fresh, she was told.

Pet helped too, always smiling, curtsying, agreeable, and taking orders with uncharacteristic amiability. But while the cook's back was turned, Pet's eyes narrowed and pried and searched every corner of the kitchen. What she was thinking, Bit couldn't tell. But some scheme was afoot.

While the bread was in the oven, the cook took Bit down to the cellar, where an astonishing array of meat hung on hooks. There was mutton, beef, and pork, rabbits, duck, and pigeons, venison, and wild boar; enough to feed a village for a year. Her heart wrenched and twisted at the thought of what the half-starved children upstairs were eating.

The cook cut a slab of choice filet, and directed Bit to carry a half dozen pigs' knuckles. Back in the kitchen, the knuckles were tossed into a pot and simmered with some limp vegetables and a few other scraps and leftovers. Meanwhile, the cook sliced off a pound of the most tender portion of the filet, and fried it in onions and butter. The aroma made Bit's mouth water, and she longed for a bite.

When the meat was done, the cook slid the filet onto a plate, pulled up a stool, and began eating. "Don't say nothing," she said with a wink, "and I'll give you some gristle to chew."

"Yes, ma'am." Bit had no desire for the gristle, but she could save it for one of the children.

After eating, the cook put the rest of the meat in a large chafing dish, and surrounding it with carrots, celery, onions, garlic, and fresh herbs, popped it in the oven to roast. Soon a delicious smell filled the kitchen.

It didn't last long. The pot of pigs' knuckles came to a boil and the rising steam carried a sickly stench. The meat had not been properly salted. Even the cook made a wry face.

Bit was certain where the knuckle stew would go. "Ma'am," she said, trying to think of some way of sparing the children from this dreadful concoction, "I think it's turned."

"Nonsense," replied the cook. "It just needs a little doctoring," and she poured in a quart of vinegar.

At noon, the roast filet came out of the oven, as succulent and fragrant a dish as Bit had ever seen in the Rose Castle. The cook sliced this up, taking out a few of the rarest cuts for herself, and laid the rest on a huge platter surrounded by hot bread and butter, asparagus, and candied yams.

Pausing to take a few bites of the roast, she carried the platter to Miss Drath's table. While she was gone, Pet sidled up beside Bit, who was stirring the knuckle stew.

"It's not fair," said Bit. "The children will eat this slop while Miss Drath eats like a queen."

"I've got a plan," said Pet. "Trust me. I'll get us out of here. It'll take a little time, a little patience."

Bit stifled a little sob. "We don't have time. Dash is dying."

"This will work. Shh, here comes the cook. At lunch, I'm going to do something. Don't stop me."

The cook returned with the platter. Some choice slices of beef remained, glistening in pale-red juices. The vegetables were gone, but half a loaf of bread remained. Hope sprung in Bit's breast that these leftovers would be given to the children. What delight and ecstasy they would feel. What gratitude. It would seem like some great holiday, and their little faces would brighten and come alive.

If only Bit could see that, once. But her hopes were dashed when the cook directed her to take the platter out to the dogs. The kennels were snug, with plenty of fresh straw. She expected the scent of the meat would set their tails wagging, but they watched her suspiciously when she entered, and bared their yellow teeth.

She quickly tossed them the food and ran back to the kitchen. There, she assisted the cook and Pet in carrying the knuckle stew up to the children, along with some stale black bread.

The cook led the way, allowing Pet to drop back a pace. "Remember," she whispered, "don't try and stop me."

Bit felt her heart flutter. What was Pet up to?

Miss Drath was waiting with Ox by the dining room door. "I understand you two have been behaving and working hard."

Pet gave a little curtsy and looked down demurely.

"Coop and strap. That's all it takes," said Drath with a

satisfied smile. "Well done, Ox."

Ox grinned broadly and winked at Bit in a way that made her flesh crawl.

The dining room was unchanged. The children sat quietly with folded hands and bowed heads. Only First Boy looked up, trying to catch her eye. She smiled at him and his face lit up.

The two lines were formed, and Pet was given the job of ladling the stew. The cook stood to her left, her big arms folded like lumps of raw dough. Miss Drath was on the other side, hands squared firmly on her hips. Bit's job was to hand out the bread. She was between Miss Drath and Pet. Ox stood at the side of the table, scratching his belly.

At the head of the line, First Boy approached the table and held out his bowl.

"Don't eat it," said Pet in a loud, clear voice. "It's spoiled."

Miss Drath's eyes narrowed to slashes. "What?" she hissed.

"You heard me. None of you eat the food."

The children craned their necks to see what was happening. Ox's jaw dropped. The cook's face turned redder.

Miss Drath's eyes narrowed to daggers. She was about to speak but Pet leaped on the table and faced her. "An idiot could run this place better."

"That's enough," Drath thundered.

"No, you'll hear me." A wild glee shone in Pet's eyes, but her mouth was set and determined. Standing with her chin raised and shoulders squared, she was not only a countess, she was a great countess, despite the rags she wore.

"Please, Pet, come down and let us eat," said First Boy. "You'll only make it worse for all of us."

"Let her, or him, or her eat the food first," said Pet, pointing to the cook, Ox and Miss Drath. "But they won't. Because they know it's bad. It's not fit for the hounds."

"You've said quite enough, Missy," said Drath coldly. "You will rue this day."

Pet laughed and Bit felt her hopes sink. What was Pet thinking? She'd be thrown in the coop, and they'd lose another day. Or more.

Pet laughed again and struck the stewpot with the ladle until the room was ringing and everyone fell silent. "You won't touch me, because in one day I can double your profit."

Ox hitched up his pants and took a step forward. "Sure. But first you'll be shoveling dog logs for a week. Come along quiet, or you'll feel the end of my belt."

Miss Drath stopped him with her hand. Her mouth was open, and she stared curiously at Pet. "How would you do that?"

"To start with, fire the cook. She's lazy, inefficient, and she's stealing from you."

The cook turned crimson to her roots and lunged for Pet's ankle. "You little minx, I'll skin you—"

"Stop," said Drath. "What inefficiencies?"

"She orders supplies in small amounts. Instead, buy fifty and hundred pound sacks, and purchase by the barrel instead of the jar. It's just common sense. You'll get a better price."

The children looked at Pet with wonder.

"Go on," said Drath.

"Take Bit and a couple of the older children and let them cook. You'll save on salary."

A bright gleam lit Miss Drath's eyes. "What else?"

"Send back the staples you bought and get your money back. It's all worthless. Even the flour for your bread is wormy."

Miss Drath rubbed her hands. "Is there more?"

"Much more. Plant a garden and fruit trees in the back

yard. You'll get more than enough for you and the children. Put up the extras for the winter, or sell it in the village so these children can have decent clothes. Do you want me to go on?"

"Yes, dear girl, yes!"

"I will." She folded her arms. "But first, everyone calls me Countess."

"Never," cried Ox.

"Shut up," Drath said to him. "What else?" she asked, turning back to Pet.

"Look at these children. They're dying of boredom and ill care. If you won't do something to help them, let them help themselves."

"These children have nothing to offer. They are dull and dimwitted."

"No," said Pet. "They're cold, beaten, and starving, not just for food, but for a little love."

"Perhaps," Drath replied, "but what can you get out of him, or her?" She pointed to the boy with two left shoes and the little girl with the gurgling cough.

"They could earn a little money. They could make things. Bit's clever with her hands. She could show them how, and you could sell what they make."

Miss Drath shook her head. "No, these children have nothing to offer. Don't blame me. I didn't throw them away. I give them a place to live out their short, sorry lives."

"I'll prove it to you," cried Pet, her eyes blazing passionately. "Give me a chance, and I'll have them paying their fare. If I can do that, will you feed and clothe them properly?"

Miss Drath stroked her chin. "First, tell me what you have in mind."

Pet hesitated. "I would . . ." She obviously hadn't thought it out this far. "I . . ."

"It's just as I thought," said Drath. "There nothing we can do for them."

"But there is, there has to be."

"You're a clever girl. But these children are beyond any of us." Miss Drath addressed the children. "Everyone, listen to me. From now on, you will address this young lady as Countess. You too, Ox, and escort the cook off the premises." She started to turn away.

"Wait," said Bit. A crazy idea flashed in her mind, a way to help the children, and also to escape. "A play."

Everyone ignored her, except Pet, who seized the idea. "A play! Let us put on a play, in the village." She lifted the ladle triumphantly. "We can sell tickets or collect donations."

"Impossible," said Drath. "They've no talent."

"All of us have something."

Miss Drath's eyes swept over the ragtag group of orphans. "Not them. They come from nowhere, and they'll go nowhere. They're mistakes, the offspring of mistakes, the dregs of the world."

At a loss for words, Pet looked at Miss Drath in dismay.

Then something strange happened. The children melted from the line and walked slowly toward Miss Drath. Those in front reached out their hands to her.

"I can sew," said First Girl. "My name is Marianna."

"My name is Ralph," said First Boy, "and I can dance."

Jeffrey stood on one of the benches. "I can play the fife."

More children stepped forward.

"I can whittle."

"I can fish."

"I can do a back flip."

From the back of the crowd, someone started singing. A gurgling cough broke in on the song, but then the throat was cleared and it started again. The voice rose higher and higher, pure, sweet, and angelic. Bit's heart swelled, and her spirit soared. She was lifted from the dingy dining hall and transported to a sunny meadow of fresh grass, wildflowers and sparkling dewdrops.

The singer drew near, and the children parted as she glided forward. Bit could see her now, the girl with the tangled hair and vacant stare. Her eyes, no longer glassy, were alive and bright with hope.

28

Several hours later, a cheerful fire

crackled in the hearth of the dining hall, filling the room with warmth and light. The children were grouped in little beehives of activity. First Boy, who now insisted that they call him Ralph, was teaching four children how to do a jig. To the rat-a-tat of a drum, they lifted their knees to the sky and skipped, pranced, and capered in happy circles.

Jeffrey accompanied the drum with a lively tune on his fife. The beat, the trills, the leaping melody made Bit tap and move her feet from heel to toe, until it was all she could do to keep from jumping off the bench and dancing with Ralph and his troupe. The drummer was none other than the boy with two left shoes. He still didn't speak. No one knew his name, so they just called him Lefty. But he kept perfect time on that drum, which was only an empty gallon tin can.

Having mastered the dance at last, they paraded around the trestle tables, which had been transformed into small work-shops. At one, Marianna led a team of busy tailors, hemming cuffs, taking in waistlines, fixing collars. At another, the chil-dren made props for the play. The most complex was a roast turkey. Under Bit's direction, they'd shaped the bird with wire and covered the outside with paper strips dipped in a flour paste. The sculpture had dried, and they were painting it with honeysuckle and umber colors Pet had found in the basement.

More props were assembled at a third table, where a group of children polished a cup and saucer, a platter, a water goblet, a wineglass, and a pair of candlesticks borrowed from Miss Drath's table. On the floor behind them, Bit had stretched out some old sheets and drawn outlines for the scenery. Using ashes, she'd dabbed on numbers to show where each color would be painted. She gave the painting job to the Fireplace Club, who followed her plan to a tee, whistling or humming as they stroked their brushes. Jeffrey's music had captivated everyone. They polished and clapped; they sewed and stamped their feet; they painted with one hand and slapped their knees with the other.

As she watched the children, Bit's heart swelled until little tears of joy salted her eyes. It was all she could do to focus on her own task, which was to write the play. Sheets of paper were scattered on the tabletop. She had a rough outline in mind, and had started writing the dialogue.

The play was to be in two acts. The first was a kind of variety show where all the children could show off their talent. There would be singing, dancing, tumbling, and a few good jokes thrown in. The second act would be about the orphanage. Jeffrey was cast as Ox, and Marianna as Miss Drath. The prize part went to Ralph. The biggest among them, he would portray the cook.

Bit wasn't concerned about everyone learning all the lines, though the play was scheduled for tomorrow afternoon. They were children. They knew how to play. They knew dress-up and tea parties and games of doctor and nurse. They knew sheriff and thieves, knights and dragons, and pirates on the high seas. And heaven knows they knew the orphanage and could pretend at that.

What troubled her was whether she and Pet could manage to escape. Pet had understood the idea instantly. Hopefully, they would draw a big crowd. Something was going to happen in Act Two that would create pandemonium. They hoped they could slip away in the confusion.

What was surprising was that Miss Drath had gone along with the idea. Pet had convinced her with an argument she could not refute. That even if the play was bad, the villagers would give donations out of pity, and, "Any money is good, if it is safely collecting interest."

Pet was downstairs with Miss Drath now, going over plans to squeeze more profit out of the orphanage. Bit felt a surge of pride for her friend, for standing up to Miss Drath, for demanding to be heard. But Bit felt a little pang of sadness for herself. Except for Pet, no one had listened to her.

She didn't want to be this way, but she didn't know what to do. Sometimes, back in Aerdem, it felt like she wasn't even in the room. Oh, everyone talked and smiled at her, but did they ever see her? No. Except for Pet, Jenny, and the Pondit, she felt invisible. Unimportant. Someone they expected to have around like a favorite chair or lapdog. She'd been this way so long she could probably live with that, if it wasn't for Dash. If she ever got back to Aerdem, if he ever recovered, what would he think of her? Could she ever attract him like Vieveeka had?

She didn't know. How could she know what was in Dash's heart? But she made a solemn vow: The next time she needed to be heard, she'd be heard.

As if to seal her vow, Bit collected her papers, put them in order, and straightened them with a determined tap on the table. Just then, Pet burst into the room and closed the door behind her with a triumphant flourish.

"I've got the old witch eating out of my hand," she said, striding to Bit, her face beaming. "I'm her 'own dear girl,' her 'clever countess,' her 'little lieutenant.' Can you imagine?" She rubbed her palms. "Everything is going as planned. She'll give us whatever we want. She's out printing handbills right now. We'll pass them out tomorrow morning after some kind of service the whole village attends." She made a megaphone with her hands and called out, "Ladies and gentlemen, presenting for your entertainment pleasure, the one, the only, the stupendous Orphan Players!"

"Whoa, Pet, slow down." Bit laughed. "Is it really all right? You're not pressing her too hard?"

"Not a bit. I've thought of a dozen ways she can make more money here. It's like pulling fish out of a barrel."

"But won't she drop you as soon as she's heard your ideas?"

"Never. I let out just a little at a time, just enough to keep her drooling, and drop hints of more to come. Did you know they have a laundry room here? It's huge. She could wash and press for the whole village. Can you imagine how much she could make? Then there are a dozen rooms on the first and second floor that are completely unused. She could rent those out. And that's just for starters. Why, look over there, Marianna could start a tailoring business."

"Careful—"

"I know, I know—we don't want Drath working the children. They need to be running around and playing and everything. I'd just throw that out to entice her, then hit her with something even more enticing. Don't worry, there's plenty to keep the old bird occupied without burdening the children. I've a million ideas bubbling in my head. I'm practically dizzy with them." She stopped at last to catch her breath. "How's it going here?" Her eyes, on fire with excitement, swept the room.

Bit smiled. "We'll be ready, I'm just putting the finishing touches on the script."

"When do you start rehearsing?" Pet's face was aglow, and a sly smile crept to her lips.

"An hour or so. Why?"

"Because I have a surprise for you."

"A surprise?"

"Yes, but give me a moment. I want to check in with everyone."

Pet rushed off to each of the workstations, smiling, laughing, patting everyone on the back, calling out encouragement. She ruffled Lefty's hair, and he looked up at her like she was his mother and it was his birthday. She draped her arms around the Fireplace Club, and they hugged her back. She marveled at Marianna's completed alterations, and Marianna grabbed Pet's hand and whisked her across the room, where they trotted along with Ralph's dancers, kicking and jumping until everyone fell on the floor in hysterics.

She watched several of the skits, and told them they were the best little acting troupe in the world. They swore they wouldn't let her down. Everything would be ready, and they'd be ready too.

At last, with sparkling eyes and a smile that poured from the heart, Pet floated across the room and threw her arms around Bit. Despite her rags, she seemed more at ease, more at home and happy occupying herself the way she had the past few hours, than at any time walking the lonely halls of her father's mansion.

"Now," she whispered slyly, "Promise not to react, at least

not in front of Miss Drath."

Bit's heart fluttered. "What are you up to?"

"Promise?"

"I promise, I promise. Don't make me wait another moment."

"I won't." Pet kissed Bit on the cheek and rushed out of the room. A moment later she returned with a small person who rolled and tumbled across the room until he fell in Bit's happy arms.

"Yalp!" Bit exclaimed. Tears sprang to her eyes and she hugged him tight. She was so glad to see him she didn't want to let him go, but at last she did and he scrambled off her lap and bowed so low his head touched the floor.

"My apologies, Your Majesty," said Yalp, his high voice an octave higher with excitement. "I tried to come sooner, but the magic wouldn't work. I don't know why."

"Then how in the world did you get here?"

"Do you know all those relics in the Crystal Room?"

"The ones Jenny's father always tinkers with."

"Right. I'd been tinkering with them too. The king and I thought one of them was a Transdevis."

Bit blinked.

"A traveling device," he said, clearing up her confusion. "Legends have been circulating for years about them. One tale describes an object very similar to one the king was playing with. The only way to tell if I had a Transdevis was to try out it. But first I needed to learn how to use it. So I studied the old stories carefully, piecing together clues and bits of information. My knowledge of magic helped, and well, I'm here."

A thrill ran through Bit. If Yalp could get here, then he could return them home safely, once they found the doctor.

"I had a pretty good idea where to find the doctor from

Jenny's stories," Yalp continued. "I figured I'd find you there too. But before I reached him, that old crow, what's her name?"

"Miss Drath," Bit replied.

"Right, dreadful woman with dreadful dogs. Did I ever tell you I'm afraid of dogs? Being little as I am, they think of me as a rabbit or a squirrel. Most unpleasant. Anyway, that dreadful Drath captured me. She thought I was a stunted child. But before she found me, someone else found me first." He paused and smiled, evidently pleased that everyone waited expectantly for him to continue.

"Who?" asked Bit, wondering how many more surprises there could be today.

"Why, Your Majesty, you of all people should know, since you have him right here." Yalp reached behind her ear where she suddenly felt a feathery fluttering. Bringing his hand around to her face, he held a little sparrow.

"Darter!" exclaimed Bit. "You're alive!"

Darter chirped happily and hopped to and fro, then flew to her shoulder and nuzzled her cheek.

She could hardly believe it. Darter. Here. Little tears of relief misted her eyes. "We better not let Miss Drath see you," she said to him, wiping her eyes with her sleeve. "We'll hide you in my pocket if she comes around. Okay?"

Everything had been going well this day. Everything pointed to success, from the moment Pet banged on the pot. The play would happen. The children were ready. She thought she'd never see Darter again. Yet here he was. And Yalp too, with a way home.

Home. She lingered on the word with a quiet joy. For the first time, she really allowed herself to believe, to hope that she could return.

But first, they needed to get away from the orphanage. She

quickly told Yalp and Darter everything that had happened, and how they planned to escape. Pet suggested Yalp could perform magic during the talent show, and that Darter could pretend to be a trained bird. Darter voiced his objections with a shrill tirade of chattering. But Pet argued it was the best plan, as it would make a strong ending to the first act. In reply, Darter skulked around one of the tables, scratching and ignoring everyone for several minutes. Finally, Bit pointed out that it would delight the children, whose future depended on the play's success. At last he agreed, which he communicated by pushing a cup of water across a table, flying several circles around the room, and then diving from the ceiling to the cup, leaving no doubt he understood the role of a trained bird.

The rest of the afternoon passed pleasantly. Pet left, having an appointment to study Miss Drath's books. Yalp gave her a list of chemicals he needed for the magic show. The first act would end with a bang of smoke, a perfect cover for their escape. Pet assured him she'd get the chemicals, if not from the old witch, then from the village apothecary.

Meanwhile, Bit put the finishing touches on the scenery. She tore pieces of wallpaper from the already torn and peeling walls, and pasted these haphazardly on the dining room scenery. She stepped back to admire her work. The set looked just like the orphanage. The turkey looked golden and glistening, like it had come from an oven. A glow of contentment filled her head to toe, something she always felt when she made things. But now it was triply special because of the pride she saw in the faces of the children.

With the props and sets completed, Bit rehearsed the second act with the children, until the play ran smoothly. Afterward, Yalp performed magic for the children. Coins disappeared behind a child's ear, only to fly out the other side. A deck of cards passed through a table. An empty cup filled with water, then drained again before their eyes. Objects expanded and shrank, were broken and restored. For the finale, he levitated Belle, the girl with the cough, until she giggled with glee.

Pet shuffled into the room, glanced at Bit, and fastened her gaze on the floor. Bit heard a little alarm bell ringing in the back of her mind, but what could go wrong? Thirty minutes ago Pet had been ecstatic. Perhaps it was just fatigue. The escape last night, sleeping in the coop, the whirlwind of activity around the play—she must be exhausted.

Pet made her way around the trestle tables, looking at the props and the costumes. Bit smiled and tried to catch her eye, but it was always turned the other way. Curious now, Bit stepped toward the dining hall scenery where Pet was standing, but her friend moved away and joined the knot of children watching Yalp.

Bit slid beside her, waiting, knowing her friend needed space. At last, Pet slipped her hand into Bit's and drew her to one of the windows. It still shone from Bit's cleaning, but the outside was spotted and dirty despite the constant rain.

Pet worried at a thread on her pant pocket. "Is the play important to you?"

"Of course it is."

Pet nodded, a little frown on her lips. "Of course." She pulled out the thread and studied it before tossing it away. "You wouldn't let anything stop the play, would you?"

"Of course not, how could you think such a thing?"

Pet looked up for a moment and searched Bit's face. "Right," said Pet, dropping her eyes again. "And you care about me, don't you?"

"You must know I do. After everything we've been

through, you're my own true friend."

Pet gnawed at the corner of her lip. She had gotten mascara from somewhere that made her eyes look darker.

"Pet, what is it? Has something gone wrong? Please tell me if it has. It's better if I know."

"Right." Pet worked at another thread, this time on her sleeve. Instead of breaking off, it started unraveling. "Don't get alarmed. It may be nothing . . ."

"Please, just tell me."

Pet nodded. "It's that old woman. The one we saw from the window. She's downstairs right now, arguing up a storm. I was listening from behind a door."

Bit fought the urge to twist her sleeve. "What did she say?"

"She wants to take us away. Tomorrow morning."

"Miss Drath won't let her," said Bit. "We're too valuable to her now."

"Right, but . . ." Pet paused and searched Bit's face again.

Bit looked back steadily, trying to show she was strong enough to hear anything. "But?"

"Something the old woman said. Something strange. She said she must have those two children—meaning us. I peeked around the door. There was a strange light in her eyes. I think she's quite mad. She said Drath does not know what she's up against. There are powers, great powers at work. Monumental things at stake. And she will have those two children."

Bit swayed on her feet and leaned against the wall for support. "Pet, I'm frightened. What does she want with us?"

"I don't know, but Miss Drath won't let us go, and we're surrounded by friends, the other children, and Yalp and Darter. They'll protect us."

"We must leave, now," Bit gasped. "That old woman is determined, she will keep trying until she gets us."

"But we're leaving tomorrow afternoon, after the play. Surely that's soon enough."

"Is it? What if the old woman has allies and attacks tonight?"

"Nonsense. If she had allies, she'd have gotten us already. No, the best thing is to stick with our plan. Besides, how could we leave now?" Pet seemed to almost smile.

"Yalp could do it. I hadn't thought of it before, but he could use the Transdevis and whisk us to the doctor."

Pet sagged. "But the play . . ."

"There's no time—"

"There is. You said we'd do the play." Pet's lower lip trembled. "The children will be disappointed, you know they will. Look at their faces. They've been looking forward to this. You have too. I can tell. You haven't smiled like this in days. Don't think I haven't caught you whistling to yourself."

True, Bit admitted to herself. She'd been surprisingly happy during the past hours. Writing the play, painting the sets, crafting the props—she felt like a bird that had just learned to fly, and was now soaring high above the trees, even to the clouds.

"Do you want to be the one to tell Belle, or Ralph, or Jeffrey that they can't do the play?" Pet asked.

"I wouldn't hurt them for the world," Bit replied. "But what good will it do if we're kidnapped? We must go. We have the Transdevis. Now's our chance."

Pet stared at the floor.

"I don't understand. You hate this place. You couldn't wait to escape."

"That was before," Pet replied, her lip quivering. "Everything has changed. I'm somebody here."

"I don't understand. You're somebody at home."

"No, I'm not," Pet cried. Her lip trembled violently. Like a stone tossed in a pond, the vibration spread through her body. She locked her jaw and clenched her hands. Tears welled in her eyes and she desperately fought them back.

"Pet, dearest, please tell me. What's hurting you so?"

Pet crumbled at last, and tears flooded her face. Heaving sobs wracked her body, and she choked and gasped for breath like a man drowning at sea.

At last the storm calmed enough for her to speak. "Please, give me this. What else do I have? You have Jenny and her family. You have the Pondit. Everyone loves you. What do I have? I'm ugly. Jenny hates me. No, don't argue, I know it's true. Except for you, no one likes me. They all laugh at me behind my back. Please, let me have the play. What else do I have? My mother ran off with a duke—"

"She left you?"

The mascara ran in charcoal streams down Pet's face. "She's been in Laskamont for a year. She never writes. She never sends for me. And my father . . . I'd be happy if now and then he said a kind word to me, or looked pleased when he saw me, and smiled a little. But he hates me—"

"You can't mean that—"

"It's true, he doesn't care if I'm alive or dead. I have nothing, no one to go home to. I might as well be an orphan. I have truer friends among these children than I ever had in Aerdem. Don't you see how they look up to me? Please, Bit, give me this. Give me these hours, and I'll follow you to the end of the earth."

29

Images of the old woman storming the

orphanage raced through Bit's mind. But the choice was clear. As frightened as she was of the old woman, she felt far more for the sake of her friend. Holding Pet, rocking Pet, crying with Pet, Bit felt her heart would break. She couldn't, wouldn't do anything to make her friend suffer.

She soothed and quieted Pet with soft caresses and hushes. They'd held on this long, she told her. They could hold on a little longer. They'd still do the play. She promised. Pet's shoulders gradually calmed, and she cried softly. Bit continued to reassure her until at last, Pet threw her arms around Bit and swore she'd follow her anywhere and never leave her side.

While the other children were distracted by Darter's acrobatic flights around the room, Yalp joined Bit and Pet to see what was wrong.

Bit quickly told him about the old woman's threat. "The escape after the play must succeed," she said. "The longer we stay here, the greater the chance of being captured. We can use the Transdevis to get to the doctor during the intermission. It's a blessing. I didn't know how we'd persuade him to go to

Aerdem. But we can prove we come from there with the Transdevis. One of us can move to another room with it. That should convince him."

Yalp looked at her sadly. "I'm afraid not, Your Majesty." He drew a copper sphere from beneath his robe, the same one Jenny's father had been tinkering with the day they first heard about the danger. The sphere was dented and spidery cracks spread across the silver mirror.

"But . . . it still works doesn't it?" Bit already knew the answer.

"No, Your Majesty. When I landed in the Plain World, I was on the edge of a rock. I lost my balance and fell. The Transdevis flew out of my hand."

Pet wiped her eyes and examined the device. "Have you tested it?"

"Many times. It's no use."

"What if we replaced the mirror?" asked Pet.

"I'm afraid this is no ordinary mirror. It's made from sheep's horn. It takes months to soak, soften, and polish so that it's transparent. But there may be other things wrong with the device."

"Months . . ." said Bit, her spirits falling. "Dash will die in a day or two."

"What about your magic, the way you got us here in the first place?" Pet asked.

"I tried that too," Yalp replied. "None of my magic works here. I don't know why."

"But you've been doing it all afternoon for the children . . ."

Yalp shook his head. "Stage magic. Sleight of hand. Tricking the eye."

"Then we're stuck," said Pet.

"No," cried Bit, feeling a flame light inside her. It was a

new feeling, and it made her feel strong. "We got off the waterfall. We found Jenny's old cottage. We've changed things forever for these children. We'll find a way. I won't give up, no matter how long it takes."

Still, she had to wonder. Would she be in time for Dash?

Dark clouds cut the sky in jagged puzzle pieces. Bit expected to see blue in between, but high above it was overcast and white, making the sky look alien. She couldn't decide if the lower clouds were leaving or bringing another storm.

Pain jabbed her feet. She was trying to rest them, hoping they'd be ready when she ran. She sat with her back against a spindly tree, with Belle perched on her lap, working at the tangles in the girl's hair. She kept an eye on the activity backstage, and watched with wonder as the audience grew.

The park was a large rectangle of thick grass, mostly green, but yellowing in places. A dirt road and a shoulder-high fence surrounded the area. The three rails of the fence, made of narrow logs, would be easy to climb through to reach the thick growth of ivy and oak beyond.

She had considered several escape routes. First, a stream bordered the east side of the park. Once there, they'd be hard to track. But it would be difficult to cross the park undetected. Worse, massive clumps of poison oak along the banks of the stream made that way impassible for Pet. It would have to be a last resort, if all else failed.

Bit had a better way. Atop a leaf-strewn embankment behind the stage was a line of picnic tables. Beyond that was a steep hill, dense with grass, shrubs, and a wall of trees. Twenty feet up, and they would disappear into the foliage. When they reached the top of the hill, they'd meet a main road out of the village.

There were two ways of getting to the hill. The first was a set of thirteen pale brick steps to the left and rear of the stage. This led to the picnic tables. The second was a trail that started behind stage right and circled past the picnic tables. A quick climb over a sagging retaining wall and they'd be up the hill and into the trees.

The main obstacle to this plan was the stage, which was really a grand and airy gazebo, probably used more for concerts than plays. Built in a square, twelve narrow, rust-red columns held up a gray shingle roof. This angled up steeply to a rectangular tower, which was trimmed with finely carved molding and thin horizontal slats. A clock had been set on each wall of the tower, but the hands had either fallen off or were never added, giving Bit the eerie feeling that time had stopped.

The stage was open on all four sides, giving the audience a clear view of the escape route. New trees had been planted on either side, but they were still slender and provided little cover. Bit solved this problem with the scenery. Based on Jeffrey's description of the stage, Marianna's crew had sewn thick twine into the upper and lower edge of the scenery sheets. Leaving plenty of twine on the ends, the scenery was tied onto the inner columns from stage left to right, effectively blocking most of the view beyond. True, they couldn't stretch sheets from floor to ceiling, which was a good fifteen feet high. But the eye goes where it is directed, as Yalp pointed out, drawing on his experience with sleight of hand. Everyone would be watching the show.

The other obstacle was Miss Drath and Ox. If they were backstage, there would be no way to leave unseen. They had to be lured and held in the audience. To do that, Pet would call for them to sit out front, and dedicate the play to them. After that, Bit could only hope their innate curiosity would hold them when they saw themselves portrayed on stage. And still later, when the play took an . . . *interesting* turn . . . they would be forced to watch despite themselves. They'd be angry, but how could they stop the play with the whole village watching?

Bit smiled to herself. No one would listen to her before, but they'd hear her now. The play was her voice.

And it was ready. The stage had been set for an hour. Pet had been everywhere, supervising the placement of the sets, organizing the props backstage, making sure everyone was in the right costume, and a hundred other details Bit never thought of, but that needed to be done.

While this happened, Miss Drath fawned over Pet. She was her clever child and sweet countess, her little lieutenant and her little miracle. Pet smiled and curtsied, and turning away, rolled her eyes with disgust when Miss Drath wasn't looking.

As for Ox, he'd wanted to bring the hounds.

"Oh, leave the babies," Miss Drath had said. "We can get them fast enough if anyone runs."

"But Miss," Ox had replied, "I really think—"

"Think? I don't pay you to think. You're not clever enough to think. The children ate steaks last night, and pancakes this morning. They've never had such a meal. They won't run off."

Ox had winced and grumbled under this tongue-lashing. Now he and Miss Drath walked around the park, passing out handbills, "to assure maximum profit," according to Drath. A crowd of a hundred people had already assembled in front of the stage. They sat on blankets and clustered under big umbrellas lest the rain started again. Rain or shine, everyone had come for a good time. The lawn was a sea of picnic baskets, roast chicken, big bowls of potato salad, pies, and pitchers of iced milk and beer. Laughing children ran to and fro chasing dogs and balls. Parents scolded them mildly, and the children screamed back in delight.

Excitement crackled through the air. The audience craned their necks to look at the sets. Backstage, the children pulled into groups of two and three for some last-minute rehearsal. Their faces were fixed with determination. Every role, every task, no matter how small, was treated as important. Pet was everywhere, adjusting a child's costume, fixing makeup, going over and over the scenery changes with the stagehands.

The excitement was contagious. Pet was at her peak, and to see her friend so happy tripled Bit's joy. Still, she couldn't help thinking of the escape, and a nervous knot twisted in her stomach. She couldn't shake the feeling that she was being watched.

She scanned the faces of the audience, wondering if the old woman was there. No one looked her way, and she didn't see anyone with the drooping eyelid or the mass of wrinkles. Her eyes swept the park. Couples bundled in coats strolled arm in arm on the dirt road. Families clustered under trees at the edge of the grass. On the south end, wagons and buggies were parked in a dirt lot. On the north end, a yellow building housed a carousel, and Bit could hear the barrel organ piping in the distance.

It all seemed innocent and festive. Still, she couldn't shake the feeling that she was being watched. Turning, she stared into the dark shadows behind her, where a short time from now she would run. There was nothing. Only trees, dried grass, and fallen leaves.

Two birds flew from one of the trees and landed on the edge of the gazebo roof, where they warbled a hopeful song.

Belle stirred in Bit's lap.

"Must you go?" Belle asked. "I don't want you to."

After working on the play late into the night, Bit had gathered the children and told them about the escape plan. She had to, because they needed to continue the play while she and Pet ran. Afterward, Miss Drath would be furious, but if Bit reached the doctor, he'd protect the children.

"I know," Bit replied softly, working a comb through her little friend's tangles. "I don't want to leave you either."

"Then stay," Belle said plaintively.

"Hush, you'll see me again, I promise. If I can't get to Aerdem, I'll stay with you always. But if I do get there, I'll come back for you and take you there."

Belle stifled a little sob. "What's it like there?"

"Like a fairy tale, with pink towers and gay flags and fields of scarlet flowers, and wonders and magic and handsome princes—right out of your dreams."

"Then when you come back, I'll go there."

"Yes." Bit fought back tears and hugged the little girl tight. Pet trotted toward them.

"Better get backstage, Sweetie," Bit said to Belle. "We're going to start."

Belle ran backstage, stopping to throw her arms around Pet on the way.

"Everything's set," said Pet. "How are your feet?"

Pain still stabbed at Bit's toes, but she ignored it. "Don't worry. When it's time, I'll run."

"Right. I'll get Drath seated and we'll start." Pet gave her a quick hug and kiss, and helped Bit to her feet.

Once they were backstage, the children gathered around.

"Before we give the dedication to the old bird," Pet said, "we're going to give the real one."

"What do you mean?" Bit asked.

"Only this. We're dedicating the play to you."

Bit felt her face burn. "But everyone worked on it . . ."

Pet waved aside the objection. "Enough of that modesty. The play is yours. You wrote it. You directed it. You painted the sets. You designed the props. You were on your feet rehearsing late into the night, and even a few minutes ago, you were painting details on the scenery and helping Marianna with some last stitching."

"I couldn't have done it without all of you."

"No," said Marianna, the dark circles under her eyes sagging from lack of sleep. "We couldn't have done it without you."

"We made you something," said Ralph, his little whistle answered by the two birds on the gazebo roof.

He held up a patchwork shawl.

"It has a piece from each of our clothes," said Marianna, "to remember us by."

"I'll never forget any of you," Bit cried, tears running freely down her face. She wrapped the shawl around her shoulders. "I'll treasure it always."

Without saying a word, they drew together in a ball and hugged for a full minute. Then, as if reading each other's minds, cried out, "Let's do it!"

Pet ran onto the stage. Bit peeked around the edge of the scenery and watched, while the three clowns for the first variety act gathered behind her.

"Ladies and gentlemen," Pet cried. "May I have your attention, please!"

The hum of the crowd subsided. All eyes turned to Pet.

"Before we start, we'd like to dedicate this play to Miss Drath. She provided us with everything you'll see today. We thank her for that, and the opportunity to do this production."

Pet extended her hand to Miss Drath, who sat next to Ox in the first row. The orphanage director stood with clasped hands and rosy cheeks, and nodded and smiled to warm applause.

"And now," Pet exclaimed, "from far and wide and parts unknown, without further ado—the Orphanage Players!"

Bit signaled the clowns with a pat on the back and they tumbled onto the stage. Yalp led the way. He wore a big red nose and a pair of gigantic shoes with the soles flapping open in the front (a grudging donation from Ox). A second clown followed, played by a big overweight boy named Alexander. His face was painted white. He sported a blue wig, striped knee socks, and yellow suspenders. A wide, star-studded tie swung back and forth while he twirled a tattered old umbrella. A short boy named Mikey played the third clown. He wore an oversized pair of Ox's boxer shorts with flower pockets from an old tablecloth sewn on. An old pot without a handle was strapped to his head, and he did flips and cartwheels across the stage.

Meanwhile, the big clown walked to a stepladder and, looking sadly at the sky, opened his umbrella. Yalp put his fingers to his lips and winked at the audience, then sneaked up the ladder with a watering pot. The audience laughed as Yalp sprinkled Alexander through the holes in the umbrella.

The big clown scratched his head and moved to the other side of the stage. Mikey and Yalp went, "Shhh," to the audience and quietly brought the ladder behind Alex. Running up the steps, Yalp sprinkled him again. This went on several more times. Finally, Alexander saw Yalp and chased him up the ladder, where he leaped off and splashed into a washtub full of water.

The audience roared and applauded, especially three little children who'd crept to the front of the stage and giggled and laughed with delight.

Riding a tiny tricycle, Alexander chased the other two clowns off the stage. Bit signaled Ralph's dancers to enter, with

Lefty and Jeffrey right on their heels. With a one, a two, a one, two, three, Jeffrey launched into a rousing jig on his fife. With Lefty smacking steadily on his tin drum, the dancers kicked and strutted and stomped across the stage.

The Fireplace Club followed with their comedy act, and soon had the audience in stitches with joke after joke.

Then came Belle. Her tousled hair still fell across her face, and she looked at the audience with big eyes, like she was about to bolt. But every other child from the orphanage walked on stage and formed a semicircle behind her. With her friends there, she nodded to Jeffrey that she was ready. He played a single note to give her the key, and she began to sing. Someone had turned off the carousel music. There wasn't another sound in the park. Even the two birds on the roof cocked an ear and listened.

It was a slow song, about a yearning heart and a lover lost at sea. The first verse was sung a cappella. The second verse Jeffrey accompanied softly on the fife, and they were like two birds crying to each other across a vast, empty sea. The other children joined her for the chorus, and together they sang the third verse. Belle's voice lifted above them all, with sadness, hope, and longing. It surged and fell like ocean waves, it caressed like a sea breeze. The choir suddenly stopped, and there was only Belle's sweet voice, rising higher and higher, like an angel from heaven.

The audience sat in stunned silence. Then everyone clapped, and jumped to their feet, crying, "Bravo!" and, "Encore!"

Bit couldn't be sure whether the explosion of applause startled the two birds on the roof, or if they heard Belle as a call from heaven, but they burst into the air above the park, chasing each other with happy wings until at last they spiraled to the sky.

Bit had no time to watch them leave. The choir rushed off stage with Belle, who threw herself into Bit's arms.

Bit was almost bowled over, but laughed and kissed Belle while signaling Yalp on stage for the finale of Act One. He had changed out of the clown costume and back into his magician's robe. The audience soon gasped as he pulled a steady stream of chickens out of a small cooking pot, then put them all back and held up the empty pot. He levitated two feet off the ground; broke a stick and restored it; made himself look taller, then smaller; and passed a feather through solid rock.

Finally, he placed a kerchief on his hand. Whisking it away a moment later, he revealed Darter. "Ladies and gentlemen, observe closely. This sparrow has only half a wing on one side." He held the bird aloft and spread out the wings. "By all rights, he should not fly. But watch. With a little magic dust . . ." He sprinkled some powder on Darter's back, which made the bird sneeze. "He flies!"

Darter was tossed in the air, and immediately circled around the stage. The audience applauded enthusiastically, but one heckler called out, "Aw, he's a trained bird. I seen it done in Puluth."

Darter landed on Yalp's finger and started chattering angrily.

Yalp smiled. "I think you've insulted him."

The audience laughed.

"His brain's about as big as yours," said the heckler.

"Then you won't mind assisting me, sir," replied Yalp. "Please step on stage."

A tall man in dirty overalls and muddy boots rose out of the audience and joined Yalp on stage.

"I will prove," said Yalp, "that this is no ordinary trained bird. My learned friend here," indicating the heckler, "will call out the commands. I, through the highly cultivated powers of mental communication, a feat even the great magician Jestagali was unable to achieve, will relay the commands to this bird."

The heckler looked smug and pointed. "Fly to that woman with the straw hat."

Yalp placed his fingers on his forehead in a pose of intense concentration. A moment later, Darter flew to the woman and landed softly on her hat.

"Come back and hop down this rail," said the heckler.

A moment later, Darter flew to the center of the stage and hovered in midair.

"The right one or left?" asked Yalp with a grin, indicating the wrought iron banisters on either side of the steps leading to the front of the stage.

"The right," the man replied.

"His right or yours? I wouldn't want to confuse him."

The man held up his right hand, then his left, looking confused himself. The audience laughed. "I reckon my right."

Darter flew to the correct banister and hopped down.

The audience applauded and the man's jaw dropped. "I wish I could get my son to mind me like that," he said.

The audience laughed. Darter took more commands. Hopping up the stepladder; circling three times around the stage, then to a maple tree and back; plucking a coin from the hand of a freckled-face boy with red hair.

It was then that Bit heard someone softly calling her name. The voice came from behind. Turning, she saw the old woman climbing down the embankment behind the stage.

 **30**

Bit looked around for the other

children, but they had melted into the audience to watch the rest of Yalp's show. None of her friends were nearby.

The old woman was down the embankment now, and approached on the dirt road that ran in back of the stage. Over hunched shoulders, she wore a plain brown cloak, the material so worn it was tattered and rent with holes. Her legs trembled, and she walked with such difficulty that Bit felt a pang of pity.

The old woman's face was kind. From a distance, the drooping right eyelid had looked sinister. Up close her face was soft and sweet, despite the deep crisscross of wrinkles, and the ridges across the bridge of her nose. There was worry, not malice in the eyes. She stopped a few feet away and clutched her hands earnestly.

"Don't be frightened," she whispered. "I'm here to help."

"Who are you? How do you know my name?" Bit asked.

"Medlara sent me. She knew you'd come here seeking the doctor, and would need help."

This made sense. If Medlara could warn Jenny that something was going to happen to the family, she could see Bit's fate too.

"I know you're stuck here," said the old woman. "I can get you home."

"How do I know you're a friend, and not . . ." She started to say Naryfel but thought that unwise. "And not an enemy."

The old woman took a step forward. "Look deeply in my eyes, Bit. Tell me what your heart says."

Bit searched the woman's eyes. They were soft and gray, and some green from the surrounding trees was mirrored there. Beneath that, Bit sensed the woman carried a burden. And a deep, abiding pain. But there was also warmth mixed in, like from a relative who sees you for the first time and instantly cares about you, even though you've never met.

"What do you see, Bit?"

"A friend."

The woman relaxed and a little of the worry faded. "Good."

"How will you get us home?"

"I'll explain later. I must go now."

"But when will I see you again?"

"Soon, child. I'll meet you at the doctor's. These old bones don't move very fast. I must start ahead of you if I'm to get there in time." The old woman turned to go.

"Wait . . ." Bit called.

The old woman turned back. "You're worried about your friend."

"Yes."

"She is good, but she is troubled. You're right not to alarm her now. Wait until you're away from here, on the way to the doctor's. Then tell her about me."

The old woman hobbled back up the embankment and disappeared into the shadows and the trees. Bit felt a whirlwind of excitement. She was certain the woman was good. And she promised a way home. There was still hope of returning in time to save Dash. If only they could reach the doctor and convince him.

Laughter from the audience drew her attention to the stage. Darter flew back to Yalp. Standing on top of the magician's bald head, he flapped his wings as if he were urging the audience to applaud more. They obliged him by whistling, cheering, and slapping their hands together until at last he seemed satisfied and sat down.

"And now, ladies, gentlemen and children," Yalp cried, "I leave you in the manner of the great wizards. There are few, precious few, who dare commune with the vaporous spirits of day and night. Few who understand the tangible qualities of mist, or the power of clouds. Before you stands one humble magician who has devoted his life to these arcane branches of sorcery. And so, without further ado, I bid you farewell."

Yalp bowed. There was a flash of light. Red and gray smoke swirled around his feet, then rose and billowed over his head until it blocked him from view. When the smoke cleared, he was gone.

The audience roared its approval. All the Orphanage Players rushed on stage and bowed. Pet gave a brief speech asking for donations, and the children circulated through the crowd with buckets.

From her seat in the front row, Miss Drath rubbed her hands and slapped Ox on the back, evidently pleased at the audience's generosity. The children returned backstage. The stagehands untied one end of the scenery sheet. Walking in a circle, they quickly tied it again so that what was painted on the back was now in front and facing the audience. The scene was a forest with tangled roots and tangled branches and giant spider webs.

A yellow sun tied on a fishing line was slowly drawn up to

signify morning. A boy limped on stage, his clothing torn and muddy. He hugged himself and shivered.

"Uncle! Uncle! I pray I am not too late," he cried. "I have wandered and circled through this godforsaken forest, and still find no way out. Or help for you. If only you could have walked with me, you would have known the way. If only our carriage had not overturned, we would be safely home now before a warm fire, and would have eaten these past three days and nights. But to leave you there with a broken leg . . . I could barely tear myself away." The boy sobbed. " 'Twas cruel, cruel of fate to do that to a sweet old man. Don't give up on me, Uncle. Hold on a little longer, you're all I have . . ." Another sob from the boy. "I swear, Uncle, I'll find help. But listen! What's that? Dogs barking! A hunt perhaps! I shall hide in these bushes and see."

He hid behind a papier-mâché bush. Four children wearing dog masks and tails rushed onto the stage. Marianna, dressed in pants and boots, and Jeffrey, with stuffing padding his middle, followed closely behind.

"Ah, my little babies," cried Marianna to the dogs, "you smell a prize for Mommy? Where darlings, where is it? Find it for Mommy."

The dogs began yipping and snarling near where the boy hid.

"I think there is something here," said Jeffrey.

"I can see that, you idiot." She reached her arm into the bushes and pulled out the boy.

"Oh Miss, you must help me," cried the boy. "My uncle has a broken leg. Our carriage overturned and he cannot walk. We must go to him or he will perish."

"Poor baby," said Marianna. "You look like you haven't eaten in days."

"I haven't, ma'am. I've been wandering these woods, trying

to find a way out."

"Come with me then. You shall have a hot meal and a warm bath."

"But my uncle, we must go to him at once."

"Don't worry your little heart. I shall send Pig to find him."

Here she winked meaningfully at Jeffrey.

"Do you have something in your eye, ma'am?" Jeffrey asked.

Marianna winked again, bigger, more exaggerated.

"I have a handkerchief, ma'am," said Jeffrey. "It's a little yellow from my cold and brown from chewing tobacco, but you're welcome to it."

Marianna knocked it out of his hand and pulled him aside. "Pretend to go into the forest and look for his uncle. Then meet me back at the orphanage."

"You always was a clever one," said Jeffrey. "Just like a fox among little chicks." He put his hand on his heart and spoke philosophically. "Like a spider to a fly. A cat to a mouse—"

"Pig!" roared Marianna. "Go!"

Pig hurried off stage.

"Little one," said Marianna to the boy. Her voice was sweet as sugar again, and she put her arm confidentially about his shoulders. "These woods are filled with wolves and bears."

The boy swallowed. "Wolves and bears?"

"Yes, my dear. And headless ghosts riding headless horses. A little lamb like you, so young, so innocent, must trust to the kindness of strangers. Oh, what a cold, cruel world is out there. But you're safe with me! Yes, you're safe with me! Come along, and soon you'll see your uncle again."

She led the boy off stage. The stagehands had already untied the inside-of-the-orphanage sheet and quickly covered the forest with it.

Scene Two was just beginning when Pet ran to Bit, followed closely by Yalp with Darter on his shoulder.

"Ready?" Pet asked.

"Ready," Bit replied. There was no time for goodbyes.

She rose. In a few moments they were up the stairs, over the retaining wall, and disappeared into the shrubbery.

They found the road out of the village. It was muddy, and they had to step around deep potholes and ruts. More than once, Bit looked back wistfully, wishing she could have seen the rest of the play. She contented herself with seeing the whole production in her mind . . .

The boy meets the other children in the orphanage. It seems a cold, dark, damp place, and he wonders aloud if maybe wolves and bears and ghosts might have been better. In front of Marianna, the children tell him what a wonderful place he has come to, with pancakes for breakfast and chocolate cake for dinner, there's never any school and nothing to do but play all day. What could be better!

Marianna leaves with a satisfied smile and the boy tells them he must leave. It's all a mistake. He doesn't belong here and he must save his uncle, who is rich beyond their wildest dreams. The orphans only laugh. In the dining room he receives his first meal. On one half of the stage, Marianna eats turkey and drinks wine from a crystal goblet, while the cook serves the children. The boy looks into the pot and it tips over. Out tumbles an old shoe and a loaf of green bread. Afterward, he is shown a spot on the cold floor to sleep on.

The sun is lowered. On other lines, a moon and some stars are raised to signify night. The boy climbs out a window, but is captured by Pig. Scene change to the coop. The boy is beaten (with a strand of velvet while a real belt smacks wood backstage).

Afterward he shivers and swears he will find his uncle.

If the play is allowed to go on—how could Drath stop it with the audience all around—the scene changes to the forest where a kindly woodsman finds an old man by an overturned carriage. The woodsman sets the old man's leg and promises to help him find his nephew. They go to the orphanage first. The uncle repeatedly inquires if his nephew is there. Each time he is turned away. At last he is told he may have any boy he chooses, for a price! Three hundred rugdas. He pays the price instantly, but the boy will not go unless all the children are freed. So the uncle buys the orphanage and puts the old lady out of business.

The End.

Bit could imagine Miss Drath's face during all this. Frowning, grinding her teeth, digging her nails into the grass, but smiling stiffly whenever someone looked questioningly her way. It was only a matter of time before Bit would hear the bloodhounds. She shuddered, thinking about their hateful eyes and sharp yellow fangs.

She'd considered ending the play with the children scattering in every direction. That would confuse the dogs and keep them busy. But she didn't want to get the children in trouble. In case she failed.

But she couldn't fail. There was too much at stake. The children at the orphanage. Her own freedom, and Pet's. And life or death for Dash and his father.

Darter repeatedly cocked an ear behind him. As yet there was no sound of pursuit. They had a little time. Miss Drath would have to bring the children back to the orphanage, get the dogs, and hitch a horse to the buckboard. Bit figured she had an hour's head start.

They traveled in silence. Yalp's eyes lingered on Pet. And

Pet darted furtive glances back at him. He'd turn away, smile at Bit, and scoot out of the way of a deep cart-rut. But his eyes returned to Pet and hers to him.

Bit had seen a little of this earlier that day, and yesterday too, Yalp giving Pet an odd look, as if he was trying to figure something out. Pet kept a wide berth, but at stray moments she studied him.

As they traveled up the road, Bit tried several times to start a conversation. Each time there was a short answer, followed by silence.

Bit hardly knew what to think, so she focused her thoughts on what to say to the doctor. Her story was so incredible, she'd hardly believe it herself if someone told it to her. And yet, she had to hope the doctor would see Yalp as an adult midget, rather than a child. This would give her some credibility. Then there was the old woman. Perhaps she would reach the doctor first and explain everything. But that would be just as strange a story. Explaining her own presence there, being sent by Medlara. It was all too fantastic.

On the other hand, they might pass the woman on the road. Bit would have to explain everything to Pet. But how could she explain what she'd felt looking into the old woman's eyes?

Only that she trusted her.

"Bit, slow down," Pet called from behind.

Bit stopped and turned, not realizing she had pulled ahead of the others. Pet was only a few steps away, but Yalp was a good way down the road, scrambling up a steep grade.

Pet was breathing hard from the climb. "No, keep going," she said, catching up to Bit.

"But we should wait for them."

"In a minute. I want to talk to you first."

They started walking again. Redwood and eucalyptus trees

marched up a slope on the left and plunged down steeply on the right. The trees swayed with a slow groan and creak. Low, dark clouds still cut jagged pieces out of a white, overcast sky. The glare hurt Bit's eyes, forcing her to squint.

"Have you ever done something you regretted?" Pet asked. She carried a canvas bag, the strap slung over her shoulder. It was filled with a few supplies, in case they had to run and hide.

"Lots of things," Bit replied. "Who hasn't?"

"Right," said Pet. She pulled the strap out and let it snap back. "What if someone did something really bad? Should they get a second chance?"

Bit felt a few raindrops on her cheek. The wind picked up and she wrapped the patchwork shawl more tightly around her. "Wouldn't it depend on what they did?"

"Take Miss Drath or Ox. After what they've done to you."

"A second chance would be hard. They weren't just cruel to me. They hurt you, and the other children. Still, if they really changed, I would try to forgive them."

"What about someone close to you?" asked Pet, twisting on the strap. "Someone you didn't expect to hurt you."

"I guess that would be harder. It would depend on who it was and what they had done." Bit wondered where Pet was going with this.

Pet gave a nod. "Right." She walked along silently, seemed to be wrestling with something. "Take Dash."

"What about Dash?" Bit felt her heart jump.

"After what he did with Vieveeka."

Images of the masked ball flooded Bit's mind, of Dash with his arms around Vieveeka, mesmerized, spellbound. All the hurt and sadness seized her as if it all had just happened. "I . . . don't know. I love him. I can't stop loving him."

"Right, but if he chooses you, will you accept him back?

Will you forgive him?"

"With all my heart," said Bit earnestly. "Isn't that what you do when you love someone?"

Pet looked at her in some surprise. They walked along quietly for a spell, and Bit tried to quell the pain these questions awoke.

"What if you were betrayed?" Pet flashed Bit a sideways glance and held her eyes a moment.

"Pet! What on earth are you talking about?" Bit started to feel alarmed.

Pet gnawed at a corner of her lip. She gave another sidelong glance, but this time tears formed shiny pools on the surface of her eyes.

Bit couldn't stand it any longer. Stopping suddenly, she faced Pet and held her hands. "Please, just tell me."

Pet swallowed. "This won't be easy."

"It's better that I know."

"It's my father."

"I know. You explained. He doesn't love you."

"It's more than that. I don't know where to begin. He used me . . ."

"How?"

"Did you ever wonder how Vieveeka knew about your castle carving?"

"So that's what this is about. Relax Pet, I figured that out a long time ago."

"You did?"

"Of course. You and Jen were the only ones who knew, and Vieveeka was staying with you."

Pet gave a little sob. "Then why did you stay my friend? I might as well have stabbed you in the heart."

"Because I know you didn't do it on purpose."

"But I was spying—"

"Your father must have made you. You never would have done it on your own."

"It's true. I didn't know he would tell Vieveeka, or that she'd make one, too."

"Of course not."

"Wait. There's more. Father told me something, right before I came to the Plain World . . . either you didn't come back, or I shouldn't bother coming back."

Bit caught her breath, feeling scared for Pet, not for herself. "But see, you didn't do what he said."

Pet burst out crying. "But I did. I sent the guards away so we'd enter the Plain World alone. Then on the waterfall, you stood on the edge. I was behind you. Don't you remember? And again when we were climbing down the shaft, and on the roof of Miss Drath's. My hands were out."

"But you didn't push me."

"But I thought about it."

"Of course you did. You had to, after what your father said. But you could never hurt me. You're my friend."

"I don't deserve your friendship."

"Don't be silly."

"But after everything I've told you—"

"If you've done anything bad, you've more than made up for it. You saved me from tumbling off the roof. Without you, we'd still be trapped in the orphanage." Bit squeezed Pet's hands. "Dear Pet, do you know what I see when I look in your eyes?"

Pet could only look back. On her lower eyelashes, tears formed a little necklace.

"I see a girl who hates being a countess, who could care less about body butter and fine clothes, a girl who wants to jump into the world and use her mind, to be so much more than what everyone expects. I see a girl who longs for friends and love and acceptance. That's the girl I see, and the girl I'll always love and trust."

Pet threw her arms around Bit. "Then you forgive me?"

"With all my heart."

"It won't go so easy for me if we get back to Aerdem. Yalp will accuse me of pushing him. But I swear, I slipped."

"Of course you did. You wouldn't want to get stuck here. Don't worry about Yalp. When the story is told, you'll be a hero. But listen, Pet. I trust you. Now you have to trust me about something."

"Anything."

Bit told her quickly about the encounter with the old woman.

Pet shook her head. "I don't like it. How do we know Medlara sent her?"

"Because I know she is good, just as I know you are."

"I still don't like it."

"But you'll follow her?"

"Anywhere you go, I go."

"We stick together like glue—"

"No matter what may come. But if she does anything to you . . ." Pet balled her hands into fists.

Bit reckoned they were close to the doctor's house. As yet, there was no sound of pursuit. Only their labored breathing, the scrape of their feet, a rolling pebble, and the creak of the trees broke the silence. Bit wondered why they hadn't caught up with old woman, unless she'd already reached the doctor's. Bit hoped so. Maybe the doctor would be ready to go when she arrived.

The rapid beat of wings made her turn. Darter hovered in the air, facing the road behind. He streaked to Bit's shoulder and tapped sharply at her neck like a woodpecker. She hushed him, cupped a hand behind her ear, and listened intently. At first there was nothing but the rustle of the woodland. Then she heard it, like the muffled wail of an approaching storm. The hounds!

Bit grabbed one of Yalp's arms and Petunia the other. With the little man dangling between them, and Darter flying ahead, they raced up the road.

31

Bit and her companions approached

the doctor's house, which was at the bottom of a gravel road. To the right was a red barn. The door had been taken off the hinges and leaned against one of the walls, waiting to be repaired. A square of white fencing marked the border of a muddy corral. There were no horses in sight, but Bit heard one snort in the barn. To the left, apple, persimmon, and peach trees were scattered about a small field. Some of the fruit had been put in burlap sacks, but most of it lay ripe, rotting, and uncollected.

In front of the house was a neatly trimmed lawn. Lonely posts rose from the ground, waiting for the pickets to make them complete. The rest of the fence, raw and unpainted, lay under a canvas tarp. The house was one story, made of clay-red bricks. Narrow diamond-lattice windows with white shutters were evenly spaced on either side of the door.

A man wearing overalls and a straw hat was seated on the ground below one of the windows. He worked at the dirt with a trowel. Set out beside him were a dozen tired-looking flowers, struggling to bloom.

"Excuse me," Bit said. "Is the doctor in?"

The man looked up. He had a long face that made his eyes look small. But they were alert and intelligent, and roamed over Bit and Pet, taking in their orphan clothes. He raised an eyebrow when his gaze reached Yalp, with Darter on his shoulder.

"I'm Doc Jenkins. But the office is closed." His voice had the maturity of a man in his early fifties.

Bit clutched her hands. "Please sir, we need a doctor."

The doctor finished digging a hole and placed one of the flowers into the spot. With the back of the trowel he slid some soil into the hole and tamped it down. He took some white powder from a sack beside him and sprinkled it around the flower. "You all look healthy enough. It can wait until tomorrow."

"No sir, it cannot. A young man and his father are dying. At the most, they'll last a day. You must go to them."

The doctor rose quickly and dusted off his pants. "Where are they?"

"A long way from here."

"Are there no doctors who are closer?" He looked longingly at the other flowers waiting to be planted.

"They've been consulted. None can help."

Doc Jenkins frowned, which deepened the grooves on either side of his mouth. "Why do you think I can help? I'm just a country doctor."

Bit gave a quick glance up the doctor's road. The howling of the bloodhounds had waxed and waned for the past half an hour. She didn't hear them now, but knew they were getting closer. "Please sir, can we go inside. I'll explain everything."

"Very well." Doc Jenkins rose. He knocked his boots against a stone birdbath to dislodge clumps of dirt, and led them into the house.

"Have a seat," he said, nodding to the living room on their left. "I'll be right back."

Bit sat on a brown sofa against the wall with windows. There was a stone fireplace on her left, and in front of her, a low table with magazines fanned out like cards. *Reel and Rod, Gill and Benson's Farmer's Almanac, Modern Knitting.* Across from the sofa were an overstuffed chair, an ottoman, and an end table with a collection of pipes and a humidor. A pendulum clock ticked on the opposite wall, a reminder that time was running out.

Still, Bit needed to pace her story. The old woman wasn't there yet. If the doctor wanted to go immediately, Bit would have no way of getting him to Aerdem.

Doc Jenkins returned a few minutes later carrying a tray of cookies and three glasses of milk. He had changed into brown pinstriped pants with matching vest and coat. His hands were scrubbed clean and the nails shined. His hair was gray, cut short, and beginning to recede.

"Don't be bashful," he said, nodding to the cookies. "Mrs. Jenkins made them this morning. They're the best in three counties."

Bit hadn't eaten since breakfast and was famished. She downed the milk in two gulps and devoured two cookies. Yalp and Pet followed her example.

Doc Jenkins sat on the edge of the ottoman and watched them with interest. "You're from Drath Orphanage?"

"Yes," Bit replied, wiping her mouth on a cloth napkin. "She captured us three days ago."

She told him how they'd been captured going to his house, and how the children were treated at the orphanage. She begged him to help them.

"I've suspected Drath was abusing the children," he

replied. "I've wanted to close her down for years. But none of the children would speak up. She generally keeps them away from me. The last time she brought one here was a little over three years ago. A boy named Timothy Rattner. He had a strange break in his arm. How's he doing?"

Bit looked at Petunia. Her friend didn't recognize the name either.

The doctor winced. "He's gone? Dear God . . ." Doc Jenkins shook his head. "Don't worry. After what you've told me, I'll shut her down forever. The sheriff is a friend of mine. Well, you best tell me about the young man and his father."

Bit launched into her story. She started with the storm, the attack in the darkest hour of the night. The frantic knell of the alarm bells, the rush of soldiers to the king's chamber. The kidnap of Jenny and her mother. Then going to see Dash, the smell of the creatures in the air, even though the floor had been mopped and mopped. It stank, like rotting cactus.

And Dash and the king, side by side on the bed, the creatures coiled around their bodies, their faces pale and still like corpses.

Bit turned the story to Jenny. How she had left the Plain World using a magic key. How she had been reunited with her mother and father, and found her half brother, Dash. How they all lived in a castle in a land so glorious it made the Plain World look like a pale ghost.

When Bit finished, her throat was dry and quiet tears streaked her cheeks.

Throughout the story, the doctor listened carefully, his eyes probing hers. Occasionally he got up and paced. When she got to the attack, he stopped her and asked her to repeat the description of the creatures. And when she mentioned Jenny, he looked startled, like someone had thrown ice down his back.

At last he sank to the chair, shaking his head. "It's all too fantastic."

"Every word is true, I swear it," Bit replied. She held one hand tightly in the other, accenting her words with them to show she was earnest.

"I thought Jenny was dead. The day she disappeared, a vicious wolf pack showed up, the first seen in these parts for a hundred years. You don't know how many nights I tossed imagining those creatures tearing her up. Or that she fell off a cliff. I've regretted every day not doing more when she came to see me. That was the day her guardian, Nell, died."

"She loved Nell very much."

"She did. She doted on the old woman, doing all the chores for both of them. But the idea that she went to another world . . . You must understand. I'm a man of science. I deal in practical facts. Simple cause and effect. What I can see, hear, and touch. Not in fantasy."

"But you cared about Jenny."

"Yes."

"Then care now about her father and brother."

Doc rose, walked to the window, and looked out. He removed a watch from his vest pocket, and, opening it, stared at the face. He closed it and tapped on the gold lid, then opening, closing, opening the watch several more times, at last he snapped it shut. "Very well. Give me a moment to get my hat and bag."

He left the room and Bit turned anxiously to Pet. "Where is the old woman?"

"I told you we couldn't trust her," Pet replied.

"But she was our way home. I can't tell the doctor we have no way of getting there."

Before Pet could reply, they heard the sharp baying of the

302

bloodhounds. Perhaps a hill or a bend in the road had masked their cry before. It mattered not. They poured down Doc's road, yapping triumphantly.

"These children belong to me," Miss Drath said. She had changed into pants tucked into tall boots, and stood in the entrance to Doc's living room, arms akimbo.

"They are in my care now," Doc replied. He faced her from the middle of the living room, arms folded firmly.

"You have no authority over my business. These are run-aways." As if to accentuate the point, her dogs whined just outside the door, where Ox had them leashed.

"You have no authority in my house. You'll have them after a full investigation."

"I'll have you arrested."

"On what charge?"

Miss Drath smiled triumphantly. "Stolen property."

"These are children, not property."

"Children with no homes or families. I am charged by the State to provide that."

"They tell me they have homes."

"And you believe them?" Miss Drath rolled her eyes and laughed. She pointed to Bit and Pet. "Do these look like children that belong to anyone?"

Doc Jenkins glanced at the children, his eyes lingering on the patchwork clothing. His shoulders sagged a little.

"They tell me there's a medical emergency," he replied at last, his finger running slowly over the handle of his black medicine bag.

Miss Drath slapped her thigh and laughed again. "And you believe them?"

"I admit it's strange."

"Strange? It's the most preposterous tale I've ever heard. This one is supposed to be engaged to a prince. And that one is a countess. It's the make-believe of children trying to forget their grim circumstances. Don't blame me if the world brings them to my doorstep."

The doctor sank into his chair, and Bit felt her hopes sink with him. "I am duty bound to help," he said. His voice, like a deep red wine before, weakened to a pale tincture, as if Miss Drath had poured in a gallon or two of water.

"They've probably told you I'm abusing them. Do you see one bruise? Do they look unfed?"

"No . . ."

"No. Of course not."

Doc Jenkins kneaded the sides of his head, as if he were working out a problem. Then his eyes lighted on Yalp. "How do you explain him?"

Miss Drath gave a nervous giggle. "He's a stunted boy, anyone can see that."

"Ma'am," said Doc sternly, "he's a midget. I studied them in medical school. But I never saw one that small."

"Very well. I grant you, he's a midget. But do you actually believe he's the magician of a king in a far-off world?" She pointed to the long robe that Yalp wore. "He's crazy. Didn't you study *them* in medical school? Delusions of greatness, magical powers, the ability to travel in the wink of an eye. Grand illusions, wouldn't you say?"

Doc winced. "Still, I must approach this logically." He turned to Yalp. "Can you tell me nothing to verify your tale?"

Yalp rose from his seat beside Bit. "Sir. Every word this child has told you is true. We come from a place called Aerdem, and the king and prince there are dying."

"And how did you propose to get there," Drath asked. "Fly?"

"With this," Yalp replied. He removed the Transdevis from his robe and handed it to the doctor.

The doctor studied the Transdevis carefully and handed it to Miss Drath.

She gave a sly smile. "Then take us there with it."

"I'm afraid I can't," Yalp said. "The device is broken."

"How convenient," Drath replied. "Come," she said to the doctor, "there's your proof. It's nothing but an antique mirror. Give me back the children, and we'll lock this little man up where he won't do any harm."

The doctor shook his head. "I've never seen a mirror like this."

"Which proves nothing," Drath replied. "He already believed he was a wizard. He was happy to take up the rest of the children's tale."

"I don't know."

"Then you are as mad as—"

The dogs outside snarled and barked viciously, cutting off Miss Drath's words. A heated argument erupted just beyond the door. Bit recognized the old woman's voice rising fiercely above Ox's.

Despite Miss Drath's protests, the doctor helped the old woman into the room. Her clothes were soiled with mud and leaves.

"I'm sorry I'm late," she said to Bit. "I felt dizzy and stopped by the side of the road to rest. I must have passed out and tumbled down the hill."

Leaning on his arm, Doc Jenkins led her to the chair. "Let me fix you a cup of tea," he said.

"Thank you, no," she replied. "There's no time. We must leave at once."

She was breathing with difficulty, and the doctor held her

wrist and took her pulse. "You shouldn't be going anywhere until that heart rate goes down." He felt her head. "And you have a slight fever."

She pulled the tattered cloak around her shoulders even though the room was warm. "My life means nothing. It is the lives of these children that matter."

"You know these children?" The sun was beginning to fade outside, and Doc lit one of the lamps.

"I know of them."

Miss Drath snorted and straightened one of her sleeves with a sharp pull. "There, you see? She has no business with them."

The old woman struggled to her feet. Her eyes reflected the lamplight in two points of gold. "I have everything to do with them. You do not know what you are dealing with."

"She's a fanatic. Been threatening me for days," Drath said to the doctor. "She should be arrested."

Doc looked startled and shot a concerned look at Bit. Pet leaned against Bit and whispered in her ear, "She looks crazy to me. If things go sour, you'd better run out the back door."

Bit didn't think the woman was mad, but Pet's comment alarmed her. Pet hadn't said "we" better run. Was she thinking of staying here in the Plain World, despite Bit's assurance she wouldn't be viewed as a spy or a traitor?

"Do you know this woman?" the doctor asked Bit, drawing back her attention.

"Yes, sir," Bit replied. "She promised to get us home."

"How?"

"I . . . I don't know."

"There," snorted Miss Drath again. "It's all a fairy tale."

The doctor shook his head, took a deep breath and sighed. "This is all confusing."

"Sir," said the old woman, rising out of her seat and gripping his arm, "we must go, we must leave. Now. Time is running out."

"First tell me what this is all about," replied Doc, coaxing the old woman back into the chair. "How did you become involved with these children?"

"That is too long a tale. I can only tell you that they do not belong here. They belong to a world far, far different from this. They only came here to find you."

"Why me? Are there no doctors in their world?"

"There are, but they are crude. Leeches, bloodletting, lodestones, amulets. One traveled from here to our world three years ago, the child Jenren."

"Then you know Jenny too?"

"No, but she told her parents about this world. All kinds of wonders we know nothing about. Trains and boats running on coal and steam. Messages clicking in code from plain to valley over thin wires. Miraculous cures for diseases."

"Nonsense," interrupted Miss Drath. "Jenny had no parents. She was an orphan dumped on a woman every bit as feeble as this one. If she had parents, wouldn't they have come for her years ago?"

"They would have if they could," the old woman replied. "That's another long story, and there's no time. No time—" She struggled to her feet and, weak as she was, tried to pull the doctor to the door.

He calmed her back to her seat again. "How do you know of these children?"

"I was told to come here, to help them."

"By whom."

The old woman hesitated. "It doesn't matter. Please, sir. If we don't leave now, more than the king and prince will die.

307

Jenren and her mother are in danger too. We must make haste."

"You see," said Miss Drath. "The more you probe, the more ridiculous it becomes. Next thing you know, their whole world will be destroyed."

"Not destroyed, but thrown into a long age of darkness. Many will live in misery. More will die."

"I rest my case," said Miss Drath, smiling with satisfaction. "If you don't commit her now, you're worthless as a physician."

Doc Jenkins' face reddened and he glared back at her. "And yet, where has Jenny been all this time? And these people seem to know her."

"There are strange legends about the mountain above you," Miss Drath replied. "You've heard the stories, I warrant. Tales of a giant waterfall. Animals as intelligent as humans, and the like. I've long held the theory that Jenny found a cave up there. That she remains in hiding, coming down only to find children to join her band. She has set herself up as their leader. She's the princess. There's the countess." She pointed to Pet.

"I do recall tales . . . and children have disappeared . . . from your orphanage."

Drath slapped her knee. "There you go. She's collecting homeless waifs and turning them into a band of thieves. I found these two stealing food out of Nell's cottage."

The doctor sank onto the ottoman and looked from Miss Drath to the old woman, and from her to Bit and Pet, and from there to Yalp, and around the room again to each of them until his eyes stopped at Darter. The little bird was scratching in the ashes of Doc's fireplace.

The old woman held his hands between hers and beseeched him with her eyes. Miss Drath stood with arms folded, a triumphant smirk spreading across her face.

Again, Bit felt her hopes sinking. All arguments were in and the doctor was still undecided. It was up to her. "Please, sir, you must trust her. She's the only way back to Aerdem."

"Another world, magic, little people, it's all so incredible." Doc Jenkins spoke more to himself than anyone in the room, and shook his head.

Pet leaned against Bit's shoulders and whispered. "Better run."

But Bit was watching the doctor, as was everyone in the room. He walked to the window and looked out. The only sound was the tick of the clock, and Darter scratching in the fireplace. Bit tried to hush him, so the doctor could think undisturbed, but Darter only hopped deeper into the center of the hearth where the ashes had piled into a little mountain. He kicked with his feet, sending plumes of ash onto the gray stone lining the front of the fireplace.

"Darter. No," Bit whispered.

But Darter dug and scratched and kicked at the ash, sending out a flurry so thick it settled on the stones like a blanket of snow.

The doctor turned from the window and watched the little bird, his face wistful and a little sad. "Leave him be. It needs sweeping anyway. One more thing I haven't gotten to."

Darter hopped off the grate. Fluttering to the ash-covered stones, he began to scratch.

"Doctor," said Miss Drath, "I am taking these children."

She walked toward Bit and Pet, her arms out, ready to sweep them up. The doctor's head fell and he waved in resignation.

"No," exclaimed Bit. "Wait."

"It's over," said Miss Drath. "Come along."

"It's Darter," Bit cried. "He's writing something."

Darter scratched at the ash with one toe. Then he hopped aside. He had written as plain as day:

32

Doc Jenkins' horse looked too weak

to pull the carriage. Her legs were rickety, her joints swollen. Her back looked ready to cave in. The pelt on her belly was pocked with holes, making her look a little moth-eaten. The stiff hair on her mane and tail was dry, thinning, and streaked with gray. She seemed to have only enough strength to hold up her ears. These were long, and stood straight like a rabbit's. But her eyes were soft and bright, and she nickered with anticipation while Doc hitched her to the carriage.

Pet scanned the horse with a skeptical eye.

"She's old, but she'll get you there," said Doc, following her look. He stroked a half-moon blaze on the horse's forehead and put a straw hat on her head. Then he gave her some hay, which she chewed delicately.

Bit was grateful they were taking a carriage. The high, white clouds had turned gray, the low gray ones dark. They were so low it seemed she could almost touch them. A few rain-drops splatted on the ground.

They helped the old woman into the front seat. Bit, Pet and Yalp squeezed into the back. Doc climbed in next to the woman. He gave the horse a tap, and the carriage rolled and jangled up the road.

Bit looked out the window behind her. Miss Drath followed in a buckboard, Ox trotting alongside with the hounds. When she saw Bit, Miss Drath's eyes narrowed to two black slashes. She flicked her horse's flanks with a whip and smiled.

Bit swallowed. She understood the look, which said, "When this is all over, I'll make you pay."

After Darter wrote "Aerdem" in the ashes, the doctor had been swayed. Nothing Miss Drath said would deter him. The old woman said she had a way to the other world. They needed to go to Nell's cottage. There, the old woman would show them. The doctor swore he'd see for himself. He'd written a quick note to his wife, grabbed a hat and slicker, and got out the horse and carriage.

"Tell me about the creatures again," he'd asked, looking sadly at his unplanted flowers.

Bit told him. He'd nodded to himself and filled a pouch with the powder he had sprinkled around the flowers. Then he put the pouch in his medicine bag.

"What was that long object I saw above your fireplace?" the old woman had asked.

"A rifle," he'd replied.

"Is that a weapon?"

"Yes. A powerful one."

"Better bring it."

Doc had frowned.

Now he drove the carriage with the gun across his knees.

Nestled at the knee of the mountain, Nell's cottage looked as lonely as before. The dark and dirty windows. The leaves stirring on the porch. The weeds overrunning the garden. And near the well, the ax handle reaching like an arm from the woodpile. A squirrel perched on the crossbeam of the well looked at them quizzically. He scampered down one of the supporting beams and disappeared into tall grass beyond the yard.

Doc parked the carriage. He and Bit helped the old woman down. Pet, Yalp, and Darter joined them. Miss Drath's buckboard rattled to a stop nearby and Ox, red-faced and panting, ran up with the bloodhounds.

The sun had set. Twilight softened the shadows. The clouds were shot with indigo, the edges crimson. They collected in a towering mass against the mountain above, where they seemed to roll and bubble.

"Well," Miss Drath said to the old woman, "show us."

The old woman drew them to the well, where they formed a semicircle. "The well is the way. It has a deep connection to Jenren."

Everyone peered down the well. The ring of inner stones disappeared in the fading light; the bottom was lost in darkness. A breath of cold air exhaled from below and caressed Bit's cheek.

She shivered.

Miss Drath smiled to herself. "What are you going to do?" she asked the old woman. "Jump in?"

"Yes and no."

"Explain yourself, madam."

"I'm going to open a passage." Reflecting the blues and reds of the clouds, the old woman's eyes shone.

Pet slid up to Bit and whispered. "She's mad."

No one else seemed to hear.

"This well is almost dry," Miss Drath said to the doctor. "I tested it a few days ago. Thirty, forty feet down, there's nothing but mud."

In reply, the doctor drew up the metal bucket. It was empty. He removed the rope from the pulley and let the bucket fall. Bit counted slowly to five before she heard a muffled bang below. Doc pulled the bucket back up. It was dented and bent on one side. He retied the rope and attached it to the pulley. The bucket waved back and forth before settling to a stop. He shot a worried glance at Bit.

The old woman looked at the clouds, which had deepened to midnight blue, magenta, and vast columns of charcoal. "It is time." From beneath her cloak, she removed a parchment packet and opened it.

Yalp stepped forward to examine it. "If you please, may I—"

Muttering to herself, the old woman didn't seem to hear. Fluttering her hand, she emptied a fine powder down the well.

They waited, Bit knew not for what. There was a low rumble of thunder in the distance. Then only silence.

Bit's throat went dry. She didn't want to look down the well again. It drew her back to the lonely times, the blank times, of falling, falling into oblivion . . .

She dug her nails into the rock of the well until she could feel her fingers, then steadied herself, forced herself to look until the fear passed.

"You see," said Miss Drath to the doctor. "Nothing. I hope you're satisfied."

"There," said Bit. "Something's happening."

Strands of mist appeared along the inner well wall. They seemed to drift out of the rock, as if the stone had exhaled. The mist collected in fingers, caressing, licking the wall. It snaked into the darkness, and more mist rose to meet it. The entire shaft was soon covered in a thick blanket that glowed, as if illuminated from behind. The dark shadows that hid the bottom disappeared. Now there was only one, long, endless tunnel.

The old woman climbed on the edge of the well. "The opening won't last long. We must go."

Dumfounded, Miss Drath looked down the well. She recovered quickly. "It's a trick. The magician did the same thing two hours ago. A few chemicals, and poof, he disappeared."

"It's not a trick," said Yalp. The size of a small child, it was hard for him to say things and have anyone take him seriously. But he looked stern now. "Chemical smoke would have dissipated by now. And how do you explain that?"

As far down as Bit could see, the tunnel of mist slowly rotated counterclockwise.

"I don't know, but it's a trick, I'm certain," said Miss Drath.

Doc shook his head. "I don't know . . ." Doubt and confusion troubled his face. "What about the bird's writing?"

"I told you. He flew around the park doing exactly what he was told. He's been trained."

Darter objected, chattering like a monkey until Miss Drath covered her ears.

"Was he trained to do that too?" Pet asked.

Miss Drath cast a wary eye at Darter. "Probably."

Darter looked ready to argue, but Bit hushed him.

"Come, little one." Miss Drath extended her hand to Pet. "I won't be mad at you. I won't punish you. I understand what you are doing. And you're right. There is a better way. I see that now."

Pet gazed back, searching Miss Drath's face.

"Dear Countess. Precious Countess. Together we can do wonderful things. There'll be plenty for the children, and more than enough for me." She sounded so sincere Bit could almost believe her.

Again, Pet gazed back, but this time there were tears in her eyes.

The old woman drew everyone's attention back to the well, where she paced on the edge, wringing her hands. "Time is running out. We must go, now, or many good people will die."

The doctor looked down the well again, uncertainty still written on his face.

Miss Drath latched on to that. "You're a man of science. You said so yourself. You can't seriously think there's anything else at the bottom of that well but a dark, cold grave. If you leap, I won't bother to fish you out."

"Nay," the old woman cried, "you do not know what you are dealing with. There are powerful forces at work. I am only a humble servant. But if you follow me, I will show you." A gust of wind blew her veil free and her hair, thin and white as finely spun thread, spread out in disarray. Eyes shining, balanced precariously on the edge of the well, she did look mad.

The doctor took off his hat and turned it round and round in his hands. Sensing his uncertainty, the old woman spoke to Bit. "My part in what comes is near. I must go. Follow if you can. Don't be frightened by what you see."

She leaped into the well. Bit bent over the edge to look and counted slowly. She could no longer see the old woman. When she reached five there was a roll of thunder from the storm clouds, masking any sound if the old woman smacked on the rocks below.

Everyone crept to the edge of the well and peered down.

"I heard her hit bottom," said Pet.

"I didn't," said the doctor.

Neither had Yalp. Bit couldn't be sure.

"That wraps that up," Miss Drath said, rubbing her hands. "Come along, children." She moved toward Pet and Bit with outstretched arms.

Doc Jenkins stepped in between. "You're not taking them."

"I am."

"You've been abusing them."

Miss Drath's laugh sounded like the cry of a vulture. "I'll take them by force." The bloodhounds snarled, low and mean, at the change in her voice.

Doc Jenkins drew himself up to his full height. "You wouldn't dare."

"Ox, set the dogs on him."

The dogs pulled hard at the leashes, slavering, foaming at the mouth. Ox grinned savagely and let them go. They raced to the doctor, their paws kicking up a wake of mud.

"Heel," Drath cried.

The hounds stopped within a few feet of Doc Jenkins, growling with bared teeth. He backed slowly away. Miss Drath's hand shot out and snatched Pet by the collar. Pet struggled to free herself, but Miss Drath locked her in cross-armed. Doc continued to back away toward his carriage.

Panic gripped Bit's throat, cutting off air. Why was the doctor leaving? Who would save them if he left?

A rumble of thunder close by made her look at the clouds. A gray curtain of rain rushed toward them.

"Grab Bit," Miss Drath said to Ox.

Ox leered at Bit and lumbered toward her with outstretched arms. Bit back-stepped around the well.

"Stop!" Doc cried. He stood by the carriage, rifle on his shoulder and aimed at Ox.

"He won't shoot," Miss Drath said. "Go ahead."

Ox hesitated, then moved toward Bit.

Doc fired his rifle in the air. Ox froze.

"Release the girl," Doc said.

Miss Drath laughed, and began dragging Pet to the buckboard. Doc fired again, and she stopped.

The gunshots were like explosions in Bit's brain, explosions she'd heard before . . . Terrible flashes of red, bursts of fire . . . smoke burning the eyes, the lungs . . . crying babies, people screaming, running . . . terrified eyes, knowing they will die . . .

Soldiers thundered through the village on horseback. A rain of flaming torches fell on the houses, passed through the windows, or ignited the thatch like tinder. Arrows rose in a dreadful arc and landed like strange, sprouting flowers . . . Two faces, a man and a woman, racing toward Bit, yelling, "Run, run!" She knew them. Her parents! Two sweet faces seized with fear for her. They ran beside her. Then they were gone . . .

She needed to hide. She saw the well and leaped. Then she was hiding, looking up through a circle of light. The explosions, the screams, the red smoke swirled above. She was quiet. She knew she needed to be quiet. So quiet. Only the lap of cold, inky water . . .

While this scene gripped her, Bit was vaguely aware she still stood by another well. A curtain of rain hung like a filmy veil, and everyone, Pet, Doc, Miss Drath, faded to gray ghosts. It was like being in two places at once, like seeing with two sets of eyes. The yard at Nell's cottage, cast in gray, the burning village in sepia and umber.

Then a third image floated before her. It started small but it grew. It was a face. She couldn't see the features, but she knew who it was. Dash! She needed to be with him. She needed to be free of the burning village so she could see Dash's face, so she could hold him. She dug her nails into the stones of the well. She looked down at her fingers. They were gray, ghostly. But they bled. And where they bled she could feel, and the feeling spread up her fingers, up her arms. The burning village faded, the face faded. Her hands and arms and legs were solid again, her flesh was her flesh and the color restored.

No one noticed Bit. An argument raged. Everyone yelled at once. Ox urged the hounds to attack. They coiled tight to the ground, readying to spring, snarling, roaring more than barking. Darter faced them. Streaking about their heads, pecking viciously, he held them at bay. Pet twisted against Miss Drath's arms, screaming that there was an Aerdem, that it was real. Yalp voiced his agreement like a shrieking pipe, then broke off into a series of incantations in the hope that he could spirit them back home. Doc still stood with the rifle butt on his shoulder, aiming at Miss Drath, telling her she had no business with the girls and to let them go. Miss Drath swore they were all crazy. Maybe she'd lock the doctor up beside the mad magician. Maybe she'd just let them all fall to their death down the well and just be done with them.

"Please," Bit said, trying to get their attention.

No one listened.

"Wait, please," she repeated.

No one heard. The argument intensified. Miss Drath threatened to throw the doctor in jail for attempted murder.

"Listen to me, please," Bit said.

It was like she was still invisible. But she never felt more alive, more determined.

She dashed to the woodpile and pulled loose the ax. Leaping on the well, she banged on the metal bucket with the ax head until it rang like a giant bell, and her ears were numb, and everyone gaped at her.

At that moment, Miss Drath relaxed her grip. Pet wrenched free and moved a safe distance away.

Miss Drath took a step toward Bit. "Come down, dear, you'll fall."

"Stay back," Bit cried. She felt a little crazed, but was past caring. She pointed down the well, which was still lined with slowly rotating mist. "I'm going. Don't try and stop me. I have to believe there is something there."

"This is madness, girl," said Miss Drath, reaching out, inching forward.

Doc tried to sound reassuring, reasonable. "Come down, we'll talk about it."

Bit struck the bucket again until everyone drew back. "Do you believe in nothing? Have your hearts grown as cloudy and gray as your skies? Have you no dreams, nothing you long for? I long for a place—though it seems little more than a dream now. A place far, far away, where the plenderil push their little faces through the last snow and paint the hills crimson. Where towers and spires of rose greet the morning sun and bathe the world in a pastel glow. Where flower petals carpet the garden paths, and the people are kind and gentle. I long for a place where there is love and magic—magic that rides on the wings of a bird or floats through the air like a whiff of jasmine. That is where my heart is. I have to believe it is there. I'd rather die at the bottom of this well than not believe."

She turned to Pet. "I understand if you'd rather stay here."

Pet looked at Miss Drath. "I could almost pretend that you really love me. It would be more than I'd ever get from my father. But I go where she goes."

Pet climbed on the ledge of the well beside Bit.

"Follow me," Bit said to Doctor Jenkins. "But if you don't, at least I'll see my love before he dies."

She threw the ax aside.

Taking Pet's hand, they leaped . . .

Part Five

33

The stream rushed out of the sewer

and exploded into foamy rapids. Water tumbled and dashed against the rocks, which rose up like row upon row of gnashing teeth. Something swirled and spun in the current. It could have been a piece of driftwood, making no motion of its own. The water commanded its fate, bobbing and dunking and rolling it on a watery back. There was no fight here, no sport, and at last the river flung it aside, where it settled in a shallow side pool along a jagged shore.

The waves rocked it gently now, only a round coconut-head floating on the surface. Perhaps that's where it would have remained, but a seagull circled down to investigate. The object didn't roll underfoot like a coconut. A taste with the beak, and the object rose a little out of the pool. Slowly, two hands grew out of the water like the branches of a tree. The hands clawed at the sharp rocks and pebbles on the shore. With a complaining squawk, the gull flew off.

The hands clawed forward, and a tousled head and shoulders emerged from the pool. With a violent heave, water poured from the mouth.

Sputtering, coughing, Jen crawled a few feet and collapsed facedown on the rocks.

A foul odor penetrated the blanket of fog, and the fog slowly lifted from her brain. Sharp pebbles jabbed her cheek. She opened her eyes. The world was a blurry pattern of light and dark. What was that horrible smell? Her eyes focused, and Jen pulled her nose out of an old shoe.

She rolled on her back and her head throbbed. She closed her eyes. When the throbbing stopped, she opened them and sat up. The rest of her body felt pummeled and bruised, but nothing seemed broken.

Fighting off the urge to lie down and sleep, she looked around. In front of her, a river rolled swiftly. Across the water, a dirt road followed the bank. Beyond that was a grassy field. Another lay behind her.

She was out in the open here. The Desert King would be combing the riverbanks with sniffers. By the sun, it was about ten in the morning. She was lucky she hadn't been found. She had to stay in the water where they couldn't smell her. But she could be spotted here. The only thing to do was to go back into the sewer. But what then? She couldn't hide in there forever. Eventually they would send in boats and search for her.

What chance did she have? She'd be caught. Either fall into the hands of the Desert King or slave her life away on a galley.

Her mother was four hours ahead, at Naryfel's Pass by now, or already at the Ice Falls. Either way she was out of Jen's reach. Maybe already dead. A wave of despair hit her.

What could she do? Who could she turn to in this strange land? She'd never felt so alone, tiny, helpless. Tears welled up, but she was too exhausted to cry.

This was her worst fear. To end as she'd started. An orphan. If she'd never found her family, it would be different. But to have found them, to be wrapped in their love, only to lose it—was more than she could bear.

Naryfel was bent on killing them. That was clear. It seemed strange at first that she'd left Aerdem. Now the plan was clear. Kill Jen's mother. Dispose of Jen. Wait for Dash and Father to die. Without their leadership, Naryfel could march into Aerdem like she'd waltzed around Count Pompahro's ballroom. Jen's people were gentle and innocent. None of them would put up a fight if the royal family was gone.

If only Blue was still with her. She'd only known him for a few days, but she felt as close to him as she did to her own family. He'd remained by her side, risking his own life over and over to help her. Even when she'd treated him badly.

What he'd done at the carriage house was clear. He'd shoved her down the pipe on purpose. He'd allowed himself to get captured so she could get away. Who knows what Naryfel was doing to him. She could be skinning him. Or worse.

Jen couldn't turn her back on him now. She clenched her hands. Maybe she couldn't save Mother. But she could rescue Blue.

She needed a way to evade the sniffers. She looked up and down the riverbank. The rocks, no higher than her waist, would give little protection. The few scattered reeds growing between the rocks wouldn't help, either. The river ringed the shallow side pools with foamy yellow scum. Higher up on the rocks, larger waves and floods had left a second ring, dregs from the city above. Broken glass, a rusty doorknob, a torn jerkin. Wedged between two rocks was the head of a doll, cracked on one side, but still smiling.

Jen's eyes lighted on what she needed, a dead fish rotting in the sun. She batted away the flies and rubbed the fish over her legs, arms and hair. She tore off a piece and stuffed it in her waist. Let the sniffers try and track her now. She still had Tubole's knife. Just in case, she cut one of the reeds. As she hoped, it was hollow.

Stepping into the river, she trudged upstream. She'd leave less scent in the water. Less sign of her passing.

The sun beat down, and the flies followed her. *Good*, she thought. *As long as the flies think I'm a fish, so will the sniffers.*

The tough part was getting back into the castle. She was pretty sure Blue would be in the lowest level, in one of the prison cells or in Naryfel's torture chamber. She could go back through the secret passage she and Blue used to escape. But what if she couldn't unlock the trap door? She could also enter through the garbage chute by the kitchen. But the sewer was a hopeless maze. She wasn't sure she could find the secret passage or the chute. There had to be another way in.

Roaring cut her thoughts short. The sniffers! On this side of the river. Just on the other side of that low hill.

Jen charged into the river. Just before ducking underwater she pulled out the reed and put it in her mouth. She sucked air from the reed and waited. The sniffers would linger at the spot where she had been. Finding nothing, they'd move on, figuring she was on the run below them. That would take five, ten minutes. She gave it fifteen, counting the seconds in her head.

Finally, she risked a peek. They'd moved on, but she could hear them in the distance. They might be combing the river in teams, so she continued wading through the water. She took the piece of fish from her waist and rubbed it on her arms and face, just in case the scent had washed off.

The sewer didn't seem like a good way into the castle. She could search for hours and never find an entrance. Worse, she could get lost. There had to be another way.

What would Blue do? The answer hit her, and she charged upstream toward the city.

Jen dashed from the bushes. With a leap, she landed like a cat on top of the marble fence. The back yard before her was deserted. No one appeared at the windows of the mansion beyond. A quick spring, and she landed on the manicured lawn. She headed first for the pool. Slipping quietly into the water, she rubbed herself thoroughly, trying to wash off as much of the fish smell as she could. Then she headed to the clothesline, which was suspended between the bathhouse and a walnut tree. She pulled off a towel, and quickly dried herself. She hung the towel back up and spotted what she needed. A pair of boy's pants and shirt, and a full-length dress for a girl about her age. She snagged these and headed for the bathhouse. In one of the rooms, she took off her clothes and put on the pants and shirt. Then she stepped into the dress and pulled it up over her shoulders.

She checked herself in a mirror on the wall. The dress would have been too big for her, but with the clothes underneath she imagined she looked as hefty as the girl they belonged to. The dress was white. It desperately needed ironing, but with dozens of pleats, lacy ruffles, and silken gauze, maybe no one would notice. The rope-soled sandals were a problem. They had to go. And her hair, chopped and ragged, would give her away.

She checked the other room and found where the ladies dressed. A maroon bonnet hung on a wooden peg. A pair of shoes had been thrown beneath one of the benches. Burnished red leather, gold buckles and laces, shiny-black heels. Jen could imagine what one of the Bluebacks would give for a pair like this.

She took off her sandals and tried on the shoes. They were a little big, but they'd do. She put on the bonnet and scanned herself in a full-length mirror. A smile crept to her lips. Petunia Pompahro never looked finer.

Jen pulled the dress up a moment and stuffed the sandals into her pants. Then she darted out of the bathhouse.

Flutters danced around Jen's stomach, but she marched boldly through the front door of Naryfel's castle and entered a crowded foyer. Foot traffic streamed both ways. Soldiers, guards, nobles, servants. Exactly what Jen wanted.

Be like Blue, she told herself.

She glided along the marble floor with her chin tilted up. She savored the air, as if inhaling a perfume only her refined nose could appreciate. Nobles bowed as she passed. Servants stopped and curtsied. Guards and soldiers dropped their eyes. Jen nodded slightly to the nobles and ignored the servants and guards. Her part wasn't hard to play. The Rose Castle had plenty of haughty models. The Grand Duchess Lyntabelle. The Lady Hyacinth. And greatest of all, Countess Petunia Pompahro.

Jen's confidence grew as she reached the stairs and descended. She figured all the sniffers were combing the river and roads out of the city. The Desert King would be with them. The last thing anyone would expect was for her to return to the castle. Her mother had left. They'd figure she was trying to follow the carriage.

At the bottom of the stairs she ran smack into the guard with the bloody knife tattoo. He looked her up and down and his eyes narrowed.

Jen ignored him and studied her sleeve, which hung down over her wrist. "Direct me to the closest seamstress." It was a command, and she said it through her nose. Some of the nobles would live in the castle. She was pretty sure each floor would have a dressmaker for a popped button or hasty alteration.

Bloody Knife pointed down the hall and shuffled off.

Jen exhaled in relief. The dress had worked. But what if she met Naryfel? Her aunt would see through the disguise instantly. Jen had to take the chance. Blue needed her.

She made her way down to the next floor, stopping only to drink a cup of milk and get two éclairs from a passing servant. When the servant asked for payment, Jen referred the woman to her father's butler. The woman raised her eyes a moment to glance at Jen's face, then turned away with knitted brow. Jen knew the look. The woman was confused, too frightened to question someone above her.

Jen felt a sharp pang of guilt for taking the food. If she got the chance, she'd give the woman a cow.

Workers labored on scaffolds, and the halls smelled of fresh paint. A faint blue still showed through the walls. Jen wondered idly how many coats it would take to cover the old color.

She made it to the servants' floor. She'd be out of place in this gown. A guard might question if she was lost and offer to escort her. She couldn't take that chance. Ducking into a closet, she took off the dress, bonnet and shoes, and stuffed them behind a box. She found a laundry hamper beside a basket in the corner. Rummaging inside the hamper she found some sheets. She folded these and put them in the basket, stashing the pastries on the bottom. She slipped on her old sandals, grabbed the basket, and stepped into the hall.

She made her way to the dungeon stairs. A voice from behind made her turn.

"You! Boy! Where you going with those sheets?" It was the fat cook. A servant or a guard wouldn't question a countess.

But they'd take any opportunity to lord it over another servant. At least her boy disguise worked.

"To the dungeon," Jen replied.

The cook folded ham-like arms and looked Jen up and down. "With sheets? The queen don't give sheets to the ones livin' below."

Jen shrugged. "There's a bloody mess down there. I was ordered to clean it up."

"Who ordered you?"

"Bug off," Jen shot back. "You're not my boss." She hoped the laundry servants wouldn't be under the cooks.

The cook glared. "No, but I can talk to your mistress. She'll skin you alive."

"Fine. I'll report you to the guard who ordered these sheets. He'll skewer your fat hide."

"And who might that be?"

"You know him. Bloody Knife."

Color drained from the cook's face.

"If I don't get down there, my hide is hash." Jen pointed her finger. "I'll make sure you get your share."

The cook snorted, but waved Jen away, grumbling that she was too busy to bother with laundry urchins.

With a sigh of relief, Jen hurried down the stairs. She thought she heard moaning, and followed the sound down a narrow, dim corridor. There were dark prison cells on either side. From one, someone reached a withered hand through the bars. The sound came from ahead, so Jen pushed on. Whoever it was started whimpering. Jen bit her lip, hoping it wasn't Blue.

The walls were wet. Water dripped from the ceiling, tapping a sad accompaniment to the moans.

She found the cell and looked in. From the shadows a pair of hollow eyes stared back.

"Blue?"

A man crawled toward her. He was as thin as a skeleton. "Food," he croaked.

Jen gave him her pastry. The other she was saving for Blue.

"Have you seen a boy? Brought here this morning?"

The man sat at the bars, too weak to stand. He bit a small piece of pastry and chewed slowly. "He's in the torture chamber."

"Did they . . . ?"

The man lowered his eyes.

Jen winced. "Where is it?"

"Turn left at the end of the corridor. You'll run into it."

"Why are you here?"

"I'm a Blueback."

Jen didn't understand. Why would Naryfel imprison her slaves?

The man saw her confusion. "She calls us vermin, maggots, a disease. She can't bear to look at us. She'd wipe us out if she could. She can't. We pull her ploughs like horses, and harvest the crops until our hands bleed and our backs break. All she can do is slake her hatred on a few of us."

Jen reached in and held his hand. "Is there anything I can do for you? Do you need water?"

The man smiled through cracked lips and took another tiny bite of pastry. "This will last all day. So will your touch."

The tapping water urged Jen on. She was like a reluctant soldier, the water a patting battle drum. The walls were scarred with rusty watermarks. Long thin streaks. Peeling blisters. Broken sticks. One looked like a face, eyes bulging, mouth a wailing O. The drip, drip, dripping seemed to beat faster as she stepped down the corridor. Lacy streams and rivulets of water wept down the walls.

No light came here and the corridor grew dim. A sour smell emanated from the walls, like the inside of a meat shop at the end of a hot day.

A black door loomed before her. She pushed it open, but dazzling brightness made her draw back. Slowly her eyes adjusted. Dozens of torches blazed, focusing intense light on every corner of the room. It was as if someone wished to miss no detail of what occurred there.

The first thing Jen saw was a whip lying on a table, the five strands hanging over the edge. Beneath, three drops of blood glistened like rubies on the pale white floor.

She looked up, her heart in her mouth. Blue hung from his wrists on a whipping post, his body a limp washrag. His back was bare and bloody, as if a small child had smeared red finger paint. No one else was in the chamber.

Jen rushed in. "Blue. Are you all right?"

He didn't reply. She cut him down with Tubole's knife and eased him to the floor. She spotted a bucket of water near a fire pit and brought it to him. Raising his head in her lap, she dribbled a few drops into his mouth.

His lips twitched and he licked them. "Miss me?" His voice was hoarse. Cracked.

Tears poured from Jen's eyes. "You know I did."

"I told Naryfel to pluck her eyebrows . . . a mistake, huh?"

Jen laughed and cried and rocked him. "Shh. Don't talk."

"Leave me. You can't carry me."

"I'm getting you out."

"No. The guards will be back any minute."

"Can you walk?"

He shook his head. Jen eased his head off her lap and he winced. She grabbed one of the sheets and spread it out on the flagstones. Then she rolled him facedown onto the sheet and folded it over him. She tore another sheet into long strips and tied him in. Grabbing the end of the sheet, she dragged him to the door.

"Wait. My harp. It's in my shirt pocket."

Jen found the shirt and stuffed it under his head like a pillow. She couldn't find the harp.

"Forget it. Naryfel took it," said Blue.

Peeking out the door, Jen looked both ways down the corridor. There was no one there, but she heard laughter echoing through the halls. Men. Coming this way.

"Which way to the cell we were in?"

Blue raised his head and looked around. "Left. Then left again."

Jen could hear footfalls now. Grasping the sheet she dragged him down the hall. By the time she reached the first turn, her legs quivered.

This had to hurt Blue, but he wasn't complaining. She reached the cell and tried the door. It was locked. The laughter grew louder.

"Can you pick the lock?" she asked.

"If I can reach it I can pick it."

He got on his knees. Lifting him under his arms she leaned him against the door.

"Give me your knife," he said.

He took the knife but it was too big for the lock. The laughter stopped and there was angry shouting from the torture chamber.

Blue reached through the bars and pried the blade along the edge of the door. When he reached the lock he twisted and the door sprang open.

Jen heard the drumming fall of boots coming toward them.

She pulled Blue into the cell and dragged him to the trap door. Rushing to the opposite corner she jiggled the rock on the wall. Racing to Blue, she slid back the flagstone and revealed the crawlspace. The guards were just up the hall. She heard Bloody Knife barking orders.

She eased Blue into the crawlspace. She jumped in after him and reached for the flagstone.

34

Jen pulled the flagstone in place just

as heavy feet tramped into the cell above. Three terrifying seconds passed, and the trapdoor locked with a click. There was a pause in the footfalls above. Then one set of feet rushed to the trapdoor. She heard scratching about the seam of the flagstone. She waited a few seconds, then scratched nearby and tapped her nails against the wall. The guards could pry open the door with a crowbar. But if they thought it was a rat they'd go away. They'd expect anyone escaping down here to stay quiet. Jen scratched again.

The guards tramped out of the cell and the footfalls faded. She waited another minute before moving. Then she dragged Blue down the dark tunnel. He still couldn't walk so she left him at the bottom, then sloshed through the dim sewer to retrieve the boat, following the colored markers. She rowed back through the heavy air and stench, then rolled the sheet into a pillow and eased him into the boat.

Dripping water, the echo of the paddle, Blue going in and out of a swoon—these marked the next hours. She rowed until her shoulders cramped, and still rowed on. She had to get away from the castle and the city. Guards and sniffers would be everywhere, combing the river and sewers. There'd be checkpoints on the roads.

During the precious moments he was awake, Blue guided her to an underground stream. The air was stifling. At times she thought she'd pass out. She seemed to be floating down an endless tube. Mineral light, oppressive and ghostly, haunted the passage.

Pain shrieked in her arms and back. Still she rowed and the pain numbed and she rowed numb. At last, she burst out of the cave. The sun was blinding. When her eyes adjusted, she guided the boat ashore, climbed out and collapsed.

In the distance she thought she heard roaring.

Blue hissed.

"Sorry," said Jen. She patted gingerly at his back with a wet piece of the sheet. A mask of dried blood coated his skin.

He sat on a rock, dangling his feet in the stream. On either side of the water a thick forest clung to the shore like a thirsty animal.

"I guess you blame me," said Blue.

"For what?"

"For messing up your mom's rescue."

"How could you know about Tubole's daughter?" Jen rinsed the cloth in the water and patted a new spot.

Blue winced. "I should have seen it coming."

"Hush. You did the best you could."

His shoulders relaxed. "I'll make it up to you."

Tears came to Jen's eyes. How he could help now? Mother was far away. Maybe dead. But it was good to have Blue here. Jen didn't want to face the future alone.

The blood dissolved from a section of Blue's back. She

traced her finger on a series of scars, thin white lines that crossed the fresher cuts and weals. "What are these?"

"Naryfel's Tears. From before," he replied.

Jen bit her lip. "She whipped you before?"

"There it is. Any nuts in my pocket?"

His shirt lay on a nearby rock. She fished in the pocket, found a few nuts, and handed them to him.

"That's all?" he asked sadly.

Jen wished she could give him a barrel full. She dabbed lightly at his left shoulder blade.

He stirred. "Leave it be."

"I'll be careful."

"That's enough, I said. Just give me my shirt."

"I can't. It'll get infected."

"Jen, please—" His shoulders tightened again.

"Shh." She sponged the area. At first it looked purple. She felt a growing alarm as the blood wiped away and she saw another color underneath. On a patch of skin was a piece of the sky.

"I'm sorry," she cried. "I didn't know."

"How could you? I didn't tell you."

"You seemed to like the name. Why? Why did you let me?"

"You never called me a Blueback."

"I might as well have. Anyone hearing me would have thought I was."

"Forget it."

"I can't keep calling you that."

"I like the name—when you say it."

Jen's heart trembled.

He agitated the water with his feet. "You must look down on me—"

"No—"

"—hate me, for being a slave—"

"Never."

"But you're a princess and all."

"I hate the people who've done this to you. It's just skin." She brushed her fingers lightly on the patch. "It's beautiful."

"Not everyone thinks so."

Jen wiped the blue patch, cleaning away the last layer of blood. The skin in the middle looked lighter and wrinkled, like a scar from a horrible burn.

She traced her finger on the spot. "What's this?"

"I don't know. It's always been there."

"Blue? What happened to your parents?"

He looked down, his feet churning the water. "What difference does it make? They're gone."

"You were right. I should have trusted you sooner. Don't you trust me?"

"I do. It just hurts to talk about it."

"Mother says talking helps." Jen dabbed at another spot with the cloth.

Blue was quiet, and she gave him time.

"I never knew my real parents," he began at last. "I don't know what happened to them. I was brought to Astor and Meloryn when I was a baby. I was very sick. Almost died. But they nursed me back and raised me as their own.

"I remember gathering herbs with Meloryn, then helping her make stew. You should have smelled it—leeks and savory and forest roots. There was nothing like it. After dinner, she took out her lyre and stroked it with her slender fingers. Then she'd sing, coaxing me asleep. Only an angel could sound like that.

"Astor was a master carver. The wooden statue you saw was his. He used to take me into the forest to gather burls for his carvings. Some he left out for five winters before he'd touch them. He wanted them to be as weathered as driftwood. I loved to ride on his big shoulders—when I was with him I was ten feet tall. I wanted to be just like him. He was starting to show me how to finish the pieces with files and sandpaper when Naryfel's army swept through our village. I don't remember much of that night—I was just five. But the red sky from the burning rooftops. The shrieks from the women and children. The men pleading for their families. That I remember.

"My parents tried to get me out of the village, but it was too late. We were surrounded and herded into a slave pen. Rats live better than we did. I think my parents gave me their scraps of food so I would survive. They died three months later."

"I'm sorry you lost them," Jen said softly.

Blue nodded. His voice was a little strangled when he spoke again. "At the end, Astor must've known he didn't have much time and he had to give me one lesson that would stick. He took me to the edge of the pen, which was perched on the side of a hill. About twenty yards away, another hill sloped up and there was a small cluster of blackberry bushes. It was the end of summer. Everything was drying up and there wasn't much food around. But there must have been a few berries on that bush because a squirrel tightrope-walked on the top vines. 'You see that?' Astor said, pointing to the squirrel. 'Only he can do that.' I watched, fascinated. I couldn't figure out how he jumped from spot to spot without falling in the thick brambles below. Sometimes he'd land and shake there a moment, but he always found his balance and grabbed a berry in his paws. The thorns never stuck him. 'Be like that squirrel,' Astor said. 'No matter what happens, be like that squirrel.' "

Jen felt a lump growing in her throat. She tried to swallow, but it stuck there. The story stirred an old, unnamed yearning.

Old, but not forgotten. Something as present on her mind as the need to keep her family safe. And somehow, the two yearnings were tied together. She couldn't do one without the other. That's what drove her to use Wyndano's Cloak in the first place. That's what drove her to the water tower, the day she'd met Bit among the plenderil.

She pulled out of these thoughts and glanced at Blue. "He loved you very much."

"He did." Blue stared at the trees on the other side of the stream and fell silent. His feet floated in the water, the current bobbing them lightly up and down.

"Remember when we were in prison?" he said at last. "What did you mean by, 'Your harp gave you away?' "

"I was told to beware if I met a harp." She described Medlara's warning.

"She's a sorceress, like Naryfel?"

"No, I don't think so. She's as old as the hills. Sometimes I think she wasn't born like the rest of us, but came out of the earth."

A flock of sparrows settled on the trees he'd been watching. "But she can tell the future?"

"Yes." Jen rinsed the cloth. Now only a little pink floated down the stream. "Once I saw her blow on a powdered root. It streamed out like dragon fire, and glowing sparks floated to the table below. Hills and mountains thrust from the tabletop; rivers flowed and forests grew—it was like looking at the world from a cloud. Then Medlara sent a mist across the little world, and when that cleared, I saw a carriage turn over in a rainstorm. Three months later my mother and I barely escaped a flash-flood."

"Spooky. But if she's that powerful, why doesn't she stop Naryfel?"

"Her power doesn't extend beyond her valley."

"She got a message to you in Aerdem."

"True. Maybe her power is growing."

Blue studied the birds across the water. "And you trust her?"

"Completely."

He turned and gave her a red-toothed smile. "She meant you were to trust me."

Jen smiled back. "I think so now."

He bit into another nut. "What else did she say?"

"To seek the answers. I think it's some kind of riddle."

"Strange. Maybe something got cut off—like the rest of her message." He looked intently at the birds.

"What do we do now?" Jen asked at last.

With drumming wings the sparrows took flight. Blue sprang to his feet, his nostrils flaring.

"What's wrong?" Jen asked. Then she heard it. Even at this distance, the roaring was filled with the ferocity of a pack that's found the scent.

35

The sun was ferocious. Heat waves

rippled across a fierce sky. A hot wind blasted from the north, as if the gates of hell had opened to greet the sniffers rushing from the south.

"We need to get out of here," Blue cried. "The wind will carry our scent." He pulled Jen toward the boat.

"Wait," she said. "We've got to cover our scent." She told him quickly how she'd evaded the sniffers with a dead fish.

"It'll take too long to spear one," said Blue. "But unka might work."

"Unka?"

"Like garlic, but stronger." He pointed out a plant with long flat leaves, and flowers like a buttercup.

They pulled them out by the roots, then mashed the bulbs on the side of the boat to make a paste. The smell made Jen's eyes water. Blue was about to smear his skin when Jen stopped him.

"Wait. Let's throw them off our trail."

"How?" Blue asked.

"We're taking the boat, right?"

"For a while. Then we need to cut through the forest, or the stream will take us back to Purpura.

"Perfect," said Jen. "Can you run?"

"I can if I eat this." He bit into a clove of unka. "It'll close the wounds in no time." He smiled when he was done. "You won't come near me now."

"I will." Jen chewed into a bulb like it was an apple. "Two unkas cancel each other."

The herb seared through her nose and burned her throat. Tears streamed down her cheeks and she swayed from a wave of dizziness. But a moment later the soreness in her muscles faded. She felt alert. Clear headed. Like she could run all day.

Blue felt ready, so she had them run a quarter mile into the forest and climb a tree. Then they doubled back to the boat and rubbed the unka over their skin. Jen gathered the used plants and threw them in the boat. Then they shoved off and attacked the water with paddles.

"Nice," said Blue. "They'll think we disappeared up the tree. Where did you learn that trick?"

"My brother." Jen thought of Dash and Father and Mother. Was it already too late? She threw her whole body into paddling.

Blue guided the boat into the middle of the stream. A rocky shore lined the stream on either side, except where the forest marched down to the water. There, the roots of pine trees gnawed at the water. The air was hot and sticky. Jen's clothes clung to her skin. The smell of unka hung over the little boat.

Blue kept up a casual chatter, but seemed to keep an ear cocked to the forest on their left. "Are you afraid of anything?" he asked.

"Lots of things."

"What scares you the most?"

"Losing my family."

"Right. But what about things you have to face?"

Jen hesitated. *He opened up about his parents,* she thought. *What could be more painful than that?* "Wyndano's Cloak," she said at last.

"What's that?"

She told him about the cloak. How her father used it to turn into different animals.

"Why are you afraid?" asked Blue.

Jen bit her lip. "I got hurt using it."

He gazed at the scar on her eyebrow. "That's how you got that?"

She nodded.

"What happened?"

"I was with my father. He was showing me how to use the cloak. We were standing on a water tower—thirty feet up—and he turned into a flying squirrel."

"He really looked like a squirrel?"

"Just like. With little hands, whiskers and silky fur. And big round eyes, black as coal. The white skin between his front and back legs made him look fat. Then he took off, and that skin suddenly spread out. He looked like a kite as he glided to a tree fifty yards away."

"Is it hard to do?"

"Changing into animals is easy. Really being that animal, doing what they do—that's the hard part. He says you can't really practice—you just have to be ready. A moment comes, and you know what to do."

"How?"

"Father says you have to grow into the cloak. It only reflects something deep inside you, something great and wonderful that wants to come out." Jen pulled at the oars, listening for sounds of pursuit.

"What happened?" Blue asked. The current churned about their oars, sweeping the little boat along.

"He came back to the tower. He gave me the cloak . . ." Jen's mouth went dry. "We argued. He wanted me to do a squirrel. I wanted an eagle."

"Why?"

Jen looked up at the sky, bright and deep. "Up there, you leave it all behind."

Blue shot her a questioning look.

"No slaves," said Jen. "No shanty towns."

"No burning villages." Sweat beaded on Blue's forehead. "You argued . . ."

"I won. I threw the cloak over my shoulders. My body grew. Talons sprouted where my feet should have been. I felt his hands on my back, grasping feathers. He told me to flap my wings. I did and lifted into the air. But I wasn't ready. I tried to stop—I thought he was holding on . . ."

"He let go."

"I flapped desperately. For a moment I thought I had it and I'd be all right. But I had a terrible thought: Nothing's holding me up . . ." Jen swallowed. Despite the heat, her skin felt cold, clammy. "The last thing I remember is the ground spinning. Then it sprang at me with a shriek."

They rowed in silence for a while.

"He didn't mean to hurt you," Blue said softly.

"No . . . but I never tried it again."

Blue eyed the tree to his left.

A moment later Jen heard roaring in the distance. "What scares you?"

Blue wiped the sweat dripping off his brow. Then he cocked a thumb toward the forest. "They say one bite from a sniffer and you'll go blind. But there's something scarier. Something we might have to do."

Jen stopped paddling. "What do you mean?"

"I think I know what you're supposed to seek."

"Medlara's warning—to seek the answers."

Blue looked at her, and he wasn't smiling. "The beginning got chopped off. She meant the Dancers."

Blue steered the boat to the shore on the right. "We can't take the stream any farther. It hooks back to Purpura."

The side of the boat knocked against the roots of a pepper tree, which twisted into the water with gnarled arms. Jen grabbed one of the roots and held the boat steady while Blue hopped off. She quickly joined him on the bank.

He pointed at the boat. "We've got to ditch it. If they find it, they'll know we came this way."

Jen rubbed her chin. "Let's sink it. That'll cover any trace of our scent."

They threw in the paddles and broke a hole in the bottom with a rock. Then they piled in more rocks and pushed the boat downstream. They watched until it drifted away and sank. Then Blue led the way on a faint trail through the forest.

"Who are the Dancers?" Jen asked.

"There's a forest knoll on the mountain up there." Blue pointed northeast to a craggy mountain, visible through a window in the foliage.

Jen saw no greenery. Only jagged-tooth rocks biting a snowy summit. "There are trees up there?"

"That's part of the mystery. In the middle of the snow is a patch of forest that surrounds a hill. At the top, there's a clearing with three dead oaks. No one goes there."

"Why?"

"It's haunted."

"Have you been there?"

"I've seen the knoll, but I never went in. Gypsies and wild men of the mountains shun it. Even Naryfel steers clear."

"How do you know?"

"She and her soldiers chased me up there. I had no choice but to hide near the knoll. She was close behind and I buried myself under a drift of snow. I heard horses ride up and stop near to me as that tree." Blue pointed to a pine ten yards away. " 'Let Them get him,' she said. But she sounded scared. She turned around and went back down the mountain."

"What does this have to do with the Dancers?"

"They haunt the knoll."

"What are they?"

"Witches or demons, I suspect."

The air was oven hot, but Jen felt a chill go through her.

"Some say they suck out your blood," said Blue. "Or turn you into a spider and doom you to spin thread for their robes. Forever. It's hard to say for sure. People who go there never come down."

Jen shuddered. "What do you think?"

"That a yawning cavity opens up and swallows you—"

Roaring cut him off. He looked east and listened. "Sniffers. They've found the fake trail we left. We better hurry."

Jen spied some unka and pointed. "Let's rub on more, just in case."

They rubbed on unka, and hurried down the path.

Jen wondered. Was Blue right about the Dancers? If so, it didn't make sense. Medlara wouldn't send her into danger. She told Blue so.

"Tell me Medlara's words again," said Blue.

Jen thought back. " 'If you meet . . . a harp, you must . . . If the worst happens, seek the answers—' "

"Fill in the blanks. 'If you meet a boy with a harp, you must trust him. If the worst happens, seek the Dancers.' "

"She knew I'd meet you."

"Right. And that I'd help you. If I couldn't free your mom, if Naryfel sent her to the Ice Falls, I could guide you to the Dancers. There's nowhere else to take you."

"But what does that have to do with my mom?"

"We need a way to get to the Ice Falls. The Dancers can get us there."

"But they'll kill us. You said so yourself."

"Look, if you don't want to go, I'll take you into the mountains. I have friends up there that'll protect us. But if you want to save your mom, the Dancers are the only ones powerful enough to get us to the Ice Falls."

The roaring had moved parallel to them. Then a burst of excitement from the sniffers.

Blue grinned. "They found the tree we went up."

"That won't hold them long. If the Desert King's with them, he'll return to the stream and have a closer look. He'll see we dug up unka."

Jen quickened her steps while she battled over what to do. Never had so much rested on her. If the Dancers were demons, how would she get them to help? Asking would put her and Blue in danger. But if she didn't try, Mother would die.

"Are you sure about the Dancers?" she asked.

"Positive. I've lived in these hills my whole life."

"Then take me to them."

Jen kept up a determined trot. There was a clear goal now, and the forest streaked by as in a dream.

Blue peppered her with questions about the cloak. "That thing deep inside. What do you think it is?"

"I wish I knew."

"It's got to be something all your own."

"Father says we all have a gift."

"Like a talent. I guess I know what yours is."

Jen turned to him in surprise.

Blue's teeth shone. "When we were in prison. The way you tackled Bloody Knife. You would have taken him out if the other guard wasn't there."

Jen shrugged. "It's a wrestling move. Dash showed me."

"He didn't show you how to leap. Jen, that guard was twice your size. Once I saw a mountain lion chasing a stag. The lion had the speed. But the stag headed for a deep gully and sailed over it in a big arc. That's how you looked when you sprang onto the guard's back."

"What happened to the stag?"

"The lion skidded to a halt at the edge. The gap was too much for him." Blue stopped to catch his breath. He pulled up a couple of unka bulbs and stuffed them in his pocket. "You're a moonjumper."

"What's that?"

"In the days before Naryfel, the Bluebacks had a festival. All the great athletes competed. Throwing spears, archery, footraces, jumping. Every once in a while, someone won every event. That was the moonjumper."

Jen rubbed her scar. "Then why did I fall?"

"You lost confidence. I watched you at the carriage house. You went up the wall like a cat."

Jen remembered. She'd allowed herself only a moment to feel the thrill. A thousand wings fluttering inside. "All I could think about was my mother. Blue, sometimes I feel that if she died, some of the light would go out of the world."

The two days up the mountain, Jen

barely slept. Neither did the sniffers. They were closing in. Soon they'd be nipping at her heels. She clutched only a thread of hope that Mother was alive.

At last, dead tired, Jen parted the pine branches and scanned the clearing beyond. Flattened, sun-dried straw covered the ground. Otherwise, the area was empty, except for three dead oak trees in the center.

"Is this the spot?" she asked. She rubbed her hands, trying to bring warmth to her fingertips. She'd been plowing through snowpack all afternoon.

Blue's teeth were chattering. "That's it."

Jen turned to him. "I'm going alone."

"No," said Blue.

"I can't put you in any more danger."

"There's plenty of danger coming up behind."

True. Jen had watched the sniffers gaining on them all afternoon. The roaring was not more than half an hour behind.

"I can take my chances with the Dancers, or get dragged back to Naryfel's dungeon," said Blue.

Jen shuddered. "The Desert King wants me. You can slip away."

Blue put his hands on his hips and cocked his head to one side. "And miss all the fun?"

Jen bit her lip as she looked back at the clearing. She could see how this spot got its name. The three oak trees looked like dancers, leaning from the waist with outstretched arms. Their branches almost touched, forming a triangle. And a deep, almost tangible silence hung over the knoll.

"Are you sure no one comes back from here?"

"Some of the gypsy women do—but they're practically witches themselves. Their own men fear them."

That didn't sound reassuring. "How do we talk to the Dancers?"

"We need to leave an offering in the middle of that triangle. Then lean up against one of the trunks. I've got some unka in my pocket. We can offer that."

Jen nodded. The roaring from behind took on a note of excitement and prodded her forward. She led the way down to the three trees. As she entered the clearing, everything became sharply focused. The rustle of her feet on the dry straw. The soft hiss of air as she breathed. The rough and wrinkled oak bark, with deep trenches and pits, ancient like the earth. The air felt warmer. The chill she'd been feeling for the past hours melted away.

Blue handed her the unka and she laid it in the middle of the triangle. She sat facing the offering, with her back against the widest tree. Blue sat beside her. He gave her a bold smile, but she felt his arm trembling. She waited, and the roar of the sniffers grew louder—then faded.

Tendrils of mist rose from the ground at the outer edges of the circle. It reminded Jen of the mist she'd seen the day of the warning, only this was pure white. Soon the ring of pine trees that surrounded the clearing was covered, as if someone had drawn a curtain. She felt strangely at peace.

A shadow fell across her face, and she looked up. There were green leaves on the oak trees, and ivy cascaded down the trunks. One of the vines caressed her arm as it brushed by.

Jen glanced at Blue. His eyes were closed. His breathing had slowed and he seemed to be sleeping. For a moment she wondered if she was dreaming too, but knew she wasn't. She felt more awake, more alive, than ever in her life.

The earth shook, drawing her attention back to the clearing. The ground was now covered with a carpet of grass, clover and wildflowers. Through the mist beyond, hanging ghost-like, she saw huts with thatched roofs, a well, and a blazing fire pit— the central square of a village. A drum started beating . . . and the murmur of voices. Little girls ran among the buildings with baskets filled with berries. Women faded into view, hoeing at a garden, grinding grain with mortar and pestle, or feeding their babies. An old woman sat at a loom, chanting.

One of the girls put down her basket and skipped into the clearing—becoming less ghost and more real as she drew near. She capered and leaped about the clearing, arms flying, flaxen hair swinging free. She was five or six, and her eyes were wide, sparkling, and innocent.

"This must be one of the Dancers," Jen murmured. The little girl tipped her head to one side and curtsied.

"Yes," Jen heard in her head.

"I'm here to—" she began.

The girl circled her arm through the air and brought her finger to her lips. "Hush."

The word floated in Jen's mind, and she realized the girl was communicating through dance. Somehow, Jen could understand the motions.

"We know why you're here," the girl continued, touching her forehead and gesturing to the ground.

A second dancer capered out of the misty village and joined the first. This one was a woman. She had full hips and breasts, and her belly was round and swollen. But she spun and twirled across the clover as lightly as a butterfly, her long hair, as green as the trees, floating behind her.

A wave of calm passed over Jen. She was certain the Dancers were good and turned to nudge Blue. He wouldn't want to miss this.

"Do not awaken your friend. What you see is only for your eyes. He is not ready to meet the Dancers." The woman dipped and swayed, also speaking through dance.

"Did you—" Jen began.

"Enchant him?" Laughter flowed into Jen's mind from both dancers. "We are protecting him," they said.

A third dancer joined the first two. This one was an old woman, gray and wrinkled like oak bark, but she danced as spryly as the first two. Her sky-blue eyes twinkled, reminding Jen of Medlara.

"Do not be afraid, Jenren of Aerdem," said the old woman.

"Is my mother alive?" Jen asked. She realized she spoke to the Dancers in her mind.

"She is alive," said the old woman. "We will open a way for you to the Ice Falls."

"But the rest you must do on your own," said the younger woman.

"What can I hope to do against Naryfel?" Jen asked.

"Remember when you were little?" said the girl. "The world was filled with wonders. You couldn't wait to run through fields of daisies, to splash through a mountain spring, or watch a butterfly idle on a leaf. The world was safe and—"

"Filled with possibilities," said the younger woman. Bread dough appeared in her hands and she started to knead it.

Jen remembered. Diving into the creek on hot summer days. Wondering if she could climb to the top of the bay tree in Nell's back yard—then doing it. Making cookies with Nell on rainy afternoons. Nell singing Jen to sleep with lullabies. Then memories of the last years flooded Jen's mind. Losing Nell. Searching the wide world alone for a mother she never knew. Finally finding her family. Then her kidnap. The maze of fire. Naryfel's prison. Almost drowning in the river. Jen started crying. "That was torn from me."

"Yes," the younger woman soothed. "But you can't bake bread without heat." The dough in her hand expanded, turned golden and brown. She handed Jen the loaf. Finding it too hot to hold, Jen dropped it in her lap. The steam carried up the fresh, yeasty aroma.

"You are powerful," Jen said. "Please, save my mother."

"We can only guide you," said the old woman.

"But Naryfel's magic is strong."

A wooden matchbox appeared in the old woman's hand. "Yours will be stronger. Fight her with this. But you must not look inside or open it until the right moment. Otherwise, you may lose faith in its power, for it will look like there is nothing there."

"What is it?" asked Jen.

All three dancers leaped about the clearing like deer. "The truth."

"Give me something more. Naryfel will laugh in my face and throw me over the Ice Falls right after my mother."

"Trust yourself," said the little girl.

"But how will I know the right time?"

"You will know," they all answered. "Go. Now. Before the door closes. Trust that you will know." They began to fade, their last words echoing, fading with them . . .

"Wait," Jen cried. "How am I to get there?"

The village was gone. The old woman and the young woman had disappeared. Just before she evaporated with the mist, the little girl reached above her. Pulling her arm down like she was lowering a shade, a large piece of the clearing changed. The motion was similar to the one Naryfel used to turn into Vieveeka. Only when the Dancer did it, it was like she had turned one huge piece of a jigsaw puzzle, with a different picture on the other side. At that spot, Jen looked on a stark, icy world. The wind was blowing there. Snow drifted into the Dancers' clearing.

A roar of triumph jerked Jen to her feet. A pack of snarling sniffers charged out of the trees, followed by Bloody Knife.

Blue sprang up, a dazed look on his face.

"Follow me," Jen cried. She raced to the jigsaw opening, Blue on her heels.

With a piercing howl the sniffers tore across the clearing to cut her off.

37

Half a dozen sniffers charged across

the clearing, kicking up dust and straw. They ran silently, tusks bared and flashing like knives. Jen dashed for the snowy doorway. She clutched the little box in one hand. With the other she grabbed Blue, still unsteady on his feet, and practically dragged him across the clearing. Jen glanced back. Bloody Knife locked eyes with her and smiled.

Now Blue was running on his own, but the sniffers were only a dozen feet behind, gaining ground every second. The one in the lead was larger than the others. He had a misshapen head, like a huge block of wood cut by a blind axman. Yellow-brown saliva foamed and drooled about his jaw. What riveted Jen's attention was his front teeth. A piece of fang had broken off, leaving a gap. Wedged into the space was a human forefinger, which crooked and flopped, crooked and flopped with every stride. As if the former owner were summoning the next victim to pass down the dark gullet beyond.

Jen could smell his rotting-carcass breath, felt the hot puffs hit the back of her neck. Spurring her feet to fly. Barely touching the ground.

Blue stumbled. She heaved him up. There were just a few more steps—

"Now!" she cried. Holding Blue's hand they leaped through the opening. Cold air stung her face. She kept running, listening for sounds of pursuit. Hearing none, she glanced back. The opening to the Dancers' clearing was gone. So were the sniffers and Bloody Knife.

Blue pulled up beside her to catch his breath. "That was close."

"Too close." Jen leaned on her knees and gulped air until her heart slowed. Finally she straightened and looked around. She was on a road on the shoulder of a mountain. Below stretched a vast, empty expanse of snow and ice, cut with dark shadows. The sun hung in the western sky like a cold ball of copper.

"Do you know where Naryfel took my mom?"

"Probably to her Keep."

"Have you been there?"

Blue shook his head. He pointed where the road turned a hundred yards ahead. "I'd guess it's in that direction. There's nothing back that way."

"What's that down there?" Jen pointed west to a half dozen black specks in the valley below.

Blue shielded his eyes from the glare and stared. Whirling, he pulled her down behind a drift of snow.

"What is it?" Jen's heart bolted to a gallop.

Blue's pupils dilated. "Sniffers."

"It can't be. They didn't follow us through the opening."

"I know. But those are sniffers."

Jen swallowed. "How can you tell this far away?"

"The gypsies call me Hawkeye." He tried to smile, but his voice was strained.

"But how'd they get here so fast?"

"I don't know."

Jen peeked above the drift and studied the specks. "Did they see us?"

Blue slithered up beside her. "I reckon not. They're not running."

"We better get moving or we're good as grave grass."

"Right." Blue led the way. They followed the bend in the road and climbed a series of switchbacks. The wind rushed past Jen's ears and snapped her shirtsleeves. She jammed her hands into her pockets to keep warm.

A mile later, she heard something above the wind. Roaring, far deeper than sniffers. The ground trembled beneath her feet. "What's that sound?"

"I don't know. It's coming from beyond that hill."

The road skirted the hill. They followed it cautiously. Rounding a corner she saw a cave set in a steep embankment of the mountain. The opening was dark and forbidding, and looked like a head turning away.

"The sound is coming from that cave," Blue said. He led the way in. A dozen steps in, the passage turned. There were torches set in the walls, which appeared to be carved from solid ice.

"What happened back there with the Dancers?" Blue asked.

"Were you asleep for all of it?"

Blue hesitated, and gave her a sheepish grin.

"It's hard to explain," Jen said. "They gave me something to fight Naryfel." She showed him the box.

"What is it?"

"I don't know."

Blue stared at the box. "Let's open it and see."

"No. They said I wasn't to look until the time was right." She put the box back in her pocket.

The roaring grew louder as she moved forward. The cave sheltered her from the wind outside, but the air inside was cold and her toes felt numb. She reached a fork in the passage. A tunnel turned off to her right and the sound came from there.

"Which way should we go?" she asked.

Blue pointed to the right tunnel. "Let's follow the sound."

Jen agreed. The roaring grew as she went, like a constant roll of thunder. She looked at Blue.

His eyes widened and he took a little suck of air. "A pretty picture. Sniffers behind. That ahead."

They emerged from the tunnel onto a narrow, diamond-shaped ledge. It protruded fifty feet from a vertical wall of the mountain. On the right was a tumbling mass of blue and white. Jen blinked. At first it looked like a waterfall, but she realized it was an avalanche of snow and ice blocks.

"The Ice Falls," said Blue, his eyes round with wonder.

Jen followed him to one edge of the cliff and looked down. It appeared to fall endlessly, with no bottom in sight.

The cascade poured close by. Jen looked up and had the sensation there was no top. The Ice Falls reached to the blue-black sky.

Two ice boulders crashed, the exploding pieces flying dangerously close. Blue pulled her back. "No surviving a fall down there."

Jen swallowed and could only nod. "Come on. My mom must be down the other tunnel." If her mother hadn't already been killed.

Jen looked out the exit to the tunnel. There was no one on the path ahead, which wound down the mountain a short distance to a cliff. Perched on the edge was Naryfel's Keep, glistening like a block of ice in the setting sun. Beyond and thousands of feet below stretched a vast, snow-covered waste. In the distance, a range of hazy mountains ringed the horizon.

Jen looked apprehensively behind her, wondering if the sniffers had caught her scent. If they had, she couldn't hear them over the Ice Falls.

She started down the path toward the Keep. Blue reached out and stopped her.

"We can't just march in there," he said. "We need a plan."

Jen fingered the box in her pocket. She had to trust that the Dancers had given her something powerful. A plan was beginning to form in her mind, but she needed to know more about the Keep. "My guess is there aren't any soldiers around. It would be hard to attack here, and why would anyone bother? There's nothing here."

Blue smiled. "We'll have to sign you up for the Resistance."

"If we get my mom back, we won't need a Resistance. Come on." Jen led the way. She kept checking behind her for sniffers, but none came charging out of the tunnel.

When she reached the Keep, it was little more than a cottage. The path led to the front door, then split to circle around the building.

Jen decided to scope out the path around the house. Peering into the first window, she saw a kitchen, and beyond it a pantry lined with jars. Next was a bedroom with a large bay window. A bathroom followed, with a sunken marble tub. Curiously, two heavy curtains, now pulled aside, hung at the window. Next came the master bedroom. Like the other rooms, it was unoccupied. A huge, egg-shaped bed dominated the chamber. The same heavy curtains hung at the bay window. When closed, there would be complete privacy.

The path turned to the back of the house, giving another

view into the bedroom. A large triangular terrace thrust over the cliff edge like the bow of a ship. On this side, the house was built over a two-step cascade, but the water had turned to ice in the act of tumbling. What must have been bubbling falls now were a series of icicle spears and daggers. The whole house looked like a boat, frozen in a beat of time while plunging through churning water.

The wind whipped across Jen's face from the northwest. She had to get moving. Her scent would go right to the sniffers.

Along the back wall, a second room faced the terrace. She crept to the edge of the window and looked past another set of heavy curtains. A thrill went through her. Mother! She was alive! Naryfel stood at the end of a table, glaring down at her.

Blue tugged Jen's sleeve. "Let's check out the other side of the house."

"Wait." Jen scanned the room for a way in. A row of louvered windows near the roof might do, but there was no way of crossing the terrace without Naryfel seeing them. She doubled back and checked out the other side of the house. The first rooms were empty servants' quarters.

Blue scratched his head. "Why no servants?"

"I think Naryfel comes here for privacy," Jen replied.

Moving on to the next room, she saw the Steward. He sat on a bed with his head in his hands. Lines of worry creased his forehead. Again, Jen had the feeling he had kind eyes.

After the Steward's room, a bridge crossed the frozen cascade and led to the rear terrace, so Jen doubled back to the front door. Taking a deep breath she turned the knob. The door swung open on well-oiled hinges. She crept inside. Blue followed close behind.

A long hallway led to the living room, where she had seen Naryfel and her mother. The door was ajar, and she peeked through the opening by the hinges. Her mother was still seated. The setting sun streamed through the bay windows. Naryfel squinted at the glare and drew the western curtains closed. She strode to the northern windows and reached for the curtains.

"Leave them open," said Mother.

"You like the view?" Naryfel asked.

"Yes."

Naryfel smiled and closed the curtains. The room would be dark save for the candelabras lining the walls. She returned to the table. Before her were a bowl of apples and dates, a paring knife, a block of cheese. She popped some dates in her mouth. Mother gazed longingly at them.

"You want some," said Naryfel. It wasn't a question.

"I'm hungry," Mother replied.

Naryfel stroked her chin. "Perhaps a last meal for the condemned."

"You won't kill me."

"After all I've done, you still believe that?"

"I do. We're sisters. Family."

"Half sisters."

"Yes, but connected through Father. He loved you as he loved me."

"He didn't."

"He did. He gave you all you desired."

"Father was a weak fool."

"No, he was wise."

"Wise men don't lie."

Mother shook her head. "He would never lie."

"But I tell you he did."

Mother stared. "Father was good. Don't blame him for what you've become."

Naryfel laughed. "I don't. And I don't regret what I am."

"You must," Mother replied. "Your kingdom has decayed. Your people are crying for your care. It's not too late. You can love them still."

"Love?" Naryfel sneered. "I'm not interested in love."

"There is good in you, Naryfel. You can choose."

"I do choose. I have no regrets."

"Good can still come of all this."

Naryfel's jaw dropped. "You believe that?"

"I do. Something good can come from something bad."

"Then you're a bigger fool than I thought."

Jen had heard enough. She pulled Blue back down the hall and out the front door. "Can you find a way to blow out the candles without being seen?" she asked.

Blue flashed a red-toothed smile. "Of course."

"Good. Here's the plan."

Jen strode boldly into the living room. Naryfel's head snapped up. She held a handful of dates. They slipped through her fingers and dropped to the floor.

"You . . . how did you get here?" she asked.

"The Dancers sent me," Jen replied. She glanced at the curtains. Good. The second set of curtains had been pulled. She smiled inwardly when they stirred a moment. There was no breeze in the room.

"It's over, Naryfel. I know your dirty little secret." Jen was bluffing. But the lack of servants here, the heavy curtains around the bathroom and bedroom. The servants dismissed when Naryfel went to bathe. Painting and repainting the walls of her castle. All pointed to a dark secret.

Naryfel staggered back on the word "Dancers," and turned white. "What do you know of the Dancers?"

363

"That they're more powerful than you." Jen turned to her mother and beckoned with her hand. Mother started to rise from the table.

"No!" Naryfel snatched the knife, leaped, and drew the edge against Mother's throat.

Jen heard footsteps behind her and moved aside.

The Steward rushed in unarmed. "What! What is it?" His eyebrows rose into domes when he saw Jen. She kicked the door shut and moved farther into the room.

"Arrest her," Naryfel commanded.

The Steward took a tentative step toward Jen.

"Stand back," she cried, pulling out the Dancers' box and holding it up. The Steward stopped, and shot a questioning look at Naryfel.

Jen nodded toward the box. "A gift, Naryfel. From the Dancers. Let Mother go, or I'll release what's inside."

Naryfel sneered. But one eye twitched as she gazed at the box. She pressed the knife closer to Mother's throat. "You're bluffing. A child doesn't survive the Dancers, and they don't give away magic."

"No?" Jen cried, holding the box high. "Behold the power of the Dancers!"

A blast of wind blew out the candles and plunged the room into darkness. Then a tiny unwinking eye of red floated toward Naryfel.

Jen heard a stifled scream. Bootsteps dashed toward the door. Jen followed as best she could. The door was flung open and she saw Naryfel's silhouette running down the hall, Mother in tow, the Steward close behind. Jen ran after them and caught them at the front entrance.

"Stop," she cried. "Or I'll unleash the wrath of the Dancers."

Naryfel shook her head. "It can't be . . ." She edged away, the knife cutting a groove in Mother's throat.

Jen held the box aloft. "Let Mother go."

Naryfel looked from side to side like a caged animal. There was nowhere to go but up the path to the ice cave. She backed away, pulling Mother with her. Jen followed, holding the box before her, but Naryfel wouldn't release Mother. Instead, she backed all the way up the path, through the cave, onto the cliff beside the Ice Falls, holding the knife to Mother's throat.

An avalanche of snow and ice plunged and crashed around the little outcropping as Jen walked half its length. The Steward stood to one side wringing his hands, looking from Jen to Naryfel.

Naryfel stepped toward the precipice. "Stop!" she cried. "Or I'll throw her over!"

A roar of triumph sounded over the falls as the sniffers rushed from the cave, followed closely by the Desert King.

38

The sniffers growled, straining at their

chains to get at Jen. The Desert King held them back with a tight grip.

He leered at Jen. "I split up the sniffers. Half went with palace guards to track you. The rest came with me through Naryfel's Pass. I've been biding my time, knowing you'd find a way to come for your mother. You're very resourceful."

Jen fought the urge to back away. She needed to look strong, show she was in command. She held up the box. "You're too late."

The king darted a questioning glance at Naryfel, who still held the knife at Mother's throat.

"Tell him to wait south of the tunnel," Jen said to Naryfel. The queen eyed the box uncertainly.

Jen took a step forward. "Tell him, or I'll open it."

"I won't go without my prize," said the Desert King.

"I told you already. I'll pay you when I return to Aerdem," Jen said. "Go while you can, or feel the wrath of the Dancers."

"You're bluffing," said the king.

"Am I? Then why is Naryfel standing at the edge of a cliff

with a knife to my mother's throat? Why is her steward standing helplessly, wringing his hands?"

"I don't believe it," said the king. He yanked back on the chains. The sniffers foamed at the mouth, red eyes glaring at Jen, hooves kicking up snow to reach her. "I have only to let go. They'll tear you up."

Jen reached for the lid of the box.

"Go," cried Naryfel. "I'll pay you later."

"You promised me the girl," said the king.

"Go," shouted Naryfel. "We'll settle up later."

Shrugging, the king led the sniffers back into the tunnel.

"Go with him," Jen said to the Steward. "Make sure he waits south of the tunnel. Then come back."

"No," said Naryfel. "Stay with him."

Jen thought that was odd. Why would Naryfel want to be alone up here? Unless there was something she didn't want the Steward to hear.

"Come back, or I'll open the box," Jen commanded.

Naryfel's shoulders sagged and she nodded in agreement. As Jen watched him disappear into the cave, she wondered where Blue was. If the Desert King had seen him on the way up here, he would have been captured. But would the king capture Blue on the way back down? She could only hope Blue would evade him.

The roar of the falls lessened. Then two mammoth ice chunks crashed together, sending a spray of shards near Naryfel. She moved a step away from the cliff edge, drawing Mother along.

"Let her go," said Jen.

"Put down the box first," replied Naryfel.

"Why should I trust you?"

"Because I'll throw her over the cliff if you don't."

367

"You could do that anyway."

Naryfel smiled. Jen felt the upper hand slipping away. "Mother?" Jen asked.

"I'm her sister," said Mother. "She won't kill me."

All Jen's instincts told her that Mother was wrong. But what choice did she have? She started lowering the box to the ground.

"No! Don't trust her," cried a familiar voice.

"Blue!" Jen exclaimed.

Blue ran to her from the tunnel. The Steward also emerged, and stood a few paces away.

Naryfel's smile grew. She let go of Mother and broke into a deep mocking laugh. "You almost had me," Naryfel said, with a shake of her head. She pointed to Blue. "I assumed you were still in prison. But you made the eye of red."

Jen held the box back up. "It's true, he faked the eye. But this is real. It came from the Dancers."

Naryfel ignored Jen. Instead, she drew Blue's harmonica out of her pocket. "Miss this?" she asked with a laugh. "How about if I toss it over the cliff?" Her voice turned cold. "The jig is up. Arrest them," she said to the Steward.

He nodded and moved toward Jen with outstretched arms.

"Stay back," Jen cried, holding the box aloft.

The Steward continued forward, forcing Jen to back away. The jig did seem to be up. An icy hand gripped her heart. She had no doubt Naryfel would throw Mother over the cliff. If Jen wasn't thrown over too, she'd be given to the Desert King.

She had to hope the Dancers had given her something powerful.

Now! she thought, and opened the box.

The Steward stopped. Naryfel watched, one eye twitching. Jen looked inside. It looked like ordinary dirt. It felt like an hour had passed, but it was only a moment and the Steward was moving again.

Jen wasn't sure what she'd expected, but there had to be more to it. The Dancers had promised her. "Behold, the wrath of the Dancers," she cried.

She flung the dirt before her. The wind should have taken it up, swirled it in the air. Instead it fell straight to the snow and an ear-deafening explosion rocked the cliff top. A cloud of blue smoke erupted from the ground. The Steward backed away, his face white, his eyes as round as coins.

Jen heard a scream from behind the smoke. It wasn't Mother. Must be Naryfel. The smoke began to clear, revealing a stout figure. At first, Jen thought it must be one of the Dancers. No more than four feet tall, with a squat body and bowed legs, she resembled a gnarled oak tree. More smoke lifted. Now a simple peasant dress and apron were visible. Her gray hair was wrapped in a bun and covered with a kerchief. She turned a pair of twinkling blue eyes on Jen and smiled.

"Medlara!" Jen exclaimed.

"Are you all right?" Medlara asked.

"Yes, but Naryfel has Mother."

Medlara chuckled. "We'll see about that." With a wave of her hand, the blue smoke spiraled up and faded.

Naryfel looked on like a statue, frozen where she stood. Slowly her color returned. "Fool. You have no power outside your insignificant little valley."

"I have the power of the truth," Medlara cried. She pointed at Naryfel. "And it's time to face yours." Her voice rang out above the thunder of the falls.

"This is your end, you meddling old crone," Naryfel spat back. "That's the only truth." She nodded at the Steward. "Arrest her. I'll take intense pleasure in roasting her over a spit."

The Steward hesitated. "I have no weapon. No ropes or chains."

Naryfel tossed him her knife, which landed at his feet. He picked up the knife and took a step toward Medlara.

"Stay," said Medlara with a gentle motion of her hand. "All the fathers in your line, back to the first steward, devoted their lives to serving the crown. It is the air you breathe. Your reason for being. Upholding tradition, the law of the monarchy, that's your sworn oath. You'd no sooner abandon your duty than these falls would flow up. So stay, my good steward. I especially want you to hear what I have to say."

The Steward cast a hasty look at Naryfel.

"If you can't arrest her, fetch the Desert King," she commanded, her eyes staring coldly at Medlara.

"Why? So he won't hear the truth?" Medlara asked. "Stay, good man," she said to the Steward, her eyes never leaving Naryfel. "For you owe no allegiance to her."

Naryfel gnashed her teeth. "Blast it, man, do as you're told."

The Steward shuffled uncertainly. "What is she talking about?"

"For the last time, leave," Naryfel shouted, her face enflamed with rage, "or I'll hang you for treason."

"I'll stay," said the Steward quietly. "If there is something concerning the well-being of Purpura, I'll hear it. If it's nothing, I'll fetch the king."

"You're relieved of your post," Naryfel hissed. "You can spend your remaining days planning your funeral."

"You can't relieve me of my post without a vote of parliament," said the Steward. "That is the law, established by your father. It is also the law, established by his father's father, that the Steward shall hear all matters concerning the welfare of the kingdom, lest any king or queen think they are above counsel."

Medlara pointed to Blue. "Now that's settled, let's start with this boy."

Naryfel appeared ready to charge at Medlara, but this stopped her in her tracks. "What about him? He's a menace. A guttersnipe. A rat slinking in the sewer."

Blue glared at her.

"This boy," said Medlara in a voice turned hard, "who you blithely insult, whose tender flesh you whipped, who you sold to slave aboard your galleys—"

"What does his life matter?"

"—This boy, I say, who was robbed of the loving guidance of parents, of the good people who took him, who was left on their death to forage like an animal for food—"

"A tragedy of war—"

"To live on grass and insects and seeds, to beg in the streets—"

"He's good for little more—"

Medlara shot an accusing finger at Naryfel. "This boy with no name, no country, with only the stars for a roof and trees for a home, this boy you hate and scorn is none other than your own son."

❧❧

Bit plunged through the tunnel of mist, hair whipping about her face. She counted slowly to herself, bracing for impact at five. Nothing happened and she continued falling. Pet's hand, clammy with fear, gripped Bit's tightly.

The tunnel stretched endlessly to a tiny point of light in the distance. As she whisked through the shaft, the point grew quickly in size, as if they had passed through miles in a matter of moments. Looming ahead she saw the pale white disk of the bottom. She braced for impact, knowing how futile that was.

There would be no pain; her life would end instantly. Fear, hopes, dreams, all her love would wink out.

Instead, she hung in midair. Time froze. Then started again, ticking slowly, gently, and Bit floated down.

The surface of the disk was translucent, hinting at the vague, ghostly outlines of something beyond. The disk appeared solid. But she watched in fascination as first her feet, then her legs, arms, and waist, passed through freely, a sensation of cloudy coolness on her skin.

When she reached her neck, time sped up and she plunged the rest of the way through. She fell a few feet and landed on a hard floor. The impact was minimal and she looked around. She was in another tunnel, this one solid. The walls were blue, but so pale as to be almost white. They were rounded, and rose eight feet to a rounded ceiling. At first she thought everything was ice, but that seemed impossible. It must be a translucent marble. To her right, several passages branched off into dark shadows. A dim light came from the left, suggesting this was a cave and she was near the opening. All was stark, cold, hard, like the grim labyrinth of the underworld.

Her breath plumed in the icy air. Fright pierced her growing confusion. This was not Aerdem.

"Great. Just great. I told you we couldn't trust her." Pet blew into her palms and rubbed them.

The old woman glided from a shadow and held out her arms to Bit. "Sweet one, you've come. I knew you would."

Pet stepped between them, her face as fierce as a lion protecting her cub. "Don't you come near her."

"You must listen to me—"

"Listen to you? I'm done listening to you. You promised you would take us home."

"I have, this is the way—"

Pet shook her head. "Lies. We're no closer to Aerdem than we were before."

The old woman reached her hands out to Bit. "Please, let me explain—"

"Not a step closer," warned Pet. "I'll scratch you to pieces if you try."

"Hush," said Bit, putting her hand softly on Pet's shoulder. "She's our friend."

"She isn't, I tell you. She tricked us and dropped us in the middle of a glacier."

"It's a cave." Bit looked deeply again into the old woman's eyes. "I trust her." With a soft pressure on Pet's arm, her friend stepped reluctantly aside.

"Fine. But if she harms one hair on your head—"

"She won't."

The old woman clasped her hands. "Listen, oh listen. We have little time. You must do what I say—"

Before she could finish, two little feet appeared at the ceiling, followed by short legs and a small torso. Yalp fell to the ground, and a moment later Darter landed beside him.

Bit clapped her hands with joy. "Yalp! Darter!"

"Your Majesty," said Yalp, with a quick bow. "We stayed as long as we could and tried to convince the doctor to follow. But the tunnel was going to close . . ."

"Tell me he's coming," Bit cried. "Please, is he coming?"

"It doesn't matter," Pet grumbled. "We're not in Aerdem. The old witch fooled us."

Yalp looked about him, startled. Darter flew to Bit's shoulder and glared at the old woman fiercely. "But why?" Yalp asked.

"You don't understand," the old woman cried. "I need, we need—"

Motion drew Bit's eyes to the ceiling again. "What in the world . . ."

A circle of the ceiling had turned translucent again, like a thick slab of glass, or a block of ice. Beyond, something moved, growing larger and more distinct. Bit watched in fascination until at last she saw, vague and ghostly, the doctor. He hung from a rope tied around his waist and peered down at them. He held his medicine bag in one arm; the other cradled his rifle. He probed the disk with the rifle, and it passed through as if nothing were there. A moment later he untied the rope, passed through the ceiling, and landed on his feet beside them.

The old woman grabbed Bit by both arms. "There's no time to explain. You must do what I say. Exactly what I say. All of you."

After silencing Pet's protests, Bit promised they would.

"Then listen," said the old woman. "I must go now. Bit, you must follow me partway, but remain hidden. Don't come out of the cave until I call you."

Pet shook her head. "I'm not letting her go alone."

"You may accompany while she waits, but when I call, only she may step out."

The old woman stared at Pet with the same immovable will she must have shown Miss Drath. Pet returned the stare, stubborn and obstinate.

Bit laid a hand on Pet's shoulder. "I'll be all right. I promise."

"You will. I won't be far behind," Pet said. She leveled her eyes fixedly on the old woman.

"The rest of you must stay here," the old woman said to the others. She pointed in the direction of the shadows and dark passages. "There's a bad man, a very bad man down there." She looked at the doctor. "If he tries to come this way, use your weapon."

The doctor tapped his gun, a grim look on his face. "Don't worry about that. Best shot in three counties."

"Good. I know I can count on you." The old woman put her hand on Bit's shoulder. "Come along, sweet one."

Bit was about to follow, but paused. "What about Dash and his father? We must help them."

"We will. That's why we brought the doctor. But we must do this first. Please hurry." The old woman urged Bit along and they hastened through the cave, Pet following close behind. A few steps took them to the cave opening, where some large rocks gave them a place to hide.

"You must stay here," said the old woman, drawing her cloak around her shoulders against the bitter wind streaming through the entrance. "Don't be frightened. All will be well. Listen for my call."

The next moment she was gone.

"I don't like it," said Pet. "It's a trap."

The cold gnawed at Bit's toes.

❦

The torrent of ice plunging over the falls slackened, shushing now like wind through the trees. Naryfel's face went blank. After an endless minute she spoke in a hoarse whisper. "Impossible. I have no son."

"There he stands," Medlara said, "rejected from birth."

"Impossible." Blue spit an arc of red onto the snow and folded his arms.

"I'm sorry," Medlara said softly, "but it's true."

"She's mad," Naryfel said to the Steward. "She can't prove any of it."

"I can. First, the whole sad tale must be told. Ever thinking of a glorious empire that would last thousands of years, you knew you needed an heir. Your hopes for marriage were dashed when Jenny's father refused you. You became bitter. The idea of tying yourself to any man repulsed you. Marriage became an unthinkable atrocity. But you needed an heir, so you scoured the kingdom for a suitable mate. You found him in a dashing captain in your army. Secrecy was paramount. You only needed a few days with him to conceive a child. Then you shipped him out to war, where he died valiantly for his queen."

Naryfel turned to the Steward and gave a short laugh. "She's making it up. How could she know all these details?"

Medlara chuckled wryly. "In my years, I have come across powerful roots and powders. They give me vision beyond time and distance."

Jen stepped forward. "It's true. I've seen her do it. She told me Naryfel would attack my family."

"Yes, I saw that," Medlara said, nodding her head sadly. "But that's the end of the tale. Going back, you, Naryfel, did indeed conceive a child with your freckled young captain. But you needed to keep it secret. The law forbade children born out of wedlock to inherit the throne. You planned in time to change that—it wouldn't be hard. Your father was a forward-thinking man, beloved by all. You had only to dedicate the new law to his memory. Then you would step forward with your child, and behold, a legitimate heir."

"She's raving," Naryfel said to the Steward. "How could I convince anyone the child was mine?"

The Steward stroked his chin. "True. And how could you keep your pregnancy from me?"

"That's the easiest thing for a shape shifter," Medlara replied.

Jen gave a triumphant shake of her fist. "I've seen that too, when she changed into Vieveeka."

"You know her power," Medlara said to the Steward. "I dare say, she'd have turned me into a toad by now, except all her magic is back home. Now she's nothing more than a snake without fangs."

Naryfel glared at her. "This is a preposterous tale. Suppositions. I had no child. You haven't a shred of proof."

Medlara smiled, lifting the bumps on her cheeks. "Oh, but I do. There's someone who did know you were pregnant. Someone who had to know, so when the time came, you could prove the child was yours. Someone you've been seeking for many years, because she knows all the secrets you must keep silent." Medlara cupped her hands and called, "Faith!"

A moment later an old woman hobbled out of the tunnel. She wore a simple brown dress that fell from collar to foot. A veil worn over her head fell to hunched shoulders, but left her face visible. Her cheeks were sunken and crisscrossed with deep lines and wrinkles. The eyebrows were thick and dark. The left eyelid drooped. Big puffy folds of skin surrounded the right eye, which turned upward, as if looking to heaven.

Jen eyed the woman's cloak. The material was worn and nappy, tattered at the edges and moth-eaten in the middle. A gasp came from behind, and Jen turned to see Naryfel stagger back.

"Ah," said Medlara. "You know her."

"I've never seen her in my life," Naryfel hissed.

"Have I changed that much?" Faith asked, her voice shaking from old age.

"For the last time," Naryfel said to the Steward, "I demand you stop this."

"I will hear her story," the Steward replied firmly. "Begin, good woman. You have nothing to fear here."

Faith bowed. "If my broken body and face looked like they

once did, perhaps you would know me, my Steward."

"Perhaps so," he replied. "What can you tell me of this boy?"

"Of this boy, I cannot be certain. Of another child, a babe, born to the queen, that I can tell you. She kept her pregnancy secret. Then, in the last two weeks she feigned illness and took to her bed. Perhaps you remember that."

"I do," replied the Steward. "All business was conducted from her bedchamber."

"Yes. And when the baby came, she refused any midwife save me. I had some experience, and delivered her a healthy child. But when she saw him, she screamed in horror."

"Why, good woman?" asked the Steward. "Was he deformed in some way?"

"No, he was big and fat. Soon he cooed and gurgled happily. I never saw a sweeter temperament. He was perfectly fine except for his left shoulder."

"What was wrong with his shoulder?" asked the Steward.

Faith swallowed and looked at Naryfel. "It had a patch of blue."

Naryfel shrieked. She rushed at Faith, hands out to strangle.

Medlara stepped in her path. "You'll have to get by me first."

"I'll pull out your lumps with my bare hands." Naryfel slashed at Medlara with her nails, but they passed through the old woman as if she were smoke.

"My lumps, my lumps," sang Medlara, as Naryfel tried to grab her.

Red with rage, Naryfel screamed and lunged. Each time, Medlara, flimsier than mist, appeared a few feet away. Laughing, she lifted her skirts, kicked up her heels and danced a jig. Out of breath, Naryfel backed away, eyeing her warily.

"You can't harm someone who isn't here," said Medlara.

"Do you think I would risk coming here directly? I'm still safely in my valley. But the same magic that brings my form is more
than enough to quell you." Her voice turned hard. "No more
stunts. We will hear the rest of the tale."

"Continue, Faith," she said gently. "You are safe."

"My life is almost over," Faith replied. "I have borne the
weight of her secrets too long. No matter what the danger, I will
be free of them."

"Then speak now," said Medlara. "Tell us only the truth."

"I will. After the baby was born, the queen changed. She
spent hours wringing her hands until they were raw. She began
muttering to herself. Sometimes, if I passed in the next room,
I thought there was someone with her. When I peeked in, it
was only the queen arguing violently with thin air. I locked the
doors leading out of her apartments so she wouldn't wander the
castle at night. Still, she padded up and down the hall like a
sentry, one minute laughing like a loon, the next moaning and
wailing.

"All this time, she refused to see the babe. If only that had
continued. He was the sweetest child you ever saw, never
fussed, hardly a cry out of him. But one night she asked for him.
Said she would give him a bath. I gave him to her reluctantly.
What could I do? I was only a servant. She asked for hot water.
I brought it . . ."

Faith swallowed, her lower lip trembling. "She sent the
water back. She wanted it boiling hot. I begged, pleaded with
her. She was adamant. So I brought water from a stove I kept
in the next room. Once more I pleaded. The water needed to
cool. I doubt she heard me. She muttered to herself, placing
the baby naked in a small tub. Then she . . . she dipped the cloth
in the water . . . and scrubbed and scrubbed and scrubbed his
pretty blue back."

Faith shook her head from side to side, as if to erase the memory. Tears flowed freely over her face. When she found her voice, it was high and pinched at the throat. "No one should ever hear what I heard. Nor see. It is too horrible, too brutal to tell . . . I will spare your ears. Just know that I tried to stop her. I cared not for my own life, but if I could, I would save the babe. I latched onto her hand with all my might, trying to restrain her. You see how big she is. She sent me flying to a corner of the room like a rag doll. My head must have struck something. I saw the rest in a nightmare daze."

The sun, a flaming ball at the horizon, bathed the snowy cliff crimson. The Ice Falls barely whispered now, as if the mountain itself wished to listen to the strange drama unfolding below, where all stood motionless.

At last the Steward spoke. "If the child lived, he would bear a scar."

Jen felt a charge ripple through her and looked at Blue. But he stared intently at Faith.

"The baby lived, barely," said Faith, wiping her eyes on her sleeve. "The queen asked for him every day, but I put her off, saying he suffered from pneumonia. Meanwhile, I nursed him as best I could, feeling him slipping from me daily. Only one thing could save him."

"What was that?" asked the Steward.

"Another Blueback baby, just gone from this world. It would be two weeks before I found one. But at last he came into my hands. After that, it was easy to switch my poor sweetheart. I told the queen her baby died and showed her the dead one." Faith looked directly at Naryfel. "She seemed relieved."

"What happened to her baby?" asked the Steward.

"I brought him to a Blueback woman renowned for herb craft and healing. She and her husband were simple, good people, without a child of their own. They were overjoyed to take him in."

The mountain above rumbled, and larger chunks of ice began falling again. A chill wind picked up. The Steward kneaded the top of his bald head, as if he was trying to work into his mind all he had heard. "Did the boy live?"

"I know not. I ran away shortly afterward and never learned his fate."

"Do you remember the names of the good people you left him with?"

"I'll never forget them. They were poor, but filled with love. He worked wood. She played a lyre like an angel. Their names were Astor and Meloryn."

Jen felt another charge rush through her. Those were the names of Blue's adoptive parents. She tried to catch his eye, but he didn't notice. Instead he swayed slightly on his feet and stared blankly at Naryfel. Despite the cold, little beads of sweat formed on his brow.

The Steward drew himself up to his full height and looked at Naryfel. "Before I question this boy, do you have anything you would like to say in your defense, Your Highness?"

"The whole thing is a farce," Naryfel sneered. She pointed at Faith. "And this woman is an imposter. She's put together pieces of the truth, but the rest—the story of the Blueback baby—is all fabrication and slander. If this were the real Faith, she would know I had a son—and a daughter. I gave birth to twins."

All eyes fixed on Naryfel, who smiled back triumphantly.

The Steward massaged the top of his head again. "Then you admit having children."

"I do."

"Where is the girl now?"

"She died at birth."

"With your permission, sir," said Faith, "I can explain. She gave birth first to a daughter. I was able to save the girl, but not the boy."

"I don't understand," said the Steward. "If the girl died and the boy was placed elsewhere . . ."

"I was unable to save the boy from her fear. You heard what she did to him. But the girl—the girl was spared."

"Fear? Spared? Explain, good woman."

"I knew giving birth to a Blueback would be intolerable, impossible for the queen to bear. I feared for months what she would do—you've heard how right I was. When she gave birth to twins, I switched her daughter with a Blueback girl that had died. Alas, at that time I could not locate another deceased baby. I couldn't save the boy until later."

Naryfel held her belly and laughed like a bad actor. "Preposterous. She adds one lie on top of another. Switching babies. Blueback children. It's all flummery. Even if that boy has a scar on his back, what of it? It would be easy to make up a story about that and present him as 'evidence.' "

"Perhaps, Your Highness," said the Steward. "But I will hear the rest. What became of the girl?" he asked Faith.

"Farmers in Laskamont raised her."

"Is she with them yet?"

"Nay, the parents were killed when the queen invaded the land. But the girl survived!"

"How do you know that?"

Medlara smiled and answered for Faith. "Because I found her. She's waiting over there in the cave." She turned to Naryfel. "The blood of her adoptive parents is on your hands. Witnessing their death, she became a shaking, mewling thing. When at last starvation lashed her out of her stupor, she sought aid at villages and farms. There, the sounds she made frightened people, and she was shunned as a witch-girl. Orphaned and alone, she wandered aimlessly through the wilderness, eating grass she found buried under the snow. At last, refugees fleeing more of your dirty work, Naryfel, took her in and brought her to Aerdem. That, Naryfel, is what you did to your own daughter—a girl as sweet and pure as nectar. A girl you publicly humiliated, that you paid to have murdered. Open and trusting, her heart is full to the brim with love, a heart you broke as casually as you'd flick a flea."

Medlara nodded to Faith, who turned to the ice tunnel and called. "Bit!"

As she watched her friend walk out of the cave, Jen's heart broke into a gallop. She swayed on her feet, her mind a dizzy whirlwind.

Bit's eyes were wide as she approached, but she broke into a smile when she saw Jen. Jen looked from Blue to Bit. Why had she not seen it? The same chestnut eyes, the same round cheeks sprinkled lightly with freckles.

"What's this all about?" Bit whispered as she hugged Jen.

"I'll explain later," Jen whispered back.

Blue's mouth was open and he had turned a little green. Only his eyes moved, roving and searching over Bit's face. Standing beside him, Bit gazed back curiously and gave him a shy smile.

Medlara pointed to them. "Do they not look like your handsome captain?" she asked Naryfel.

Naryfel, staring blankly at Blue and Bit, didn't reply.

The Steward rubbed his hands. Jen had the feeling it was not from cold but because he was warming to his work. "Your tale brings me to tears, but one thing doesn't fit," he said to Faith. "Why would the queen mate with a Blueback when she loathes them so?"

"Because," Faith replied, "a Blueback father might pass on the blue patch, but the mother always does. The young captain was a pure son of Purpura, his family line long and august." She pointed to Naryfel. "There's your Blueback!"

"Careful," warned the Steward. "You've been a credible witness up to now, despite your strange tale. But what you suggest now—"

"I understand your skepticism," Faith said. "You have known the queen since you were children. Known her as the daughter of King Brodellorn. But hark, this is the strangest part of the tale. For here is a secret the queen has only guessed at. A secret that twisted inside her like a viper. Born out of fear, it became a hateful thing that burrowed deep and ate at her soul. There is only one place hate like that can go. Out. At the thing most despised!"

Faith broke off into a wrenching cough. Jen scooped up some snow and offered it to her. The old woman took it gratefully. She spoke again after several bites had melted down her throat. "Before that angel was born," she pointed to Jen's mother, "the king and his first wife tried for years to have children. They sought the advice of physicians, to no avail. At last, resigned to the fact that they would never have children of their own, they decided to adopt one.

"Shortly after, it came to the king's attention that a young groomer in his stable was raising a baby alone. This stable hand was too embarrassed to say how he came to be the sole parent. But the king was kind, reassuring the man he was there to help, not judge. The man broke down at that and confessed. He had fallen in love with a girl who danced in one of the taverns. She was a wild thing, with a bewitching smile and smoldering eyes. Their affair was short. When she grew with child, she refused to marry him—her sights were set higher. After giving birth, she left the baby with him and ran off with a soldier. The groomer tried to raise the girl as best he could, but he needed to work. So he kept her at the stable, feeding and changing her as best he could while currying the horses.

"The king took pity on the man and offered to adopt the girl. At first the man refused. He loved the baby despite his desperate circumstance. But the king was also desperate—the queen cried every night, longing for a child. So he promised he would raise her as his own, as First Princess of Purpura, and that she would inherit the throne. How could the good groomer refuse this chance for his daughter? His only condition, no one must know the baby's true origin. He wanted to guarantee she was truly accepted in the king's household, and not treated ill.

"Besides the king and queen, only I knew the secret, as the baby's nursemaid, and the one who told the king about the groomer. After a few months, the birth of the princess was announced. There was much banter about court, how the queen had hidden her pregnancy so, and the other ladies wished they could keep from showing.

"The girl grew. I never saw such a clever child. She counted at twelve months, and soon could separate money into different denominations. She named all the colors at two. I'll never forget the day she giggled at me because I was wearing a blue sock on one foot and red on the other. She painted pictures of everything she saw: her rocking horse, the view out her window, her mother and father. I never saw a better likeness.

"As soon as she could walk, which was early, she explored the castle from head to foot. She spent hours looking at the Royal Gallery. She asked dozens of questions. Why did she live in a castle? Where did the servants come from? Why were father and mother so old when the other children had young parents? She looked at herself in the mirror, and asked why she didn't look like Mommy and Daddy. I'll never forget the day she came to me, she couldn't have been older than three, and asked, why did she have blue on her back? It wasn't for me to answer. I took her to her father, who told her it was something special that she must never show or tell anyone. 'Do you and Mommy have a special mark?' she asked the king. No, they didn't, was the answer. After that came hundreds of questions. Why didn't Mommy and Daddy have the mark? Was there something wrong with the mark? Where did the mark come from? Why was it a secret? Was it something bad? If it was special, why couldn't she show it to people? Days and weeks and months went by, and still the questions came. Then one day they stopped. It was the day her half sister was born."

Faith pointed to Jen's mother.

The Steward nodded. "I understand. The king's first wife had died of a fever. He remarried, and his second wife gave birth to a daughter. If what you say is true, then Naryfel is not the queen at all. Her—"

"Half sister is," Jen exclaimed. "My mother!"

Naryfel's knees buckled and she swayed backward toward the edge of the cliff. Her face was chalk-white, her eyes glassy. She tried to speak, but no words came.

The Steward rubbed his hands again and turned to Blue. "I must know everything to determine if Faith's story is true. Do you bear a scar on your back?"

Blue reached for his collar. Slowly he pulled his shirt off and let it fall to the snow. There was the wrinkled skin for all to see, the lingering mark of a terrible burn. The Steward approached to examine the scar, but Blue walked by him like a sleepwalker, his eyes wide and fixed on Naryfel's face.

"My name . . ." he asked her. "What is my name?"

Naryfel sagged to her knees. "Barthal," she replied, her voice a hoarse whisper.

"Barthal." He repeated the name slowly, softly, as if it held a thousand wonders, as if it were a snowflake of sugar that might dissolve, lost forever.

His body shook from the cold. Faith took off her cloak and wrapped it around his shoulders. The sun had fallen below the horizon. The last violet glory was fading as a deeper indigo spread across the sky.

"There remains one thing left to do," said the Steward to Naryfel. "To inspect your back."

Mother wiped tears from her eyes. "No. She's been burdened enough. Can any of us know what she felt? Knowing your parents were not your real parents. Pretending they were. Pretending you were something you weren't. Keeping the secret to please your father. Keeping the secret for fear some disaster would befall the family." She turned to Naryfel. "I understand why you tormented and hated me. After I was born, if your secret came out, you would no longer be First Princess. Or heir to the throne."

Naryfel rose. "Do you understand now, sister?" she asked, in a little girl voice.

"I do. Naryfel, I never wanted the throne. I always thought it was yours. If it had been known you were adopted, I would have given it to you gladly. I still would, if only I knew you'd use it for good. All I want, all I need is in Aerdem. Naryfel, we can be a family."

"A family . . ."

"You have a son and a daughter. Choose love, Naryfel. Choose them." Mother pointed to Blue and Bit.

The Steward drew himself up to his full height and squared his shoulders. "That's all well and good, but the law is clear. She must stand trial for her crimes. She can choose to be a family behind bars."

"No," said Mother. "The throne is mine to give. I can change the law. My father wanted her to be queen."

"But her crimes, they are too extreme to overlook."

"Punishment will not heal Purpura. Only forgiveness and compassion," said Mother. "Let her true talents and the fullness of her heart—smothered and buried since childhood—let these come out now. Let her be the great queen she was meant to be."

Jen had the feeling that Mother's light, which brightened rooms, penetrated the growing twilight on the cliff top.

"Would you do that for me, sister?" Naryfel asked, her voice still high and innocent as a child.

Mother smiled. "I would, gladly."

Naryfel held out her arms, her face glowing. "Come to me, sister."

Mother smiled and glided to Naryfel.

Jen felt a cold finger trace an icy line down her neck. "Mother, don't." It was more a thought in her mind.

Mother and Naryfel hugged. They held each other gently. After a moment, Naryfel's hands shifted.

"Fool!" she shouted. With a violent twist, she sent Mother careening toward the precipice. Mother grasped Naryfel's arms, pulling her along. They caught their balance at the brink and Naryfel wrestled to throw Mother over.

"Mother!" Jen ran. Her feet were numb. She willed them to move faster, but the muscles in her legs cramped from the cold. She knew it wasn't so, but it felt like she was running in place and the space between her and Mother was a fixed distance that wouldn't close.

She saw Blue running. He was closer, and reached Mother

and Naryfel in a few quick steps. He grappled, trying to break Naryfel's hold. The cloak slipped from his shoulders and fell to the ground, and the three of them rocked and swayed on the precipice like a trio of drunken dancers—and pitched over.

"No!" Jen raced to the cliff edge, grabbed the cloak mid-stride, and leaped off.

39

Jen hung in the air, everything strangely

quiet. Even the wind held its breath. Then she tumbled. At that moment the mountain erupted, and a violent avalanche of snow and ice crashed and thundered around her.

She fell end over end. Sky, cliff and clouds spun madly. Dizziness socked her in the belly. Her stomach lurched. Sour bile scalded her throat.

She had to stop tumbling. Hugging her knees in a tight ball, she thrust out her arms and legs. Now she dove headfirst, cutting the air like a knife. She held the cloak tight. It snapped and whipped against one arm and the side of her head. The wind lashed her face and tears sprang to her eyes. She wiped them and saw Mother, Blue, and Naryfel below, falling head over heels like potato sacks. There was no bottom. Only clouds and the falling curtain of ice.

The wind pummeled and batted her right and left. She fought back, pulling her arms down and drawing the cloak around her shoulders.

Nausea twisted her gut, but there was something else now, deeper, stronger, bursting to come out. It rushed like hot flames to her toes and the crown of her head. Her arms were gone. Instead, a pair of glorious wings unfolded, spreading, reaching, twenty feet to either side. Her chest expanded, covered with a thousand feathers that shimmered like opals. Now the wind was her friend. It lifted her and she was riding, skimming, sailing on a river of air.

Wyndano's Cloak! She didn't know how Medlara had gotten it to Faith, but Jen recognized it the moment she saw it. Now she drew her wings in and shot down like an arrow.

Tumbling boulders of ice blocked her path. She looped and glided past them with the fleet grace of a falcon. Mother and Blue somersaulted below, holding hands. Naryfel was there too, but she'd spun away and was rolling dangerously close to the wall of falling ice.

They disappeared into a cloud and Jen followed. Slicing into the cool white, she flew blind. She held her breath, praying she didn't crash into an ice block, and that none hit Mother and Blue.

She burst out of the cloud, and Blue and Mother were closer. She called out, but it was the piercing cry of an eagle. Blue looked up and scowled. As Jen neared, he let go of one of Mother's hands and balled his fist.

He doesn't know it's me, Jen thought. Blue swung his fist at her. *He's plunging to his death. But he's protecting Mother to the last.* She veered near him and he swung again.

"No!" Mother cried. "It's Jenny!"

For a moment, Blue's face went blank. Then a smile stretched from ear to ear, and he waved to show he understood.

Jen pulled away so she could circle below them. She completed the turn when she saw two ice boulders crash together. A large chunk broke off and hurtled toward Mother and Blue.

Jen let loose a fierce eagle-cry. With a powerful stroke of

her wings she swooped below Mother and Blue. She had to hope they understood, and for a breathless moment she waited, hovering below them, watching while the chunk rushed headlong toward them like a cannonball.

Then she felt two sets of feet land on her back, and hands burrowing into her feathers, holding tight. Tipping her wings, she veered right, and the ice chunk whistled by.

"Jenny," Mother called, "save Naryfel."

Jen circled back and saw Naryfel drifting toward the twilight-blue curtain of the falls. Sheets of snow sprang in silvery fountains. Explosions of ice roared and crashed, launching frozen missiles and spinning shrapnel.

Jen dodged the zooming chunks and flew as near she could to Naryfel, but blocks of ice and flowering cascades of hail kept her just out of reach.

Someone shifted to the edge of Jen's back. Out of the corner of her eye, she saw Blue's bare arm stretch out, reaching a hand to Naryfel.

Naryfel shook her head. "I'm too far."

"Try," Blue screamed.

Naryfel drew something from her pocket that glimmered golden in the fading light. She held it out to Blue by her fingertips. His harp!

She smiled and said his name. "Barthal."

He reached as far as he could and his fingers grasped the other end. For a moment the harp connected them.

Then a massive chunk of ice swept by. Naryfel was gone. Only three drops of blood remained, floating in the air like glistening rubies.

Part Six

40

Jen paced in an anteroom off her mother

and father's bedroom. She paused a moment by the inner door, listening for sounds from within. Hearing nothing, she resumed her patrol along the border of a floral throw rug, and darted a look across the room. Blue sat on one side of a sofa, watching her. Bit sat on the other side, twisting her sleeve. Pet had pulled up a chair, and was hovering beside Bit.

With a knock from the outer door, Sally came in carrying a tray for tea, and set it on a low table in front of the sofa. Pet rose and lifted the lid off the teapot. The scent of wintergreen, spearmint, and tilia flowers drifted across the room.

Pet pulled Sally aside. "She needs something stronger," whispered Pet, nodding toward Bit.

Sally nodded in agreement, but Bit called out, "It's okay. I like this."

"You're sure?" Pet asked.

"Yes. Sally, you must sit down. You're as frightened as any of us." Bit started to rise, looking absently for a chair.

Sally pointed to the spot between Bit and Blue. "But that's Miss Jenny's seat."

"I'll get her one," Pet said, and rushed out of the room, returning a moment later with a chair, which she placed beside hers.

The walls swirled and glowed, as if hot flames burned within. Bit and Jen locked eyes.

"Are we too late? He's been in there a long time." Bit sank back into the sofa. She stared at the inner door, eyes wide and red-stained.

"It's only been a little while," Jen replied, but it did feel like a long time since Doc Jenkins had gone in. Medlara had opened a tunnel at the Ice Falls, and they returned to the Rose Castle in a heartbeat. They'd rushed Doc to Father's chamber, where Father and Dash had lain unconscious since the attack. Doc would only allow Jen's mother and the Pondit inside, saying he needed room to work, and quiet. Jen got one terrifying look at her father and brother. Their faces were peaceful, with the slightest smile, as if they dreamed. But they were as pale as ghosts.

"What's wrong with all of you?" Pet asked. "This isn't a funeral."

Bit gave a little cry. "Please don't talk of funerals."

"I'm sorry, it's just that they're not dead yet—"

At the word dead, Bit shot Pet a look of anguish, as if she saw Dash being lowered into a grave.

"Pet's right," Jen said. Her fists clenched into balls. "I've got faith in Doc Jenkins. He's the best doctor I know. He pulled old Nell out of all kinds of things. Our old mare too. And Dash and Father? They'll fight. You can't kill them so easy. If the Pondit says five days, I give them a week."

Bit looked at her hopefully, but Jen was pacing again. There was a hollow feeling inside she kept pushing away. What if she lost them? She bit her lower lip. Hard.

Blue watched her, his big chestnut eyes brimming with an emotion Jen couldn't quite name. But it felt gentle, soft. "I give them two weeks. Why don't you sit, then?" He tapped the sofa.

Jen crossed the room and slumped in the spot beside him. The walls flared up again, as if they felt Father and Dash's pain. She reached to braid her hair and found nothing. Remembering Naryfel had chopped it off, her arm fell, defeated. Blue's hand slipped over hers. It felt warm and comforting.

A voice from the bedroom made her freeze. More voices, reassuring, answered. The first voice grew louder, insistent. Jen and Bit bolted to their feet.

"Something's happened," Bit cried.

Silence fell in the next room. Everyone listened. Jen's heart rose to her throat and stuck there.

The first voice spoke again, louder. Others answered, again trying to calm, but the first voice argued, weak and hoarse, then with growing heat. Footsteps stumbled across the floor. Stopped. More arguing. Then footfalls slapped the floor and someone crashed against the door. A moment later it was flung open and Dash leaned against it. His knees trembled and he could barely support his weight, but he pushed off the door and lurched across the room until he swayed drunkenly before Bit. He reached a hand out to her, as if he saw her far away through a sea of mist.

"She's here . . . She's safe . . ." His voice shook, a shadow of Dash's vigor.

Bit reached out to him, ready to throw herself into his arms, but he drew back. "No," he cried. "I can't . . . Not yet . . ."

Tears sprang to Bit's eyes and she looked at him in fright. "Dash, it's Bit. Don't you recognize me?"

He swayed again on his feet. Jen and Blue rushed to support him. Now Doc, Mother, and the Pondit were in the room.

"He needs rest," Doc said. "We must get him back to bed."

"No rest . . . not until—" A series of wrenching coughs seized him. When he stopped at last there was blood on his hands. The doctor tried to escort him back to the bedroom, but he twisted away.

"Stop him," Doc said. "I'll administer something to calm him."

"Never," Dash cried.

Jen and Blue held him up. He flailed. He was so weak she could easily stop him, but he looked at her so desperately that she didn't have the heart to. She nodded to Blue and they let him go. He staggered to the door.

"He must rest," Doc pleaded.

"Son?" It was Father. He leaned against Mother at the bedroom door. "What is it, Son?"

It was all Jen could do to keep from running and hugging and kissing him. But Dash came first.

"Something . . . I must do," Dash insisted.

Father inclined his head, gaunt and pale, but still kingly. He glanced at Mother.

She smiled. "The danger has passed."

Father breathed a sigh of relief. "Go, Son."

Dash stumbled at the door. Jen and Blue rushed to his side and helped him out and down the corridor. His cheeks were sunken, and he felt light under her hands. Every few steps he needed to rest, but he pushed on.

"The most precious bloom . . . the sweetest flower . . . Fool! Selfish fool! Oh where is it . . . Where?" He staggered on.

"What, Dash? What are you looking for?" Jen asked. "I'll help you find it."

He didn't hear. "Blind! Blind fool! Where? Yes! They would take it there!"

He stopped a passing butler and gasped, "Water, man. Bring water. And food."

The butler ran off and found them a minute later in another hallway. He carried a jug of water and a platter of rolls. Dash paused long enough to drink the water, half of which he sputtered over his shirt and on the floor. Flinging away the jug, he crammed a few rolls into his mouth, and took off down the corridor.

"Bring the biggest hammer . . . to my room," he said to the butler. "And canvas. A giant piece of canvas."

He grew stronger at every step, but still he rambled. "Heartless . . . cruel . . . blind fool."

At last they reached his room, and he rushed in. On a table was the big replica of the Rose Castle that Vieveeka had made to upstage Bit. Some servants, not understanding its significance, must have moved it from the Count's mansion. With a burst of love for her brother, Jen understood Dash's goal.

A moment later the butler returned with a large roll of canvas. A workman accompanied him, holding a long heavy hammer, the kind wielded with two hands for driving wedges and posts, and breaking rock.

Dash spread the canvas, and it nearly covered the floor. He leaned the hammer against the wall and dismissed the servants, but not before ordering more food and water, a broom and a dustpan.

"Help me," he said to Blue. Together, they carried the glittering replica to the middle of the canvas. Then he spit in each palm and picked up the hammer. His arms trembled as he tried to lift it. Jen and Blue begged him to let them help, but he waved them aside. At first only little chips of quartz broke off, but with fresh draughts of water and three or four more rolls, he regained his strength. Soon towers and battlements cracked and shattered and flew like missiles. Even when the castle was reduced to rubble he kept pounding with the hammer until even the largest pieces were smashed into dust.

Pausing only to mop sweat from his brow, he walked carefully around the perimeter of the canvas, looking for stray pieces that had escaped him.

"Do you see any?" he asked Jen and Blue. "Nothing must be left behind."

They searched the room while he swept and swept with the broom, catching tiny shards and fragments in the dustpan.

When at last the floor gleamed and every chip and splinter had been found, he folded the canvas, taking care that nothing spilled, until all was wrapped in a neat ball. Then he collapsed in a chair. "Saddle Nightflyer."

"You're too weak," Jen said.

He lifted the ball of canvas and shook it. "Bring him. I can't rest until this is out of Aerdem."

Jen clutched Blue's arm. "Go with him."

Two days later, Jen was eating breakfast in the Crystal Room with Bit, Mother, Father, and Petunia. There was a tap on the door, and the Pondit, face red, breathing hard, ducked his long noodle body into the room.

He looked so excited Jen thought he'd do a cartwheel across the floor. "Prince Dashren has returned and approaches the front gate!"

Everyone rose. Trays turned over. Jams, sweet rolls and hot cocoa erupted into a fountain. Cups and saucers clattered to the floor.

They rushed from the room and through the castle. Bit's face was aglow, hopeful. Jen was just as excited to see Blue again. Down staircases, across bridges and walkways they flew, until they reached the wide steps that led down to the outer courtyard. And stopped.

Dash rode through the front gate. He held a rope in his hand. The other end was tied around the chest of Petunia's father. He stumbled, trying to keep his feet. Benden rode at a respectful distance behind the Count. Blue brought up the rear, driving a wagon piled precariously with clothing, patent leather pumps, a crate of jangling wine bottles, another of brandy, a third of fine china peeking out of straw, a rolled-up rug, candelabras, paintings, a pair of teak chairs, several chests, a locking jewelry box, a gold mirror. All the most valuable items Jen had ever seen in the Count's mansion.

Father led the way slowly down the steps, stopping three from the bottom. Dash rode up. Leaping off Nightflyer, he dragged the Count before Father.

"Look what I found trying to slink out of Aerdem," said Dash.

Father fixed a stern eye on the Count. "Untie him."

Dash did. The Count rubbed his arms, then held them out, appealing. "A misunderstanding, Sire. I was merely toting a few things to my country estate."

"A lie," said Dash. "He was trying to slip over the border."

"Only to bring a few trifles to my wife in Laskamont."

"At night?" said Dash. "You were conspiring with Vieveeka. Why else would you run with a painting of your mother?"

The Count held out his hands again in supplication. "My wife misses my mother as much as I do."

Dash laughed. "She hated your mother. Everyone in court knows that."

The Count colored. "You'd do well not to listen to idle gossip, young man."

"Enough," commanded Father. "I've been looking for you

ever since I found out Vieveeka was Naryfel. You fled without even saying goodbye to your daughter."

The Count glanced at Petunia, and gave an almost imperceptible shake of his head that she ignored.

"He's a traitor," said Dash. "He's coveted the throne for years. He harbored the enemy. I can't believe they weren't thick as thieves."

The Count stared at his nails, polishing them on his velvet vest. "Ridiculous. Why would you say such a thing, after the nice party I threw you?" He shot another brief look at Petunia, as if he sought some subtle confirmation from her.

She took a step down. "Tell them, Father."

"I have nothing to confess."

"They'll be merciful."

His eyes flashed a warning. "Daughter, not another word."

Father shook his head sadly. "Petunia's told us everything."

The Count froze, his face ashen. He collapsed to his knees. "It was that little minx, Vieveeka! Lying, conning, trapping me. She bewitched me, made me do it. I never wanted anyone to get hurt. Never."

"Your crimes deserve the severest punishment," said Father. "Conspiracy. Treason—"

"I didn't know, I didn't know." Gone was the bravado. He looked like a small child.

"Attempted murder of myself and my family."

"I didn't have anything to do with that. I swear."

"Perhaps. But what you told your own daughter, what you made her do. Sending her with Bit to . . ." Father choked; stopped to recompose himself.

Silent now, the Count hung is head, avoiding everyone's eyes.

"For that alone," continued Father, "you deserve the severest penalty."

"Be merciful," the Count whispered hoarsely. "Please be merciful."

"He doesn't deserve mercy," Dash said.

Father shook his head. "Everyone deserves mercy, no less the Count. He was under duress. Financial burdens that Naryfel exploited." He sighed, put his hand on Mother's shoulder. "Who knows greater than I what she was capable of? How she could twist minds."

"Yes, yes," said the Count. "She was a trickster."

Father silenced him with a look. "Still, you could have come to me. Warned me. I would have helped you. Given you money. Instead, you sent your only daughter on a perilous journey from which she might never have returned. Only one thing stops me from banishing you forever from Aerdem, allowing you only what you can carry on your back."

The Count waited, trembling, wringing his hands.

"If your daughter accompanied you, she'd be subjected to the hardship of your punishment. If she stayed here, she'd be deprived of her father. I can live with neither option. Instead, I have confiscated all your property. The mansion, the country estate, the vineyards, all the carriages and horses." Father waved his hand at the loaded wagon. "All of value there."

The Count burst into tears. "But where will I live? How will I survive? What will become of me?"

Father shrugged. "You'll have to take that up with the new owner. Perhaps they will be charitable and let you stay in the servants' quarters."

"New owner?"

"I have sold the property."

"I shall perish. I shall starve," the Count sobbed.

Jen was tired of his blubbering. She pointed an accusing finger at him. "You haven't once asked about Petunia. You haven't asked what would happen to her."

Pet looked at him impassively. Waiting.

Bit stepped beside Pet and clasped her arm. "Do you know what your daughter is?"

The Count's face went blank.

Jen took the other arm. "Do you know how funny she is?"

"Do you know how smart she is?" Bit asked. "How loyal?"

"Petunia?" said the Count, as if they were talking about someone else.

Pet pinched her cheeks until they were rosy. "Do I please you now, Father?" She fluffed her hair, batted her eyes. "Or now? Do you see nothing else worth noticing? Nothing else to love?"

He still looked blank.

"Count," said Father, "meet the new owner of the Pompahro estates. Did you know? She has a capital idea to cart farm produce into town? I'm in for thirty percent. I'd do more, but she insists on a controlling interest."

"Petunia?" The Count leaned forward and stared at his daughter as if he were trying to bring her into focus.

Father stepped down and put his hand kindly on the Count's shoulder. "There's been too much suffering. It's a reprieve. But make no mistake, old friend. You've bungled your finances. She's in charge of them. I've emancipated her. She can do what she likes in Aerdem without your permission."

"Petunia?"

"Yes, Petunia." Father gave him a little push. "You better go to her. She needs you."

The Count shuffled toward her, still looking dazed. When he reached her, his eyes roamed over her face. At last, he raised his hands tentatively toward her, as if he expected her to slap them, and whispered, "Forgive me."

Petunia hooked her arm around his and began leading him up the castle steps. "Come along, Father. I have so much to tell you. So many ideas. I'm going to open a school. And an orphanage. We're going to have a theatre group. Bit will be the artistic director. Then there's the vineyard. No one has ever exported your wine. Why shouldn't we? It's the finest. Then the wagon project . . ."

Jen slipped next to her mother. "Will she forgive him?"

Mother smiled. "She already has. But will he forgive himself when he realizes what a treasure she is?"

❧❧

Bit took a jug of cider and two glasses from the basket and set them on the picnic blanket. Two plates, cloth napkins, and a platter of cheese were already arranged. The air was cool under the fruit trees. Their arms touched the ground, heavy with pears, oranges, and peaches. A chorus of birds serenaded in the branches above, accompanied by the bubbling waterfall.

A few paces away, Nightflyer and Snow Dancer nibbled the tall grass. Dash gazed at them intently. He had barely looked at Bit since they left the stable.

Before they mounted, Pet had marched up between them and looked him squarely in the eye. "Before you say anything, let's get one thing straight. She's worth a thousand of you."

"I know," he'd replied, but he rode all the way here without saying a word.

Bit poured the cider and handed him a glass.

"There is something I have to tell you." He set the glass down without sipping any, avoiding her eyes.

She waited. Jen's mother had told her to give him time, but her heart trembled.

"The night of the storm, after we returned from the ball . . .

I tried to see you," he began. "I went to your door. I begged and pleaded for you to open it. I could feel you just on the other side, so close I could hear you crying—"

"There is no need now—"

"There is." He rose, began pacing before her. "That night, I wanted to explain. I cursed myself for a fool. Heartless, cruel, blind—"

"It's over now. You mustn't—"

"No. You must hear. Leaving your door at last, I wandered toward my apartment, thinking only what my penance should be. The nighttime glow of the castle was particularly bright, but couldn't penetrate my gloom.

"I was by Father's bedroom when screams from within pierced the night. I rushed inside. It was dim, but the translucent walls burned crimson, as if angry flames flashed and flickered inside the stone. Enough light was cast to throw sharp silhouettes. There was Father, standing on the bed, a broadsword in his hand, fighting off a mass of shadowy figures. I drew my knife and leaped into the fray, attacking the assailants from behind. I fought to Father's side, and together we battled to protect the queen, who drew back to a corner behind us.

"Whirling our blades, we felled ten, twenty, thirty of the attackers. It was like mowing wheat, but more streamed in from the windows, and more. The room became a sea, and wave after wave crashed on us, only to be beaten back. My arm tired. I tried to breathe, but it felt like all the air had deserted the room. Still I fought, my knife forcing me to work at close quarters.

"Through a red haze, I saw most of the assailants charging at Father, who appeared tireless. I had never seen Father—or anyone—fight like that. His jaw was set. His eyes fearless. He roared like a lion, and his sword spun a vortex of death. Dozens of enemy weapons went flying, sparks rained down like fireworks, and all the majesty and glory of Aerdem sang in his blade."

Dash's eyes were like bright flames. "I felt a surge of pride. The honor of dying beside such a man, of showing him what his son was made of. I cast fatigue aside. My knife sprang to life, and attacked with a will of its own. The enemy drew back, but struck again as reinforcements poured through the open window.

"The enemy was small, between four and five feet tall. Hoods obscured their faces, save for their eyes—lidless and red—which burned with hate. The room was awash with their blood. The sticky stuff stank like rotting cactus, and I fought off the urge to retch.

"The attackers cared nothing for their own lives. A dozen threw themselves on Father's sword, while more jumped on his back, dragging him down. I hacked and chopped and stabbed to free him, but the enemy piled on and dragged me down too—"

"Hush—" Bit reached to soothe him, but he continued to pace.

"I was weak, but somehow found the strength to throw them off. I rose, dizzy, sick, but still wielding the knife. I looked for Father. He was down, a dozen assailants holding him. I watched in horror as something slid along the floor and wrapped around his feet. Coiling round and round and round like a snake, it moved up his legs and torso until he was bound head to toe."

"I went berserk," he swung his arms as if he still held the knife, "and ploughed through the enemy to reach Father. They surrounded me quickly. Striking from all directions they dragged me down, kicking and clubbing me. I struggled to my knees, my feet. Blood trickled down my face and into my mouth—"

"Hush. We're safe now—"

"Three or four assailants held me, spun me across the room. I tossed them off. I swayed on my feet. The motions of the battle slowed, faded. I saw the open window and the wind-driven rain. For a moment, two giant clouds parted, revealing the last fragile arc of the moon. Then the queen was carried through the window. The clouds closed, burying the moon, and the queen disappeared into a grave-black night.

"I was tackled. Something struck my feet. Another creature, coiling, coiling, around my ankles. I fought back, driven not by self-preservation but by something far more precious. I kicked free, but the creature struck again, biting my ankle. Warmth traveled up a vein in my leg. Somehow I rose . . . my feet were like anchors but I willed them to move. I staggered toward the door . . . the floor tilted and rose. The room faded . . . but one idea, one thought, one passion still drove me: To protect my love, my heart, my . . . ."

"Hush, hush, hush."

She looked into his eyes . . .

She looked into his eyes and held him in her arms, and only heard the waterfall and the birds, and the beating of their hearts.

❧

Three months later . . .

The Orphanage Players rushed off stage. The audience remained standing, pounding their palms in an attempt to coax the actors back for a fifth bow. Jen clapped until her hands hurt, but the curtain closed and the applause faded. The chairs were cleared. Servants rushed in with cloth-covered tables. Waiters brought bowls of punch, and platters of appetizers and desserts. People clustered in little knots, smiling, laughing, clinking glasses.

Jen hovered on the periphery, looking for Blue. She'd seen him arrive late, preventing them from sitting together. He had to be somewhere in the crowd that eddied about the Royal Theatre. They were supposed to meet after the play.

Count Pompahro rushed from group to group, his eyes beaming. "Did you see my Petunia? She was the emcee. She produced the play." He grabbed the Pondit's arm. "Did you see, did you see? That was my daughter's company." Jen never saw a prouder father.

The Pondit smiled. "She was magnificent."

Jen's father and mother joined them.

"That's a lovely suit, Count," said Mother. She ate from a bowl of ice cream. Three scoops topped with blueberries, chocolate-covered cherries, and about a million dates.

The Count wore green velvet pants and a maroon vest. "Petunia selected it for me." He dropped his voice. "Confidentially, she has me on a stipend. But I give her half to invest. I'm sure to double my money in six months."

"She's hooked me," Father said. "The wagon business is going so well, we plan to expand it to Laskamont. Are you in, Pondit?"

"Absolutely."

Jen smiled to herself and moved on. She still didn't see Blue. But there were Darter, Yalp, and Doc Jenkins talking with Bookar and Penrod.

"I'm glad you could make it to the play," Yalp said.

"Thank God you fixed the Transdevis, or I wouldn't be here," Doc replied. "How are the orphans settling in?"

"Beautifully," Yalp said. "They're staying at the Count's mansion until the king can build a proper place, with a school and playground. I hear you're in the business too."

"Yes. I've taken over Miss Drath's establishment for all the children who wanted to stay in my world."

"What happened to the old coot?" Darter asked, hopping from Yalp's shoulder to the top of his head.

"I hear she's raising bloodhounds."

"And Ox?"

" 'Spect he's shoveling dog logs."

Darter tittered, then cocked his head. "I've been meaning to ask you. When you cured the king and prince. What was in the sack?"

Doc pushed his hat high on his head and smiled broadly. "Weed killer."

Jen moved on, looking through the crowd. A stranger stared at her from across the room. He looked like one of the gypsies who had recently camped outside Glowan. He was tall and lean, his face weathered and cut with deep wrinkles.

Jen wasn't surprised to see him here. Father always opened his doors to everyone. But where was Blue? She still didn't see him, but there were Dash, Pet, and Bit. Belle, the little girl who'd sung so sweetly in the play, held Bit's hand and looked into her eyes. Jen sidled up to them.

Dash was asking whether Pet had dated anyone. Pet shrugged. Dash nodded toward Endare and Benden, who were looking at her from across the room. "They're more than interested. You're suddenly the talk of the castle."

Pet waved the notion aside. "I'm too busy for boys. Jen, what do you think? Do we have a hit?" Her strawberry curls were tied in a ponytail, and she glowed in an effusive gown of scarlet chiffon.

"You bet." Jen smiled. She was thrilled for all of them, but her mind was on Blue. Did he slip out before the play was done? If so, why?

"Bit wrote it," Pet said. "We wouldn't have a troupe without her."

Bit blushed. In a gown of snow-white tulle, she looked radiant, like a flower floating on a cloud. "Have you heard? Dash is—"

"Tonight's the night. I'm—" he cut in.

"Hush," Bit said, laying her hand lightly on Dash's arm. "Let me tell it. He's going to set a date with Father."

"A date?" Pet asked. "A date! For the wedding! You must let me plan it. I'll order the flowers. Seppe will give us a good price. Roses, of course. And lots of big plenderil. What about the cake? We'll need enough for an army, and . . ."

Everyone hugged Bit and Dash and congratulated them. Jen moved on. She needed air, and made her way to double doors that opened onto a patio. She leaned against one door and looked out. The setting sun cast a cool glow on the garden. A gibbous moon hung pregnant in the sky.

The gypsy stepped from a nearby shadow. He whispered with an accent. "Do you want to see Blue?"

Her heart galloped. "Yes!"

"Follow me." He led her behind some shrubbery at the edge of the garden and took a handkerchief from his pocket. He folded it several times and gestured toward her eyes. "Blindfold."

She took a step back. "Why?"

His lips pulled away, exposing yellow and missing teeth. Even with the grin, his face was expressionless. He fixed piercing black eyes on her. "Do you trust him?"

"Completely."

In reply, he blindfolded her. Then he took her wrist and led her along a footpath. His fingers were callused, but held her lightly, just enough to guide. Laughter and tinkling glasses faded behind. The air was warm, and a slight breeze rustled the surrounding plants.

They left the garden, went up stairs, and down a long corridor. She thought they must have entered the northeastern wing of the castle, but they turned down another corridor, and another, and she was lost. Then she felt air on her face, and they were outside again. *This must be a walkway*, she thought, *and a bridge*, as they arced up and down again.

"Wait here," he said.

Footsteps faded and returned. Her hand was grasped, but the fingers that held hers weren't callused.

"Blue!" She'd recognize his hand anywhere. Over the past months, she'd held it on starlit walks through meadows and orchards.

She laughed. "Why all the mystery?"

"You'll see." He led her over another walkway, down a flight of steps, and into another courtyard. She heard the familiar tinkle of a fountain, her fountain, and the fragrance of oleander, and knew she was in her own little garden.

They stopped and he put her hands on a narrow tree trunk encircled by thick vines. "Climb. Don't take off the blindfold until you're inside."

"What about you?"

"I'll be right behind."

She began to climb, grasping vines, feeling for places to wedge her feet. The light beyond the blindfold was pink and dimming. But the air felt clean and crickets sang below her and she felt wondrously free and alive.

As she rose, the tree bent under her weight, but her hand felt the bottom of the veranda, and a moment later she climbed over the rail. Blue joined her, and she felt her way to the open door. Her curtain had been pulled. She pushed by and took off the blindfold.

The room was dark. Four silhouettes stood in the shadows.

Jen laughed, recognizing her family instantly. "Why aren't you all at the party?"

Father lit a lamp. "This a private ceremony."

"Why here? Shouldn't we go to the Crystal Room?"

Mother cocked her head, as if she were listening. "Something is going to happen. I've been watching the nest on your eaves."

- "The Starbirds?" Jen had forgotten about them until a few days ago, when she heard scratching from their nest.

With some effort, Dash lifted a cedar chest onto a table. "I've known all along this was yours."

Father tapped the lid of the chest. "I tried to deny it, but I knew too. This was destined for you."

The wood was stained scarlet, and polished until it shone. Wooden handles were attached to the sides, and two copper strips were fastened across the lid and the front of the chest. Shaped like a plenderil, more copper surrounded a keyhole.

"What is it?" Jen asked.

"Don't you know?" Bit's eyes sparkled in the lamplight. "What you've longed for."

Mother placed her hand over her heart. "The purest, truest part of you."

Jen looked to each of them, trying to plumb their meaning. They only smiled back. Outside, Jen thought she heard one of the Starbirds cooing.

Dash smacked his fist into his palm and laughed. "This is better than a birthday! You really don't know?"

"Not a clue," Jen replied.

Blue took her arm and led her closer to the chest. "That yearning," he whispered in her ear. "To find that thing deep inside, and let it fly."

A thousand candles blazed in Jen's mind, and her heart

thrilled, like leaping from a boulder into a mountain lake. "You can't. It goes to Dash."

"I'll stick with my sword." Dash nodded toward the chest. "With that, I'll fall like a rock."

"Maybe I will too." Jen laughed, because she knew deep down she wouldn't. "I haven't used it since the Ice Falls."

Father took a key from his pocket, opened the chest, and took out Wyndano's Cloak. A breath of wind from the open doorway made the cloak flutter. "You did just fine against the Desert King. Remember?"

How could she forget? Before leaving the Ice Falls, she'd used the Cloak to change into a dragon. She'd run the Desert King into a snowy shoulder of the mountain where there was no escape. There she made her terms clear. He was to return to his kingdom and never leave it. Breathing fire, she'd blasted away a berg of ice to show what she'd do if he ever did.

"It's just like riding a horse," Father said. "You never forget. Besides, if Blue hadn't been distracting you these months, you'd have been pestering me to use it long ago."

Father straightened to his full height and beckoned Jen forward. He draped the Cloak over her shoulders. "Henceforth, you are Keeper of the Cloak. It only reflects something deep inside you, something great and wonderful that blesses you in abundance."

Jen smiled up at him, unable to find words for what she felt. She was filled with possibilities. It didn't matter what life threw at her; she'd glide above the flames.

Mother drew them onto the veranda. The sun had set, and they lingered as the sky deepened from indigo to black, and a spill of stars twinkled above. The air was cool, but the Cloak felt warm over Jen's shoulders.

A noise above made her look to her eaves. The pile hung

there like a great, hard, volcanic egg. From within sounded a restless scratching, tapping, knocking. With a burst, the Starbirds broke out of the pile and soared into the air, shimmering in a feathery rainbow.

Mother gave Jen a little shove. "Take them home."

Jen crouched with a swirl of the Cloak. Then spreading rainbow wings of her own, she took off.

She rose in the cool night air until the candles and lamps below twinkled like jewels.

The Starbirds wheeled to meet her. She led them, dancing, spiraling upward. Sailing, higher and higher. Reaching, reaching, for a piece of the sky.

GLOSSARY

Aedilac Mountains, the (AE- (rhymes with may) deh-lack). The range of mountains encircling Aerdem on the west, south, and east.

Aerdem (AIR-dem). A jewel of kingdoms, Aerdem is a lush valley, situated between tall mountains on the west, east, and south.

Baden. The name children teased Jen with in the Plain World.

Benden (BEN-den). Son of Aerdem's Captain of the Guard, and best friend of Prince Dashren.

Bloody Knife. Jen's name for one of Naryfel's guards.

Bluebacks. A derogatory name for Turlians, a people enslaved by Queen Naryfel.

Bookar. A friend of Jen's that helped her find her mother when she first arrived in Aerdem. Also called Booker.

Crispels. A fried pastry drenched in honey.

Darter. A sparrow that followed Jen from the Plain World. Once he reached Aerdem, magic there enabled him to talk. He helped Jen find her mother and father.

Dashren (DASH-wren). Prince of Aerdem. Nicknamed Dash, he ruled as a boy during the long years his father was missing.

Deastyer (DEE-stee-er). A condescending name for someone born in Deasty, the northeastern province of Aerdem.

Desperation. The name of a Blueback shantytown just outside the capital of Purpura.

Divida (DIH-vih-duh). Wife of Naryfel's carriage driver.

Elan (E- (rhymes with may) LAN (rhymes with gone). King of Aerdem, and father of Jenren.

Endare. A young baron of Aerdem.

Geoffrey. Count Pompahro's butler.

Glindin Lake. A lake near the Rose Castle, and just outside the walls of Glowan.

Glowan (GLO-when). The main city of Aerdem, situated just below the Rose Castle.

Gold petal(s). One of Aerdem's coins. A grand petal is a thousand gold petals.

Ice Falls, the. A vast avalanche of snow and ice.

Jenren (JEN-wren). Princess of Aerdem. Nicknamed Jen, or Jenny. She lived in the Plain World from age two until she arrived in Aerdem at age eleven.

King's Loop, the. Also called the Loop. The main roadway in Aerdem, it encircles the kingdom. Starting at the Rose Castle, it passes through Glowan, goes up the east side of the kingdom, runs along part of the northern border, and loops back around on the west until it returns to the Castle.

Kishwar (KISH-wahr). A monster as tall as a two-story house.

Large Kingdom, the. A vast forest on the northwestern border of Aerdem.

Laskamont (LASK-a-mont). A kingdom neighboring Aerdem.

Medlara (Med-LAR-uh). An old woman with magical powers, some call her an earth spirit. Also known as Bumpy on account of the small tumors that cover her face and body.

Morslittes (MORE-sleets). Candies made from various roots and the rinds of fruits. These are boiled; infused with spices or oils from mint, cardamon, cinnamon, clove, vanilla, and different flowers; and crusted with melted sugar. Wet morslittes are served in syrup. The melted sugar is allowed to harden on dry morslittes.

Naryfel (NAR- (rhymes with where) eh-fell). Queen of Purpura, half sister to Jen's mother, and a powerful sorceress.

Naryfel's Pass. A pass Naryfel created through magic that transports objects and people to distant locations.

NB. Initials for Naryfel's Bane, one of Blue's names.

Nell. An old woman who raised Jen in the Plain World. She died when Jen was eleven years old.

Penrod. A friend of Jen's who helped her find her mother and father when she first arrived in Aerdem. Nicknamed Penny. Penrod is also the First Poet of Aerdem.

Plain World, the. The name Jen gave to the world she grew up in when she lived with Nell.

Plenderil (PLEN-dur-il). The national flower of Aerdem, plenderil have crimson petals.

Pondit, the (PON-dit). Counselor to the King of Aerdem for many generations.

Portarien Pool (Poor-TAR-ee-in). A pool by the east side of King's Loop. The water there has magic properties.

Purpura (Purr-POOR-uh). A kingdom far to the north of Aerdem, ruled by Queen Naryfel.

Rose Castle, the. The home of Aerdem's royal family. The Rose Castle is situated at the bottom of a sheer cliff. The cliff is one wall of a tall mountain. The castle was built from a single stone. While it is crystal-like in appearance, it is quite hard. Fire-like colors flicker inside its translucent walls, which makes the castle glow at night. The colors change and intensify during times of danger.

Royson. A raisin from a large, sweet purple grape.

Rugda(s). A denomination of money in the Plain World.

Sally. Bit's servant in the Rose Castle.

Sniffers. Ferocious creatures with a highly developed ability to track prey.

Transdevis (Trans-DEH-vis). An antique device capable of transporting objects or people.

Trilafor (TRILL-uh-for). A kingdom neighboring Aerdem.

Tubole (TOO-bowl). Naryfel's carriage driver.

Turlian (TUR-lee-in). A person from Turlia, a small kingdom neighboring Purpura. Turlians, derogatorily called Bluebacks, were enslaved by Naryfel. They are known as master artisans, musicians, and artists.

Vieveeka (Vie- (rhymes with eye) VEE-kuh). A duchess of Trilafor.

Wyndano's Cloak (WIN-dah-no's). A magic cloak capable of transforming the wearer, usually into an animal.

Yalp. First magician of Aerdem.

ABOUT THE AUTHOR

A. R. SILVERBERRY, the pen name of Peter Allan Adler, holds a BA in music and a PhD in psychology. Ever feeling the call of a creative life, he's a watercolorist, pianist, and composer, and he has been dreaming up stories since childhood. He lives in Northern California, where the majestic coastline, trees, and mountains inspire his writing. *Wyndano's Cloak* is his first novel. Stay tuned for two novels in the pipeline. Visit his website at www.arsilverberry.com.

NOTE FROM TREE TUNNEL PRESS

THE AUTHOR will donate a portion of profits from the sale of this book to agencies that serve needy children. He also conducts school visits to encourage creative expression in young people. The author welcomes inquiries from interested agencies and schools. Please visit his website to learn more: www.arsilverberry.com.

ABOUT THE FONTS

WYNDANO'S CLOAK was set in Aquiline, Principe Normal, and New Caledonia. Aquiline is a cursive italic style inspired by the great 16th-century writing masters Ludovico degli Arrighi and Gerardus Mercator. The font is historically correct, emulating the adventurous and elegant writing of the late Renaissance.

ABOUT TREE TUNNEL PRESS

TREE TUNNEL PRESS publishes fiction and nonfiction books. We are interested in the power of art and culture to positively impact society. We create products that entertain, encourage, and inspire.

Additional copies of this book may be ordered from your favorite online or brick-and-mortar book dealer; or ordered directly from the distributor, Atlas Books, at 800-247-6553.

Requests for rights or permissions should be directed to:

Tree Tunnel Press
P.O. Box 733
Capitola, CA 95010

Visit our website, www.treetunnelpress.com, for more information.